D0456999

SUPER HOST

SUPER HOST

– A Novel –

Kate Russo

G. P. PUTNAM'S SONS
NEW YORK

PUTNAM
— EST. 1838 —

G. P. PUTNAM'S SONS
Publishers Since 1838
An imprint of Penguin Random House LLC
penguinrandomhouse.com

For Tom

THE DEMONS YOU'RE STUCK WITH

In the hierarchy of linen stains, blood is at the top. Everyone thinks semen is the worst, but they're wrong. They only think this because of that popular TV show where inspectors take a black light to a hotel room and it lights up neon yellow, indicating bodily fluids all over the bedding. Since that report, people automatically throw off the bedspread in hotel rooms, assuming it's drenched in some stranger's spunk. It probably is; that's why Bennett Driscoll prefers to use duvet covers in his rentable four-bedroom house. Soap, hot water, and a rigorous spin cycle will scrub all the manhood out of a duvet cover. It's the stains you can detect with the naked eye that are the real problem. When Bennett throws back the duvets on checkout day, it's the sight of blood he fears most.

Fuck.

And there they are, halfway down the fitted sheet. Only a couple drops' worth, but on Bennett's bright white sheets they stand out like a red scarf discarded in snow. Their removal will require bleach and a lot of scrubbing. Recently, he bought a nailbrush or, for his purposes, a blood brush, to combat the really stubborn stains. In the beginning, he would just throw away the visibly soiled sheets and buy new ones, but now a year into renting out his suburban London house on AirBed, he has thrown away five sets of perfectly good sheets. Bleach is cheaper. He pulls the fitted sheet up from the corners, wadding it into a ball in the center of the bed. If the blood has transferred onto the mattress pad, that's double the work.

Dammit.

Recently, Bennett was awarded the status of "Super Host" on the AirBed website—an honor he earned for having a quick response rate and excellent reviews. Though it's never been his aspiration to become a host, he'd be lying if he said that the little medal next to his picture didn't fill him with pride. Until two years ago, Bennett was a full-time artist who never stuttered over answering the question, "What do you do?" In fact, nobody ever needed to ask him. He was the well-known painter, Bennett Driscoll. Everyone knew that. Okay, maybe not everyone, but enough people that he didn't have to worry about renting out his house to tourists. Unfortunately, things change, tastes change. It used to be that anything he painted would sell. In 2002, there was a waiting list. Now, sixteen years later, there are more than a hundred of his paintings in storage. His last solo show was in 2013. The critic for the *Guardian* wrote, "Driscoll cares so little for the current trends in painting that one wonders if he concerns himself with the contemporary art world at all." That pissed Bennett off, mostly because it was true. But a bad review is better than no review, he realizes that now. Since art critics don't review his work anymore, Bennett pores over each AirBed review as though it's the *Sunday*

Times, scouring each for a new and nuanced understanding of his hosting skills. More often than not, they go like this: "Bennett was a welcoming and gracious host," "Bennett was very helpful," "Bennett has a beautiful home," and "Looking forward to staying at Bennett's house again the next time we're in London." They're not exactly *Times* quality, but nevertheless, it's nice to be reviewed favorably. Hey, it's nice to be reviewed, full stop. Sometimes he wonders if his ex-wife, Eliza, ever goes on AirBed to read his reviews. Probably not. She left a year ago to live in America with a hedge fund manager named Jeff, taking with her the steady salary from her publishing job that, until the divorce, had been paying their bills. That's when Bennett decided to move into the studio at the end of the garden and rent out the family home on AirBed. He doesn't think his Super Host status would impress Eliza. Almost nothing impressed her. He wishes someone would write, "Bennett has a beautiful home. He was the perfect host. No, the perfect man—exciting, interesting, and handsome in equal measure. He would make an excellent husband. I even bought several of his paintings because I believe they are the pinnacle of contemporary art." No such luck yet.

‖‖‖‖‖‖‖‖‖‖‖‖‖‖‖‖‖‖‖‖

As he rounds the corner from the bedroom to the hallway, hip-hop is quietly thumping in the distance from the other side of the house. He carries the big wad of sheets down the wide staircase, careful to peer ahead of him from the side of the load. As he walks through the large, open-plan living space, the music grows louder. Bennett sings along confidently, although he can't quite bring himself to rap the lyrics. Instead, the words always come out melodically, each one dragging on a millisecond longer than it should. He discovered rap music around the same time he started letting the house, around the same time Eliza moved out. Though unable to name a single song, she claimed to hate hip-hop.

On the night he discovered the rapper Roots Manuva, he'd been out to dinner with his daughter. They were at some trendy Shoreditch restaurant, the kind of place that claims to sell street food, but in the comfort of the indoors. The music was, of course, too loud—he knew that even without Eliza there to point it out. He had to shout to be heard, which was difficult considering the task at hand was explaining to Mia why her mother had just fucked off to New York. At one point, Mia, needing to collect herself, went to the ladies' room. He hated the idea of his daughter crying alone in a stall, but he sat patiently, fighting the urge to follow her into the women's loo and check on her. At the time he was one of the few people on earth for whom the mobile phone wasn't an obvious distraction. Why pull out your phone unless you needed to make a phone call? Instead, in need of entertainment, he started listening intently to the restaurant's music:

> *Taskmaster burst the bionic zit-splitter*
> *Breakneck speed we drown ten pints of bitter*
> *We lean all day and some say that ain't productive*
> *But that depend upon the demons that you're stuck with*

He had no idea what a "bionic zit-splitter" was (he still doesn't), but something about how we "lean all day," and "the demons that you're stuck with" resonated.

"I can't stand still with you anymore," Eliza had said two weeks previously. Divorce papers had since been served. He was now doing his best to explain to his then eighteen-year-old daughter something even he couldn't understand himself. Had he been standing still for the last twenty years and not realized it? Their whole marriage, he thought he was being reliable—a good father and husband. That's what women wanted, right? Reliability? *Wait.* He should be *asking* women what they want, not *assuming.* Eliza was forever pointing that out. His own father was anything but reliable. Well, that's not strictly true, he was reliably drunk all the time—a miserable man who was only happy when he was listing all the ways you'd wronged him. Bennett *was* happy, or so he thought. He loved being an artist. He loved Eliza and Mia with all his heart. Why not stand still? Where else would he want to go? Eliza thought he was stuck. "The demons that you're stuck with . . ." What were these demons that destroyed his marriage and why hadn't he noticed them? This was what he was pondering when Mia returned to the table.

"What is this song?" he asked her.

A die-hard Father John Misty fan, she just shrugged in ignorance as she sat down.

"Excuse me?" Bennett stopped a server moving quickly by with a plate of Mexican grilled corncobs. "Can you tell me what this song is?"

Mia, embarrassed, put her face in her hands.

"Roots Manuva, 'Witness,'" the girl said, her tone implying *Duh.*

Bennett pulled out the little black notebook he kept in his blazer pocket and wrote down *Routes Maneuver. Witness.* He had no idea which was the artist and which was the song title, but he'd figure that out later on Google.

At the end of the night, Mia burst into tears as they hugged good night. Though she'd only moved away from home the previous month, she told him she'd move back to keep him company.

"No, I won't let you do that," he said, holding her tight. "Besides, without your mum's income, I'm going to have to put the house on AirBed."

She cried even harder at this. The guilt weighed heavily on him. He might be stuck, but he wasn't going to let Mia be stuck with him.

He went home that night and bought Roots Manuva's "Witness" on iTunes. He played it twenty times on repeat before finally going to bed.

||||||||||||||||||||||

The music fades out as he reaches the laundry room—an annex off the kitchen with a large, American-style washer and dryer. When Eliza ordered the appliances from John Lewis ten years ago, he thought she was crazy. The environmental impact *alone* of these fuck-ing things! Eliza loved to live like an American in London. Big house. Big car. Big fuckin' washer and dryer. "They understand convenience in America," she liked to say. "They don't *enjoy* suffering over there." It had long been Eliza's belief that misery was Bennett's preferred mode. And not just him, but all British men. All that floppy-haired, self-deprecating, Hugh Grant nonsense from the nineties had pene-trated their psyches and they were all irreparably damaged. But, even-tually, the car, the house, and the washer/dryer were no longer enough. Eliza needed an actual American man.

Bennett spreads the fitted sheet over the top of the dryer. After pulling down a bottle of bleach from the shelf overhead, he pours a little over the stain. Grabbing the blood brush, he braces himself by stepping back on one leg to get more traction. The dryer rocks back and forth as he scrubs, a few strands of hair falling down in front of his eyes. He's been lucky to keep a lot of his hair, though it's thinning on top. His solution is to brush it back. A little product usually holds it in place. Eliza found the product sticky. Bennett finds satisfaction in the fact that her new bloke, Jeff, is completely bald with a shiny dome to match his shiny, fitted suits. *Twat.*

Bennett stops scrubbing and regards his progress. Barely a dent. He goes back at it, bending his front knee more to bring himself closer to enemy number one. Engaged with the task in hand, he's startled when his phone, in the front pocket of his jeans, starts to ring.

"Mia! Hi, darling." It's particularly difficult to control his heart swells these days.

"You're coming tonight, right?" she chirps, skipping the pleasantries.

"Of course I am." He starts working at the stain again with his free hand. "I've just got to get the new guest checked in, then I'll be on my way."

"Ugh. Okay." Mia makes no secret of her disapproval regarding her childhood home being on AirBed.

"She'll be here at four. I'll give her the keys and then catch the Tube. Should be there about half-five. Is that alright?"

"Yeah, that's fine."

"I can't wait to see your paintings."

"I had a good crit this morning."

"Great!" He can't help but beam with pride.

"But the tutor told everyone in the crit that Bennett Driscoll is my dad. Cunt."

"Is that so bad?"

"I don't want to ride your coattails."

"I'm currently scrubbing blood out of bedsheets. Those coattails?"

"Eww, Dad! I'll kill you if you tell any of my classmates about that."

He smiles wide. Horrifying his daughter has long been one of his greatest pleasures. At nineteen, it is easier than ever to send her into frothy outrage. Why would Bennett Driscoll confide to a bunch of art school pricks that he's letting his house on AirBed? Is there anything worse than admitting that his paintings no longer sell? He'd rather watch Eliza and Jeff have sex. On second thought, no he wouldn't.

"Can I take you out for dinner after?" he asks.

"Can I bring Gemma and Richard?"

No. No. No. No.

"Of course, darling, whoever you want to bring."

||||||||||||||||||||||

His next guest is Alicia, a young woman from New York. Originally, she said she'd be traveling with a group of friends, which gave Bennett pause. He prefers families, but there is something trustworthy, maybe even a little naive, about Alicia in her smiley profile picture in front of the Brooklyn Bridge. When she booked the house a month back, she said there could be anywhere between three to five friends with her, she wasn't yet sure of the numbers. Bennett had explained that the house slept six comfortably, but please don't exceed eight people. **That won't be a problem**, she wrote back two days ago, explaining that it would be only her staying after all. He didn't want to pry, but what was a twentysomething young woman going to do in his big, suburban house all alone? It had been a good-sized house for three people. It's an enormous house for one, as he knows all too well.

That first day, when it came to him that Eliza and Mia were gone for good, the silence had been unbearable. Hip-hop now constantly follows him around the house like an entourage, sweeping the solitude under the carpet. He felt kind of silly the morning after he listened to "Witness" twenty times in a row. Bennett suspected that what Roots

Manuva was rapping about probably had to do with racial injustice and that he shouldn't equate those "demons" with his own, but he couldn't help it. He loved the song's sense of urgency, and before long he owned the entire Roots Manuva catalog. The old Bennett was a Billy Bragg kind of guy. A Jeff Buckley fan. All that "depressing, nostalgic wallowing," Eliza called it. Musical evidence that he'd never change. He'd spent his whole life avoiding the things that weren't "meant for him," diligently adhering to the middle-class white man's algorithm for taste and respectability. But staying the course is rubbish, he's decided. He's trying not to "give any fucks" (a phrase Mia taught him) but in reality, he gives so many fucks. Like, a truly debilitating number of fucks. He can't even work up the courage to tell anyone besides Mia (is there anyone besides Mia?) about his recent obsession with the rapper. What would they think? Is his newfound love of hip-hop a "fuck you" to Eliza? He tells himself, no, it's more than that . . . but yeah, sort of.

The older he gets, the more impossible it becomes to live in the present as Eliza wanted him to. The past is too vast to ignore and the present is too close, like staring at your pores in a magnified mirror. Last year, even his gallery of thirty years suggested that he'd be more valuable to them when he's dead. Libby Foster Gallery began representing him in 1988, right after he graduated from the Royal College of Art, but over the last decade, his sales had waned. Libby insisted that it wasn't just him. Lots of artists were suffering from the economic downturn. Just before Eliza left, a letter from Libby had come through the post. "Dear Bennett," it read, "We regret to inform you that, after much thought, the gallery has decided to no longer represent living artists. Given rising rents in London, the time has come for us to give up our formal exhibition space and redirect our focus on representing the estates of William Warren, Christopher Gray, and Tyson Allen Stewart in the art fair market."

He called Libby, immediately.

"You got the letter," she answered. "I love your work, Bennett. You know I do. But it's not selling, not right now. If interest piques in the future, the gallery would be very interested in representing your estate."

"You'll be interested in representing me when I'm dead?" he clarified.

"We no longer represent living artists, so, yes."

Fuck the present.

|||||||||||||||||||||||

Alicia arrives right at four o'clock as planned, pulling her suitcase behind her. She has a thin frame and her straight, sandy-blond hair is in a ponytail. Her eyes are visibly tired through her thick tortoiseshell-rimmed glasses. Bennett watches her approach through the front window of the living room. He likes to observe his guests as they arrive, hoping to catch some glimpse of their true selves before he greets them. Bundled up in a double-breasted navy blue wool coat, Alicia hunches over, dragging her suitcase up the pebbled drive. She bites her lower lip as though she intends to confess something. Since becoming profoundly lonely himself, Bennett now feels he can spot it easily in others. Alicia is lonely. Halfway to the door, she stops to tighten her ponytail by taking a section of hair in each hand and tugging. He remembers both Eliza and Mia would do this, too. He adored all their strange habits, all their alien feminine rituals. He can't help smiling to himself as he opens the front door.

Noticing his smile, she smiles back, relieved.

"You must be Alicia."

"Bennett?"

He nods. "Please, come in." Despite inviting her in, it takes him a moment to move out of the way. He's struck by her tired eyes, glazed and a bit dark. He's always been attracted to heavy eyes. Eliza, he thought, was always at her most beautiful at the end of a long day. Alicia steps forward with one foot, looking at him expectantly. He gestures grandly when he finally moves out of the way, revealing the large entryway and contemporary, open-plan living space.

She looks behind her and hoists her heavy suitcase over the front step.

Take the suitcase, you knob.

"Let me get that." Reaching for the handle, he grazes her hand; it's soft, but cold from the winter air. Uncomfortable with the sensual thoughts that are now suddenly and unwelcomely flooding his brain, he clears his throat. "I'll put this upstairs in the master bedroom. I assume that's where you'll want to sleep?" And now he's thinking about her lying naked in his bed.

Pervert.

He runs his hand over his hair, a nervous habit he's had since he can remember.

"I guess," she says, looking around the house. "This place is huge."

He smiles back from the bottom of the stairs, not quite sure how to respond.

"Where do you live now?" she asks.

Bennett points to the window behind her. Through the glass there's a small building at the end of the garden, not much larger than a shed, though certainly more solid.

"Oh."

"You won't notice I'm there, I promise. I'm an artist. That's my live/work space."

Her eyes are drawn to the paintings on the walls around them. "Are these yours?"

"That one is." He points to a large red-and-blue painting of an intricate pattern, not unlike a Persian carpet.

"Wow. Beautiful." She seems unsure of what else to say. "I feel bad taking up your house all by myself."

"You shouldn't. You paid for it." He starts up the stairs with the suitcase. Was that curt? he wonders. He turns to face her again. "Make yourself at home."

"All my friends backed out after I booked the place," she explains. "Nobody has any money at the moment."

He nods, understanding. "Any plans while you're here?"

"Hoping to see some old friends. I did my master's at LSE a few years ago."

Nostalgia, Bennett thinks. Everyone chases it. He can see that Alicia already knows her mistake: you can't go back.

"I'll get this upstairs," he says, pointing to the suitcase. "Then, I'll leave you to it. Obviously, you'll know where I am if you need anything."

"Great. Thanks," she says, wandering into the large kitchen.

He watches her as she aimlessly opens the cutlery drawer. When she looks up at him again, he grabs the bag's handle and hoists it up the remaining stairs.

||||||||||||||||||||||||

Bennett opens the back gate of his garden onto Blenheim Road at four-thirty. He tucks his white earbuds into his ears and spins the dial on his iPod. He still uses the now-antiquated device that Eliza and Mia bought him for Christmas in 2006. "You can get rid of it, Dad. It won't hurt my feelings," Mia's told him many times. He can't throw away anything she's given him. In his studio, he still has the first little clay sculpture that she made him when she was four: a bust of a man on a pedestal. He thinks it's supposed to be him, but he's never been quite sure. It's been sitting on the same windowsill for fifteen years, too brittle to move. "You can put all of your music on your phone now," she'd added, sounding more like the parent than the child. "It's easier." He hadn't used the iPod much when Eliza was around, mainly because they traveled most places together and he didn't need the distraction. Now that he is traveling everywhere solo, it's become his closest companion.

Turning onto Priory Ave., Bennett makes his way to the Tube. Bennett and Eliza bought the house in 1994. One of the few detached houses in Chiswick, Eliza's heart was set on it. It was the same year Bennett was nominated for the Turner Prize. He didn't win, but sales still skyrocketed. His series of life-size nudes reclining on intricate fabrics that reflected the rich history of textile design in London's Spitalfields neighborhood were an instant hit. He hadn't even needed a mortgage. When the crash of 2007 happened, they'd lost a lot of money, both in investments and paintings sales. Eliza's salary from publishing was thankfully steady, but the financial stress, Bennett now believes, was the beginning of the end. He was willing to forgo the nice dinners and shopping sprees at Selfridges, the giant appliances, and the fancy car so long as they were able to keep the home he'd made with his family. Maybe it would even be romantic. It wasn't that Eliza loved money more than she loved Bennett, but she felt he lacked the ambition it would take to get back on top. She was worried that he'd run out of good ideas. He was worried she was right. He still is.

He taps his Oyster card to the reader at the station and the gates open. Truth is, if he could have lived anywhere, he would have bought one of the old Victorian terraced houses in London's East End. Whitechapel, maybe, with all its history, its old shops, and the dark pubs. He'd grown up nearby in Hammersmith, and was desperate to leave the suburban feel of West London behind. During the nineties, he watched with jealousy as his artist friends cultivated a creative hub in the East End. Back then, he would travel the length of the District Line—west to east—at least three times a week, visiting studios and exhibitions. Once Mia was born, the journeys to Whitechapel felt impossible. Even his own studio in Ealing was difficult to get to. Eliza wanted him to spend more time with his daughter, but at the same time, was frustrated by his lack of productivity. And this was just one of many mind-fuck conundrums of their twenty-five-year marriage. When he suggested that they build him a studio in the back garden, Eliza was initially against it.

"It'll be an eyesore," she protested. "It will devalue the house."

"But we're not planning to sell the house," he'd replied. "Who cares about the value?"

She frowned at that. God knows why. He had thought she loved the house.

"You're constantly throwing up roadblocks," he said. "You have to help me solve problems, my love." He'd always called her "my love," thinking it was endearing. He was deeply wounded when, in the middle of a row last year, she told him she found it patronizing.

Lately, it's been hard to remember the good times with Eliza, but like a swift kick to the gut, those memories come flooding back every time he takes a seat on the Underground. From day one of their relationship, whenever they rode the Tube together, Eliza would slip her arm through his and rest her head on his shoulder. He'd smooth her hair back and kiss her on the top of the head. Eliza always wore her hair down in long, thick, wavy brown curls. She never cut it, like so many women do when they get older. It always smelled of sweet pea blossoms. God, he loved that about her. She'd nuzzle into him and kiss him on the arm. Every damn time. These days, when he sits down on the train he looks like a lunatic entertaining an imaginary friend. Without Eliza to lean into, he sits awkwardly, shifting in his seat, unable to find the sweet spot. Today, he fiddles with the dial on his iPod, hoping to find the ideal volume to drown it all out.

He changes lines for King's Cross, the relatively new location for Central Saint Martins School of Art and Design, where Mia is in her first year studying painting. King's Cross would never have housed an art school when he was nineteen. Thirty-five years ago it was one of London's dirtiest, most transient neighborhoods, a gaping wound between Bloomsbury and Islington, filled with seedy pubs and even seedier hotels harboring tramps, drug dealers, and prostitutes. As a boy growing up in the leafy suburbs, hearing stories about King's Cross was like hearing stories about Vietnam: atrocities happened there, true, but at least it was far away. As he and his friends got older and started taking the Underground by themselves, trips to King's Cross became a rite of passage. It was so easy to tell your parents you were going to see a film in Leicester Square. King's Cross was only another four stops. He remembers the first time he and his friends—all of them fifteen—went there. Bennett was such a wimp that his mates didn't even tell him beforehand where they were going. He still remembers standing up when the speakers announced, "Leicester Square," and his sniggering friends remaining in their seats. He didn't have to ask where they were actually going. He already knew.

||||||||||||||||||||

His mate Stuart nudged him as they rode up the escalator at King's Cross Station. "How much money you got?"

"I don't know. Thirty quid, maybe." He knew it was exactly that much. His neighbor, Mrs. Garvey, paid him thirty pounds to clean out her pet budgie's cage while she was on holiday.

"Bennett's got thirty," Stuart shouted down the escalator. "What can he get for that?"

The other boys, farther down the escalator, started laughing. Owen and Jay—idiots—were the masterminds of this mission. Stuart was the middleman, the one that communicated Owen and Jay's plans to Bennett. It was also Stuart's job to convince Bennett of everything they had in mind. The other three boys had tried going places without him before this, but as it turned out, Bennett Driscoll brought credibility to any scheme. Their parents were far more apt to give permission if they knew do-gooder Bennett was going, as well. "Such a lovely lad," they all said.

"He can get a blow job from that, I bet," Owen shouted up the escalator. No need to whisper. Nothing to be ashamed of.

"Wait, what?" Really, he shouldn't have been surprised. They'd been talking about prostitutes for weeks, ever since that night at Jay's house, when his brother, Neil, bought them beers and told them they were stupid to wait for the girls at Godolphin to put out. "Fifty quid will buy you everything you need," he'd assured them.

"My brother said his mate Jeremy got his finger up a girl's cunt for twenty," Jay said, adding a handy visual demonstration that involved sliding his index finger through a hole in his fist.

"Yeah, I brought the full fifty," Owen said, proudly.

"I don't want anything," Bennett said, regretting the statement immediately.

"Don't be a poof," Jay shouted loud enough for people on the down escalator to turn around, though he knew Bennett was anything but. He'd watched Bennett pine for Beatrice Calvert, the blue-eyed brunette whose dad taught English at their all-boys school. Bennett had worked out that she came to meet her dad after school on Mondays and Thursdays, so he joined the Shakespeare Society, which met then, and he'd have a reason to stick around. The problem was he hated Shakespeare. Hated him even more when Beatrice ultimately started going out with Jay a year later.

They exited the station into hot, thick summer air that smelled of cigarettes, vomit, and piss. At first glance, there seemed to be more tramps than prostitutes around, not that Bennett could tell the difference. According to Jay's brother, Neil, the prostitutes approached you. That was the extent of their plan: wait for a prostitute to approach. They'd heard Caledonian Road was the best place, so that's where they went and stood around awkwardly—four teenage boys in Chelsea football gear, sticking out like dolphins on safari.

A woman in high heels and trench coat came toward them. Owen, confident, stepped forward. "She looks like a prossie," he said to his mates over his shoulder.

She looked him over without even breaking stride and walked straight past them. "Eat shit, you little twat."

This, Bennett thought, was probably the best outcome he could have hoped for. "We can probably still make the film, if we leave now," he suggested, hoping to capitalize on Owen's bruised ego.

"No fuckin' way, mate. I came here for pussy, not abuse."

They stood in silence for another fifteen minutes before a young woman in a tight black dress, clearly high as a kite, approached them. As she got closer, Bennett thought she couldn't be much older than they were. She looked bizarre, like a little girl playing fancy dress with her mother's makeup.

"You got money?" she asked Owen, her eyes straining for focus.

"I got fifty."

"Alright." She looked at the other three. "Wait. I'm not doin' all of you for fifty."

"We've got one hundred and eighty total," Jay chimed in.

Her eyes lit up. "Yeah, alright then." She led them toward Pentonville Road. She walked fast, both cold and jittery.

Bennett grabbed Stuart's arm and they lagged behind. He pulled out his wallet. "You can have my money. I'm not doing this."

"We know, mate. We need you to keep watch for coppers or angry pimps."

"You're serious?" There was really no worse task to assign Bennett, a scrawny kid with a reputation for being skittish, except for maybe fucking a prostitute.

"'Fraid so."

Owen already had his hand on the prostitute's bum as she led them down a dank mews with a metal door at the end of it. On the other side of the door was a dark hallway and an even darker staircase. The four boys followed her up the stairs, single file and silent, Bennett, of course, bringing up the rear. At the very top, four stories up, she opened another door where a skinhead stood. Bennett suspected he was the only person thinking about fire exits. The skinhead looked at Owen, then at the other three boys. To judge by his expression, he'd seen this a million times before.

The skinhead held out his hand for Owen's money. "Fifty quid. You pay first. You go in one at a time."

The prostitute was already in the room. Was it *her* room? It would be nice, Bennett thought, if she had her own room, at least. Jay and Stuart leaned up against the wall in the dingy hallway, so Bennett followed suit. A strip of flowery wallpaper came cascading down on his head when his back made contact with the wall. He was careful to keep his hands in front of him. Even though this was long before he learned about black light technology, he suspected these walls were covered in semen. The hallway reeked of weed, BO, and another smell that Bennett would now identify as sex, though he couldn't at the time. The three boys didn't say a word to each other. It wasn't long before they could hear a bed creaking. Then some moaning. It had to be Owen. The girl hadn't made so much as a peep since she'd picked them up. In the hallway they looked at their feet. It was possible, Bennett hoped, that the other two were chickening out.

The creaking and moaning stopped and the skinhead asked, "Who's next?"

They all looked at each other. The color had drained from Jay's and Stuart's faces.

Owen opened the door, buttoning his trousers. He didn't even look at his friends, just headed straight down the stairs.

Bennett immediately went after him—partly to check on his friend, but mostly to get the fuck out of there.

"If you're not going to pay, piss off," he heard the skinhead say to the other two. Seconds later, Jay's and Stuart's footsteps clattered down the stairs behind them.

Outside in the mews, Owen just kept walking, picking up enough speed that Bennett had to run to catch up.

Owen looked back at him, but kept moving. "Fuck off, Bennett."

"What happened?"

"Wouldn't you like to know. Get your own pussy, mate."

Finally Bennett got ahead of him, stopping him in his tracks. "You ran out of there like you were upset."

Owen tried to get around him, but with skittishness comes speed, and Bennett was able to block his path.

"Fine. I couldn't do it. You happy?"

Bennett looked at him, confused. "We heard you."

"I fucked her tits," he whispered. *This* he was ashamed of.

If this was the same young woman they picked up on Caledonian Road, her tits wouldn't fill a thimble. Bennett's face must have expressed his disbelief, because Owen was quickly on the defensive. "Yeah, I know, mate. Mostly I just rubbed my cock up against her rib cage." He looked back at the other two, who were catching up. "Don't tell them anything." They never discussed it again. Owen went off to university in Australia a few years later and never came back.

||||||||||||||||||||||||

As the train pulls into King's Cross, Bennett can't help but wonder what Owen's reaction would be to the area now. Does he ever think about that girl? Nobody even asked her her name. Bennett himself doesn't think about her much. She's only returned to his memory over the last year when he pictures his own daughter walking down Caledonian Road. The mews is gone now, replaced with blocks of luxury flats.

Lingering memories of King's Cross in the eighties aside, Bennett was nervous when Mia announced her intention to study art at St. Martins. He'd hoped that she'd follow her mother's path into publishing. Though hardly the stable force that it once was, it's still a hell of a lot better than the art world—Penguin hasn't yet announced its intention to publish only dead writers. Yes, he is worried about Mia navigating the ultra-competitive and male-dominated gallery scene, and he doesn't want her to feel the constant financial uncertainty he now feels. But there's another issue: he isn't sure how much talent she really has. It's a horrible thought, he knows that, one he dares not utter to anyone. When he looks at her work, he isn't sure he sees its potential. It's only her first year, he tells himself, and his opinion is hardly the be-all and end-all of art criticism. He's probably too close. And what does he know? He's out of fashion, better off dead.

He exits the station, adjusting his coat and scarf against January's piercing damp. Only in London can mist feel angular and aggressive. He thinks about his new guest, Alicia. Maybe he should send her a message to let her know there is a spare blanket on the top shelf of the upstairs linen closet. He pulls out his phone, but hesitates. No, she can probably figure this out. She mentioned her master's degree. Linen closets won't be an elusive concept to her. Still, he can't help but think of her, alone and shivering. He types a message as he weaves through the throngs of commuters. *Hi, Alicia, it occurs to me you might get cold tonight . . .*

Alicia responds quickly: *Thank you, Bennett. I suppose I didn't pick the best month to visit. :)* He remembers that sweet, self-deprecating smile she gave him when he opened the door to her earlier that afternoon.

Change gears, Bennett.

A few minutes later he's standing in front of St. Martins. He takes a deep breath. His own alma mater, it's the last place he wants to be, given his recent decline. He stops in front of a large water fountain in the school's courtyard, where water squirts up in patterns from the cobblestones, lit by spectacular colored lights. Equipped with motion sensors, the water stops when someone attempts to step into the stream, so a person can walk through it without getting wet. This concept is currently blowing the mind of a four-year-old girl, who runs back and forth through the fountain, squealing. Her mother watches on, impatient.

To Bennett, this kind of opulence at an art school makes no sense. War heroes get fountains, not art students. They'd surely be more interested in a giant cigarette machine. This is further evidenced by the four students who are currently huddled together, lighting up a single fag and blocking the entrance to the school. Mia, thank God, isn't one of them.

"Pardon," Bennett says to the group, removing his earbuds. The students ignore him at first, preoccupied with protecting their solitary rollie from the mist that threatens to put it out. They take notice only when Bennett pulls out his old-school iPod and holds down the pause button to turn it off. They watch, captivated, as he flicks the switch on the top to lock it, before wrapping the earbuds around the device and sticking it in his pocket. They look him up and down. A stylish and distinguished-looking man, his clothing is in direct conflict with the iPod. One girl focuses on his jacket, a dark grey wool peacoat with tortoiseshell buttons. She passes the cigarette to the guy next to her, who takes a drag while inspecting Bennett's checkered wool scarf, the kind you see Brad Pitt wearing in celebrity magazines. The other young man focuses on Bennett's dark indigo jeans. They look expensive, because they are. Bennett washes them inside out and on delicate, just like the label suggests. The final young woman hones in on his polished brown leather boots with waxed khaki laces. All of the clothes are several years old; he can't afford Selfridges anymore, but these little shits don't need to know that. They all look up to catch his gaze at the same moment.

"Alright, mate?" one of the young women asks. She's wearing a pair of denim dungarees with just a mustard-yellow lace bra underneath. She's chosen a red-and-black flannel shirt, unbuttoned, to wear over the dungarees and a bright orange wooly cap over her purple-dyed hair. She's hopping around uncomfortably in the cold.

He wants to tell her to button up her shirt and that he is not her "mate."

"You Mia's dad?" she asks.

"I am." How can she possibly know this? "Are you all in her year?"

They all mutter some form of "yeah," then stare down at their inadequate footwear; three pairs of canvas sneakers and a torn pair of leopard-print ballet flats.

"I'll take you in," says one of the young men, wearing black skinny jeans and an INXS sweatshirt, after taking a drag. "I share a studio with Mia." It's impossible to tell by his expression whether this is a good or a bad thing. He hands the rollie to one of his mates. "Follow me, *Bennett Driscoll*." He draws out the name, his voice suddenly going fake-posh, like he's Piers Morgan. He opens the door, gesturing grandly for Bennett to enter, while his mates snigger. What is so fucking funny? Bennett wonders. Is it possible these kids know that the name "Bennett Driscoll" doesn't open as many doors as it used to? Is that why this kid is flamboyantly opening this door for him now? Sarcasm?

Bennett looks back into the courtyard one more time. The little girl still runs through the fountain, shrieking in wonderment. Why is he following this grimy-looking boy into the building? *He* could use a run through a fountain. The kind that actually gets you wet. Reluctantly, Bennett follows him in.

"You went to St. Martins, right?" the kid asks. His skinny jeans are so tight they shorten his stride.

"Once upon a time."

"Then the Royal College?"

Has this weirdo been reading my Wikipedia page?

He's not sure whether to be creeped out or flattered. Maybe this night could be the ego massage he needs.

"That's right."

"Nice. Pretty ideal, mate."

I spent the morning scrubbing blood off white sheets. Not ideal, mate.

"I'm Evan, by the way."

When was the last time you washed your hair, Evan?

"Pleased to meet you." He gives Evan the professional smile he used to give collectors at openings. It feels unfamiliar. He hasn't had to use those muscles in a while.

Evan opens a fire door, which leads to a narrow hallway, once again letting Bennett through first. "Second door on the right." He points for good measure.

The door is wide open and voices are pouring out. Bennett pokes his head around the corner of the large studio, set up for around eight students to share. The grey-painted floors never change from art school to art school, decade to decade. The smell of turps and glue makes him feel twenty years old again. For a second.

"It's cool. Go on." Evan smiles, sensing Bennett's lack of confidence. "You're Bennett Driscoll."

Stop saying that.

"Can I get you a beer, Mr. Driscoll?"

You can fuck off.

Bennett meets Evan's eyes and immediately feels guilty. The sticky kid looks genuinely honored to fetch him a beer.

"Dad!"

Oh, thank God.

He turns around to see Mia. She is waving aggressively from the corner of the room, clearly not wanting to approach Evan.

"I'll check in with my daughter first," he says, leaving Evan standing alone in the center of the studio.

He scoops Mia in his arms, but stops just short of lifting her off the ground. She's still light enough to swing around, but that doesn't mean he should, even though it allows him to think, however temporarily, that's she's still six.

"Evan is the worst," she whispers in his ear, mid-hug.

Yes, he is.

"He's not so bad." He hopes his daughter will be more tolerant of other human beings than he is, though so far it's not working out.

It occurs to Bennett that, unlike her classmates, Mia has made an effort in her appearance this evening, wearing a red wool dress and thick black tights. Her hair is halfway down her back in long brown ringlets, just like her mother's, only Mia has a curly fringe. She smiles brightly, the freckles on her face always seeming to exude enthusiasm. He realizes now who the little girl running through the fountain reminded him of. In his mind, Mia will always prefer to run, squealing, through a fountain over sharing a cigarette with a group of ironic idiots.

"Which piece is yours?" he asks.

Mia steps out of the way to reveal what appears to be a five-foot-square painting of . . . a vagina. All the innocence of his previous thoughts is annihilated. She says nothing and lets him take it in. Suddenly, the thought of his daughter smoking a fag with ironic idiots is preferable to contemplating the origins of this painting. The silence pounds in his head as he stares at it, unsure of what to say. He shoves his hands in his jacket pockets, any bare skin now feeling too exposed, and tries to convince himself the painting is depicting a flower, a Georgia O'Keeffe kind of thing, but it isn't. It's *definitely* a vagina. For all his worry about her God-given talents, or lack thereof, she has, in this case, effectively captured the essence of her subject matter, its depths conveyed, its contours rendered.

Was *this* what Evan and his friends were laughing about? Maybe they weren't laughing about him being washed-up. Maybe they were laughing because they knew what his daughter was about to present him with. It *would* be bloody hilarious, if only it wasn't happening to *him*. He keeps his eyes focused on the painting, but now he wonders if he's spent too much time looking at the vagina, like, a creepy amount of time.

Jesus, is it hers?

"You're speechless," Mia finally pipes up.

Does he look at her or keep staring at the oil-paint clitoris? Is he capable of looking back and forth between his daughter and the giant minge she's painted? He doesn't know. He's never had to ask himself this kind of question before.

"Yes," he finally spits out, deciding to keep his eyes on the clitoris.

"You painted nudes, Dad. Same thing."

No, it's not.

He removes one hand from its sheltering pocket to check if his hair is still in place.

Yep, it's still in place. Now what? Say something not creepy.

He can only think of one question. "Is it painted from . . . life?"

So much for not being creepy.

He finally turns to look at her, her expression fighting back laughter.

"Photograph."

"Right . . ."

"From a medical journal." She indicates the large textbook sitting on her desk. "I'm getting really into anatomy."

At last, he can smile a little. "I should say so."

He's relieved, although he doesn't really understand why. It's still a five-foot vagina painted by his own daughter. In fact, if she told him that she was a lesbian and this was her lover's vagina, he'd probably, weirdly, be thrilled. Lesbianism would certainly be preferable to a lifetime with one of the Evans of the world. Or one of the Bennetts, for that matter. He's always been suspicious of his own gender's cruel nature, so much so that he suspects his daughter purposely doesn't share any of her love life with him. She knows he doesn't have the stomach for it.

He puts his arm around her. "I'm proud of you." He kisses her on the head. Her hair smells just like Eliza's. "So what are you working on next? Or don't I want to know?"

"Feet are really hard." She points to a stack of drawings on her desk, all of feet and toes from different angles. "A lot of these are from life."

He flicks through them, relieved to be looking at something else, and stops on one particular charcoal drawing that looks like a man's foot, hairy with deep grooves in the toe knuckles. He smiles to himself before asking, "Is this Evan's foot?"

"Eewww. No!"

How can it be so easy to horrify the girl who is voluntarily exhibiting giant genitalia on her studio wall? It warms his heart that he can still send her from zero to completely flustered in two seconds.

"That's Richard's foot, Dad! Don't you recognize it?"

"Thankfully, no, I don't."

The thought of Richard's bare feet makes him uncomfortable. Bennett's been aware for the last few years that Richard, Mia's good friend from childhood, fancies him. He's long past being flattered by it. He'd hoped that Richard would go off to university and direct his misguided sexual energy on to one of his professors, but he's still in London working in an antipodean coffee shop in Soho and sharing an ex-council flat with Mia in Dalston, along with their other friend from school, Gemma.

"Mr. D!"

Speak of the devil . . .

Bennett turns around to see Richard, a rail-thin, walking oxymoron in a mesh tank top and a tweed jacket. He arrives with Gemma, a loud and lanky girl whose greatest aspiration in life is, as she puts it, "to tame a banker." Tonight, she looks ready for a photo shoot in heavy makeup and three-inch heels. She clocks the painting and shrieks. "I can't believe you actually painted it!" she says, shaking Mia's shoulders.

"Looking sharp!" Richard steps back and takes in Bennett's style with genuine admiration. "I love your scarf." He reaches out and thumbs the fabric. "Where can I get it?"

"Selfridges." He holds out his hand to Richard, hoping the kid will stop stroking him.

"Damn. I was hoping you'd say Primark!" Richard skips the handshake and comes in for a hug. He smells like a grammar school gym class: sweat, mesh, and cheap cologne.

"How's the coffee business?" Bennett asks, trying to wriggle out of the embrace.

"It's good." Richard lingers on the words, nodding contemplatively as though being a barista were a career choice rather than just a job. "Brilliant celebrity spotting in Soho. Why haven't you come in? I'll make you the best flat white you've ever had!"

The only flat white I've ever had.

"I don't make it to Soho much anymore." Not a lie, actually.

"Not even for me?" Richard slaps him playfully.

Oh boy.

Bennett is forced to turn to the vagina painting for relief. "What do you think, Richard?"

Richard looks at the painting and jumps back.

"Terrifying!" He turns to Bennett and, with all sincerity, he says, "That's my worst nightmare."

||||||||||||||||||||||

Occupying the same courtyard as St. Martins is London's hippest vegetarian restaurant, Acreage. "They make vegetables taste just as good as meat!" Gemma exclaims after Bennett enquires where they should have dinner. "It's all small plates," she adds, her tone suggesting this is a good thing. Mia has been a vegetarian for the last five years, so when his daughter's face lights up at the idea, Bennett is happy to oblige.

"You haven't been yet?" Bennett asks, arm around Mia as they exit the school.

"I can't afford Acreage!"

You can't afford small plates of vegetables?

"Good." He pulls her in. "Glad we could do it."

Gemma and Richard are several strides ahead of them, walking as though they're running late. Bennett and Mia adopt a more leisurely pace.

"Have you ever walked through it?" he asks, gesturing to the fountain as they pass it.

"Yeah, we all did on the first day."

"I saw a little girl running through it earlier. She reminded me of you when you were small."

Mia cringes. He knows she is weary of his post-divorce sentimentality.

"Try it. It's fun," she says, giving him a little shove.

"Nah. We're all hungry, let's eat."

"It'll take two minutes."

He looks at the water shooting up to the sky. There is no one around now, he'd have it all to himself, but he can't admit to his daughter that the fountain makes him nervous. He knows it's irrational, but he's convinced the water won't turn off when he steps in. Why does he so consistently believe that certain "givens" are not given for him? He's certain the water will continue to shoot up in his face and soak his clothes. The kind of experience that would have had his schoolmates Stuart, Jay, and Owen in stitches if such a fountain had existed in their youth. He stares up at the dark sky. He must look like he's praying, which means he looks ridiculous. But this, he decides, is his only defense against the water. Could such a fountain even be able to detect the presence of a man who's been standing still for the last twenty-five years and didn't even realize it?

"Do I need to hold your hand?" Mia asks.

Cheeky little shit.

"Go stand in the middle." Mia pulls out her phone. "I'll take your picture."

He walks over, stuffing his hands in his pockets. He closes his eyes and puts one foot on a spigot. All the spigots around his foot suddenly turn off. He opens his eyes and looks down at his beautiful brown boot, dry as a bone. He looks back at Mia, who wills him on like he's a small child making his first attempt on the monkey bars. He walks in cautiously, savoring each trail of water that shuts off in his presence. Finally, at the middle, he turns to face his daughter, who's taking photos as water shoots up in the air from a safe radius all around him. He takes his hands from his pockets and reaches to the sides, waving his arms around and commanding the jets of water to stop and start, stop and start. He's detectable. He's alive.

IIIIIIIIIIIIIIIIIIIIIIIIIII

The restaurant is heaving. They'll be waiting forever for a table, but Bennett doesn't mind because it means extra time with Mia. They hover around the host stand, surveying the cavernous warehouse space; open kitchen, long bar, large windows, exposed bricks, and . . .

Wait, what the fuck?

"Dad, isn't that one of yours?" Mia points to a painting on the back wall. It's a large still life of aubergines, courgettes, and tomatoes on a table covered by an intricate fabric that could only have been painted by Bennett Driscoll.

Seriously, what the fuck?

"Yeah." He squints in disbelief. "How long has this place been open?"

They all look at Gemma, since she's the expert. Well, she acts like she is.

"Not long, six months, maybe."

Bennett hasn't received money for a painting in more than a year, but he's not about to admit that. They all look at him now. He shrugs, confused.

"You didn't sell that to them?" Richard asks, scandalized. He's always excited when a plot thickens.

"I did not."

Bennett stuffs his hands back in his coat pockets, making fists in secret.

The host returns to his stand; he's a young man, wearing a stern expression more appropriate for marching troops into battle than organizing seating charts.

"How many?" he asks, coming face-to-face with Gemma's disapproving eyes.

"Where did you get that painting?" Gemma points to the artwork like a dog owner would point to a puddle of piss. She wants to rub his face in it.

"Pardon?" He looks at her like she's insane.

Gemma raises her voice. "Where was that painting purchased?"

He glances at the painting. "I can't say that I know." He returns his focus to the seating chart. "Four of you?"

Gemma ignores the question. "This man, here"—pointing to Bennett—"he painted it, and you didn't buy it from him."

Shut it, Gemma.

The host looks at Bennett and waits for confirmation.

Bennett nods, silently. Yes, he did paint it.

"I can ask my manager where it was purchased, but I'm not sure he'll know, either." What else can he say? This is way above his pay grade.

"It's okay." Bennett briefly removes his hand from his pocket to wave this off.

"You can give us a good table for now," Gemma continues, with her authoritative tone. "But your manager will be hearing from this man's representatives in the morning."

What representatives?

||||||||||||||||||||||||

It wasn't long after being nominated for the Turner Prize that Bennett decided to abandon nudes in favor of produce. By then, he'd been married for a while and had a daughter on the way. Inviting strange women to undress in his studio didn't feel right anymore. After all, the nude paintings had happened, sort of, by accident, anyway. During his own time as a student at St. Martins, Bennett had fallen for Henrietta, a Scottish student two years above him. A sculptor, Henrietta spent all of her time in the "life room," drawing and molding figures in clay. She had crazy, frizzy ginger hair and wore her terra-cotta–stained apron everywhere. She bit her fingernails until there was almost nothing there. Henrietta represented everything Bennett imagined a serious artist to be. Plus, she liked to stroke his wavy blond hair. What else was an impressionable young man supposed to do except toss aside his interest in still lifes in order to spend a few extra hours a day sketching strangers' limbs alongside the woman who infatuated him? For a year, he followed her around like a puppy that needed feeding. As it turned out, the side benefit of his infatuation was that he became an excellent figure painter. His paintings earned a lot of attention from his tutors, so he started entering competitions and they got in. At the end of his first year, when Henrietta buggered off to Glasgow without so much as a goodbye, he saw no reason to quit the figure painting. In fact, this weird thing was happening: other women were starting to use the life room to be near him. Who'd have thought?

Switching to produce presented certain new challenges, all of them exciting, especially the new palette. The deep purples of an aubergine, the bright reds of a tomato. A banana is never the yellow you think it is. The still-life installation in his studio was ever changing based on what was available at the farmers market. "Why don't you bring some vegetables home when you've been to the market?" Eliza had asked him one night. She had never minded his models much. She never asked him to stop painting naked women. So far as he could tell, she never felt the slightest bit threatened by them, whereas, the fact that he would go to the farmers market every day and never brought home so much as an apple to his wife and daughter . . . *that* bothered her. Maybe she wouldn't have wanted the fancy car, the giant washing machine, or loud, American, hedge-fund Jeff if it had only occurred to Bennett to bring home just *one* of the fucking aubergines instead of taking them all to the studio?

||||||||||||||||||||||

"Mr. Driscoll?"

Bennett turns around, a braised leek on the end of his fork.

A bearded thirtysomething man in suspenders hovers over him. "I'm Chris, the manager. I understand you enquired about the painting?"

No. She *did.*

Bennett looks across to Gemma, who is on the opposite side of the fantastic window table that her insolence secured them.

Chris pulls on the end of his beard. "I've spoken to our designer."

Gemma sets down her cutlery and looks up at Chris like she means business.

Bennett scrapes the leek across his tiny plate, releasing it from the fork which he still grasps, tightly.

"She's informed me that the painting was bought at auction. Sotheby's, she thinks." He puts his hand on the back of Bennett's chair in a far too personal gesture. "If you like, she can pull up the paperwork? E-mail it to you?"

"That's not necessary." He takes a sip of his wine, needing to find a purpose for his free hand.

Confused, Chris looks to Gemma for confirmation.

"Have her e-mail it, definitely." she chimes in.

Mia looks at her dad, her expression somewhere between embarrassment and compassion. Either way, it makes Bennett's heart sink.

"She says it'll likely have the name of whoever put the painting up for auction," beardy Chris adds, his thumbs in his suspenders like he's ready for a hoedown.

"Really, it's alright." Because Bennett doesn't want to know who put it up for auction. He definitely doesn't want to know if the bastard got more money for it than he did. He stabs another leek with his fork, despite not having eaten the first one.

"Seeing as we love the painting, we're sending over a double portion of our special beetroot ravioli to show our appreciation."

Sounds like you hate me.

"That's very kind. Thank you."

"He is FIT," Gemma says as she stares at Chris's ass walking away, the fight over the painting forgotten.

"You're such a flirt!" Richard is, once again, scandalized.

That was flirting?

Bennett looks over at Mia, who smiles back at him.

"Poor Dad. You hate beetroot."

"But you love it. You can have mine." He can't go back in time and bring home apples and aubergines, as Eliza had wanted him to. But he can give his daughter all his beetroot ravioli. With pleasure.

||||||||||||||||||||||

Even with the free beetroot ravioli, Acreage had been staggeringly expensive. Bennett's wallet aches as he heads to the Tube, hoping, at the very least, the three nineteen-year-olds are going home happy and full. Truthfully, he knows they're not headed home. Their night is only just getting started. Though Mia was polite and only checked it once, her phone vibrated several times during dinner. He glimpsed a smile when she looked down at the screen. He didn't enquire who it was, but he hopes desperately that it's someone who is good to her. Someone who wouldn't balk at buying her three hundred quid's worth of braised vegetables.

Dinner has cost him roughly what one night in his house is costing Alicia. He can't help but wonder which one of them got the worse deal. All night it's been difficult to get the vision of Alicia, alone in the house, out of his head. At one point it occurred to him to order an extra plate of beetroot ravioli to bring back for her. Although it's not uncommon for Bennett to feel the entirety of any emotional spectrum all at once, it's confusing to feel both fatherly toward and sexually attracted to Alicia. He decided not to order her the ravioli, because he prefers the sexual fantasy to the fatherly impulse. As he steps onto the down escalator at King's Cross, putting in his earbuds, he thinks that, inaction, for once, was the right choice. Young women don't like gifts from strange old men, especially when that gift involves beetroot.

||||||||||||||||||||||

When Bennett changes to the District line, he has the carriage all to himself. Faced with all the empty seats, he decides to remain standing, recalling being in the center of the fountain earlier this evening, arms outstretched. He grabs on to the central pole. He pulls the ancient iPod from his coat pocket and with his thumb, turns up the dial on Roots Manuva. The old train lurches, throwing him forward and causing him to strengthen his grip. He looks around him, still self-conscious, as the music vibrates through the empty train car. He taps his foot and bobs his head. After a few seconds he can't help it, his lips move . . .

> *Taskmaster burst the bionic zit-splitter*
> *Breakneck speed we drown ten pints of bitter*
> *We lean all day and some say that ain't productive*
> *That depend upon the demons that you're stuck with*

He taps hands along on the handlebar, keeping the beat, surfing the train.

> *'Cause right now, I see clearer than most*
> *I sit here contending with this cheese on toast*
> *I feel the pain of a third world famine*
> *Segue, we count them blessings and keep jamming*

"Ravenscourt Park," the woman's voice says over the intercom. The doors creak open and a dignified man in a flat cap about ten years Bennett's senior boards the train. The older man hears the hip-hop and looks around the carriage, searching for its source. Holding on to the iPod in his pocket, Bennett's thumb finds the wheel and the volume drops. Regardless, the flat-capped man takes a seat at the far end of the carriage. Deflated, Bennett stares down at the train's speckled flooring for the rest of the ride.

〡〡〡〡〡〡〡〡〡〡〡〡〡〡〡〡〡〡〡

Lights are glowing from the ground floor of his house when Bennett returns. He stops at the garden gate, looking, covertly, through the windows to find where Alicia might be. He sees her shadow moving through the living room, the TV flickering in the background. He squints to see if he can tell what she's watching. It looks like some sort of comedy panel show. She walks past the window again, her blond hair down now, draped over a mustard-yellow hoodie, zipped up tight. Bennett hastily fiddles with the latch of the gate, hoping to seem as though he has been in perpetual motion and not, in fact, spying on her. He doesn't think she's spotted him. He wonders whether he should close the gate quietly or announce his presence by slamming it shut? He's never asked himself this question about any other guest. In the past, he's always closed the gate quietly, not wanting to invite any interaction. If he does slam it, what is he hoping to achieve? Does he want Alicia to see him? To invite him into his own house for a drink? He has a bottle of amaretto locked in the study. Women like amaretto.

Sexist assumption? Probably.

Nevertheless, amaretto is a better gift than beetroot ravioli. Sexier. He's not thinking about being fatherly now. He doesn't want to go in the house to, say, read her a story. He'd like to kiss her. If she's as lonely as she seems, then maybe they could both benefit.

He sees her take a seat on the couch, covering herself with the blanket from the linen closet. It warms his heart to know he helped in that regard, at least. It looks like there is a bottle of wine on the coffee table and maybe a plate.

Good, she's eaten.

The fatherly impulses return. Either the constant fluctuation of emotion, or possibly Acreage's crispy kale, is making him queasy.

He closes the gate quietly behind him and jams his cold fingers back into his coat pockets. In that split second, he remembers the security light in the back garden. The lamp illuminates all of the yard, including Bennett, who stops abruptly. Another reminder he's not so invisible after all, his movements traceable for the second time tonight. He can't help it; he turns around.

There she is, having stood up from the couch, looking out the window at him. She tucks her hair behind her ears, apprehensively, maybe even a little frightened.

He smiles his gentlest smile—the exact opposite of his professional one that he gave Evan earlier. He nods with a little wave, a guilty kind of wave. One that attempts to apologize for all his perverted thoughts. She smiles back, but it's an embarrassed smile. However unwisely, Bennett feels in this moment that if there is anyone to whom he could convey his uncertainties, his solitude, his stagnation, Alicia is somehow that person.

Seeming to share in his uncertainty, she quickly looks away.

He doesn't have to tell her about his vulnerabilities. She already knows. His burdens are just that, his burdens. No sexier than beetroot ravioli. Nothing for him to do now but turn back around and keep moving.

BEGGARS CAN'T BE CHOOSERS

Alicia's never seen sheets this white before; they're unnaturally so, like the teeth in whitening strip commercials. Her tired eyes survey the large bedroom. There's a cream-colored chaise lounge in the corner, a white-painted parquet floor and a chest of drawers that's been painted white, but then sanded back to give it a distressed look. Above the chest is a small square painting of white flowers in an antique white bud vase. In the painting, the vase sits atop an intricately detailed ivory-lace doily on a whitewashed wooden table—a hundred different shades of white in one painting. It was painted by her AirBed host, Bennett, a middle-aged bachelor, who put a tiny little "B.D." in the lower right-hand corner of the painting, barely visible in yet another shade of white. She wishes she knew more about art. She thought she'd learn a lot more through her job at the online auction house, Virtual Paddle, but she's just there to crunch the numbers and in actuality, there's very little art in the art world, anyway. She knows the hashtags that sell—#abstraction, #photorealism, #landscape—but she doesn't get to see the art, not beyond the little thumbnail that accompanies her stacks and stacks of spreadsheets. Still, something about Bennett's painting speaks to her, its intimacy. He really knows that vase, that doily, that whitewashed wooden table. She can't imagine knowing anything that well. She can't imagine having anyone know her that well, either. She wonders what it's like to sleep with a guy that pays that much attention to detail. It's an odd impulse, thinking about sex with her AirBed host—he could probably be her father—but it's been a while. Five years.

She lies in the middle of the bed, gliding her legs under the duvet from end to end, making snow angels on the white sheets. It would be nice to meet someone, she thinks, someone to push her over to one side of the bed, someone she can annoy with her restless legs syndrome the way it annoyed William five years ago in a different bed, in a different part of London. Dating William, a classmate at LSE and the heir to the large French bistro chain, Café Chartreuse, was like buying a house over budget—a giant emotional expense that she's now paying back with interest. Keeping up with a man of his privilege, charm, wit, and good looks was exhausting, and no man has looked as appealing since.

God knows what he saw in her. She never was able to figure that out. Because she couldn't figure it out, she never told her mother about him. William was the kind of guy that would have made Annette roll her eyes. "Beggars can't be choosers," her mother always said when she was growing up. Annette meant it mostly in regards to dinner—if Alicia wanted beans and hot dogs but was faced with tuna-noodle casserole—but the phrase bled into all aspects of her young life: clothes, homework, clarinet lessons (she had wanted to play the piano).

She went to the only college that accepted her—Denison University in Ohio, her "safety school." She'd wanted to go to one of those liberal arts colleges outside of Philadelphia, but none would have her. Same thing with her master's. She went to the London School of Economics, because the U.S. programs had all rejected her. And it hadn't helped that until the day he died, her father called her "Mouse," an endearing term for her dark blond hair as well as her relative invisibility. When she met William, she thought she'd finally shifted from beggar, straight past chooser, to lottery winner. Of course, lottery winners rarely stay rich.

Coming back to London was a bad idea. The plan was hatched at an Anglophile's bar on the Lower East Side, GinSmith, a place that boasts a hundred types of gin and a playlist weighted heavily in favor of the Smiths. A lover of all things British, but especially Morrissey, Alicia suggested her friends all meet there for a gin tasting—a step up from their usual Friday night "Buds with Britney" event that her friend Andrew, an Alabama native, hosts in Bushwick. While at Gin-Smith, three shots in, her friend Zoe, a short and bubbly assistant children's book editor, expressed an interest in a London trip. To the amusement of the group, she re-created the moment from *Peter Pan* where Wendy and Peter fly over Big Ben and the River Thames, in what appeared to be interpretive dance. Everyone else, also three sheets to the wind, agreed that a London getaway would be amazing. They should *totally* do it. Alicia, over the moon, said she'd look into houses on AirBed. But it was an error to interpret her friends' drunkenness as genuine enthusiasm. After she booked Bennett's house, one by one, they dropped like flies: Zoe decided it made more sense to buy a car rather than to go on vacation; Matt, a sous chef, met a beautiful girl and didn't want to risk her finding a new guy while he was gone; and poor Andrew, an off-off-Broadway actor, never had a real prayer of being able to afford the trip in the first place. Liz was the one that upset her most. A childhood friend from Southern Illinois, Liz had taken Alicia under her wing when she moved to Brooklyn five years ago, despite having almost no contact. She and Liz had drifted apart after high school, when Alicia went off to Ohio and Liz remained in Carbondale to attend Southern Illinois University. Then when Alicia was living in London, she'd never thought much about her old friend. During that entire year, she didn't really think about anyone back in America. There was a small part of her that hoped she'd never have to think about any of them again. If Alicia is honest, she knows they don't have a ton in common anymore, not like they did when they were little girls—an idyllic time when the most important thing in the world had been scoring each other's dismounts off the monkey bars.

I thought you were into the idea, Alicia replied to Liz on Messenger.

You can't hold me accountable for what I say when I've been drinking, Liz typed back. *Plus, I don't want to spend my vacation watching you pine after your dickhead ex*, she added.

That's not why I'm going.

Please. You have terrible taste in men, Alicia.

||||||||||||||||||||||

She rolls onto her side and looks out the window. The shed that Bennett now calls home is at the end of the garden. His curtains are pulled back, but she can't see him, only a few paintings propped up against the wall. She wonders what he's sleeping on in there and if the place has heat. She knows she's paid for his house, four hundred dollars a night, but still, she feels guilty for relegating him to a glorified hut, especially with all these free bedrooms. She's got to stop feeling sorry for men who can't get their shit together, but she liked Bennett when she met him yesterday, even if he is, for reasons beyond her comprehension, living in a potting shed. He was kind, eager not to be in her way. She thinks she wouldn't mind sharing the house with him. When he came home last night, she swears he was staring through the window like a sad puppy left out in the rain, though he was quick to disappear when she spotted him. Since then, she's concocted a fantasy where she and Bennett share a bottle of red wine, talk about art, cook a roast, and settle in to watch the box set of *Sherlock* together. In this fantasy, Bennett isn't annoying like most of the guys she knows. First, he'll ask her what *she* thinks about online sales trends versus brick and mortar, then how *she* likes her beef cooked (mid-rare). He won't solve the *Sherlock* mysteries out loud and he won't call her his "Watson" the way William did.

You won't notice I'm here, Bennett promised her at check-in. Relieved as she should have been to hear him say that—the men she works with are always vying for the spotlight—she was actually disappointed. After all, if she isn't meant to notice him, that means he won't be noticing *her*. That's the thing about men wanting her attention; she always gives it to them, because at least by wanting her attention, they have to admit she exists.

||||||||||||||||||||||

Showered and dressed, Alicia stands in front of the bathroom mirror wearing a black T-shirt and jeans. She ties her wispy, shoulder-length hair back in a ponytail and attempts to flatten the flyaways around her temples with some spit. She pulls her yellow cardigan on over her black T-shirt. Yellow is her favorite color. She fears that might be the most interesting thing about her. Nobody likes yellow. Just her.

For the rest of the morning, she sits at the kitchen island, perusing the Facebook pages of her favorite LSE classmates. So far as she can tell, four of them are still living in London. Judging by their profiles, they are all happy, smiley, successful people with life partners and children. By all accounts that year at LSE is long gone for them. It's been buried by newer, happier memories—milestones, accomplishments, and stupidly happy babies—cataloged, chronologically, on virtual timelines. They've all bought houses in London neighborhoods Alicia's never heard of: Bruce Grove, Leytonstone, Abbey Wood, Hither Green, where the fuck? She pulls down the *London A-Z* from Bennett's bookshelf and looks up Hither Green. It's east and south of the Thames and she is north and west of it. She turns at least twenty pages in the book before finding the map of Chiswick, where Bennett has diligently marked: "You are here!" She would never have booked a house this far west if she had known she was coming on her own. During her year abroad, she lived in Camden Town and loved the punks and goths who wandered around the neighborhood as though it was 1979, listening to "London Calling" pumping out of market stall stereos.

Growing up, she would have liked to have been a punk, if she'd had the courage, but it was hard to rebel the way the other kids did, especially when it was just her and her mother. Once her dad left them for Jesus, everything was about survival, nothing about choice. Annette was an administrative assistant at the university, making almost nothing. Alicia's clothes were the cheapest that her mom could find at Walmart or Goodwill. If Alicia had cut holes into her clothes, splattered paint on them, or pierced safety pins through them, she would have been punished.

Resolved to cheer herself up by spending the afternoon in Camden Town, she rises from her stool and looks around the kitchen for all the things she'll need to take with her. She tosses her wallet and Bennett's *A-Z* into her purse and slings it over her shoulder, then she grabs the keys from the kitchen island before looking out the back window at Bennett's studio. In the bright midday light, she can see a large propped-up blank canvas. Bennett stands next to it, holding up several fabric swatches to the light. Lost in her own narrative, she doesn't immediately notice when Bennett spots her through the window. He waves at her like he did last night, as though he has something to apologize for. He's handsome in that unfair way that only happens to men of a certain age, where all the wrinkles, scars, and barren hair follicles only add to the attraction. Bennett looks lived-in, Alicia thinks, like an old T-shirt you can't stop wearing, even though it's falling apart.

When she waves back, he opens the door to the studio and comes out into the yard.

"Sorry, I didn't mean to disturb you," she says loudly from the back door as he comes toward her.

"That's alright," he says, smiling. His button-down shirt and jeans are both covered in paint. Hands in his pockets, he stops several feet short of the door. "Everything alright?"

"Yeah, fine. Sorry, I was in my own little world."

"Not to worry." He stays put, apparently happy to chat. "Little warmer today, thankfully."

"Yeah, I think I'll head out in a bit. Hoping to meet a friend in Camden." Why is she lying to him? She'll only have to back that up later.

"Well, enjoy your day. Do you know how to get to the station?"

He strokes his hair and then points, she presumes, in the direction of the station, before stuffing his hand back in his pocket.

"I think so. I've borrowed your *A-Z*, I hope you don't mind. I prefer it to the map on my phone."

This seems to please him. "I prefer it, too, but I'm an old dog."

"Oh." Easily mortified, she rifles through her bag to retrieve the map. "Do you need it?" She holds it out to him. "I can use my phone."

"Please, it's all yours." His smile grows. "I'll be here all day staring down that blank canvas." His fingers fidget in his pocket, like he's found a ball of lint.

"How do you decide what to paint?" she asks, then quickly wonders if it was a weird question. She can tell by his expression, utter dread, that he didn't sign up for this interrogation. "That's a terrible thing to ask. Sorry."

"No. That's alright. I have a fabric collection. I work from that."

"Wow, cool." It *is* cool, but she can't help worrying if the tone of her voice suggests sarcasm.

"You can come and have a look, if you like."

"No, no, thank you, I should get going." Going nowhere, of course.

"Well, another time, if you want." He starts back to the studio, then turns around. His eyes linger on her shoulder before he speaks, long enough that she looks down at her cardigan, expecting to find a stain. "You can always pop round for a cup of tea," he says, finally, "if you're at a loose end."

He knows, she thinks. He knows she's a mess of loose ends, culminating in a giant knot, like the clump of necklaces that sits in the bottom of the jewelry box. The ones not worth untangling.

"Thanks. Maybe I will."

||||||||||||||||||||||

Camden Town hasn't changed much in five years. Stepping out of the station and onto the high street comes with a rush of déjà vu. The pubs, coffee shops, and restaurants all look the same, including The World's End on the corner—a pub that only signifies the end of the world, if the end of the world starts with a slowly decaying pub carpet. Alicia doesn't know whether to be relieved or disappointed at how familiar everything is. Looking around, she weighs her options: she could continue up the high street to Camden Lock or go in the other direction to Central London. Kentish Town Road would take her out of the chaos and into leafy North London or she could go up to Royal College Street and look at her old flat. Instead, nostalgia pulls her across Camden High Street to Parkway and plants her at the front door of the Jazz Cafe. She looks over the posters of upcoming acts. She hates jazz, but she doesn't want to ignore the place. If she walked, briskly, past every place in London that held memories, she'd be in a constant sprint. It had been the site of her and William's first date. Beforehand, he'd taken her for staggeringly expensive dim sum down the road at Gilgamesh. Throughout their relationship, he took her out for fancy meals all over London, but they never ate at Café Chartreuse because the food was, to his mind, "shit." He enjoyed spoiling her—it was so easy, considering she'd never been spoiled before. For William, Alicia was six months of fun. He knew she'd be heading back to America after the academic year, which gave him an excuse to never truly take the relationship seriously. She realized that too late. Two weeks before she was due to fly back to America, she asked him, "Would you like it if I stayed?" He answered quickly that, of course, he'd love it if she stayed, adding unconvincingly, "Too bad it's not possible."

The next weekend, lying naked next to him in his sun-filled bedroom in Islington, she said, "Maybe I could leave and come back. Apply for jobs in London from home?"

"Sure," he responded, pulling her in for a kiss. "Only if it's for you, though. Don't do it if it's for me."

He married some girl called Pippa two years ago—a tall brunette, perpetually in sunglasses. Alicia's been stalking her on Instagram.

|||||||||||||||||||||

The sushi place, a couple doors down from the Jazz Cafe, is still in business, but it's quiet today, just a couple of tables are occupied when Alicia enters. She smiles at the waiter, an older man, who gives her a swift nod. He, like his restaurant, is just the same as five years ago—disheveled and tragically unhip. Back then he was curt, bordering on unfriendly, and perpetually disappointed in his customers' taste. There's nothing to indicate any of that has changed. His face and his maroon shirt (the same shirt after all these years!) are wrinkly in equal measure.

"He's Korean, not Japanese," William used to say. "All the Asians that work in sushi restaurants are Korean." He always said this kind of thing with an authority that felt pointless to question.

"Just me," she says to the, apparently, Korean man.

Wordless, he points to a table by the window. He shows no recognition of having seen her before, which is understandable—it's been five years—but still, it makes her a little sad. She likes to think she is a memorable customer, the kind that restaurant staff want to return. Still, no heartwarming reunions happening today at Sushi Bento; this guy doesn't give a fuck. She sits down, uncomfortably, on the vinyl-coated chair at a table that is really meant for four. She puts her coat on one chair and her bag on another in the hopes of making her oneness less obvious. She opens the thick laminated menu, where every item is listed by number, both in English and Japanese; if you're still confused, there's a picture. She checks her watch to see if it's still a respectable time to order a bento box. According to William, ordering a bento box past three p.m. is as culinarily unacceptable as ordering a Bloody Mary with dinner. "Amateur hour," he would say. With William she was never an amateur. She was always in "the know," a rare and powerful feeling, the kind that subsequently led her to believe she was more important and deserving than she really was. A feeling previously unknown to her and one that disappeared like a puff of smoke several months later, after a long flight from London to Chicago, when her mother picked her up at the Carbondale Greyhound stop and announced, keys in hand, "Hurry up, the meter is running."

"Mixed sashimi bento box, please," Alicia states as confidently as she can for a loner at a table for four.

The maroon-shirted man bears down on her. "Drink?!" Somewhere between a question and a command.

"I'm fine with water," she says, losing confidence.

He takes the menu from her hands before she's had the chance to close it, then he gives her order to the chef, saying something in Japanese. Korean? She's ashamed she doesn't know. With just a little research, all of William's theories would be so easy to prove or disprove, but no one, including Alicia, ever bothered.

||||||||||||||||||||||||

She's on Kiera Michaels's Facebook page when her bento box arrives. She and Kiera were never very close at LSE, but they shared a quiet respect for one another. At least Alicia thinks they did. Kiera was shy, too, and they clung to one another for the first few days of classes, sharing nervous glances as their classmates shouted over each other for attention. Eventually, Alicia started to branch out socially, but Kiera continued to focus on academics. Kiera wasn't a big drinker, so she didn't join the post-lecture crowd that gathered at the pubs in Lincoln's Inn Fields most nights. She was very smart and driven, and though soft-spoken, she gradually found her voice. She owned her opinions and worked hard to defend them, often arguing for business models that put inclusivity at the forefront. Alicia, alas, never really found her voice. She agreed with most of what Kiera said in class about ethical and feminist business models, but she rarely spoke up. William would, though. "That's all well and good, Kiera," he'd say, "but at the end of the day, business is just business. It's not personal."

One afternoon at the pub, William said, conspiratorially, "Kiera's too competitive." His sweetness was often eroded by a few beers and an audience. "That's why she doesn't come to the pub with us. Because she sees us as threats." He'd chugged half of his pint in thirty seconds. "She should lighten up. It's not like we're competing for the same job. My dad isn't going to hire her instead of me."

To Alicia, Kiera never seemed threatened or threatening. In fact, she seemed surprisingly empathetic for a business student. "Companies with a compassionate business model do better," she argued in class, pointing out that fashion brands with charitable one-for-one models were some of the fastest-growing new businesses. She was right, Alicia thinks, realizing the glasses she's wearing are from one such company.

These days, it seems the two of them are on similar career paths.

According to her info page, Kiera is the chief financial officer at Printed Palette, an art poster brand that sells through museum gift shops. In her profile picture, Kiera looks much the same, still a big woman with cropped hair and giant breasts that are tethered by a turtleneck sweater. She's standing next to a Picasso, one of the cubist pieces where the woman is crying into a handkerchief. In the photo, Kiera neither smiles nor frowns, as if the shot is for posterity only.

Dipping her tuna sashimi in soy sauce, Alicia peruses the Printed Palette website. It seems Kiera is practicing what she preached in school—a one-for-one business model—donating one poster to a British school for every one sold. Alicia zooms in on the map she finds on the company website. Southwark Street, it says, right behind Tate Modern. Maybe she'll head to the museum this afternoon, maybe even try to locate Kiera's office when she's there.

Back on Facebook, Alicia's thumb hovers over Messenger's text box before setting down her chopsticks on the rest provided so she can type two-handed: *Hi Kiera. It's Alicia from LSE. I hope you're well.* She pauses. That's the easy part. *I'm back in London for a few days and was thinking of you.* *Thinking of you* sounds vaguely romantic. She continues, *It looks like we're doing a lot of the same things. Working for art companies. Maybe you'd like to get a coffee sometime this week? I know it's short notice, so I totally understand if you're busy. Best, Alicia.*

She takes a deep breath and presses Send, before looking up to see the maroon-shirted man watching her, disapprovingly. She piles white sticky rice onto her chopsticks and wraps her mouth around the large bite. She smiles at him, as best she can with her mouth full, nodding encouragingly.

||||||||||||||||||||||

After finishing her sushi, Alicia wanders up to Royal College Street, past her old flat, but she feels stupid. She doesn't even stop, she just glances up at her old bedroom window and keeps moving. Crossing the street, she heads back in the other direction, studying the flat one more time from the other side of the road. What is she supposed to do? Talk to a building? She hasn't even visited her father's grave back home since he died twelve years ago, because she wouldn't know what to do once she got there. This old block of flats is nothing but a stack of bricks now, just as her dad's gravestone is just a slab of granite. No spirits, no answers, just masonry and stone.

When she planned this trip, Alicia thought she and her Brooklyn friends would spend their days hopping from neighborhood to neighborhood, museum to pub to restaurant to more pubs and then, who knows, maybe a nightclub. Everyone's energy would be endless, their spirits high. To say this was an absurd fantasy is an understatement. She'd been confusing her actual friends with TV friends, those people who continuously wander in and out of each other's apartments and have boozy brunches together every Sunday. Mythical friendships. She hasn't really gotten close to anybody in the five years since she's been back in the States. Her friends are actually Liz's friends. Even if they had come with her to London, it wouldn't have been the trip she'd imagined, for the simple reason that they weren't the people she imagined them to be. Odds are she would feel just as lost and lonely if they were here.

Her high-top sneakers scraping the pavement of Camden Road, she hasn't got a clue what to do next. Feeling lost in a place you know by heart is one of life's more disconcerting feelings, she thinks. She thought she'd be happy to be back; truth is, all it's done is prove that she hasn't been happy since the year she lived here. In Brooklyn, when she's having a bad day, she closes her eyes and walks the streets of London in her mind: down Royal College Street, left onto Camden Road, down Camden Road and left onto Camden High Street. Camden High Street until it becomes Eversholt Road, across Euston Road, following it past Tavistock Square, onto Woburn Place, and then onto Russell Square until it becomes Southampton Row, past Holborn Station and it's now Kingsway, left on Portugal Street and there is LSE. It's all there in her mind. She could do it with her eyes closed; her feet are already heading that way, but she won't let them go. She'll need her happy place intact in her mind when she gets home. She can't risk losing it to this current funk of hers. If her mind can't go there, where can it go?

||||||||||||||||||||||

She heads south on the Tube thinking only vaguely of getting off at London Bridge, a ten-minute walk from Tate Modern and Kiera's office. Like Camden, the neighborhood is full of memories of William, memories she should be trying to avoid, so she tells herself that she'll only get off if it feels right. If it doesn't, she'll ride it to the end of the line to Morden; maybe it's amazing.

Seven stops later, longing proves stronger than discovery and she steps out of the Underground at London Bridge, straight into Borough Market where she used to take her fancy SLR camera for walks around the foodie market on Saturday mornings. She loved to photograph all the weird mushrooms, funky cheeses, and fish eyeballs. She often wonders, if she had a life where making money wasn't the necessary objective, maybe she might've been a food photographer. Five years ago she had entertained thoughts of being married to William, the two of them traveling the globe together, and how she'd document all the world's peculiarities with her Hasselblad medium format camera (the camera that he would buy her as a wedding present). Recalling dreams like this, she feels foolish. She tells herself that she never *really* thought any of it would happen. William, however, did travel the world after they broke up. He took pictures, too, but they were the people-smiling-in-front-of-things variety. Not the kind she would have taken. For this trip, she hadn't even bothered bringing her camera.

She makes it into the market as it's closing down. It's only four but the sun is nearly set. The vendors have been hawking since the early hours of the morning. Evening has brought a definite chill to the air, as well as a breeze that threatens to blow away whatever hasn't sold. The crowds will soon shift from the stalls into the pubs. She and William used to come down to the market on Tuesday afternoons. They'd buy fancy cheese and crackers at end-of-the-day prices, then settle, pints in hand, into a coveted table at one of the pubs and watch as the market men packed up. By the time the pubs shut, they'd be hammered but fortified against hunger with stinky cheese and quince. They'd ride the Tube back up to Islington and devour *époisse* the way others would a late-night kebab.

On busy Stoney Street, a fog starts to roll in as the temperature drops. She stands in front of the Market Tavern feeling moisture collect under the collar of her wool coat, causing her to shiver. Or maybe it's the memory of the terrorist attack that happened just outside these doors less than a year ago. Although, it's not really her memory to shudder over; she wasn't here. She was back in Brooklyn, watching in horror as the drama unfolded on CNN. As the screaming crowds spilled out of the pubs, a strange feeling came over her, one she wouldn't want to admit to—she wished she and William were in Borough Market that night. Her feelings for the place, for William, and for that warm feeling of being with your friends in a crowded pub, were so strong she wanted to be there to defend them. Those drunken revelers were fleeing all the pubs she recognized: the Granary, the Market Tavern, the Rose. Her pubs. The attack had felt personal. She was deeply ashamed of these thoughts then, and she's deeply ashamed of them now as they come flooding back. She knows how stupid and insensitive it would sound out loud, but what pissed her off more than anything was that it felt like London wasn't hers anymore. In the days after the attack, nobody understood how upset she was. Her strong connection to London was apparent to no one else but her, and the very thing she thought defined her, didn't. Sometimes she wonders if she and William had survived such an event together, maybe they would still *be* together.

She makes her way to the Rose, her favorite pub. A little set back into the darkness of the market, it doesn't draw as much tourist trade as the others. In late afternoon the outside looks quiet and secluded, particularly in the fog. The inside glows with the twinkle of Christmas lights that they haven't gotten around to taking down. If she squints, she could be in Victorian London. She imagines the men in the pub wearing three-piece suits. There could be a piano player, sawdust on the floors, and women in long flowing skirts and corsets, or some such ridiculous nonsense.

As she lingers in her fantasy, a man in a shiny grey suit stumbles out of the pub, releasing its shouting and laughter into the cold air. It's not even dinnertime and this guy is hammered. He sees Alicia near the entrance and struggles not to sway. He can't be that old, mid-thirties, maybe, balding—bordering on just plain bald. He spins around to catch the door before it closes behind him. Alicia can tell that he shaves his own head, but can't quite reach the hairs on his neck, so they've grown wild. His facial hair is somewhere between stubble and beard. The hairs are unruly, pointing at strange angles. His suit is well-fitting, though the shininess makes it look cheap. He props himself on the door and regards Alicia while fishing through his pockets.

"Coming in, doll?" he slurs.

She looks down at her feet. She wasn't really planning to go in.

"It's fuckin' cold out here," he says, pulling a cigarette out of his jacket. "I gotta smoke this before my cock freezes to the side of my leg."

She smirks, glancing down at his crotch, a knee-jerk reaction. His trousers are the skinny-fit kind, so they don't leave much to the imagination. All his manhood is scrunched up in the shiny fabric, held captive slightly to the left. She immediately regrets looking; thankfully, he appears too drunk to notice.

He struggles to get the cigarette lit. "You want to share this with me?"

"No, thanks. I'm good." She finds herself inching toward the pub entrance.

"Smart choice," he says. "Strange man and all that."

She steps past him and into the doorway. His cologne is strong.

"I'm celebrating," he blurts out, his head pivoting to catch her eye before she disappears inside.

"Congratulations," she says, hoping that will suffice.

Clearly proud of himself, he smiles, but then the penny drops. "Aren't you going to ask me why?"

He loses his balance turning around, hoping to prop himself on his other shoulder, facing Alicia. When his arm hits the door a little harder than intended, he offers her an embarrassed smile, one that she can't help but find endearing.

"Alright. Why are you celebrating?"

"Commission." The cigarette bounces around in his lips as he talks. He chases it with his lighter. "A big commission."

"Lucky you." She could ask, *A big commission for what?* But she's enjoying torturing him. Just a little bit.

"It's not luck. It's hard work." He's dead serious.

"Right. Of course."

"I'm not so popular at the office. Other blokes get jealous when I make big commissions." He gives up lighting the cigarette. Removing it from his lips, he holds it out to his side as though it's lit. "It happens a lot."

He's cocky, she thinks, the kind of cocky that suggests low self-esteem at its core.

"Do you want me to light that for you?" she's surprised to hear herself ask.

He smiles again. *This* is luck. He takes his weight off the door and backs into the nearly empty market. She follows, the pub door closing behind them, its warmth and laughter replaced by cold and silence. He puts the lighter in the palm of her hand, caressing her fingers as he pulls away. She feels a tingle in her spine as their hands touch. Whether it's attraction or fear or both, she's not sure. She ignites the lighter and lifts the flame up to the cigarette between his lips. It catches immediately and starts to glow. He takes a long drag before blowing the smoke up into the roof of the market. Moving closer to Alicia, he again offers her the cigarette. This time, he lifts it to her lips with the hope of inserting it himself, but she steps back. She shared cigarettes with William sometimes when they'd been drinking. Even though smoking killed her father, she loves the way cigarettes smell, particularly in the rain.

"Come on, now. One won't kill you."

"No, thank you," she says, quietly confident, holding out the lighter to him. Instead of taking it, he looks her up and down.

"You meeting your fella?"

"Don't you want your lighter?" She shakes it at him.

"No fella?"

"None of your business." She smiles as she says this, not wanting to be a bitch.

"You're American," he adds menacingly, as though she were a spy or a mercenary.

She tries to stand her ground, but it's obvious he interprets this as flirting. "This is *your* lighter."

"You can put it in my pocket," he suggests. Pushing back his jacket with his hand, he motions to the front pocket of his trousers.

She doesn't look at his crotch this time. Instead, she forces her gaze over to the pub and the door she unwisely let shut. Next to it is a wide windowsill, littered with empty pint glasses. She steps back and sets the lighter down next to the empties. "It's here when you want it." She continues backing up deeper into the market.

"Ah, come on! It was worth a try, love."

"Have a good night," she says. "Congratulations, again."

"Come back!" he shouts, falling forward.

She keeps going. It would be a bad idea to get sucked back in. She has to tell herself this a couple of times. *You have terrible taste in men, Alicia*, Liz's words sting.

On the other side of the market, the fog rolls in off the river. In the distance, Alicia can spot the tall chimney of the old Bankside Power Station that now houses Tate Modern. She crosses under the steel Millennium Bridge, just as a large group of students descends the footbridge's sloping ramp onto the pavement. They move chaotically, with their matching backpacks, toward the museum's sliding glass doors. Rather than follow them into the vast concrete entrance hall, Alicia keeps walking. She has her eyes out for Southwark Street. When she finds it, it's populated mostly by hotels and sandwich shops. Printed Palette, Kiera's company, is halfway down, visible only by a small brass plaque outside a modern, unassuming, four-story building. Maybe she could try ringing the buzzer and say she's an old mate of Kiera's who just happens to be in the neighborhood. No, that would be weird, Alicia *is* weird. Pulling out her phone, she's hopeful that maybe Kiera has responded to her message, but no. She turns back and regards Tate Modern. She doesn't want to go in. The advertised exhibition is some guy she'd never heard of. Still, she can't head back to the house now, not with Bennett painting away in his studio. She doesn't want him to see her return so early, so pitifully. She noticed a Starbucks along the river. She'll go there first. Maybe look up the Tate artist or maybe wait to see if Kiera writes back.

Inside, she sits down in a plush velvet chair next to a group of Italian tourists, selfie-sticks at their sides. They're scrolling through their phones and laughing loudly at the photographic evidence of a brilliant day. Alicia sugars her coffee—the coffee she doesn't even want—which will, inevitably, keep her awake and prolong this already difficult day. She thinks about flipping through the photos on her phone, only to realize she hasn't taken a photo all day. The Italians are in hysterics, as one of them holds out his phone horizontally to the group—the contents of which is so funny, one of the other guys falls out of his chair. Alicia snaps her stirring stick in half and stabs her phone screen with the jagged edge.

She takes a swig of the hot coffee, burning the back of her throat. She wishes she could go back in time and delete that drunken New York evening when she proposed the idea of a trip to London in the first place. Her Brooklyn friends were never going to come with her. They aren't even her friends; they're acquaintances at best. They are always ignoring her invitations or, worse, agreeing and then ditching her over text. Fucking pathetic. And Kiera's not going to write back, either. She's regretting the message she sent her earlier. It will likely appear out of the blue, maybe even desperate, to her old classmate. They weren't even friends after that first week. What reason does Kiera have to respond? That they shared a quiet, mutual respect is probably a fabrication. Heck, she abandoned Kiera after that first week. Maybe if, just once, she had asked Kiera to study rather than running off to the pub with William and the trust-fund gang, Kiera would have reason to think of her fondly. Furthermore, why did Alicia believe that Kiera had any respect for *her*? She had done nothing to deserve it. How was Kiera to know that Alicia believed in ethical business practices when she spent the year gallivanting around London with the heir to a mediocre French bistro chain, the very presence of which predicted the death of every community it entered?

She looks down at her stirring stick, broken into twenty or so wooden chips in her lap. The Italian tourists aren't laughing anymore; they are staring at her, nervously. Picking up her phone, she goes back on Facebook, where she systematically removes all of her Brooklyn friends. Next, she moves on to every person she knew while she was living in London, deleting Kiera first and ending on William. There, she thinks. She's no longer living a lie. These people are not her friends. They never were. Unfriended.

"Fuckers." She stands up, defiantly, brushing the shards of the stirring stick onto the floor. Everyone in the coffee shop awaits her next move.

She looks around, embarrassed, realizing that she's left the virtual world and is now back in the real one. She picks up her coffee and smiles weakly at the Italians, hoping to convey she's kinder than the wooden stirrer suggests. She makes her way to the door, where she waits awkwardly for a group of American teenagers to file in—all of them thrilled and relieved at the sight of a Starbucks in this foreign land. They don't even prop the door open for her. Alicia hates them but smiles at them anyway.

The Tate is looming outside the door, uninviting. She never looked up the exhibiting artist, maybe she never had any intention of doing so. Blackfriars Station is only a couple minutes away. From there she can get the Tube back to West London, earlier than she planned, yes, but walking the streets of memory-less Chiswick feels smarter than walking, wounded, around Southwark.

Why then, she wonders, is she heading the opposite way—back in the direction of the Rose pub?

IIIIIIIIIIIIIIIIIIIIII

He's no longer standing outside the pub when she returns. Despite having felt the impulse to flee earlier, she's now embarrassed by the disappointment that washes over her when she sees he's gone. She can't help feeling that maybe she shrugged him off too quickly. Yes, he was drunk. Yes, he was forward, but he also had those long hairs on the back of his neck, signaling he must be living alone and therefore, likely, lonely. If he had a girlfriend, she'd trim those hairs for him, as Alicia has done for every guy she's ever dated.

With the sun now set, the fog is getting thicker, frostier. London's winter air is like being wrapped in a cold, wet blanket, not at all like the dry cold she is used to in New York. Moisture beads on the sleeves of her wool peacoat. She swears she can feel it soaking into her jeans. Only smokers would stand outside on a night like tonight. There are a couple of these lingering outside the pub, two businessmen, probably in their sixties, discussing Brexit. They don't notice her hovering by the window, wiping off the condensation to peer inside. It looks warm and cozy. Maybe he's in there. If so, maybe she's meant to make friends with him. So what if he's a cocky drunk? All guys are. Besides, she could see it was all a facade. This guy has some self-esteem issues. He was overcompensating before. When he was drunk, William would do that, too. There must be *some* positives about this guy. For starters, he has good taste in pubs. Plus, he just got a big commission. For what, she doesn't know, but still, that's good. It means he's not a total fuck-up. And he seemed to like her. Nobody else has paid that much attention to her in a long time. Fuck it, she's going in.

That smell—stale beer, musky cologne, cheese and onion crisps. Memories of William flood her mind as the familiar perfume of the pub fills her nostrils. Suddenly every guy in the bar looks just like him. She glances at the ledge where they used to sit, staring out into the market.

"My sister thinks you're too quiet," William once told her on that ledge. "You're too passive."

She took a sip of her beer and shrugged.

"Like right now: Why aren't you standing up for yourself?" he wanted to know, shaking her shoulder.

"What's the point?" she mumbled. "Your sister's not here."

"You're a pushover," he continued. "It's okay to have opinions." *His* opinions, of course. Kiera had opinions, lots of them. He disagreed, loudly, with every single one.

"Maybe."

Before unfriending him on Facebook, Alicia saw that he'd recently purchased a microbrewery in North London, which meant he'd have no reason to come to the Rose anymore. It had been his dream to own a brewery. He's the only person she's ever known that always gets every single fucking thing he wants.

She's behind a group of three businessmen and one female colleague waiting to be served. They're teasing the woman, encouraging her to flirt with the bartender to get better service. Alicia watches them, envious. This woman is the type Alicia has always imagined becoming. During graduate school, she pictured her life would be a steady stream of pub-quizzes, curry nights, and karaoke weekends. She'd be the kind of girl that could keep up with the boys. They'd tease her and she'd hit back at them with her quick wit, but they'd be "her boys." They would love and respect her. "Her boys" would protect her. There's certainly none of this camaraderie at her offices in Brooklyn. Most of the employees at her pay grade are family people. No one goes for drinks after work. Everyone rushes home for dinner or to a school play or to daddy-daughter yoga.

"Go on, Val!" a handsome, grey-suited man says. His hair and beard are straight out of a box of Just for Men. "Get up there!" he adds, giving his coworker a shove on the small of her back, pushing her up to the bar.

"Undo a button, Val! I'm thirsty," a clean-shaven, blue-suited guy adds, to the laughter of his mates.

Val shoots him a dirty look. But not a *really* dirty look. Val is playing her cards carefully, Alicia concludes. Her dirty look suggests not that he's an asshole, but that he's naughty.

Blue Suit understands the game. "Steady on, love. We've got all night."

A third, Black Suit, gives him a congratulatory shove and they share a nod.

The male bartender finally turns his attention to Val and the three suits cheer. She orders everyone's drinks, flipping back her long, bleach-blond hair, and feeling, for a moment, like their hero.

Alicia finds she's smiling at the whole exchange. Yes, it's sexist, but she wants to believe that Val is really the one in charge. It's possible she has these three guys wrapped around her little finger. Maybe Val gets shit done, even if her methods are a little unorthodox. Maybe she just wants to have a laugh. What's so wrong with that? Women should get to be one of the boys. How can women expect to win "the game" if they don't play it?

"'The game' is rigged," she remembers Kiera saying in class. "We can't succeed when the aim of the game is to devalue women. To win is to beat ourselves."

The suits and Val vacate with three pints and a large glass of white wine. Blue Suit and Grey Suit each have a hand on the small of Val's back. Black Suit, staring at her tits, shouts loudly, "Alright, Val, put 'em away! Do you want us to take you seriously or not?" They all laugh, settling into a table at the rear of the pub.

"You're back."

The smell of cigarettes and fruity cologne wafts over her shoulder.

She doesn't even need to turn around; he's right behind her. Not wanting to appear eager, she ignores him and moves up to the bar, tapping
her fingers on the ledge while reading the labels on the beer taps.

"London Pride, please," she tells the barman.

"Pint or half?" he asks, his eyes wandering to the leering man
behind her. He gives the guy a nod of familiarity.

"Pint," she says, pulling out her wallet.

"Good girl," the drunk says, coming around to her side and leaning on the bar.

Alicia looks at him now. Not with a smile exactly, but an acknowl-
edgment of his existence.

He smiles back like he's won a bet. "You can put your money
away, doll." Turning his attention to the barman: "I got this, Toby."

Alicia looks at the barman, hoping he might give her a sign as to
whether or not her companion is safe, but apparently Toby can only
concentrate on one thing at a time. Right now, he's pouring a pint.

She keeps her wallet out, still prepared to pay.

"Make that two, Toby," he adds. "And two shots of . . . What's the
one I like?"

"Lagavulin," Toby says, pausing mid-pour for a moment to look
up, then resuming.

"Laaa-gavooolin," the drunk says, trying to sound either smart or
sexy, Alicia isn't sure.

It takes a moment to register that the second shot is for her. "Oh,"
she says, words failing her after that. She watches him, paralyzed, as
he takes her wallet from her hands and drops it back into her large
leather purse, which is hanging open.

"You should zip that up, love. Thieves operate in this neighborhood," he says in his best Underground-announcer voice. Chuckling

at his own impression, he pulls his own wallet from his back pocket, opening the billfold wide.

There's a lot of cash in there. He can see that she can see it.

"I got it covered." He smiles down at what looks like a thousand pounds in bills.

She glances again at the hair growing on his neck. Surely, he can afford a barber.

The barman pushes the pints and shots in front of them. Alicia tries again to make eye contact, but Toby has his eyes on the computer screen. "Uhhhh . . . twenty-four pounds eighty, Paulie."

Paulie? Seriously? Is this guy in the mob?

Paulie takes out thirty pounds. "Keep the change," he says, proudly, pulling Alicia closer to him by the collar of her coat to make space for the men gathering behind her to order. His disregard for personal space is so brazen it seems pointless to protest. Reaching across her, he pulls her pint closer, too, and she catches a whiff of sweat that his strong cologne is meant to cover up; a nervous sweat that smells more bitter than sweet.

She acknowledges the pint she's been given, but she's not ready to pick it up just yet. Once she drinks from the glass, she'll owe him something.

"People usually say 'thank you,'" Paulie says.

She runs her index finger down the condensation on the glass, stopping when she sees he's watching. "Thanks."

He licks his crusty lips. "I'm Paulie," he says, as though instructing her on basic politeness. "And your name is?"

"Alicia."

"Pleased to meet you." He tries a little bow with his pint glass in hand and beer splashes onto the front of his shirt. "Oops," he says, his tone suggesting very little embarrassment. "I guess you'll have to come back to mine tonight." He winks, adding in case his point isn't clear, "I can't wear this shirt to work tomorrow."

"Please, let me pay you for these drinks." Her voice cracks, but finally she manages a full sentence.

"Why can't a fella buy a woman a drink anymore?" he shouts, so that everyone in the vicinity can hear him. A rotund man in a cable-knit sweater, standing next to Alicia, turns and rolls his eyes at Paulie. Paulie glares back, challenging, until the man turns back to his group. "I'm trying to be chivalrous," he adds at a lower volume. It comes out "shrivelroos."

"It would make me feel better to pay for my own."

Fishing her wallet out of her bag, Alicia accidentally elbows the man in the cable-knit sweater. To her surprise, he elbows her back.

Paulie reacts immediately, shoving the guy. "Give her some space, you fat fuck."

"Lousy drunks," the man barks back.

"We're all in a pub!" Paulie shouts.

Instinctively, Alicia slides in between them, putting her hand on Paulie's chest like she's stopped more than one bar fight in her time (she hasn't). "Don't!" she pleads with what feels something like intimacy. Despite knowing him for barely five minutes, she can't help feeling she understands the stupidity this man is capable of, and that she can stop him.

Instead, the larger man concedes first, but not without saying, "Real winner you got there," to Alicia before turning around and resting his pint on his large gut.

Paulie puts his hand on hers, so that they both rest on his chest. He visibly softens. He strokes her fingertips with his own. She wants to pull away, but this seems to be keeping him calm. He smiles down on her, clearly happy with this result.

"The drinks are a kindness . . ." He lingers on that word and leans in. Releasing her hand, he slips his own through her open jacket, resting it on her hip. She can feel his thumb, wrapped in the belt loop of her jeans.

"I'd feel more comfortable if you would let me pay you."

"I'm making you uncomfortable?" He steps in closer, so close, she can taste the beer-flavored spittle flying from his lips.

"Maybe a little," she says, apprehensively.

He removes his hand, agitated. "Alright. It's no big deal to me, love." He looks around the pub, trying to appear aloof. "I just thought you looked lonely." Then, just that quickly, he changes tactic again. "Is that what you want? To drink your pint all alone?"

She glances at the pint, full and sweating on the bar. She doesn't want to drink it all alone. She came back to the pub to have a drink with him and here he is. He even just defended her with that jerk in the preppy sweater. Besides, beggars can't be choosers. Alicia takes what she's given. She should be thankful he's here. No need to expect or hope for more. She picks up the glass and takes a big gulp, like she's quaffing milk.

"We're gonna have a good night, you and I," he says, smiling ear to ear now. Once again, he steps in close, putting his hand on her face this time. His fingers caress her cheek, going up her scalp, until he has a hand on the top of her ponytail. "You should let your hair down," he whispers in her ear. His scruffy, unshaven face smells like toenail clippings. "You're prettier that way." He tugs on the elastic band.

"Leave it," she whispers, barely audible, looking down at the pint she's holding, her compensation for his advances.

He moves his hand down to the back of her neck. She flinches, thinking he might clench it, but instead, he slides his middle and index fingers under her tied-up hair, pulling off the band and redirecting her hair over her shoulder. He runs his fingers through it, root to tip, smiling. He smells the elastic band, before pocketing it.

"Souvenir," he teases.

She reaches out to reclaim it but stops just short, aware that in order to get it back, she'd have to put her hand in his pocket. He takes her extended hand as an invitation, clasping it and pulling her in. Their bodies are now flush, except for her pint sandwiched in between their torsos. He removes it with his other hand, setting it on the bar before wrapping his arm around her and pulling her in completely.

"Let's drink our whiskey and get out of here," he coos, swaying her slightly, as though they're dancing. She can feel his erection, the shock of which inadvertently causes her to clench his hand tight. "Steady on, love."

This is the exact phrase the blue-suited man said to his colleague, Val, earlier. At the time, Alicia had found it absolutely charming. Now she tries to pull away from Paulie, who grips her harder.

"Someone's eager." He reaches for the whiskeys. "Let's knock these back and then we can go."

"I'm not such a fan of scotch."

She glances over at the bar in a last-ditch attempt to make eye contact with Toby. No chance. He's captivated by the pint glass he's holding as it fills with copper beer.

With the same middle and index fingers that he just ran through her hair, Paulie pushes her chin up to make her face him. "Don't be rude. I bought it for you."

"I should go," she says hastily. "I'm meeting a friend and I'm running late." The statement is so plausible and yet everything in her voice betrays it. She doesn't even have anyone to call. The only British phone number she has is Bennett's.

Paulie leans in to reveal a secret: "People don't really like me, either," he says, while looking into her eyes to see if she understands. "I don't know why people don't like you, but I'm not going to judge you."

She thinks about her now friendless Facebook profile. Whatever friends she might have had, they're gone. Her closest friend in London, maybe even in the world, is this guy standing right in front of her.

He takes her hand and guides it to the bar, wrapping her fingers around the shot glass.

She smiles back at him, a half-cocked smile. It's just some company, and it's in a busy pub. She can leave when she wants to. It's fine.

"Ready?" Paulie asks, looking genuinely happy to have someone to drink with. "One, two, three . . ."

They both shoot back the whiskey. The glasses clink on the bar simultaneously.

"You've done that before," he says, impressed.

"You thought I came here straight from the convent?"

"Whiskey makes her frisky," he says, proud of his rhyme. "Alright, I like that." He flashes two fingers at Toby, signaling he wants another round.

Alicia leans in on the bar now. That wasn't so bad, she tells herself. They're building up a rapport. She's feeling warmer, more comfortable. She looks at Paulie and smiles. For real this time. When the shots arrive they knock them back.

"How are you still standing?" she asks him.

He smirks, eyebrow raised and pulls out a little vile of white powder from the inside pocket of his jacket. "Got plenty."

William and his mates liked coke, but Alicia could never bring herself to partake. Back when she was a kid, there were these assemblies at school, where they packed all the students into the hot, stale gymnasium and a cop would present a suitcase full of drugs. He would hold up the different powders and pills and then tell the children all the horrible things that would happen if they took them. A Christian cop no less, who went to the same church as her father, and he wanted the kids to know that if the police didn't catch drug users, God would. The only thing scarier was the other assembly where a different guy brought in all the poisonous snakes. Alicia can still conjure the mixture of sadness and sheer terror she felt at seeing a rattler in a tiny Perspex box, fiercely shaking its rattle at foolish little boys knocking on the plastic. Every school year, it was the snake assembly first then the drug one. Naturally, when it came time for the drug assembly and the God Cop preached "take drugs and your worst nightmares will come true," Alicia's mind went straight to that snake. To this day, despite prevailing evidence to the contrary, taking drugs means coming face-to-face with a rattlesnake minus the protective Perspex box.

"I'm good. Thanks."

"Let's get out of here." He pulls a twenty out of his wallet and lays it on the bar, then grabs Alicia's hand, intertwining their fingers. Her palms are sweaty, but he doesn't seem to mind. He leads her out the door and into the cold.

The smokers who were previously leaning on the ledge are gone, their pint glasses, a little left in each, still perched on the windowsill. Alicia can hear people in the distance, but there's no one in sight. The fog is so thick now that she can barely see Paulie in front of her.

"Where are we going?" she asks. She leans back toward the pub, hoping to pull him back in.

"Depends, where's home tonight, American Alicia?"

She thinks about Bennett, about the quiet smile they shared at the window last night before he retired to his studio. She doesn't want to bring Paulie back to his house. All she'd meant to do was make a friend in a pub, have a laugh, maybe a snog at a push. Paulie, now leering at her, with both hands on her ass, only has one thing in mind. She remembers the fantasy she had this morning, the one where she and Bennett curled up on the couch and binged on *Sherlock*. Paulie doesn't seem like the kind of guy you can do that with. He's neither a Sherlock nor a Watson. It occurs to her she's been drinking with Moriarty.

"I need the loo," she says, not a lie. Her Starbucks coffee and that pint of beer have gone straight through her. "I'll just be a second," she assures him, trying to break away.

He tightens his grip. "You can hold it."

Leading her around the side of the pub, he stops in between two streetlamps, one dim, the other blown out. On the other side there's nothing but dark, shuttered market stalls. He stops in one spot, abruptly, like it's marked with an *X*. Pulling her in, he kisses her, his hand on the back of her neck like a shackle.

She's led him on, she thinks. She never should've done those shots. They were meant to tell him she's game, but she doesn't want to play anymore.

"Paulie." She can barely spit it out.

When he pushes her against the outer wall of the pub, the back of her head scrapes against the bricks. His tongue fills her mouth, spreading cigarette tar and stale beer all over the inside of her cheeks. His hands are on her hips and he squeezes, pushing his erection into her pelvis. His body is like an anvil against her full bladder.

"You came back for me tonight," he whispers, looking her square in the eyes, challenging her to refute it.

It's true, she did. He's not at all what she hoped, but somehow exactly what she feared. She tries to push him away, but it only makes him more persistent. He reaches his hand under her cardigan, grabbing her breast and squeezing it so hard she wonders if he's trying to pull it off, maybe put it in his pocket with her hair elastic.

"Jesus. Fuck," she mutters, trying to wriggle out from between him and the wall, but he grabs her arms and locks them up over her head. "Please, Paulie."

"You're so polite," he says, his smile cocky.

He keeps her arms pinned to the wall with one hand and uses the other to unzip his trousers, putting the full weight of his body against her. He's pressing her wrists against the wall so hard that she loses all feeling in her fingers. The bricks continue to scrape her scalp, yanking out hairs every time she tries to move her head. She's pretty sure it's bleeding, because it feels warm, like piss in a pool.

Earlier, she'd been able to calm him by putting a hand on his chest. She'd like to do that now, but with both hands pinned above her head she can't. She tilts her head to the side, trying to make eye contact, but he's not interested in looking at her anymore. When she stops trying to shift, everything is still. She's aware of voices, but they're faint, distant, somewhere on the other side of the fog bank. There's nothing to see but the beads of sweat forming on Paulie's forehead.

"Paulie, no." It comes out as a whimper. A plea that doesn't register with him at all. He's working on her zipper now. She can feel his penis pulsing in the groove between her hip and her pelvis. Her bladder throbs under the pressure of his hand on her jeans. Lack of oxygen is making her woozy. His bald head is turning into TV static right in front of her. She knows she should probably scream, but she's not sure she can. As a girl, she'd wondered if there would come a moment in her life that really, truly warranted a scream at the top of her lungs. Is this that moment? Are you allowed to scream after you've let the guy buy you a drink? She opens her mouth, but nothing comes out.

"Stop fighting," he says in a stern whisper.

She feels like she's going to faint. He has her propped up, but her head slumps. "I need to sit down." When she hears herself, she sounds distant, as though the words were uttered by someone else.

"Fuck that. No you don't." He steps back to pull down her high-waisted jeans. The release of pressure is just enough to make her knees wobble.

"I think I am going to fai—"

Her body drops under Paulie, her head bumping along the bricks as she slides down the wall. He catches her by the fly of her jeans and holds her up, then her bladder gives way. Urine streams down her thighs, causing Paulie to step back in horror. "Fuckin' cunt," he says, as if explaining the circumstance to himself. The ground beneath her is cold, her urine warm. She closes her eyes. It's possible she loses consciousness for a second because when she opens them again she sees Paulie, or rather his shoes, rounding the corner, and she is alone. When she tries to get to her feet, they slide out from under her immediately.

Just sit here and breathe for a second, she tells herself, pulling her legs up to her chest and putting her head between them. She can smell her own piss, but she's too woozy to care. If anything, it smells comforting. She touches the back of her head and feels the patch of blood that's already congealing in the cold. She wishes he hadn't taken her elastic band. It's a stupid thing to wish at a time like this; she should be happy to be alive. She should be happy he didn't penetrate her. But she really just wants her fucking elastic back so she can pull back her hair and try to walk away from this situation feeling somewhat normal. Is this what her mother means when she says that some girls are just asking for it?

She can hear voices, like patchy radio, in the distance. "Someone's had too much to drink!" Followed by laughter. Figures emerge and then disappear again in the dense fog. She leans back against the wall. The air in front of her is thick as whole milk. It could be the ocean out there for all she knows. In fact, she swears she can hear waves. Her head slumps to the side. She closes her eyes and thinks about what her night might've been like if she'd gone to Blackfriars Station like she knew she should have. How she might have knocked on Bennett's door for that cup of tea. Maybe she would have told him about how she wanted to be a food photographer and about the Hasselblad camera she's coveted for so long. Or maybe she wouldn't have said anything. Maybe she would have just sat there quietly and watched him contemplate his fabric samples, running his fingers lovingly over the textured threads. Tomorrow, she'll have to tell him that she's going home early.

"Is she alright?"

Alicia can hear a woman's voice, but it sounds far away, like she herself is on land and the woman is in the waves. When she opens her eyes, a group of women is approaching her. She tries to lift her head, but it feels like a wrecking ball. She closes her eyes again.

"Shit." One pair of feet is rushing closer. "I know her!"

She feels a hand on her arm and flinches, confused, thinking Paulie might be back. "Alicia?"

There's a blurry, large figure in a tight black turtleneck standing over her.

The woman sits down next to her and puts her arm around Alicia, drawing her into her big bosom. "It's me, Kiera," she says softly.

Alicia lifts her head and looks up at Kiera, bleary-eyed.

"Can you tell me what happened?" Kiera asks, cupping Alicia's face in her hand.

"I shouldn't have come here," Alicia mumbles, almost inaudible.

"Here? To this pub?" Kiera tries to decipher what she means.

Shaking her head, Alicia looks away: the pub, Borough Market, Camden Town, Chiswick, London. Take your pick, she doesn't belong in any of them.

"I got your message," Kiera says, tucking Alicia's hair behind her ear.

Kiera's friends are now squatting all around her. One is rubbing her knee. Another wants to know if she should call 999.

Alicia wraps her arm around Kiera's waist.

Kiera looks down at her undone, soaked jeans and grips her tight. "It's not your fault," she whispers as Alicia starts to whimper. "Do you understand, Alicia?"

She nods, yes, and she wants to believe her. Feeling out to sea, Kiera is her mast. Alicia curls deeper into her friend, clinging for dear life, while the waves rage.

MORE VIBE

You can live in an enormous four-bedroom house with a chef's kitchen, dedicated laundry room, super king-size beds, a flat-screen TV, closets full of shit you haven't looked at in years, endless fluffy towels, and a bathroom with a rainfall showerhead and heated towel racks or . . . Or you can live in a glorified shed with a hard futon, a calcified kettle, a wardrobe you share with a mouse, and a shower—roughly the size of an upright coffin—with a rusty tap. Either way, you're alive. And that's preferable to death, Bennett's pretty sure.

Looking out the window of his tiny garden studio, across the short green grass of his lawn (it stays impossibly green, even in winter), and past the stone patio, he stares into the window of his large yellow-brick house. The futon, where he's currently perched, abuts one of two large windows of the studio, perfect for spying on guests. Today, it's the Eastons, a British guy and his American wife, who checked in a few days ago. They're booked in for a month, the longest any guests have ever stayed. The pair of them are walking around like they own the place, he thinks, bitterly. They're *artists*. "Me, too," Bennett told them at check-in, pointing to his studio across the garden. That didn't elicit a response from either of them, not even an American "No kidding." Mrs. Easton just looked across to the studio, her face scrunched up like she smelled something rotten. Though he assured them he would be no bother, her expression suggested that, yes, he would. "Don't worry," he'd said, "I'll leave you in peace." It wasn't a total lie. He hasn't interrupted them at all; it's just he can't stop watching them. After all, he hasn't got a TV to entertain him.

In the beginning it was important for the studio to feel like a home. For the first few days, he went to the trouble of pulling down the futon every evening and reassembling it as a couch in the morning. He even went so far as to cover it with a fitted sheet at night, though it was a bugger to fold up the next day. He kept the duvet and the pillows in a tiny linen closet next to the loo, pulling them out at bedtime and stuffing them back in each morning. Before long, all that became a nuisance. The frame of the futon was a problem, too. It creaked and often got stuck halfway between bed and couch. Each morning, he'd have to pull the whole thing out from the wall and then give it a good, hard shove into the couch position. Difficult to accomplish because the shove usually just pushed the futon, in bed form, back up against the wall. The key was to push it more upward and then back, but this involved getting on his knees for the correct leverage. Bennett is fifty-five, a fact he didn't want to be reminded of every single time he bent down to push the futon back into a couch. With that in mind, the futon now remains permanently upright. When he wakes up, he tosses the duvet and pillows down to the foot, where they stay until it's time to sleep again. And it's at the top of this futon where, every morning, he rests his chin and stares straight out into the kitchen window of his large former home.

The Eastons wake up late, which works well for Bennett because so does he. The winter sun doesn't stream bright into his studio until eight so he's rarely up before then. This morning, they are doing what they've done every morning so far—eating granola at the kitchen island, staring at their phones without saying a word to each other. Bennett's getting to know the routine. First, Mr. Easton comes downstairs in his pajamas. He grabs the granola from the shelf and pulls down one bowl from the cupboard. He fills it with granola and milk and then puts the box back on the shelf and the milk back in the fridge. Five minutes later his wife comes downstairs, fully dressed, her hair always tied back in a bun. She pulls down the granola from the shelf and a bowl from the cupboard. Filling the bowl with granola, she then eats it dry, which Bennett finds repulsive. They don't converse the whole time they are eating, just scroll through their phones. They never show each other articles or photos. In fact, they don't exchange a single glance until the moment Mr. Easton picks up his bowl and drinks the leftover milk, at which time his wife turns to him and gives him a look that could curdle a dairy farm.

Bennett can see all of this because he has excellent vision. Strange that he couldn't see his divorce coming from a mile away (probably because things *that* close up start to get a little blurry), but he *can* read the bottom line of letters at the optometrist's office, unaided. He believes this gift of good vision is one of the assets that makes him a good artist. In particular, he loves to stand back from whatever painting he's working on and take in all its tiny, intricate details, of which there are many. Currently, he's working on a four-by-five-foot painting of a yellow fabric he pulled out from the bottom of a heap of floral-patterned fabrics he has in the studio. He's collected thousands of fabrics over the years, as evidenced by the floor-to-ceiling stacks that populate the side wall on the opposite end of the studio. He's been painting so-called "portraits" of these fabrics for about a decade now. His "loyal subjects," as he likes to refer to them—mostly to himself, because there's no one else around. The fabric wall is organized by pattern and then by color. There's one floor-to-ceiling stack of floral fabrics arranged chromatically, starting from oranges to reds to purples to blues to greens and then yellows at the bottom. Similar stacks exist for gingham, geometric, and striped fabrics. He likes to mix and match within his paintings, overlapping different patterns and palettes.

Given that yellow is his least favorite color, this floral fabric was an odd choice. He can't even remember where he bought it. It stuck out to him a couple weeks back, after his renter, Alicia, left the house one morning in a yellow cardigan that caught his eye. He'd lingered on her jumper—not quite mustard, not quite butter, more like Colman's blended with Lurpak Spreadable and a squeeze of lemon. He had to mix it. That afternoon, he did exactly that, mixed the color from memory. Not with actual mustard and butter, but with paint—cadmium yellow, extra deep, mixed with a little brilliant yellow, pale, Naples yellow, brown ochre, and lastly some cadmium lemon. Diluting the paint mixture with turpentine, he brushed a thin wash over his canvas, staining it with what he'd come to think of as "Alicia Yellow." Once he'd done that, this particular yellow floral fabric right at the bottom of the stack leapt out at him, demanding its moment. He had thought to himself that if he bumped into Alicia the next day he'd show her the canvas. Maybe he'd even ask her to stand next to it with the cardigan on to see how close he'd gotten the match. He never did get the chance to ask her.

Though shy from the beginning, the Alicia he saw the next day was a different woman from the one who'd worn the cardigan, the one he couldn't get out of his mind since she'd checked in. She was completely distraught that morning, said something had come up and she needed to go home early. It was none of his business, so he didn't pry—probably family or boyfriend stuff, not stuff you share with your middle-aged AirBed host. She didn't ask for a refund, but he gave her one anyway. He's not sure why other than he hoped it would make her smile, which in that moment seemed more important than money. She did smile at the refund, kind of—not the happy or relieved kind, but the obligated kind. With that, he decided not to show her the painting, sensing that she'd certainly feel obligated to smile again. Yesterday was the deadline for the two-week window she had to leave him a review on the AirBed website, but she never did. He checked the website every morning, every time he made a cup of tea, and again when he broke from painting for lunch and dinner. He's not surprised she didn't leave a review, though it would have been nice to hear from her, to hear she's okay. He wrote her a five-star guest review: **Alicia was an excellent guest, kind and considerate. Would happily have her back anytime.** It was the restrained version of what he was thinking, *I wish she'd come back so I could give her a cuddle.* Anyway, hard to imagine feeling that way about the Eastons.

Today, Mrs. Easton doesn't look at her husband when he slurps the milk from his granola bowl. Instead, she takes her spoon and lightly bangs herself on the forehead with it. Bennett barks a quick laugh at her frustration. He doesn't laugh out loud much anymore. He can't get used to the sound of his own voice, which seems much louder and also foreign when he's the only one around to hear it. Besides, what's the point of registering to *himself* that something is funny? He already knows.

Mr. Easton gets up, puts his bowl in the sink, and heads back up-stairs. Bennett is quick to lie back down on the futon at this moment. After three days of watching their routine, he's learned that this is exactly when Mrs. Easton will put down her phone and stare straight out the kitchen window into the garden at his studio.

He rolls off the futon and onto the floor, landing on his feet and hands, then crawls a couple feet to the bathroom door, where he pulls himself up by the handle, groaning as he does so.

His paint-splattered jeans and tunic are hanging from a hook in the bathroom. Very rarely does he wear anything else these days. He has a few plastic containers that hold his other shirts and jeans, but they remain closed much of the time. The container with underwear and socks sits on top of the others for easy access, though possibly not easy enough. Today, he puts on his paint clothes before realizing he hasn't changed out of the underwear he slept in. He thinks for a moment about whether or not he can be bothered to take off the jeans and change his briefs. It's not the first time he's had this particular existen-tial crisis. Who is going to know, but him, if he keeps on the old ones? He doesn't want to ask himself, "What's the point?" That's a dangerous question . . . but, really: What is the point? Again he thinks of Alicia, all set to face the world that day in her yellow cardigan. If she could do it . . . He takes off his jeans and pants, dropping the dirty ones in a tiny waste bin that acts as a hamper, and pulls out a fresh pair of black boxer briefs from the plastic tub. Putting them on, he lets the elastic waist-band slap into place with pride. The underwear is brand-new. He went to Marks and Spencer last weekend to buy a dozen more pairs. With his washer and dryer in the main house, he had to stock up on socks and pants to get him through the Eastons' month-long stay.

His morning bathroom ritual is quick. He doesn't shower every day anymore. Showers in the narrow and claustrophobic cubicle are far from the luxurious ones he used to take in the house. The master bedroom shower has two rainfall showerheads and enough room to conduct an orchestra. If he stood upright in this stall, the showerhead would be at his neck. It had been Eliza's idea to install the studio shower in the first place. She despised the smell of the turpentine and oil paints, so she encouraged him to shower after a day of painting before coming back to the main house. Bennett can't smell any of it anymore. After nearly forty years of painting, he's gone nose-blind. Most mornings, he throws on his paint clothes, brushes his teeth, and splashes water on his face. He does the latter quickly, no need to labor over all the grooves that time has carved into his skin or the scar under his left eye from the night, forty years ago, when his father, half-cut, threw a ceramic bowl at his face. Eliza used to buy him this expensive face moisturizer, but he has no idea where she got it from. He could google it, but he's never bothered. Unlike clean underwear, it's no longer necessary.

Because he's proud to still have his signature waves, he spends the most time on his hair. His hairdresser recommends two products for him: some frizz-fighting Moroccan argan oil and a gel that helps give his waves definition. He squirts a dollop of each into his hand and rubs them together vigorously, before running the mixture through his hair, root to tip.

Ready for the day, he emerges from the bathroom and turns on the electric kettle. Across the room from his futon, he's set up a makeshift kitchen. He keeps the space compact and tidy so that he has more room to prop canvases along the rest of the back wall. He got a great deal on a small, electric two-hob cooker and a short fridge on eBay; with the money he saved, he splurged on a toaster oven and a microwave from John Lewis. A sink had already been plumbed into the

Formica countertop that had once been just a brush-washing station. Now, a cutting board, the kettle, an iPod dock, and a fruit bowl occupy the surface. He eats a lot of fruit these days because it's the perfect food for anyone who wants to eat while doing something else. Bennett peels back a banana while he waits for the kettle to boil. He's careful not to look out the front window again. He wants to appear aloof to Mrs. Easton, who is still sitting at the kitchen island. He wonders for a second what kind of artwork she makes. Probably conceptual, he thinks, bitterly.

Hitting Play on the iPod dock, he gazes down the length of the room, across all his canvases to the fabric stacked at the end. When the hip-hop starts playing, he can feel his shoulders drop, the silence, deadened. He's just a middle-aged man, who happens to like hip-hop, keeping the beat and eating a banana in his studio. Nothing to see here. He bobs up and down with something bordering on abandon as he waits for the water to boil. He taps his teaspoon on the edge of the counter.

More vibe, more vibe, more pressure, more vibe.
More vibe, more pressure, more pressure, more vibe.

The kettle rumbles and turns itself off. He fishes his hand into the box of PG Tips and pulls out the last tea bag. This afternoon, he'll have to go to the shop. Probably just as well, as he hasn't left the studio in days.

Mug of tea in hand, he plops down on his paint-coated rolling chair. Between the yellow painting on the back wall and the windows on the front of the studio, there is nothing but the chair. He likes to have this space completely clear so that he can engage with his paintings at any distance. To his right are the stacks of fabric and in the dead center of the room are two wallpapering tables, covered in paint tubes, a glass palette, rags, and brushes, dividing the living and work spaces. The looming problem is the lack of storage space for finished canvases. They don't go straight to a gallery anymore like they used to. They go into a locked room on the first floor of the house—Eliza's old study. It's nearly full now, with paintings stacked precariously against the radiator. Of course, the simplest answer to the storage question is to stop painting. But then what the fuck would he do with himself all day?

He wheels over to the wall of fabrics, taking a big gulp of his tea before pulling one of the yellow striped fabrics from the bottom of the stack. He'd spotted it from across the room while he was waiting for the kettle to boil. The patterns have a way of calling to him, or so he thinks, when it is their turn to be immortalized in paint. He knows that his fabrics aren't actually sentient, but he imagines himself in conversation with them. The lonelier the days get, the more personified his possessions become, especially for a man who already has a natural proclivity for assigning human emotion to inanimate objects. He holds the chosen fabric up to the painting. The yellows in the latter, which had a lemon quality before, are now ringing more orange next to the greener yellows in the striped fabric. He squints his eyes and watches a halo form between the colors, the greens becoming more orange and the oranges becoming more green. These are the kinds of magical moments he's looking for, colors glowing and changing when they're brought together. People don't do that enough.

After laying the striped fabric over the back of his chair, he squirts some cobalt blue paint onto his palette of yellows. He flattens it into the glass with the palette knife, scraping it along the smooth surface until the paint stops. Twenty years ago, when he was painting nudes, he found capturing the expression of his sitters to be the most difficult part. When painting naked women, Bennett preferred to separate himself by thinking of them anatomically, instead of emotionally. He was good at anatomy; he understood the figure and its proportions beautifully. It was mood he couldn't master. Something about painting those women's feelings felt a little bit like cheating on Eliza. To understand another woman enough that he could paint her emotions was akin to infidelity. When he painted fabric, however, or from a still life, he could extract from his subjects all of their truth, an apple's need to nourish, a fabric's desire to clothe. In fact, reviewers often complained that "Bennett Driscoll seems to care more about the fabric his nudes recline on than the nudes themselves." One reviewer even went as far as to say, "Maybe Driscoll should just ditch the nude all together?"

Where, Bennett wonders, is that reviewer now? He listened to the bastard and now he's broke. Taking a heaping palette knife full of cadmium yellow light, he spreads it across the layer of blue. Maybe it's his recent single-dom, or maybe it's being broke, but lately Bennett's been thinking about reintroducing the figure into his paintings. It could have several potential benefits, he thinks. It might get galleries interested in his work again. Collectors didn't care what the critics thought. The nudes sold.

He folds the yellow paint into the blue, methodically, like a baker folding eggs into flour. The blue and yellow, turning from two colors into one.

Also, there's the more pressing issue of human contact. He needs to start talking to more people, not just AirBed guests with inane requests for the best place to get a curry. *Try India, you knob!* Having a model in the studio would mean having someone to talk to for several hours a day. And she'd have to talk to him, because he'd be paying her.

Payment. That would be a problem. Models don't come cheap. He'd have to up his nightly rate on the house, but that's a possibility. He never did raise his rates when he became a Super Host, which most people do. And who knows, maybe the model would have sex with him? No, wait, he can't pay her *and* fuck her.

That's a prostitute, you twat.

He steps back from the palette. He's mixed a bright green, a St. Patrick's Day green. The wrong fucking green. He wanted a greenish-yellow. Resentfully, he squirts out a big blob of cadmium yellow on top of the green, as though the color has insulted him. What resembled gently folding eggs into batter, before, is now more akin to cracking eggs into a high-velocity blender. His palette knife furiously flips the paint, sending flecks of it flying across the glass. It's still too green, so he siphons off half of it and sets it to the side of the palette. He wonders if Mrs. Easton can mix color. Bet she uses the colors straight from the tube. She's *still* sitting there at the island. Doesn't she have anything to *do.*

He squints at the fabric resting over the back of his rolling chair. He needs to make his color more neutral because, now that he's looked again, the yellow he's after is actually brownish-greenish-yellow. What he needs, is brown ochre. Ninety-nine percent of the time, brown ochre is the answer. He should learn to start there. He searches around on his workbench for the color—unlike his fabrics, the paint tubes are not lined up chromatically, but rather jumbled up in a big messy pile. Given the ochre's demand, it's no surprise that when he locates the tube, it's empty.

ııııııııııııııııııııı

When he leaves the studio after lunch—a lunch that consisted of two apples and a red-netted bundle of mini Babybel cheese—he has in his pocket a note that reads: *brown ochre* and *tea bags*. He shouldn't need a shopping list for two items, but if he didn't write them down, he'd forget one. His memory, like his knees, is also fifty-five. Now that he needs paint, he'll have to go to Boss Art, the large art supply store in Soho that sells paint at prices so low it's no wonder that the people who work there can't tell a paintbrush from a pencil.

He hasn't been out of his studio since Sunday, when he checked in the Eastons. It's now Thursday. Stepping into the chilly February air, he clocks Mrs. Easton *still* sitting at the kitchen island, *still* staring at her phone. He wonders if this is what it was like for Eliza to watch him all those years; her parting words—*I can't stand still with you anymore*—are ringing in his ears. He reaches back into the studio and grabs his sketchbook and a couple of pencils, tossing them in a canvas shoulder bag that's been hanging by the door collecting dust. He's going out and he's staying out. After all, he put on new underwear.

||||||||||||||||||||

Khoury's Market, by the station, always has the door propped open, even in the dead of winter. The corner shop stocks all of Bennett's daily needs as a single man: pasta, pesto, fruit, Babybel, and most importantly, tea. He makes a beeline to the back of the store where, much to his frustration, the tea is located—past the wine and next to the washing powder. It's the Khoury daughter sitting behind the till today; she's not so friendly, so he sets the tea on the counter without a word. She's got her hair pulled back in a ponytail so tight that it looks painful. She gives him a blank look, so he pushes the box a little closer to her. It used to be her dad behind the till, but recently, Bennett's been seeing more and more of the daughter. Mr. Khoury was friendly, always looking up from his copy of the *Sun* to ask Bennett if he'd seen *Match of the Day*. Bennett has never watched *Match of the Day* in his life, but it makes him happy that he passes with Mr. Khoury for the type of man that might.

"Two quid, mate." The daughter doesn't like to make eye contact. She stares out the open door to the street. She taps her fingernails on the counter while she waits. They look sharp enough to slit a man's throat.

"Can I ask why you keep the tea all the way in the back?" he is surprised to hear himself ask, while fishing in his pocket for a two-pound coin.

She shrugs.

"It's probably your most popular item, right? Why not put it by the counter." He should stop, but it feels so good to speak to someone.

"Most people buy something else as well," she says, indifferent, taking his money. "You know, like, on the way they see stuff they didn't know they needed."

"Right." He lifts the box of tea. "What else do they buy?"

"Crisps and that." She shrugs. "Salad cream."

That sounds like a disgusting combination. "So you were hoping I'd buy some salad cream as well?"

"Not really, mate. Don't care."

Figures.

||||||||||||||||||||||||

Soho is the place to go for old farts like Bennett who still want to feel hip. It's full of washed-up guys searching for relevance. They're mostly film and television types that populate the cafes and bars of Dean and Frith Streets. Bennett has tucked himself into a back table at the Claret. Somewhere between a French wine bar and a British pub, it was a favorite of the artist Francis Bacon, and is therefore a favorite of Bennett Driscoll. He's ordered a large glass of red wine, Syrah, he thinks, but honestly he's not sure what the barmaid poured. He can't remember the last time he had a glass of wine before five p.m., but he's assured himself it isn't a big deal. He's already bought his brown ochre paint, a very quick errand for a comparatively long journey into town, and besides, he told himself he would stay out. Before he left the studio, he went to the effort of changing out of his paint clothes and into a nice pair of jeans, his favorite black cashmere jumper, and his brown lace-up boots. Francis Bacon wouldn't have given a fuck about drinking at three-thirty in the afternoon. Although, Bennett reminds himself, Francis Bacon was an alcoholic.

But Bennett isn't here to drink. He's here to draw. He's got his sketchbook out on the table, though so far it remains closed. His pencils are resting off to the side, making his intentions known—mostly to himself. Choosing a subject for his drawing is going to be difficult. There's a group of stuffy old men around the bar with nothing better to do than drink on a Thursday afternoon. A few of them have wives, all with small glasses of white wine sitting next to their husbands' larger glasses of red. He doesn't want to get punched, so it's probably not a good idea to sketch any of these mens' wives. He doesn't really want to sketch the old geezers, either, so he settles on the barmaid. Opening the sketchbook, he finds a clean page and takes a big gulp of his wine before picking up an HB pencil. From where he is sitting, he has a profile view of the middle-aged, red-haired woman behind the bar. He stares at her for a moment, trying to decide where to start. First, he draws the lines of the bar top to create a minimal environment for the figure. She's slender, which isn't surprising for a woman who stands all day. There's something strange about her, sexy even. Though it's not effortless, maybe a little awkward or nerdy, like she might know a lot about *The Lord of the Rings*. Maybe it's her fairylike, deep crimson shirt with sleeves that flare at the wrists. He'll begin there, with her hand, which rests on the edge of the counter. He follows her sleeve with his pencil until it dips below the bar. Next, he takes the line across to the pit of her elbow, then effortlessly up to her shoulder, then glides it, quickly, back down to complete the arm. All of this takes only thirty seconds. He's surprised by the familiarity of the motion. He watches her as she gabs with the two wrinkly old gits on the other side of the bar—one in a flat cap and the other with an enormous, unruly beard. In another two minutes, he's outlined most of her figure. He takes extra care to accentuate the lift in her small breasts, a detail that indicates she is younger than he had originally thought. Bennett is a fan of small, perky breasts, so he's happy to linger.

He's left the difficult task of capturing her expression for last. He works around the face by adding the details of her soft, shiny hair, which she's pulled back in a loose, low bun. He sets down the pencil and takes another sip of wine for inspiration, studying her as she laughs at one of her customers' jokes. Is it really funny or is she just being polite? This is his problem: he can't tell. He contemplates just leaving her face blank. He wonders if maybe there is something interesting or mysterious about that, but he knows there isn't. He's just being a coward. He procrastinates by looking at the photos and artwork hanging on the walls of the pub. With more than a hundred years of history, the place is half boozer and half museum—covered in old photos and caricatures of its most famous patrons. Directly above him is a picture of Francis Bacon seated in a chair just like the one he is sitting in now. Bacon looks serious, but content, his legs crossed and lips closed in a straight line. He's leaning forward in his chair in a manner that could be construed as aggressive. Bennett wonders if the artist knew, at that moment, just how important he was, how influential he would become. Photos of famous artists always carry a weight of genius, Bennett thinks. Bacon looks as though he knew all along, without a single shred of doubt, that he was extraordinary. Bennett can't think of any photos of himself that have the same gravitas. For starters, in most photos, Bennett is smiling. In many, he is grinning like an idiot. He remembers when he was a child that his father would yell, "Smile for your mother," pointing at the camera his mum was holding. Adding, "It's the only thing that'll make her happy." Every photo of himself that he can think of, even as an adult, was taken by his mother. She loved going to his openings and snapping pictures of him posing next to his artwork, smiling like a boy in a school photo, dutiful and sweet.

Recently, he's been thinking about Bacon's use of the figure and, most importantly, how he painted his own fears into his work. A man haunted by death and failure, he seems to have mixed his paint with anxiety the way other artists might mix theirs with linseed oil. It was his true medium and necessary to his enduring success. The lack of such emotion in Bennett's own work, he fears, could be a factor in his gradual descent into obscurity. He hasn't been mixing his paint with fear and doubt. He's been mixing it with safety and predictability. Bennett has purposely lived his life as the sort of man he imagined would be easy to love, the opposite of his dad, who took pride in his failures as husband and father. Bennett tried to be both supportive and stable for his wife and daughter, but still Eliza left, describing him as "fucking frustrating." Now he has no idea what kind of man he is or wants to be. What he considered "supportive and stable" was apparently "suffocating and stubborn" to Eliza, and maybe to Mia as well, he doesn't dare ask her.

Returning to his drawing, he picks up his pencil again and squints the barmaid into focus. He draws her mouth in several quick motions, slightly open, lips curved with the tips of her front teeth just barely showing. Her eyes curl with laughter, revealing crow's-feet. Bennett adds the lines like whiskers on a cat.

When she looks over in his direction, he quickly drops the pencil. She's not actually looking at him, though. She's checking the level of his wine, which is getting low. She lifts up a bottle of Syrah to him, her expression a question mark.

He lifts his glass to suggest, *Yes, please.*

She comes out from behind the bar, holding the bottle by the neck. It glides along her thigh as she strides to the table.

He closes the sketchbook.

"What have you got going on over here, then?"

"Just taking some notes," he replies, unconvincingly.

She fills his glass up to the line and looks at what's left in the bottle. Deciding it's not enough to bother with, she pours out the rest, all the way up to the brim of his glass.

"I thought maybe you were drawing," she suggests, shaking out the last drops. "You know, you're in Soho?" she adds, with a wry smile that accentuates the laugh lines around her mouth. "There's plenty of strippers around. Why bother sketching a dumpy old barmaid?" She lets the empty bottle drop to her side.

Bennett never knows what the hell to say in these moments. She's probably fishing for a compliment. Why else would she call herself "dumpy" to a stranger? But then, is it a good idea for him to comment, even flatteringly, on the figure of a woman he doesn't know? The truth is she doesn't look dumpy at all. In fact, compared to the drunken pensioners in her bar, she looks damn good. Her tits are fantastic.

"You have a lovely smile," he says.

Well done.

"Are you going to show me?" she asks, leaning over the sketchbook.

She reaches out and touches the cover, but she's polite enough not to open it. Her hands look older than her breasts would suggest, but she's a bartender—she uses them. Her short red-painted nails rest on the sketchbook, her fingers stroking it. Red hair, red sweater, red finger-nails. She looks like a life-size strawberry lollipop; he'd like to lick her.

"It's not finished," he says.

"I don't mind. I've never seen a drawing of myself." Her fingers curl around the edge of the cover to open it, but she steps back, as though something frightening has just occurred to her. "Oh God, it's not like one of these caricatures, is it?" She points up to a cartoon of writer John Mortimer, with an enormous head and powdered wig.

"No," he says, warmly. "No giant head."

Is this flirting?

"Thank God for that," she says with her hand on her chest. "I'd have to ban you from the bar." She lingers above him with a defeated smile, swaying slightly like a child asking, *Pretty please?* "Well, I can tell you don't want to show me. It's alright."

He can tell it isn't really alright.

"Want me to go away so you can finish it?"

You're a moron, Bennett.

"Maybe once I've finished this glass of wine, I'll be drunk enough to show you," he says, pulling the full glass toward him slowly, careful not to spill.

"I'll keep plying you with more until you do." She taps the table a couple times with her bright red nails. "Maybe I'll do a drawing of you on a napkin. See how you like it." She squints at him with a smile that suggests mocking disapproval.

"No giant head," he says. "That's the rule."

"You're on." She points to him, then struts back to the bar like she's on a catwalk.

He spends another hour in the pub finishing his drawing and making a few other quick sketches of the crowd that's forming. When he finally reaches the bottom of his enormous glass of wine, he knows it's time to leave. He's probably drunk close to a bottle by himself and now he really needs a piss. After putting his sketchbook and pencils back in his shoulder bag, he shifts out of his chair and pushes the table forward. It scratches along the wooden floor, announcing his departure.

He looks over at the barmaid, but she's busy serving a group of young women, one of whom shouts, "Quick! Grab it!" when she sees Bennett exiting his table.

"I can't move that fast in these heels!" another woman bellows back to her friend, through fuchsia lipstick.

Could have fooled Bennett. Heels and all, she's moving at a jaguar's pace down the aisle of the pub. He braces himself, thinking that he'll have to catch her when she reaches the table and falls, giant handbag first, into his arms. It would be his first real physical contact in days.

"You're leaving?" she asks, out of breath, when she gets to the table.

"All yours," he says, shifting places with her in the aisle.

"Don't think you're leaving without showing me that drawing!" the bartender shouts to him from behind the bar, calling him forward with her index finger. The loos are upstairs and he's bursting. He approaches the bar like a kid summoned to his teacher's desk for punishment. "Alright, let's see it," she says.

He wonders why she wants to see it so badly. If someone had done a sketch of him, he definitely wouldn't want to see it. Nevertheless, he pulls the sketchbook out of his bag and pushes it toward her, which he immediately regrets when he realizes how sticky and damp the bar is.

She shoots him playful dagger eyes before she opens the book.

You're torturing me. Also, don't stop.

She flips slowly through pages of fabric drawings, taking in each.

"These are beautiful," she says, looking up, with an element of surprise in her voice. She hasn't gotten to the one of herself yet.

"Thank you," he replies, a slight lump in his throat.

She turns the page and there she is, caught mid-laughter. She doesn't say anything, just stares at it.

Bennett shifts from leg to leg trying not to piss himself.

"Wow," she says, finally. "Hey, Nigel!" she shouts down to the end of the bar at a flat-capped man she'd been laughing with earlier. He is deep in conversation with an older woman in a low-cut top, her cleavage wrinkly. "Nige!"

Nigel looks over at her. "Bloody hell, Claire, what?"

"Look!" She holds up the sketchbook, opened wide for all to see. "This is it!" She starts down to the other end of the bar.

Bennett reaches out for the book in a weak attempt to control the situation, but leaning against the bar presses on his already suffering bladder.

She holds open the book for Nigel, who leans back on his barstool to get the drawing in focus. "Hold on," he says, fishing around in his coat pocket, "I need my glasses."

Bennett lightly raps the counter. This is the reason he doesn't draw in public. His dick is going to explode.

"Very nice," Nigel chimes in after holding the sketchbook at a full arm's length.

"My tits look amazing, don't they?"

Nigel nods, yes, they do. "Is he going to let you keep it?"

Claire looks back at Bennett, expectantly.

"The pages don't come out of that book, I'm afraid," he says in a tone that suggests he won't be ripping it out.

She frowns at this. "Maybe you can come back sometime with a book where the pages do come out?" It comes out a like a veiled threat, like, *Come back with a different sketchbook or else.*

You won't want me back if I piss on your floor.

"I can probably do that."

This pleases her so much she does a little jump, then, "Oh! You have to see my drawing of you!"

Shit.

She's cute, but she's really irritating him now. Surely, she knows how much wine he's drunk. Surely, she noticed he didn't leave his table to go to the loo at any point, but most of all, SURELY, she can see the extreme discomfort in his beet-red face.

"Here it is!" She hands him the napkin, triumphantly.

He glances at it, nervously, but not too nervously; he doesn't want to appear insulting. But he instantly sees there's no need to worry. He smiles wide at the sketch of a smiley stick figure holding a giant glass of wine.

"Well played," he says.

"Be sure to look on the back . . . later," she says provocatively.

After I've had a piss. "I owe you for that final glass." Bennett fishes for his wallet.

"On me, love." She winks at him. "Go on. You must be bursting for the loo."

He leaps up the pub stairs two by two. He hasn't shown this much athleticism in years. Even his knees know how badly he needs a piss; they offer no objection. The napkin Claire gave him crumples in his hand as he fights with his zipper. He reaches the urinal in the nick of time and unloads with a mighty groan. Out of breath, he props himself up on the wall with his fist, the balled-up napkin inside it. When the stream is finally finished, he gives his dick a shake and stands up straighter, leaning backward at the waist to stretch out his lower back. Only then does he loosen his grip on the napkin and unfold it. The stupid little stick figure makes him grin again, and when he flips it over there is Claire's name written, followed by her phone number, and two *X*s for kisses.

Well, fuck me.

Careful with the napkin now, he folds it twice and tucks it into his jeans pocket. He taps the pocket twice to ensure its safety, only then stuffing his dick back in his pants.

||||||||||||||||||||||

It's rush hour on the Tube. Bennett holds on to the top rail in the central aisle of the heaving train. He's jammed between two heavyset businessmen, both of whom insist upon reading the newspaper, despite the carriage being packed to capacity. Bennett's face is up against the soaked-through armpit of one of them. He doesn't care, though, because he just got a woman's phone number. Without even having to ask. When was the last time *that* happened to any of these *Evening Standard*–reading tossers? He looks around the train for a man more attractive than himself, but he doesn't see anyone particularly good-looking. He pokes himself in the abdomen: not rock-hard, but not bloated, either. He applauds himself for having dry armpits and wonders how many of these twats bothered to change their underwear this morning. *He* did. He runs his hand through his hair, not because of nerves this time, but because he has hair.

Fishing his earbuds out of his coat, he turns on his iPod. He doesn't need to look at it. He can make it work just by rolling the dial in his pocket—a skill impressive to no one but himself. There's only five albums on it, anyway. He's removed all the music that reminded him of Eliza, which it turned out was everything. Everything but Roots Manuva, that is. After some shuffling, he finds the song he wants:

> More vibe, more vibe, more pressure, more vibe.
> More vibe, more pressure, more pressure, more vibe.

The men on both sides of Bennett turn to give him a dirty look, but he just smiles back. He has a phone number.

Beat that, you fat fucks.

He can't decide whether to call Claire tomorrow or to return to the bar first. The phone isn't exactly his strength. The only person he talks to on the phone these days is Mia, and even that can feel strained. He could text, but that feels like a cop-out. Returning to the bar is probably best. Is tomorrow too soon? He'll need to get a sketchbook where the pages tear out, which means another trip to Boss Art. Does he ask her out on a date or see if she wants to come to the studio and model for him? She seems to enjoy being the subject of his drawings. No, they should go on a date first, *then* he'll ask her to model. If she says yes to modeling then odds are she'll be into sex, too. If he's right, then he'll have a model *and* sex, and he won't have to pay for either. He couldn't have asked for a better outcome to this day. He needs more wine.

||||||||||||||||||||

When he enters the shop, the Khoury daughter is still behind the till. She looks up but doesn't acknowledge him. Recalling that the wine was by the tea, he walks confidently to the back of the store. He looks over the reds, trying to discern the least offensive one. His wine knowledge will need some improving if he's going to date Claire, an expert. He picks up and examines the labels of a couple different bottles, thinking this will somehow improve his insight. He settles on a Malbec because it sounds more manly than Merlot and he's feeling manly. Remembering his previous conversation with the Khoury girl, he grabs a bag of Doritos and a jar of salsa (salad cream is disgusting) on his way to the till. With a big, boastful smile, he sets his three items on the counter.

She wasn't kidding before: she doesn't give a fuck. "Tenner, mate." She flicks something, God knows what, out from under her fingernail.

He pulls a ten-pound note out of his wallet. "I came in for the wine, but I saw the crisps and thought, 'I fancy those, actually.'"

Not impressed, she peels a small blue plastic bag from a stack next to the register, licking her middle finger and thumb to pinch it open.

Recoiling, he lifts up his shoulder bag. "No need!" He loads the items into the bag with his tea and sketchbook. "Cheers."

"Enjoy your crisps, mate."

"Thank you, I will." He knows she's being sarcastic, but his smile only grows. *Phone. Number. Bitch.*

|||||||||||||||||||||||

Going back through the garden gate, Bennett triggers the security light and Mrs. Easton looks up from the kitchen sink, sullen. He smiles and waves but doesn't break stride to the door of the studio. She waves back but offers no smile.

Honestly, what is her problem?

The Eastons' presence is the main snag in planning a romantic night with Claire. Suppose he does have her over to the studio. Suppose she even poses naked for him. Will Mrs. Easton be glaring disapprovingly out the kitchen window the whole time? How can he be expected to romance Claire knowing that the woman is a hundred feet away, giving him her blood curdling death stare? And he can't just wait for the Eastons to leave. They're booked for another three weeks.

"Just fuck off back home," he mumbles to himself, twisting the key into the lock.

Back in the studio, he takes his iPod from his jacket and puts it back on the dock:

> *More vibe, more vibe, more pressure, more vibe.*
> *More vibe, more pressure, more pressure, more vibe.*

He turns up the volume just a little too high and twists the screw cap off his bottle of wine, bobbing his head to the music. He glances back at the main house to see if Mrs. Easton is still watching him. She's acting like she's not, but she is. While she's still in view, he can't drink out of the bottle. He pours the wine into his tea mug instead.

Fucking Mrs. Easton.

He'd rather invite Claire to the main house. He doesn't want to have her over to this stupid little studio. If things get heavy, she'll have to wait for him to pull out the futon, which will allow her enough time to change her mind. He can't give her wine in a goddamn tea mug, either. There are fancy glasses in the main house. Back when Eliza purchased them, he had no idea what Riedel glasses were, but she assured him it was the only way to drink wine. Now he wants to use those wineglasses to woo another woman, *So fuck you, too, Eliza.*

He chugs the wine in his mug and then pours more, before

twisting open the jar of salsa and squeezing the air out of the Doritos bag. Standing over the sink, he dips a chip into the salsa, coating it completely. Starving, he shoves the whole thing in his mouth. He takes his dinner over to the futon, where he nestles the jar of salsa into the corner so it doesn't spill. He sits down, slouching into the hard cushion, crisps in one hand, mug of wine in the other. It's the kind of habit that would drive both his mum and Eliza insane. His bad quirks are getting worse, he realizes, catching himself chewing to the beat of the music.

What kind of music does Claire listen to? he wonders. If she comes around, he'll need something smoother, something with more ambience. Something feminine.

He pulls his phone from his pocket and goes into recent calls to tap Mia's name.

"Hi, Dad." She sounds busy.

"Hello, my darling Mia."

"You sound perky. Why are you perky?"

"I like hearing your voice." He makes a mental note to try and tone it down.

"I spoke to you yesterday and you didn't sound like that."

"What music are you listening to these days?"

"I don't know." Mia always sounds angry when she's confused. "Why?" Her confusion is quickly replaced by worry. "You've never asked me this before." She believes her father's mental breakdown is imminent and has not been quiet about it.

"I'd like to get some new stuff." He stuffs a crisp in his mouth while he's talking. He can sense her recoiling on the other end of the phone. "I was in Soho today. I was going past the record shops and I thought I should expand my collection." Not a total lie. He did go past the record shops. He just didn't have that thought.

"You were in Soho? Did you go visit Richard **at** the coffee shop?"

No, I didn't buy a coffee from your gay best friend who wants to jump me.

"Is his coffee shop near there? I guess I forgot that." He didn't forget.

"You're the one who listens to rap. I haven't got a clue what music you should buy." She pauses. "You alright, Dad?"

"Yeah, of course. I'm fine." He hears the pitch in his voice get higher.

"It's a little early to be drunk."

"I'm not drunk." *Well, not that drunk.* "I was doing some sketching at a pub." He knows it's much easier to be up-front with Mia. She's too smart. "It was nice to be out of the studio."

There's a moment of silence before she speaks. He knows what she's going to say, but he's also learned over the years just to let her say it.

"I understand. Just remember Granddad."

She says she understands, but she can't. Not when she says things like that. She can't comprehend that forgetting her granddad, his dad, isn't an option for him. Fucking hell, he'd love to. He wants to tell her how much it hurts him that she would ever compare him to his father. Instead, he says, "I know, love. You don't need to worry about that." She's totally killed his buzz. "Wanna have dinner next week?"

"Sure."

"Love you."

"You, too, Dad."

That bugs him, when she drops the word *love*. Hanging up, he tells himself it's not intentional.

He rolls up what's left of the Doritos and takes them, along with the salsa, back to the kitchen counter, where he screws the cap back onto the wine and pushes the bottle up against the wall, signaling the end. He looks back through the window of the main house, where Mrs. Easton is sitting at the kitchen island eating dinner by herself.

||||||||||||||||||||||||

In the morning, Mrs. Easton is sitting right in the same spot as though she never left. This confuses a groggy Bennett, when he pulls himself up to his spying perch, his head pounding from the combination of red wine and Doritos. Has he slept through the Eastons' normal morning ritual? he wonders. He checks his phone. It's eight. Where is Mr. Easton? Bennett fell asleep early last night, but still, he's pretty sure the guy never came home. It's a drizzly day. Condensation on the windows makes it hard to discern Mrs. Easton's mood, but that doesn't stop Bennett from assuming she's miserable. It's a selfish thought, but a rift between the Eastons could prove quite useful. Maybe, like Alicia, they'll leave early. Only he won't give *them* a refund. He'll keep the money and then invite Claire around to have sex in all the beds.

It's been two years since Bennett's had sex, hence the urgency. He wonders if maybe he's jumping the gun by planning a sexual encounter with Claire, a woman he barely knows, but he wants to be prepared. He glances at her stick figure drawing, which he's propped up on the windowsill. After all, she's given him her phone number without him having to ask. That's the thought he keeps returning to.

Mrs. Easton finishes her granola and pushes the empty bowl away from her. She looks at her phone again, then slides it aggressively down the marble counter of the island and buries her face in her hands. Bennett's starting to feel guilty about witnessing all of this. He remembers that first week after Eliza left. He couldn't let his phone out of his sight, he was so certain she was going to call asking to come home. Mrs. Easton's wallowing might be proving detrimental to his own recovery, he thinks. Time to look away. Besides, compared to most others, today feels like a relatively big one. There probably won't be much time for painting. The brown ochre remains unopened on his palette table. The yellow he mixed yesterday is forming a skin.

All he can think about is returning to the Claret. He wants to see the look on Claire's face when he walks in again. He thinks, from that, he'll be able to tell. Tell what, exactly, he's not sure, but something important, maybe even life-changing. Cup of tea. Shower. Clean pants. Hair gel.

Go get 'er, tiger.

||||||||||||||||||||||||

He dresses himself thoughtfully before leaving the studio. He even squirts on a little cologne—black cedar and juniper, the label says. According to the bottle, it expired a couple months back, but he doesn't think anyone will be able to tell. He puts a little extra goop in his hair to keep it in place. He is wearing his favorite chocolate-brown blazer and blue-checkered button-down shirt, both of which have been hanging on a hook in his tiny linen closet, awaiting a special occasion. Taking a deep breath, he reminds himself he shouldn't be looking to sleep with Claire tonight. He's just planting a seed.

A seed in her mind, not a seed in her . . . get a grip.

He has reason to be nervous. The last time he had sex was awful. Previous to his final attempt with Eliza, there'd been a steady decline in pleasure, sure, but nothing that could have prepared Bennett for the gut-wrenching feeling of being inside her, a woman he'd been with for twenty-five years, and knowing it would be the last time. The worst part was that Eliza had been so nice about it. As she lay beneath him, he could tell that she was, genuinely, trying to muster up some sort of passion.

Not many relationships last twenty-five years; that's what he tells himself. Yes, he thought they'd vowed to share a lifetime, but in prison, twenty-five years is a life sentence. Things were bound to go stale and when they do you can't fix them, you just have to chuck them. Just as Eliza chucked him.

ıllıllıllıllıllıllıllıllı

"Bennett?"

He hears his name being called with an American accent as he locks the door of the studio. He'd purposely waited for Mrs. Easton to be out of sight before stepping into the garden, but here she is anyway. As far as he knows, she's the first guest that's been annoyed by his close proximity, but right now, he's annoyed by hers. Normally, he's inclined to make each guest feel as welcome as possible in his home. After all, he's a Super Host, but he's not feeling super about Mrs. Easton. He musters his warmest smile before turning around.

"Sorry to bother you." Her tone suggests otherwise, her arms crossed. She leaves a good ten feet between them.

"Not at all." He matches her tone. Two can play at this. He crosses his arms, too.

"We've managed to break one of your nice wineglasses."

"Oh," he replies, surprised, having expected a complaint rather than a confession. He's tempted to tell Mrs. Easton to break the lot. He'll send the box of shards to Eliza in America. "Not to worry. I expect things will break."

"If you let me know where you got them, I can replace it when I am in town tonight."

"Really, it's not necessary." He takes a step away and then recalls her sitting morose at the kitchen island last night. "Going somewhere nice in town?"

"Some tapas place," she says with a shrug.

"Well, have fun." He makes for the gate. Claire is waiting. She doesn't know she is, but she is.

"Oh." Mrs. Easton lurches forward, stopping him before he can escape. "Just so you know, my husband won't be around much. His brother is sick and he's spending the majority of his time at his mother's place." She says this with a twinge of sadness, but mostly contempt.

"I'm sorry to hear that," he says, remembering how Eliza lost patience with him during the final year of his mother's life. "If there is anything I can do . . ."

"No, no. I just thought you might wonder. Since you're so close by."

Can't let that go, can you?

"Well, I hope everything turns out alright, Mrs. Easton," he says in his best Super Host voice.

"Thank you. And call me Emma, please," she says, more of a command than a kindness. "I didn't take my husband's last name."

"Of course. Emma."

Eliza didn't take his last name, either.

"I may not be back tonight. Depends on how late the night goes. My friend's got a flat near the restaurant. I might stay there."

Why is she telling me all of this? I'm not her babysitter.

"Honestly, do what you need to do. Pretend I'm not here."

He has no intention of telling her what *his* plans are for the night. Well, they're not *plans* so much as *hopes*, but either way, none of her damn business.

|||||||||||||||||||||||

One woman's trash is another woman's treasure, right?

Bennett's brain has become a place where positive idioms go to die.

Walking to the Claret, he's cycling through all of them. Just because Eliza chucked him doesn't mean he has no value for *any* woman. There are probably plenty of women out there who are looking for the exact traits that Eliza criticized; women who would appreciate the company of a kind, if slightly neurotic, man, who yes, arguably spends too much time in his garden shed and thinks his fabric collection has feelings. This isn't how he's going to pitch himself to Claire, because the more he thinks about it, that guy doesn't sound like much of a catch. Presenting himself to Claire as a successful, talented, caring and, dammit, sexy man (no beer gut!) will be a challenge, but maybe *acting* successful, talented, caring, and sexy will make him all of the above. Maybe, eventually, it'll come naturally to him.

You don't know until you try is the last adage that goes through his mind before checking his reflection in the pub window, careful not to look himself in the eyes where doubt is lurking. It takes a second for his focus to shift to the figure on the other side of the glass. Claire is smiling at him, beckoning him inside with her index finger.

"Hello, Bennett Driscoll," she says when he enters, as though she is saying, *Checkmate*.

How on earth does she know his name? He paid with cash yesterday. He swallows hard, facing the door, a little afraid to turn around. *What does she know?*

The bar is quiet, just a couple of tables occupied in the back and a few of the old boys from yesterday sitting in the window. Claire is behind the bar, smirking, her arms spread out, balancing on the counter. It's a splintered and sticky kingdom, but it's hers.

"I was going to introduce myself, but I see there's no need." He approaches the bar, tentatively at first, then he remembers that *tenta-*

tive is what lost him the last woman he had. He adds some swagger to his final steps, before spreading his arms across the other side of the bar, mirroring her.

"One of my regulars recognized you," she says, reaching for a wineglass on a rack of recently washed glasses. She starts polishing it. "He said he went to school with you." She watches Bennett's reaction through the glass, before placing it between them.

"Did he have nice things to say?" Bennett asks, leaning on his elbows now, trying to appear comfortable.

"He said you were always in the life room drawing naked ladies."

Feeling himself blush, Bennett drops his gaze to the floor and touches his hair, then looks up again with a sheepish smile of a boy caught stealing.

"I googled you," she adds, picking up another glass and holding it up to the light, looking for smudges.

He knows exactly what she'd have found in her search. He googles himself, weekly. His Wikipedia page comes up first, followed by several archived articles from the nineties and early noughts.

He leans in closer. "And what did you learn?"

Is she wearing more makeup today? She definitely wasn't wearing mascara yesterday. He'd have noticed because he finds the stuff disturbing, like spider legs crawling out of a woman's eyeballs.

"I think that drawing you did of me could be worth money."

Nope.

He chooses to act mysterious rather than divulge the depressing truth that she probably couldn't give the damn thing away, so the conversation devolves into a staring contest. He's going to let her win, but he's going to make her earn it first.

She sets the second wineglass next to the first and reaches behind her, without looking, to pull out a bottle of wine from an ice-filled well that runs along the inside of the bar. "You like white?"

He nods, yes, not breaking their gaze.

"Good. We normally only sell this by the bottle," she says, pushing the label toward him, hoping to trick him into looking. "Some guys convinced me earlier to sell them two glasses." Her eyes conspiring with his, she uncorks the bottle. "I need to get rid of the evidence. You'll help me, won't you?"

"A willing accomplice," he agrees. The words sound smooth coming out of his mouth. So long as she continues to flatter him, this will be easy.

She fills the two glasses with the wine, both hitting the same level, all without her having to eye it. This is some sexy shit.

She pushes one toward him and keeps the other for herself. "Cheers."

"Cheers." He clinks her glass, still careful not to break eye contact. Sipping the wine, he remembers the old superstition about seven years bad sex. He's not normally superstitious, but two years of no sex, followed by seven years of bad sex for breaking eye contact is too big a risk; plus, now he'd like to win the staring contest. He squints a little to let her know he's not backing down. Eliza never let him win at anything, it didn't matter the game, she was always better. He hated that.

Defeating Claire on her own turf is a bad idea. He reminds himself to focus on the long game. He ends the battle with a wink, before turning his focus to his wine.

"This is nice," he says, spinning the wine around in his glass.

"I don't normally drink during my shift, but I'm off in fifteen minutes."

He brings the wine to his nose. He's seen people do that. It smells like cat piss, but oddly, not in a bad way. "I was going to do another drawing for you. I brought another sketchbook, with perforated pages this time."

"Is this what you do?" she asks, but it's not quite the right question. She tries to rephrase. "Do you normally draw women in bars or don't you have a studio for that kind of thing?"

He nods. He likes this mysterious nodding business. "I do, actually."

"So you draw women in bars and then you bring them back to your studio?" She leans back from the bar and sizes him up. "They take their clothes off and you paint them?"

This feels like a trap.

"Looking for new recruits, are you?" She swirls the wine in her glass, confident that she's got him figured out.

"I used to have paid models," he says, setting his glass on the bar. He's going to tell her the truth, although there's no chance in hell she'll actually believe it. "I haven't painted a naked woman in fifteen years."

She laughs. "Please! There is a picture on your Wikipedia page of you grinning next to a painting of a naked woman reclining on some giant banquet table."

Dammit.

He points to the wrinkles under his eyes, which are more pronounced around his scar. "That was fifteen years ago."

She shrugs, conceding that, yeah, he does look older than the man in that photo. "So why were you drawing me?"

"I told you yesterday, you have a pretty smile."

This feels like the easiest answer. Certainly easier than telling her that he's suffering from crippling self-doubt, that he's hoping to rekindle his career with his old tricks, that if he doesn't start leaving the studio and conversing with other humans, he'll probably stop changing his underwear. There is a lot at stake, but she does have a pretty smile. That's not a lie.

She's questioning whether or not to trust him, he can tell. "How about this," she says. "I'll let you take me for a drink. Then we'll see."

"See" what? I haven't asked for anything. Yet.

"Let's go to Townhouse," she says, gesturing in the general direction of the posh cocktail bar down the street. She doesn't need to; he knows the place well. He and Eliza used to go there on date nights. The owners, avid art collectors, have a Bennett Driscoll hanging above the bar. They'd commissioned a painting of a nude, seated in one of their signature hunter green upholstered armchairs, recognizable by its intricate navy blue embroidery of stags' heads. (Bennett had questioned whether the portrait would give customers pause about sitting in the chairs, but apparently not.) Townhouse didn't pay him real money for the painting, but instead, with a giant bar tab. Eliza, of course, scoffed at this, but was still determined that they were going to drink every drop of the painting's worth in pretentious cocktails. He's reasonably sure it was just a coincidence that she started seeing Jeff around the time the bar tab ran out. Anyway, if he and Claire go there now, she is going to see his painting hanging above the bar. Dated 2015, it is literally the only nude he's painted in the last fifteen years.

||||||||||||||||||||||||

The five-minute walk to the bar is strange. Claire is a different woman when she leaves the comfort of her own bar. She talks faster, can't stop talking, in fact—and in a voice that Bennett swears is pitched higher than the one she uses behind the bar, like someone hit fast-forward on a cassette tape. And she also walks faster and doesn't sway her hips like she does in the pub.

Despite being nearly full, Townhouse is the kind of place that never looks busy. There is a long bar that runs the length of the room. The rest of the space feels like a hunting lodge, although the clientele look as though they couldn't tell a shotgun from a toilet brush, having never held either. The room is full of short, round, dark wood tables that can hold no more than a few cocktails and a small bowl of nuts. These tiny tables are surrounded by luxurious armchairs, like the one Bennett used to pose his nude. The armed bar seats have the same fabric upholstering. A far cry from the rickety wooden stools at the Claret. The marble-top bar glistens like an ice luge.

There are only two bar seats left when they arrive. They happen to be conveniently located right in front of Bennett's painting. Maybe she won't notice it, he hopes. Yes, it's a five-foot-tall painting of a naked woman and it's *meant* to be noticed, but she doesn't necessarily have to know *he* painted it. His signature is small, barely noticeable. (The bigger the signature, the smaller the cock is Bennett's personal philosophy.) Plus, it's not like Claire's an art historian and it's not like Bennett's personally responsible for every nude painting in London. It just so happens he painted the one currently staring down at them.

"Blimey," Claire says, stroking the bar. "I bet all this marble cost more than I make in a year." She runs the full length of her arm across the smooth surface, making a crescent, stopping just short of knocking over the drink of the man next to her. "I just want to lick it."

It hadn't occurred to Bennett until now that Claire wouldn't know how to behave in a classy establishment. He looks around at the other drinkers, mostly suits, a few hipsters. He doesn't think anyone will recognize him. "Let's get you a drink," he says, pulling out her seat for her, "before you start licking things."

When she removes her coat, he's able to take her in more fully.

She's obviously been motivated by his drawing of her breasts. After her shift, she'd changed into a black top that's cut much lower. Her cleavage spreads apart, leaving a valley of milky-white skin between her breasts. A long gold necklace with an amethyst pendant is resting tantalizingly in the valley. A pair of dark, tight jeans glaze her legs like ganache. She's got black boots that zip up almost to her knees. Does she dress like this every day, he wonders, or is she just prepared?

Shimmying onto the stool, she swivels it back and forth, testing its movement. The man to her left looks across to Bennett as if to say, *Control your woman.* Bennett looks away, unsure of how to react.

She studies the back wall of the bar, which is covered in navy blue and green tartan wallpaper, above which a large stag's head is mounted.

She leans into Bennett, who has only just gotten himself situated in his stool. "Is that real?" she whispers.

Of course it's real.

"Yeah, I knew him."

She scowls at him. Exasperated already. *That didn't take long.*

"They chopped his head off, because he wouldn't stop swiveling in his barstool. Tragic."

She punches him in the arm. "We can't all be as posh as you."

The barman, dressed in all black but for a bow tie that matches the upholstery, brings them cocktail menus.

Claire claps her hands in excitement. "I'm so excited to drink something that's not wine." She pulls the elastic band from her hair and shakes out the red waves, so that they fall just below her shoulders. The scent of orange blossoms suddenly wafts under Bennett's nose. Women get all the good smells.

"Have you been here before?" she asks. "Who am I kidding, I bet you bring lots of women here." She taps her fingers, nervously, on an empty coaster.

"I haven't been for a while," he says in a tone that implies *Let's leave it at that*.

"What? Last week? Ha!"

He glances, slyly, at the painting that she so far hasn't noticed. It's a damn good one, he thinks. Maybe he really will start another series of nudes. Not just for money, but because he's good at it.

"I'm too sarcastic," she adds. "Bartender problem. Sorry."

He'd like to run his fingers through her beautiful strawberry hair. He'd like to cup her rosy cheek in his hand and stroke it with his thumb. Anything to stop her rambling.

"Well, *I've* never been here. You're my excuse." She has to take a deep breath to stop herself from saying anything further.

"Pleasure." He slides the cocktail menu under her nose, trying to focus her.

Opening it, her eyes land immediately on the cocktail she wants. "Lavender martini! Wow, that sounds gorgeous, doesn't it?" She asks the question, but doesn't look to him for a response. "Done!" She closes the menu like she's just finished reading a thousand-page novel and only then, finally, she looks up. Her eyes hang silently on the painting before asking, "Okay, what do you think of that one?"

It's damn good.

"I'd rather know what you think." He knows it's kind of a dick move, but he doesn't want to answer her question.

"Do men think women just lounge around naked all the time?" she asks, pointing at the cross-legged nude in the chair. "Poor woman was probably freezing while that was being painted."

"I'm sure the room was heated," he says with a nervous laugh.

"Yeah, probably to the ideal temperature for the clothed artist. Not her."

Bennett thinks back to the day he painted it and wonders if she's right. He always set his thermostat to twenty-one degrees. Considering he doesn't sit around in the buff, well, ever, he has no idea if that's too cold for a naked woman. *Huh.*

"So, not a fan, then?"

"I'm sure it's well-painted and all that. She just looks . . . uncomfortable."

Bennett makes eyes at the bartender, signaling that they are ready to order. He doesn't want to talk about the painting anymore.

"Oh, I'd love one of your lavender martinis, please," Claire tells the bartender. She watches with genuine admiration as the bow-tied man scoops ice into a martini glass, like the thing he does and the thing she does are worlds apart.

Bennett orders an old-fashioned and hands him the menu with a flat, nervous smile.

"Are you?" she asks.

He swivels in her direction. "Am I what?"

"Old-fashioned."

If Eliza were here to field this question, she'd be nodding her head so furiously she'd give herself whiplash. To Bennett's mind, it's his father who was old-fashioned, a drunken armchair preacher who prided himself on never having washed a single dish in his life. So, no, Bennett doesn't think he's old-fashioned. He thinks he's decent. Unless decency is old-fashioned.

"I guess that depends on your definition?" He doesn't mean to keep turning all her questions back on her, but her questions are hard.

"You're very polite. That's pretty old-fashioned."

Polite. The compliment every man yearns for. Still, he *is* polite, his mother hardwired him that way. Bennett could be polite to a man who's stealing from right under his nose. He was never anything but polite to Jeff. *Fucking twat.*

"Well, I'd imagine you deal with enough impolite people to make you an expert," he says, yet again turning the conversation back to her.

"Tell me about it," she says, rolling her eyes. "Like most bartenders, I hadn't intended to still be doing this in my forties." She looks over at him for a reaction. "I know you must be shocked! 'How could she possibly be over forty?!'"

He looks down at her tits, which he probably shouldn't do, but they do tell a different story about her age.

She looks down at them herself. "I know, right?"

Caught in the act, he can't help but laugh. Her self-deprecating humor is gentle and strangely sexy.

The bartender places their drinks in front of them, torches a branch of rosemary, and rests it gently in Claire's drink.

She waves the smell of the toasted rosemary closer to her nostrils. "Beautiful," she says, eyes closed.

Indeed.

Bennett picks up his glass. "Cheers."

They clink glasses, looking into each other's eyes again, though it doesn't feel like a game this time.

"What do you wish you were doing?" Bennett asks. "Instead of bartending."

She laughs to herself, as though her dreams and aspirations are a private joke. "Growing up I could never decide what I wanted to be. I wanted to be a lawyer, but I'm too much of a nervous talker for that."

She holds her cocktail beneath her lips. "I wanted to be a doctor, but I hate blood. I wanted to be a chef, but I can't cook. Nowadays, I think if I could do anything I'd probably own a bookstore." She finally takes a sip.

"Really?" He wasn't expecting that, not that he knows what he *was* expecting.

"It might not be very 'highbrow,'" she says, with air quotes, "but I love mysteries. I've read all the Sherlock Holmes and Agatha Christies. I guess I'd like to own a mystery bookshop. I know that sounds ridiculous."

"There used to be one not far from here when I was growing up."

"I remember!" She lights up, happy that he knew the store, too. "My dad used to take me to see matinees on Saturdays, then we'd go to all the bookshops on Charing Cross Road." She smiles into her cocktail at the memory. "He'd never buy me sweets at the theatre, but I could have as many secondhand paperbacks as I wanted." She looks at Bennett with misty eyes. "The deal was, I had to carry them home myself."

Bennett hopes that someday, when Mia sits across from some man at a bar, she'll speak as fondly of him.

"Where was home?" he asks. It's nice to listen to a voice that isn't his own.

"Bermondsey." She puts her hand up to hold his silence while she takes another sip of her cocktail. "It was not the place it is now. I wish I still had my parents' house. It'd be worth a fortune."

She swirls the rosemary branch in her cocktail with her red-painted fingers. Christmas has come early, he thinks, focusing on the sprig resting between her middle and index fingers.

"Sorry! I'm terrible! I need to keep my hands busy. It's such a bad habit." She puts the rosemary on a cocktail napkin and pushes it out of reach. He does his best to hide his disappointment. "What about you? Where did you grow up?"

"Hammersmith."

"See. Posh," she says, as though she'd put money on it.

He remembers his dad saying, "Only poor people talk about class. We don't talk about class." But Bennett knows better than anyone that growing up with means doesn't preclude you from a miserable childhood. He can't imagine his dad ever taking him to the theatre or buying him old mysteries. To his father's way of thinking, men read the paper, that's it. Books were for girls and poofs. He once threw a Stephen King book of Bennett's into the river. He readjusts himself in his seat. "It wasn't so special."

"Where do you live now?"

"Chiswick." He smiles, knowing what's coming.

"Of course you do," she says, taking a victory sip of her cocktail.

He can tell she's imagining his big house, his studio, his expensive things, but all he can think about are the damn Eastons and their crap all over the place. He wants to be the man Claire thinks he is. The man he used to be. Well, except not married.

"I'll be right back," she says, getting up from her chair. She puts her hand on his knee before heading back toward the bathroom.

Bennett looks up at the painting and shakes his head. Pulling his phone from his pocket, he scrolls through the phone numbers until he reaches "Mrs. Easton." His thumb hovers over the "send a message" button. It's my damn house, he's thinks, then clicks it.

Hi, Emma, I have a collector asking about a painting that I have stored in the house. Would you mind if I popped in tonight to grab it?

It's a desperate move to make up an imaginary art collector. It'll likely have terrible karmic consequences for his future sales, not that they can get much worse.

Claire is on her way back from the loo, and she's swinging her hips again.

Hi, Bennett, Emma's reply pops up on the phone. *Sure. I won't be coming back to Chiswick tonight. Good luck with your collector. Good luck*—that gives him a momentary pang of guilt. *Now* she's being friendly.

He sets the phone facedown on the bar, trying to suppress an idiotic grin. Claire slides back on her stool and puts a hand on his shoulder. He turns toward her, her soft lips glistening with newly applied lipstick just millimeters from his own.

"Did she have a nice smile, too?" she asks, pointing a sexy finger up at the woman in the painting.

|||||||||||||||||||||||

Slipping his key into the front door lock is a peculiar feeling. Even when the house isn't rented he enters through the garden, but Claire is expecting the full effect of a grand entrance. She waits, gazing up at the windows on the top two floors.

On the cab ride back he plotted how to answer all her inevitable questions. "Why is there a fire exit map tacked to your fridge?" "Why is that room locked?" "Why is there a binder on the coffee table that says 'Welcome!'?" He's decided he'll say the fire exit map was a school project of Mia's, from childhood, and he doesn't have the heart to throw it away. She'll love that. The welcome book he'll try to toss into a drawer before she notices it. He'll say the room with the paintings is locked for extra security, because of their value. Then he'll unlock the door and let her have a look around, thus making her feel special and hopefully turned on. What he isn't prepared for is all the Eastons' stuff. He can't make up stories for that shit because he doesn't know what to expect. He wants to take her to the master bedroom, but the Eastons are probably sleeping there and women's clothes will be everywhere. There is no reasonable explanation for that. They'll have to use one of the other bedrooms, but not Mia's old room. Definitely not Mia's old room. He's already made up a story about tomorrow morning. He told Claire in the cab that he has to catch a seven a.m. train to meet an art collector in Edinburgh, so he'll need to leave the house by 5:45 a.m. Unable to take a hint, she suggested sharing a cab to King's Cross, which means he'll have to wake up at an ungodly hour, take a cab all the way to King's Cross Station with Claire and a *real* painting for a *mythical* collector. And, if she follows him into the station, he might actually have to board a fucking train to Edinburgh. This is a lot of bother for sex, but it's worth it.

Flipping the light switch, he braces himself for whatever state Emma has left the house in. "Blimey, this is huge!" Claire says, dropping her purse on the ground and casting her eye from kitchen to dining area to lounge, all one enormous room, all beautiful parquet floors. "I'll take my shoes off!"

The house looks untouched, like Emma's not even used it. Just one empty bowl and spoon in the sink.

Thank fuck.

The marble countertops in the kitchen glistens just like the one in the bar. His books on Victorian London are stacked on the coffee table in order of size. The herringbone throw blanket is tossed artfully over the back of the sofa.

Claire balances herself against the entryway wall as she unzips her shiny black boot. He follows suit, unlacing his shoes. They both notice Emma's ballet flats tucked under the radiator at the same time. Claire looks at him with a raised eyebrow.

"My daughter's." The lies just keep coming. "She stays here a lot."

"That's sweet. You have a daughter? How old?" She flings her boot onto the floor. It makes an awful *thunk* on the hardwood.

"She's nineteen." No more lies. The truth this time. He beams as he says it, because he always beams when he talks about Mia. *You're a massive moron, Dad.* That's what she'd say if she knew what he was up to right now.

He waits for Claire to turn her attention to her second boot, before he tiptoes over to the coffee table, locates the "Welcome!" book, and stuffs it in a drawer.

"Are you hiding all the embarrassing stuff?" she asks.

Yes, obviously. Stop asking so many questions.

He changes the subject. "How about some amaretto?" There's a bottle locked up in the room with the paintings.

"Lovely. On ice, please." She looks puzzled as he goes off in the opposite direction from the kitchen, but she doesn't follow, wandering instead into the living space and stroking everything from the light grey sofa with the soft wool blanket, to the dark wood floor-to-ceiling bookcases full of hardbacks, and then to the kitchen where she strokes the marble countertops with her whole arm, just as she'd done in the bar. He studies her from afar. She even picks up an avocado from a giant wooden fruit bowl and fondles it.

He rejoins her in the kitchen with as much confidence as he can muster and the bottle of amaretto. "I don't have your palate, but I don't think avocados and amaretto are a match made in heaven."

"Even your avocados look better in West London."

"You can have it," he jokes, secretly hoping she won't take it because he won't have time to replace it tomorrow.

Thankfully, she puts it back in the bowl and returns to the sofa, swinging her hips softly and continuing to touch everything along the way, including the leaf of a standing ficus tree. She nods to herself, impressed, when she discovers it's real.

Bennett pulls down highball glasses from a cabinet—right where they've always been for the last twenty years—and reaches into the freezer for ice. He doesn't dare remove the "in case of emergency" card on the fridge, just in case she's noticed it.

"You like textiles, don't you?" she asks, standing next to the mantel above the gas stove. She's looking up at a red and blue painting that resembles an intricate weave. "The chair in the other painting had a beautiful fabric." She looks back at him. "The one in the bar, definitely. Plus, the drawings in your sketchbook."

She's thinking about what he does, he can tell. Like he's a jigsaw and she's putting together the pieces. He likes being her puzzle.

Stepping in front of the mantel, he hands her the amaretto, then sets his own drink down next to a remote control, which he points at the gas stove and suddenly flames shoot up from what was previously a cold void. Her face screams *Magic*. It feels nice to have someone to impress. Eliza was never impressed by anything.

"Cheeeeers." He draws out the word.

She tilts her head like she's singing along. "Cheers."

He waits for her to finish her first sip before he kisses her. Her lips are cold and almondy, softer than he remembers lips being. He wraps his free hand around her and rests it on the small of her back. Her shirt is wonderfully soft and unfamiliar. She steps in closer and wraps her arm around his neck, eagerly, still clasping the amaretto glass.

When cold condensation drips from the glass onto Bennett's neck, he shudders.

"What's wrong?" she asks, worried.

"Cold glass." He reaches back for her arm and pulls it down from around his neck. Taking the glass from her hand, he sets both drinks down on the coffee table.

She pulls him in for another kiss, mouth slightly open, before he even has the chance to stand up fully. Her lips are warming up now, but her tongue is still icy. Sliding his hands down her hips, he inserts them in the back pockets of her jeans and squeezes her bum, because, as far as he can tell, she's really into this. She grabs his neck with her cold, clammy fingers and pulls him in tight, her tongue deep-sea diving all the way to the back of his throat. *Wow.* Sexy hips. Great tits. Very aggressive tongue. He's uncertain whether he wants to speed up or slow down. Slow down, he thinks, given how out of practice he is. There's no rhythm, no balance. He pulls away for a moment and returns his hands to her hips.

"What?" she asks, defensively.

More questions.

"Nothing." He smiles, stroking her face to calm her. "Just wanted to look at you."

She searches his eyes for an ulterior motive. "Do you say that to every woman?"

"Do you *always* ask so many questions?"

Bollocks. Didn't mean to say that out loud.

He masks his frustration with a grin. Why do women always assume they want answers? Does she *really* want to know that he just broke into his own house, desperate, thanks to not having been laid in two years, or does she want sex? He knows which one he wants. Best to just keep kissing her.

Intertwining his fingers with hers, he leads her along to the staircase, glancing back to make sure she wants to be led. She smiles and squeezes his hand. It's him that's nervous, not her. "I've let my daughter take over the master," he says, but it sounds like a non sequitur. "She has more clothes." *Sorry for the lie, Mia. I do love you. So much.*

He opens the door to a bedroom that he and Eliza had always used as a guest room. They'd had sex in this bed once, he remembers, when it was far too hot to sleep on the top floor. He'd caressed his wife's naked body with an ice cube that night. He tells himself not to think about that right now. The room is clean. Too clean. It looks like no one has slept in it for months, because *no one has.*

"This isn't your room," she says, conspiratorially. "Statement. Not question."

"They're all my rooms." He wraps his arms around her and mentally pats himself on the back for that comeback.

They kiss again and she guides his hand to her breast, the first thing that feels familiar. Though he knows they come in many shapes and sizes, all the best breasts feel the same to Bennett, like a ball of buffalo mozzarella wrapped in silk. *Brilliant.*

She unbuttons his favorite blue-checked shirt and flings it clear across the room.

Okay.

He pulls her silky black top over her head. It snags momentarily on the gold chain of her necklace. Underneath is her bra made of sheer black mesh. It leaves nothing to the imagination, but that's fine by him, he's happy to give his overworked imagination a rest. Her abdomen is trim, but fleshy and speckled with freckles and moles. She pushes him onto the bed and he wonders, for the first time, if maybe he's not the first customer Claire has seduced. She crawls on top of him, wrapping her legs around his. Her tongue darts back in his mouth, stabbing the insides of his cheeks. He *will* get an erection, he tells himself. He just needs a little more time. She sits up, straddling his legs, and pulls the strap of his belt out of the buckle. He doesn't want her to see that he's not, yet, up to the task, so he pulls her down again, deciding to endure that dagger tongue for a while longer. He imagined this would be more romantic, more tender. There's no real reason that they should make love. It's not like they're *in love*, but still, he didn't think it would be so . . . carnal. He thought, at the very least, that she'd let him lead. It is his house, after all. Plus, he did let her win the staring contest earlier.

He fumbles with the back of her bra and manages to unlatch it. Not in one fell swoop as he'd hoped, but rather, one little plastic clasp at a time. He flings it across the room, because flinging things seems to turn her on. Taking control, he flips her over on the bed and kisses her breasts, usually the surest route to an erection.

His mind keeps wandering to his little studio in the garden. Maybe *that* would have been better? He imagines himself lying on top of Claire on the hard futon, still in its couch position. He imagines it creaking under their weight. He thinks about waking up next to her, cramped and achy. He'd make her tea. He'd let her look through his fabrics. He'd sketch her with whichever one was her favorite. He wishes he'd done that; that would have been so much better. Besides, he's a terrible liar. Lying makes his cock soft.

He works his lips down to her waist, but looks up at her before removing her jeans. She can't be buying all his bullshit, can she? When she smiles back at him, his heart sinks. Getting away with all these lies doesn't feel as good as he thought it would.

She props herself up on her elbows, looking at him, confused. "Are you alright?"

"I'm not who you think I am," he says, defeated, head between her legs.

"You're not Bennett Driscoll?"

"No, I am." He rests his head on her thigh.

"This isn't your house?"

"It is."

"You don't want to have sex with me?" She shakes her head side to side, so that her red hair falls on her nipples, resting like feathers on sand.

"No, I do."

"Then you're exactly who I think you are."

She shifts her legs around to the top of the bed so that the two of them are now face-to-face. She kisses him again, but this time, sweetly, slowly. "I'm sure it's complicated," she says. "It's always complicated." She runs her fingers through his hair.

It hadn't occurred to him, until now, just how much he wanted her to do that.

"I don't usually touch the women I draw."

"I know." She lays her head under his, looking up at him.

"And I don't draw the women I touch." He can feel his expression growing dark.

She reaches up and caresses his cheek.

"Twenty-five years with my wife. I never did a single drawing of her."

"I bet you could, though. Every last curve and nook from memory."

What can he say to that? She's right, but it can't be something she wants to hear, not while lying on her back, exposed, on his bed. Her breasts, it seems, defy gravity.

"Will you still draw my picture?" she asks.

"Of course," he replies, "if you want me to."

He resumes kissing her, upside down, cupping her face in his hands.

"Even if?"

"Yes." He saddles up beside her and pulls her into him.

She pulls back. "I was wondering, if maybe instead of the bar, you could draw me in a bookshop?"

He rolls on top of her. He's hard as a rock now.

"Can you do that?" she asks, wrapping her legs around his. "Draw something that's not really there?"

He nods, yes. He can do that.

FEELINGS AREN'T FACTS

Theo is a jerk. Is this a feeling or a fact? Emma asks herself, her pen hovering over a small notebook, open to a blank sheet. It's certainly true, because when you act like a jerk, you are one. She writes it down on the piece of paper to fill the page, *Theo is a jerk*. She thinks about ending the sentence with an exclamation point, but her therapist has encouraged her not to use inflammatory punctuation. "Is that help-ful?" Dr. Gibson would ask. "Probably not," Emma would answer. "Sometimes the most powerful tool against anxiety is empathy." Yet another theory floated by Dr. Gibson in their last session. "Just keep that in mind, Emma. This trip to England isn't going to be easy on Theo."

Sitting at the large kitchen island, she tears the perforated piece of paper from the notebook and folds it up into a square. She creases it carefully, so that all the edges line up, before dropping it into a cookie jar full of other similarly folded pieces of paper. The "fact jar" was intended to last the full month of their trip, but it's only been a week and already it's stuffed. Over the last several days, she's had a lot of strong convictions, all of which she believes, wholeheartedly, are facts: *Theo is a jerk. Bennett is spying on me. Charlie is selfish. Sarah is avoiding me. Monica hates me.* All facts. All recorded in the fact jar. Most of Emma's "truths" center around what she believes to be her inherent unlikability; she doesn't like herself most of the time, so it's natural to think that others must feel the same. It was Dr. Gibson's idea for Emma to record and store all of her strongly held convictions while in London. This is the first time since starting therapy that she's taken a full month off, but Dr. Gibson thought it would be a good challenge for her. It just so happens that everything Emma doesn't want to do sounds like a "good challenge" to Dr. Gibson. This time around, though, Emma thinks she might enjoy not having her therapist constantly nagging her about feelings versus facts, rituals versus flexibility, fears versus evidence, yeah, yeah, yeah . . .

She wasn't diagnosed with obsessive-compulsive disorder until two years ago. Her symptoms aren't typical. She doesn't wash her hands a hundred times a day and she's disorganized—leaves all her clothes in a pile on the floor and never makes the bed. She thinks superstitious people are stupid, like the way Rafael Nadal always has to pull on his ears and nose before every point on the tennis court. Emma suffers from a growing list of what she calls her "negative obsessions"—things she simply can't abide. Other people might call them pet peeves, but in Emma they illicit intense fear and rage. The sight of anything that's cracked and ripped, tearing or peeling, makes her want to scream. It's even worse if the rip can be described as "gaping." That makes the acid in her stomach leap straight to her throat. She'll go out of her way to avoid anything that looks like it's decaying, including food, rundown buildings, and even torn upholstery. She avoids most people, too, because of the gross sounds they make, their gestures, or how they smell. To Emma's way of thinking, every human being should come with a remote control, so she can mute them, or better yet, just turn them off entirely. Because of this avoidance, she frequently feels isolated. It's incredibly lonely when you want to murder everyone around you all the time.

It's also incredibly lonely when your husband abandons you in a stranger's house for a month to take care of his selfish brother. Dr. Gibson would say: "Drug addiction is a disease, Emma." She looks at her phone and scrolls through Theo's texts. The last message her husband sent was earlier this morning: *Wish me luck xx.* That pissed her off, but she responded good luck anyway, no return kisses. His older brother, Charlie, has an appointment at Crossroads Rehabilitation Center today, which he's only agreed to attend if Theo, and only Theo, takes him. Charlie is adamant that it's completely unfair for him to have to make a decision about where to spend the next eight weeks of his life based on a one-hour consultation. Besides, according to Charlie, he doesn't have a drug problem, anyway. *If* he goes to rehab, it'll just be to get his family off his back. Poor Theo, Emma thinks. Charlie is playing him.

She should get started on a new drawing this morning, but it's difficult to focus when she's waiting to hear from Theo. *Charlie won't check himself into Crossroads Rehabilitation*, she scribbles on another piece of paper, then folds it, and stuffs it into the jar. It's hard to work when you're waiting to hear you're right.

She gazes through the kitchen window at Bennett's studio across the garden. He's been spying on her all morning, and all of yesterday morning, too, and the mornings before that. Ever since they arrived, this dickhead has been spying on her. She can just catch the top of his head disappearing below the studio window when she looks up.

There were a lot of factors that went into choosing where in London to rent a house, but only one that really mattered: no shared walls. Dr. Gibson has encouraged Emma to be more flexible on this; London is, after all, a big city and very few of its residents live without at least one shared wall. "What frightens you more," she asked, "your neighbors hearing you or you hearing them?" Emma hates the idea of both. She likes her life to be as private as possible. She feels the same about other people's lives; if they're exercising, watching television, or having sex, she doesn't want to hear it. It's grotesque, she thinks, the way other people's lives can just seep into your own and vice versa. Everyone should live in a human version of a Tupperware box. No seepage. "Remember, Emma, avoidance is a form of compulsion," Dr. Gibson told her. "The more you avoid your fears, the worse they'll get." Whatever. If Emma was going to London for a month, leaving her suburban Rhode Island house, studio, and routine behind, then she was going to have certain demands. "No shared walls" was one of them. Except for one minor concession, Bennett's house fit the bill perfectly. The owner lives in a studio in the back garden. "You won't know I'm here," Bennett wrote on the listing. Bullshit.

Hey, babe, Theo's text pops up on her phone. *Charlie doesn't like Crossroads.*

She wants to smash her phone on the marble countertop hard enough that even Theo, miles away, will feel it. She glances out to the studio and spots Bennett drinking a cup of tea by the window, pretending to be captivated by it.

Fuck sake, Theo, she responds.

Alright, don't kill the messenger, he replies.

Theo's so much more than the messenger. He's the enabler, she thinks, but doesn't text that. Instead, she writes it down on a piece of paper, *Theo is an enabler.*

|||||||||||||||||||||||||

Emma had been starting a masters program in painting at Rhode Island School of Design when she met Theo, a photography student a year ahead of her. She fell for him on an early autumn afternoon when the air was getting chilly, but she was too stubborn to switch from flip-flops back to regular shoes. The wasps were similarly obstinate, not yet ready to give up on the idea of summer. They were sluggish and flying low to the ground that day and one of them flew between Emma's heel and her sandal as she strode across campus. That was the end of the wasp, but it left its stinger embedded in her heel. The pain was immediate and horrendous. She sat on a nearby bench, waiting for the stinging to subside, but it wouldn't. She had her foot propped up on her opposite knee, inspecting the sting, her thick brown ringlets flopping in front of her, when Theo sat down next to her.

"Alright?" he asked.

"I stepped on a fucking wasp."

He looked at her, startled, not expecting such strong language.

"Sorry, it fucking hurts. Sorry."

He smiled at her, apparently amused at how American she was. "Want me to have a look?" he asked, cautiously, rummaging through his backpack. "I have some tweezers on my Swiss Army knife. If the stinger is still in there, maybe I can get it." His British accent was adorable.

When he pulled the tiny tweezers from the top of the knife, she noticed his bright green eyes. Everything about him seemed to suggest that whatever he encountered in life was an unexpected opportunity. It was charming at the time, but now, five years in, Emma admits it's fucking annoying.

"It'll feel so much better, I promise. Give me your foot."

She cringed at the thought of the metal touching her burning heel, but reluctantly, she stretched her leg across his lap. She was thankful, at least, that she'd bothered to paint her toenails the day before.

"Yep. I see the little bugger." He looked up and smiled at her. "Ready?"

"Just fucking do it," she said, fists clenched.

She punched her leg several times as the metal pressed against the thick skin of her heel.

"Hold still . . . got it!" He held up the tweezers triumphantly, the tiny stinger on the end. "Better?"

"Not really. Sorry."

"You probably need an antihistamine," he said, getting up close to the sting. "Looks red and swollen."

She removed her leg from his lap, before the bottom of her foot could become permanently etched into his memory.

"I can go to the chemist for you. I'm heading in that direction anyway."

"Really?" she asked, perplexed by his kindness.

"I'm Theo."

"Emma."

"That's my bike over there, Emma. I'll be back in fifteen."

"Thank you. I owe you."

"That's the plan," he said with a cheeky smile.

The next day, she repaid him with a drink. Sitting in a booth at the grad student bar, he challenged her to go as long as she possibly could without swearing. Fourteen minutes was her best time and that was only because he had his tongue in her mouth for most of it. She remembers there being a giant tear in the cushion of the red laminate booth with the yellowish foam sticking out. She could see it clearly as she peered over Theo's shoulder, mid-kiss. It didn't bother her one bit.

IIIIIIIIIIIIIIIIIIIIIII

On the top floor of Bennett's sprawling house, Emma sits at the small white drafting table she purchased especially for this trip. It's set up in the master bedroom because there's a lot of extra space on the third floor. Skylights surround the giant loft-style bedroom, a former attic, so she gets morning and afternoon light streaming down from all sides. Windows on the backside of the room face the garden, flooding the room with even more afternoon light. After laying out a large blank sheet of thick white paper on the slanted surface of the table, she opens her laptop on the unmade, king-size bed and clicks on Philip Glass's *Einstein on the Beach, Knee Play no. 5* in her iTunes. With the computer's remote control in hand, she sits down at the drafting table. The plastic tray attached to the bottom of the table is filled with colored pencils, one hundred and twenty to be exact, and she picks up Prussian blue, her favorite. She inspects the tip, pricking her finger to test its sharpness. She gives it a couple spins through the pencil sharpener and she's ready. She points the remote to the computer and hits Play. The sound of an organ comes in low as a choir begins to chant:

1 2 3 4 1 2 3 4 5 6 1 2 3 4 5 6 7 8 1 2 3 4 1 2 3 4 5 6 1 2 3 4 5 6
7 8 1 2 3 4 1 2 3 4 5 6 2 3 4 5 6 7 8 1 2 3 4 1 2 3 4 5 6 2 3 4 5 6
7 8 1 2 3 4 2 3 4 . . .

She transcribes the numbers in a calligraphy-like style, as the choir recites them.

1 2 3 4 2 3 4 5 6 2 3 4 5 6 7 8 1 2 3 4 2 3 4 5 6 2 3 4 5 6 7 8 2 3
4 2 3 4 5 6 2 3 4 5 6 7 8 2 3 4 2 3 4 5 6 2 3 4 5 6 7 8 1 2 3 4 2 3
4 5 6 . . .

When the choir finishes the eight-minute recitation of numbers, she pauses the music. She glances at the wall that her drafting table abuts, where a thin hairline crack runs through the white paint. Seeing the crack bothers her, but not as much as facing the window that looks onto Bennett's studio. He's an artist, too. This information had apparently been available in the "About the Host" section of the AirBed website, but she hadn't bothered to look, because at the time she didn't give a shit. Besides, when Bennett wrote, "You won't know I'm here," she'd taken that to mean he'd be at work all day. Bullshit. Facing the window when he is working is far too distracting. He's a painter in that old-fashioned white guy way—large, colorful, bold canvases. The way he holds the brush, it looks like it all comes easily to him. Too easily. He has an annoying rhythm when he paints (mix paint, dip brush, mark canvas, step back, wash brush, mix paint, dip brush, mark canvas, step back, wash brush . . .) and it disrupts her own rhythm. "How can you even see what he's doing?" Theo asked her when she complained about it. "I just can," she said. "You know I can see everything."

Emma sets the Prussian blue into an empty tin box, with divots for the individual pencils, that sits atop the adjacent dresser. Next, she holds up two colored pencils, considering, before finally deciding on scarlet red. She hits Repeat on the remote and once again the choir starts reciting the numbers, which she transcribes, this time, with the scarlet pencil. Now that she's recorded the sequence once, she *could* just copy it rather than repeat the song each time, but that's not how she works. There are lots of *easier* ways to do all kinds of things, but Emma's not interested in any of them.

The composer, Philip Glass, was a revelation. She'd heard of him—in fact, she'd been recommended his music on many occasions because of their mutual love of repetition—but she always shelved the suggestion. Being handed something is not nearly as rewarding as finding it yourself, Emma believes. She finally found Philip Glass on a Thursday in December. Therapy day. When she pulled out of the driveway, the radio was tuned to NPR. She didn't really want to listen to it, but she's a nervous driver and kept both hands tight on the wheel, at ten and two, until she got to the doctor's. Next up was a segment called "Music That Moves Me." The piece in question, that moved some guy called Craig, fifty-eight, from Warwick, was Philip Glass's *Einstein on the Beach, Knee Play no. 5.* She can't remember a single thing about what made the music special to Craig. She didn't care. From that moment on, the song was no longer Craig's, it was hers. The counting soothed her on the frigid roads, stained white from the grit of previous snowstorms. The sides of the road were piled high with banks of dirty decaying snow, but she kept her eyes ahead. Two female voices started speaking over the chorus of numbers, repeating nonsensical phrases like, "Will it get some wind for the sailboat? / And it could get for it is / It could get the railroad for these workers / And it could be where it is / It could Franky / It could be Franky / It could be very fresh and clean / It could be a balloon . . ." For those eight glorious minutes she felt she was actually in control of the car and not the other way around. The music felt like a message, some kind of Morse code, pure chaos for most, but perfect order for the chosen few. Emma felt she was one of those. She was at Dr. Gibson's office five minutes after the piece ended, but whatever she and the therapist discussed in the session, she doesn't remember. It wasn't important. She was careful not to say anything about the song. She didn't want to dissect the swell of emotion she felt for it, particularly the part at the end where the violin and the man's voice came in, seemingly from nowhere asking, "How much do I love you? Count the stars in the sky. Measure the waters of the oceans with a teaspoon. Number the grains of sand on the sea shore." Yes, she thought, exactly—the immeasurable, the immense, if she could quantify it all, she would.

IIIIIIIIIIIIIIIIIIIII

When *Einstein* ends again, she hits Pause, putting down scarlet red. She already knows she's going to go for cobalt green for the third sequence and then probably caput mortuum for the fourth, maybe Payne's gray for the fifth, but she doesn't want to get ahead of herself. It's hard not to get excited by all the possibilities. She's working on an application, an open call for a solo show at a Providence gallery, where she wants to exhibit a series of drawings influenced by *Einstein on the Beach*. The problem is, she hasn't exhibited since graduation five years ago. It's hard to get her work seen, so much harder than she anticipated. Her drawings are subtle—quiet and contemplative. They don't photograph well. Posting images of her work on Instagram is pointless; it looks like nothing at all, making her wonder why she bothers. But this song, it opened up something in her, made her feel sure of herself and what she wanted to do—interpret the music visually. The deadline for the exhibition is at the end of the month—ten images and a statement, but this is only drawing number one and already doubt is creeping in. Do the drawings look better in her head than they do on the page?

Back in Providence, to ward off the encroaching doubt, Emma procrastinated on her application. Then a month ago, the shit hit the fan. Charlie was found unconscious in a pub bathroom. Though Emma had long suspected that Charlie's drug use went far beyond recreation, Theo and his mum were slow to accept it. According to Theo, it had been a long-running joke in the Easton family that Charlie had an addictive personality, though it was always portrayed as harmless, even "adorable" how addicted he would get to things like cigarettes, coffee, tattoos, and even running. "It was a mistake," Charlie told Theo over the phone after he was released from the hospital. "I was at Simon's leaving do. You know Simon . . . I took some co-codamol because my back was really hurting. I got there and, you know, there was cocaine, there was vodka. I got carried away." His back injury was the result of falling off his skateboard while attempting kickflips at Acton Skatepark, an injury Emma had very little sympathy for to begin with. Two weeks after being found unconscious at the pub, Charlie was evicted from his flat for starting a small fire. He'd taken more painkillers (far beyond the recommended dose), lit a cigarette, and promptly passed out. Now he was back living with his mum. As Charlie spiraled, Emma and Theo both stopped working creatively. Every day, they waited, half expecting to hear that he'd lethally overdosed. But every day he was getting by, his mother supplying him with a small regimen of co-codamol to keep him from going out to get the harder stuff. One afternoon, over the phone, Monica admitted she was struggling. Despite her attempts to keep him calm,

Charlie's cravings won out and when he was in withdrawal, he could be mean. "Don't worry, he's not violent," Monica said. "He just doesn't know his own strength." For Theo, that was it.

"He'll kill her," he told Emma with a wild stare. "I can't be here. I need to be there."

The tip of the cobalt green pencil snaps under the pressure of Emma pushing it into the paper. She hadn't realized how hard she was pressing. This can happen when her mind wanders. Dr. Gibson is encouraging her to be more mindful, to really focus on whatever she's doing, but that can be difficult when the things she's doing are so repetitive. "Maybe you should try making less repetitive work," Dr. Gibson suggested in one session, but then backed down when she saw the panic in Emma's eyes. Emma hits Pause on the music to sharpen her pencil. The broken end looks wounded, brittle, and angry. She twists it through the sharpener hastily, eager to smooth the jagged edges.

She checks her phone before resuming the music. It's noon and Theo hasn't called. He's spent only three nights in the house with her, so far. Mostly, he's over at his mother's helping babysit Charlie. The idea had supposedly been to spend the afternoons there and come home to Emma in the evenings, but Monica clung to Theo when he arrived, and before long she wanted him there until Charlie went to bed at night and again as soon as he woke up in the morning. Eventually, it just seemed easier for Theo to stay overnight. Easier for everyone except Emma, that is.

Last night, though, he said something on the phone about meeting at a pub, the Elk, for lunch. Getting hungry, she's frustrated at having to wait for him all the time. All there is in the house to eat is granola, cheddar cheese, crackers, and an avocado, but she's been avoiding the avocado ever since she found it facing the wrong direction in the fruit bowl a few days ago. She doesn't like it when her food is pointing right at her, like the barrel of a gun. Avocados, bananas, eggplants, zucchini, all have to be laid out lengthwise. This, according to her therapist, is one of her compulsions. A few nights ago, when she went into town to meet Theo's friend, Sarah, for dinner, the avocado was pointing toward the laundry room—the way she likes all the fruit and vegetables to point, because she's rarely in the laundry room to receive their harsh stare. But when she came home the next morning, the avocado had been pointing toward the window and out into the garden. The previous evening, she'd given Bennett permission to come in and retrieve a painting from the house, so obviously, he touched it. Why on earth he'd want to manhandle her avocado, she has no idea. She'd taken it to the sink and examined it for possible lacerations, even running it under a hot tap to remove any residue he might have left behind. There didn't seem to be anything wrong with the avocado, but she still hasn't worked up the courage to eat it. She wrote *Bennett touched my avocado* on a piece of paper and added it to the fact jar. She wanted to throw the thing away, but she knows that it would be a good challenge for her to keep and eat it, if only to prove to herself that Bennett and the avocado aren't conspiring against her.

Just as she's about to hit Resume on the music, her phone rings.

"Hi," she says to her husband, purposely grumpy.

"Hi," Theo matches her emotionally. "It's been a shit morning."

"Come back."

"Charlie says he'll lose it if I leave."

Emma releases the cobalt green pencil into the plastic tray, before she can snap it in half. "'Lose it'? What's that supposed to mean?" she asks, making a fist.

"I'm not sure I want to find out."

She wants to ask Theo why he lets his brother threaten him like that. She can feel the anger rising inside her, like from deep in a volcano. She punches herself in the leg, harder than intended. She'd meant to hit her thigh, but she missed, catching the side of her kneecap. "Ouch. Fuck."

"You okay?" Theo asks, seemingly more out of frustration than concern.

"I'm fine." She rolls up her jeans to examine her knee, which is red on the left side.

"Good. I can't take care of both of you at once."

And the volcano erupts. Her ears feel like hot magma, her eyes like balls of fire. "Bye, Theo." She hangs up, raising the phone above her head, preparing to smash it facedown on the wooden floor, but that would be the third screen she's rage-shattered in a year. Instead, she chucks it hard on the mattress, where it bounces high and then disappears into the duvet.

She retrieves the cobalt green pencil and hits Play on the song.

2 3 4 2 3 4 5 6 2 3 4 5 6 7 8 2 3 4 2 3 4 5 6 2 3 4 5 6 7 8 . . .

She can hear a muffled vibration from the phone in the duvet, but she ignores it. Theo thinks he's such a saint. She reminds herself to write that fact down later. What would she and Charlie and Monica do without him? Everyone's savior. Oh, please. He's only making things worse. Doesn't he get it? Charlie needs to hit rock bottom and he's not going to with Monica and Theo propping him up. Charlie's not even in therapy, for Christ's sake. He can't even admit he needs help. If she picks up the phone right now she'll cry, maybe even scream at Theo. She's doing him a courtesy by not answering.

2 3 4 5 6 2 3 4 5 6 7 8 1 2 3 4 2 3 4 5 6 . . .

She pauses the music again, takes a deep breath, and digs the phone out of the duvet. "Voicemail from Theo," it reads.

"Emma, I'm sorry. I was trying to make a joke. It was a bad one. I'm not comparing you to Charlie. Want to meet for lunch at the Elk? I could really use a burger. I miss you."

Sure. When? she texts him back, adding a kiss to show she's calmed down.

||||||||||||||||||||||||

There are two distinct crowds in the Elk. The front part of the pub is populated with solitary older men. They don't talk to each other; in fact, they take no notice of each other at all. Each man occupies his own small, round wooden table with a bottle of red wine or a pint, noses bright red like Rudolph. Some have newspapers to hide behind, but most make no attempt to hide their purpose—drinking to forget.

Toward the back, the young mothers gather, their strollers pushed up against the back wall of the pub. They've pulled tables together, so they can sit in groups of six and eight. Toddlers and babies are bouncing on their mothers' knees: some cooing, others screaming. It bothers Emma that at thirty years old, she still feels complete indifference to such a sight. Being diagnosed with OCD has made her wary of her ability to be a good mother. It's hard to see how she could succeed at motherhood when so many other seemingly normal tasks are such a challenge. She's already had to stop herself from smashing her phone twice, just today. What if she can't stop herself from spiking her baby on the ground when it won't stop crying? How do you explain to a child why perfectly benign sights and sounds, like the tap of a hammer or the sight of peeling paint, terrify you? What kind of example is that for a child? *Be afraid, kid, be very of afraid of everything all the time.*

Theo is sitting at a small, round table sandwiched between the two groups. He stands up when he sees her coming, his green eyes beaming with the look of sweet freedom. He wraps his arms around her waist and gives her a big squeeze. "Did you leave your drawing to meet me?"

She shrugs. "Yeah, that's okay."

"How's it going?"

She sits down across from him. "Too soon to tell. It's hard to get momentum."

"I know." He reaches his hand across the table and takes hers. "I'm sorry."

She shrugs, again. She knows he's sorry. She feels guilty that he's always sorry.

"Mum thinks you should come stay with us."

Emma pulls back.

"She says she could clean off some of the dining room table for you to work."

"You're not serious?"

"I know it's not ideal, but at least we'd be together."

"We spent a lot on this house. Someone needs to sleep in it. Half of that money was your mum's!"

"Yeah, Mum was thinking maybe we could cancel the remaining nights and get a refund. You don't know until you ask."

"Yes, I do." She pulls her hands away from his.

He shrugs. She wants him to say she's right, but he doesn't.

"Is Bennett still spying on you?" Theo grins as he asks the question, hoping to lighten the mood.

"I'm serious about that," she says defensively, but a smile breaks through. "He's watching me. Did I tell you he touched my avocado?"

"Yes, you told me. He probably didn't."

"If you were home . . ." She takes a sip from her water. "You'd see it."

"I don't think the guy means any harm. You're both artists, maybe you should hang out?"

She pulls a face like he's crazy. "Sarah said he used to be kinda famous. Like part of the Damien Hirst crowd."

"Really?"

"Yeah." She shrugs. "Bit of a fall from grace, if true."

"I don't know, I think you need to investigate. Invite him round for tea."

"No way! Not with you gone. He'll probably think I want to sleep with him." She puts on her best porn star voice. "Oh, Bennett, can you come over and fix my faucet, it's leaking . . ."

"Yeah, alright," Theo concedes. "Just thought he could be a friend."

"I'd rather have you."

||||||||||||||||||||||

Lunch is too quick. Theo leaves the Elk after a text from Monica. Emma wonders what Monica will do when they head back to the States? Theo can't come running every time his brother wakes up from a nap. Deep down, Emma's worried Theo's not planning to return to America at all. She doesn't envy him the task of trying to get his brother into rehab, but still, she's envious that when he walks through the door of his childhood home, he'll be needed immediately. When she opens the door to Bennett's house, she'll be on her own again, until the next time Theo can get away, and those gaps seem to be getting longer and longer. She hadn't anticipated feeling so useless. She thought marriage would secure her from this kind of loneliness.

She passes Khoury's Market on the way home and sees that among the fruit and vegetables displayed outside the shop are a bunch of avocados. She thinks maybe she'll buy another one for the fruit bowl. Once there are two, hopefully she'll forget which one Bennett tainted. Standing over the crate, she sees each avocado is nestled in its own foam nest. She looks for one that reminds her the most of the avocado at home, selecting a plump one with dark green, coarse skin.

She hesitates going into the market, noticing the gross black-and-white-checkered linoleum floor inside. It's peeling and curling up at the edges, shriveling and decaying like a dead leaf. She steps in, holding her breath. Good challenge.

She heads straight to the register with the avocado, doing her best to ignore the floor and stare straight ahead at the girl behind the register. The young woman's long, plastic, bejeweled fingernails are wrapped around a tattered copy of *A Midsummer Night's Dream*. They look sharp, like the kind of fingernails that *cause* tearing and peeling, possibly even big, gaping wounds. They're painted pink with white and purple rhinestones glued to the surface of each nail, save for the right index finger, which is missing the purple rhinestone. That's disconcerting, Emma thinks, knowing that little jewel could have attached itself to any number of things in this shop. Instinctively, she checks her avocado, then holds it up to the girl, who regards Emma, curiously.

"Quid," she says, then continues reading.

Emma fishes in her wallet for a pound coin.

"You look smart," the girl says, eyeing Emma. "You read this book?"

Emma shakes her head, pushing the pound coin across the counter rather than handing it to her. She doesn't want to make contact with those nails.

"I read *Romeo and Juliet* when I was in school," Emma says.

"That one's dumb," she chirps back. "Bitch killed herself for no good reason. Try this." She lifts the book. "Willy was trippin' when he wrote this one."

"Right. Maybe I will."

She definitely won't, she thinks, putting the avocado in her coat pocket.

"I'll be done with it tomorrow." She shakes the book. "If you want to borrow it."

She imagines the purple rhinestone sandwiched in between the pages. No way she wants to borrow that book.

||||||||||||||||||||||

She rinses both the new and the tainted avocado in the kitchen sink, before putting them both in the large wooden fruit bowl that lives on the marble countertop island. She grips the bowl on both sides, spinning it so that the avocados dance around inside, stopping when she feels like she doesn't know which is which. Once they've stopped rolling, she points them both in the direction of the laundry room. If Theo were here, he'd tell her she's acting insane. Whatever. He's not here. And he never tells Charlie when he's acting insane.

Hovering over her small notebook, Emma thinks about all the thoughts she had on the walk home, wondering which deserve to be in the jar. Only one stands out, but she's scared to write it down. The point of the exercise, Emma knows, is for her to distinguish between mere feelings and reality. "Feelings aren't facts," Dr. Gibson reminds her nearly every session. "What you believe may not be rooted in truth, but actually in fear." She's convinced that Theo doesn't intend to return to Rhode Island at the end of the month as planned, despite the fact that Theo has said nothing to indicate that this is true. It's not just a feeling she has, it's a truth so inevitable that she believes she's powerless to stop it. *Theo's not coming home with me,* she scrawls.

"Where's the evidence?" Dr. Gibson would ask her.

"He has nothing to go home to," Emma would answer, convinced that their marriage and his job at RISD don't have the same pull as Charlie, his mum, and his childhood home. Hell, she followed him all the way to London and she's barely seen him.

She folds the piece of paper and stuffs it in the jar, her eyes welling up with tears. Some facts are cathartic to write down, but not this one.

Looking out the kitchen window, she sees that Bennett has just started a new painting. Yesterday, he spent the afternoon in the garden, where he laid out a giant sheet of linen across the grass and proceeded to staple the fabric around a large stretcher a hundred or so times. The staple gun was loud, but more annoyingly, every time he fired it, he would clear his throat with a phlegmy groan—phlegm that could have tainted her avocado. She couldn't work because she kept imagining herself chucking the avocado at his stupid face. "You won't know I'm here." Bull. Shit. Bennett. After he finished stretching the canvas, he coated it several times with gesso, a process that wouldn't have bothered her except that he was humming along to music coming from his headphones the whole time. It was annoying. Today, he's coating the canvas with a bizarre yellow wash. She remembers her painting professor advised her to start with a darker more neutral color as a wash, then paint her way to the light colors at the end. Bennett seems to be doing the opposite. Has he forgotten the basics? She wonders if the painting is a commission. Does it already have a destination or someone who desires to own it, before he's even painted it? His career clearly isn't where he wants it, otherwise he wouldn't be renting out his house; still, he seems to be applying this saturated Subway sandwich yellow with all the confidence of a man who has done this a million times before to great effect. Is this the definition of success? Total abandonment of the basics and not giving a shit? What must that be like? To be so sure of your work and have others so sure of it, too?

She's determined that if she looks back at the fruit bowl now, she won't be able to tell which avocado is which, so she tests her theory. If she had to guess, she'd say the new one is on the left, but she knows she shouldn't guess; they're both just avocados.

When she turns back to look into the garden, a red-haired woman is coming through the gate carrying what appears to be a blackout curtain. Emma looks down at the sink before the woman has a chance to make eye contact with her. When she looks up again, Bennett is greeting the redhead at the studio door with a kiss—an exaggerated, heavy-on-the-tongue kiss that you only get at the beginning of relationships. Emma cringes, watching them out of the corner of her eye and pretending to concentrate on wiping down the countertop with a damp sponge. When Bennett pulls away, he looks over at the kitchen window in time to see Emma wringing out the sponge, high above the sink. Taking the redhead by the hand, he leads her inside. Emma can see through the studio window that they're still kissing. The redhead is undoing the buttons on his shirt when he pulls back. Glancing in Emma's direction again, he reaches for the blackout curtain, lifts it up, and runs a metal rod through it, before placing it in front of the big studio window. And just like that, Bennett and the redhead are gone. Emma should be thrilled.

||||||||||||||||||||||

Back at her drafting table, she tries to focus. She's managed to use only three of the one hundred and twenty total colors she intends for this drawing. Grabbing the caput mortuum pencil, she hits Play. She writes just the first four numbers of the sequence before hitting Pause and staring back at Bennett's blacked-out window. Something is happening behind that curtain that he doesn't want her to see, and after all the crap he's subjected her to, that really pisses her off. How dare he want privacy now? She wanted privacy yesterday when he was grunting out in the garden. She takes a deep breath and turns away from the window, and then right in front of her is the crack in the wall. It looks deeper, somehow, like it's widening. She wonders if Bennett knows about it. She'd like to stride across the garden, bang on his door, and tell him. She'd like to demand that he stop whatever secretive thing he's doing and come over here and fix this hideous crack.

"Is it really about the crack?" she can hear Dr. Gibson asking. Yes, Emma thinks. The crack is horrible. Fact. She follows it all the way up to the high corner of the wall. Pushing her chair into the corner and still holding on to the colored pencil, she climbs up to inspect the source of the split, tracing it with her finger until the crevice drops low enough for her to step off the chair. The tip of her finger follows it as it carves its way above the drafting table and zigzags down into the far low corner on the other side of the wall. She's sitting in this same corner, where the crack meets the molding, her head against the wall, when Theo calls.

"What's up?" she asks, knowing that something is.

"We're in the car. Me and Charlie and Mum. We're on our way to Bristol."

"What? Why?"

"Don't get mad." This has to be the most pointless phrase in the English language. She fumes at the very suggestion.

"Charlie wants to see Dad." Theo's father, Martin, is buried in Bristol. He had been a documentary filmmaker, who produced many pieces for the BBC before dying, suddenly, ten years ago, from complications after a routine heart operation. That Charlie takes after his father and is, himself, a talented filmmaker is one of the Easton family's agreed upon lies. Charlie talks a lot about making a documentary about Martin making documentaries. He's yet to shoot a single frame. "He wants to visit Dad's grave and talk to him. He thinks it might help."

"Help him with the drug problem he claims he doesn't have? He's stalling."

"Maybe."

No, not maybe. Theo says *maybe* too much.

"There's another rehab place just outside of Bristol, a twelve-week program. He said maybe he'd prefer it because he'd feel closer to Dad. It's worth a try."

"I guess," she says, knowing full well it's not going to work.

"We're going to stay overnight. Visit the clinic in the morning."

"Is Charlie packed for a twelve-week stay?"

"No."

"Right." She takes the sharpened end of the caput mortuum pencil and jams it into the base of the crack. "I wish you'd told me you were going."

"I'm sorry, it just happened so fast."

"Maybe I would have come with you," she says, digging the pencil tip into the crevice so that bits of the plaster chip away. The maroon pigment transfers to the white surface.

"Really?"

"I've never seen your dad's grave."

"Now probably wouldn't have been the right time." He pauses. "I'll call you tonight," he says in that finalizing tone.

"Okay," she says, even though she doesn't want to get off the phone at all.

When the line goes dead, she lets the phone drop onto her lap, then brushes it off onto the floor. She grips the pencil with intent, like she would if she were working on her drawing. Scooting along the floor on her butt, she traces the crack with the pencil, as she had done earlier with her finger, pressing the pigment into the gap. She's careful to keep the tip of the pencil inside the crack, not letting the drawn line stray off the predetermined path. The color coats both sides of the crevice. She shifts to her knees and then, when she can no longer reach by kneeling, stands up, continuing to follow the line up over the desk. When it gets too high, she steps back up onto the chair. From there, if she stands on her tiptoes, she can reach the farthest corner, the color stretching all the way to the end of the crack. She jumps down from the chair and steps back to look at what she's done. The result is vulgar. The wall looks like it has a pulsing vein running through it. Tonight, she'll sleep in one of the other bedrooms, let the vein throb in peace.

||||||||||||||||||||||

The next morning, she wakes up thinking about the crack and wonders why she'd been so stupid to trace it. If Theo hadn't gone to Bristol, she wouldn't have done that. It's his fault, she tells herself, sitting at the kitchen island with her granola, staring across at Bennett's still blacked-out studio. Theo hasn't even sent his usual good morning text. She could text *him* "Good morning," but she's not the one who keeps leaving. She's right where she's been all along, in this giant house by herself, where even the annoying neighbor has decided to ignore her. She just needs to focus. If she can forget about the loneliness and forget about the crack, she can put all her energy into her drawing. She'll just work really hard, maybe so hard that if Theo calls she'll be too busy to answer.

|||||||||||||||||||||||

By early afternoon, she has, technically, worked hard. She's traced the crack with half of the one hundred and twenty colored pencils in her case. What was a small crack, no thicker than a strand of hair, now looks like a chasm; the Grand Canyon on a suburban, white wall in London. The drawing on her table remains as she left it yesterday with just three sequences recorded, plus the very beginning of a fourth. She sits on the floor, staring up at the graffitied wall, watching it like one might stare at a burning building, with a mixture of fascination and terror. Somehow, when she woke up this morning, she knew she would do this, just as she knew she'd regret it and the result would be grotesque. And yet . . .

She can hear Dr. Gibson's voice in her head. "What bothers you about it, Emma?"

"It's pulsing," she'd tell her. "It's alive."

All sixty colors together have coalesced into a thick, purplish-brown, like a bruise.

"Except, it's not, really? Is it?" the doctor would probably ask. Sensitive, not confrontational.

"It looks like it's rotting," she'd explain. "Only living things can rot."

The Crack, she thinks—a proper obsession deserves a proper noun.

|||||||||||||||||||||||||

Starving, she stands in the kitchen, staring at the avocados. It's definitely the one on the left, she thinks. She knows she's not really going to eat it. Maybe if she gets good news from Theo, like Charlie's checked in to rehab, then she'll challenge herself to eat the fucking thing, but she can't be brave all the time. Now, it's Charlie's turn.

She opens a cabinet and pulls out a box of Ritz Crackers, a little taste of home, although they're not as salty in the U.K. and always taste a little bit stale. From the fridge, she grabs a block of cheddar cheese, which she slices on a big wooden cutting board while staring out the window, watching the sun shimmer through the newly budding tree branches. Bennett's studio is still blacked-out. She's beginning to wonder if they'll ever resurface, when the studio door opens and the redhead appears. She spots Emma in the window and gives her a big wave, but Bennett is quick to come up behind her, clearly embarrassed.

Emma smiles back, weakly, but doesn't wave. She doesn't want them to see her cheeks flush from finally being noticed. She continues to chop her cheese into rectangles and arranges them on the cutting board in a herringbone pattern.

Bennett and the woman seem to be having a disagreement on his front step, but Emma can't quite hear what it's about. "Just ask her," she thinks she can hear the redhead saying.

"No, let's not bother her," Bennett replies, dismissively.

"She's right there!" She points to Emma at the window, but Emma pretends not to notice.

The redhead goes back inside and comes out again a few seconds later with a balled up duvet and cover. She walks defiantly across the yard with the huge wad. She waves again at Emma as best she can with her load, beckoning her to the back entrance.

"Hi," she says, chipper, as Emma pulls open the door to the garden. "I'm Claire. Sorry to bother you. Emma, right?"

Emma nods, yes, and leans against the entrance, making it clear to Claire not to cross the threshold.

"Is there any chance we can borrow the washer and dryer? We had a red wine incident last night and this duvet has absorbed easily half a bottle of pinot noir. A good one, too!" She slaps at the duvet, like it's been naughty.

"Okay." Emma stands upright with a groan, pretending that Claire is putting her out, even though she's relieved to once again have human contact. Being annoyed is better than feeling alone. Anything is better than feeling alone.

"Thank you, you're a star," Claire says, barging right in. "Bennett said not to bother you, but I was sure you wouldn't mind. You seem like a reasonable person."

Emma stifles a laugh. If Theo were here, he'd howl at the thought of anyone thinking she's reasonable.

Claire stuffs the duvet and its dark blue cover into the top-loading drum, then locates a bottle of bleach and pours in a capful. Emma stands silently at the edge of laundry room, wondering if this woman knows what bleach is.

"He says this is one of those industrial American type washers."

Claire stares at it, confused. "There's so many buttons on here. You're American, right? Do you know how this thing works?"

"Um, kinda. I've only used it once. I think it's probably a heavy load, right?" She points to the spot on the dial that reads: "Heavy."

"Maybe I should ask?" She breezes past Emma to the back door. "BENNETT!"

Emma watches from behind Claire, as shirtless Bennett appears at the door of the studio in a pair of jeans covered in paint. Throwing a T-shirt over his head, he pulls it down quickly when he realizes Emma is looking. "Yeah?" he asks, embarrassed, running his hand through his hair.

"IS IT A HEAVY LOAD?" Claire shouts from the door.

"Give me a sec," he says, flustered, looking at the floor around him for his sandals. He slides into them and strides across the garden, head down, hands in his pockets.

Claire returns to the laundry room. Putting her weight onto the washer, she peers into the drum for answers.

"Do you mind?" Bennett asks Emma before stepping into the house.

She gestures for him to come on in. It's not like she really has a choice. "You always have a choice," she remembers Dr. Gibson saying. How come it never feels like it? She looks over at the avocados. They're currently pointing right at her, so she takes a step back.

Bennett looks into the drum. Then at Claire. "Did you put bleach in here?"

Emma can tell he's pretending not to be upset.

"I put in laundry soap," Claire replies.

"This laundry soap?" he asks, grabbing the bottle of bleach.

"Bollocks."

"Right." He shakes his head, closing the drum, then sets the washer to Heavy Load, Hot. "Sorry, Emma. We'll get out of your hair for now."

She can't stop thinking about the sixty colored lines she's drawn on his bedroom wall. She really shouldn't have done that.

"Nice to meet you, Emma," Claire says, wrapping her arms around Bennett's waist. He flinches, like he's being attacked, but gives in and puts an arm around her.

"Come on," Bennett says, taking Claire's hand like he's leading a small child. Adding as they step out into the garden, "I hope things are okay with your husband's family, Emma."

Emma shrugs. "Not really, but what can you do?" The phrase "her husband's family," registers with her. It feels that way. Despite their marriage, Theo's family isn't hers.

||||||||||||||||||||||||

Back in the master bedroom, she sits down at her drafting table, but doesn't want to pick up a pencil. She just stares at the barely started drawing. She tries calling Theo, but it goes straight to voicemail. Unable to concentrate, she switches Bennett's laundry from the washer to the dryer when she hears the machine buzz. An hour later, he knocks on the back door.

"Thanks, Emma," he says, sheepishly, opening the door when Emma waves him in. He's holding a bottle of wine, which he forces into her hands as he enters. "For the trouble."

"That's alright," she says, looking down at the label—Bordeaux.

"Claire knows her wine, she assures me that it's good. I have the palate of a pillock, so . . ."

"Thanks." Emma's surprised to feel a smile come across her face.

"I actually put the duvet in the dryer for you. I hope you don't mind. I heard it ding." She looks at the timer—two minutes. "It'll be done soon."

"You didn't have to do that," he says, running his hand over his hair.

"I thought you were probably busy."

"Thank you. Yeah. I'm working on this painting. Lost track of time."

"A painting of Claire?" She hasn't seen the canvas since he coated it in yellow paint, but Claire reminds her of the kind of woman that modeled in Emma's life-drawing classes in college—gutsy and a little overly theatrical.

He nods. "It's been a while since I've done a portrait. It's challenging."

"Well, I sucked at life-drawing class."

"Of course, you're an artist." His tone is slightly patronizing.

"Trying to be," she says and leaves it at that, thinking that tracing the crack on his bedroom wall is probably closer to vandalism. She doubts he'd find any artistic merit in it.

"You're young," he says, "you've got time." It comes out entirely unconvincing. Of course he asks her nothing about her work. Typical.

Finally, the buzzer goes off. Bennett steps into the laundry room and crouches down in front of the dryer. Opening the door, he pulls out the duvet, but drops it on the floor quickly when he realizes how hot it is. "Mind if I borrow the basket?"

"Go for it."

He groans as he stands up, basket in hand, attempting a half-smile. "Back to work, I guess. Can't hide from the painting."

"Or the model," she says. It just comes out, but thankfully he smiles for real this time.

"True." He looks down at his bleach-stained duvet cover and sighs.

||||||||||||||||||||||

Ten minutes later she's looking up at The Crack, bulging and throbbing in front of her—open bottle of wine in one hand, the sixty-first colored pencil in the other. She wonders if Bennett is *really* challenged by his painting, like, actually frightened that it might be no fucking good. What's he really, truly afraid of, she wonders. What problem can't he bear to face?

"Why are you so frightened of cracks and tears?" Dr. Gibson asked her at their first therapy session.

She cringed. Jesus, if she knew the answer to that question, would she be paying a hundred-and-fifty dollars an hour for therapy? "I just don't like them. They remind me of disease."

"Have you ever had a visible disease or known someone that has?" the doctor asked.

"No," Emma said, shaking her head fiercely at the thought of it.

"I think if you got one, you'd be able to handle it," Dr. Gibson said encouragingly. "Our fears are often worse in our minds than they are in real life. That's what you're here to learn."

Emma shook her head again, unsure.

"Are you worried about something in particular?" Dr. Gibson asked, leaning forward in her high-backed armchair. "If you or if Theo had, say, shingles, how do you think you'd cope?"

"We won't. I made sure we both got the vaccine."

"Okay, but say it doesn't work." The doctor treads carefully, seeing Emma's face go ashen. "Sometimes we get the flu even when we've had a flu shot. How would you cope if Theo got shingles?"

"Badly."

"How badly, Emma?"

"I'm worried I'd skin him alive," she confessed.

‖‖‖‖‖‖‖‖‖‖‖‖‖‖‖

When all the wine is gone, she's traced The Crack with all one hundred and twenty colors. She still tries to convince herself that it was a "good challenge." She should be proud of herself for confronting something that scared her, even though it's actually more terrifying now. It's meant to be frightening, she reminds herself—that's how she learns. Most importantly, she assures herself that this is nothing like what happened three years ago, when she traced all the veins on her arms and legs with a ballpoint pen, every day, for weeks, until her skin bruised and cracked. That was compulsion. This is therapy.

She turns her back to The Crack, sitting up against the wall, sliding her socked feet along the white-painted floor. The herringbone pattern is only visible through the intervals where the floorboards meet and the paint dips ever so slightly into the joint. She traces one of the floorboards with her finger. Finally a text comes through from Theo: *Horrible Day. Charlie ditched us. Got on a train to fucking Manchester to buy black market Vicodin. We'll go after him tomorrow. I'll call you in the morning. Just need to sleep. XXX.*

She reaches up to her drafting table to pull down the indigo pencil. She draws a light, thin indigo line on the short end of one of the planks. It fits ever so snuggly in the dip.

"Don't, Emma," she whispers to herself.

‖‖‖‖‖‖‖‖‖‖‖‖‖‖‖

In the morning, as she pours her granola, she stares at Bennett's studio. The blackout curtain is finally pulled back. He's alone today, working on the painting of Claire. The yellow canvas from a couple of days ago is now full of color. Claire's naked body is cross-legged in a rocking chair with one hand on the arm of the chair, the other holding open a book; Emma can't make out the title. She knows he's not finished yet, but Claire looks somewhere between human and porcelain doll, not exactly the woman she met yesterday—not loud or theatrical, but still, inorganic, classical. Her fair skin seems to glow with light purples and cool pinks, contrasting and complementing the yellow background. It reminds her of a lecture from art school, when her professor showed the class an image of John Singer Sargent's *Madame X*—one of his most famous paintings—a woman with her flesh so pale against her black dress, it was cool as ice. The lesson, she remembers, was that skin tones are inherently cool; the blood coursing through our veins is blue, not red. Maybe Bennett does know what he's doing with that yellow, after all. It's remarkable how much he's been able to accomplish on the painting in just forty-eight hours. How does he work *every day* with such ease and confidence? He works like it's no challenge for him at all. Maybe last night's insecurity was just an act. She thinks about her own drawing upstairs, how she's barely touched it. Inspired by Bennett's work ethic, she wants to push forward on her *real* drawing today, but she knows she'll have to move her drafting table; she won't be able to concentrate with The Crack pulsing above her.

||||||||||||||||||||||

She drags the base of her table down the staircase to the second floor and into the small bedroom, where she's been sleeping for the last two nights. She rebuilds the table next to the door of the room, in a tight space that's not much wider than the table itself. The overhead light glows weakly with one of those eco-bulbs. It's dark, too dark. Still, claustrophobia and darkness are preferable to The Crack. It's frustrating, not gaining any momentum, she thinks, laboring back upstairs to fetch her colored pencils. She wants to blame Theo's brother. *If* he could just stop being so selfish, *if* he could just get into rehab, *if* she could have her husband back, then *maybe* she could get some work done.

||||||||||||||||||||||

Three years ago, after Theo and Emma got married, they were still living in Providence, where Emma was waiting tables at one of the Italian restaurants on Federal Hill and Theo was working as a darkroom technician at RISD. They were ships passing in the night that year; Theo worked days and Emma evenings. She crawled into bed at one a.m. and he got up at six. For Emma, daytime in their tiny apartment was hellish. She'd set up her drafting table in their living room, but the room shared a wall with their neighbor, a jazz pianist, who spent the afternoons practicing his craft, sometimes playing the same riff a hundred times a day. At the time, she was working on a series of grid drawings, all done with ballpoint pen. Mornings, she'd sit at her drafting table, playing David Bowie or Leonard Cohen on her headphones—anything with lyrics that she could get lost in. In one hand, she held a ruler and in the other, a Bic pen. Placing the ruler on the paper, she'd line it up with the light pencil marks denoting where the ink lines would go. Then, she'd breathe deeply, regard the wall she shared with the pianist, and drag the pen down the edge of the ruler from one marked point to the next. If the pianist didn't make a sound, she'd draw another line. This is how it went all day, every day. After a few months of this routine, Bowie and Cohen were too mellow to drown out the pianist or, more importantly (as Dr. Gibson would later point out), the fear of the pianist, so she started listening to the Pixies and Sonic Youth, which produced the wall of noise she was craving—a strong barrier between her and the jazz man. The problem was, she couldn't draw. All that sonic distortion didn't exactly provide for visual clarity. And her head hurt.

"Doesn't it strike you as ironic that you need sound to drown out sound?" Theo asked her on one of those rare nights when they were both at home, curled up on the sofa. Emma had the night off and piano man was out playing a club. She had his website bookmarked on her computer, so she always knew when he had gigs and scheduled her nights off accordingly. He was out of her ears, yes, but not out of her mind.

"I can't concentrate when he's playing," she responded, defensively. To her, this was a fact, no matter how strange or ironic Theo found it. "Why can't he find someplace else to practice?"

He put his arm around his wife, sensing her need for comfort. "He probably can't afford to. Same as you can't afford a studio."

"Yeah, but I'm not bothering anyone when I draw. What he does affects other people."

"You're both artists. Maybe you should collaborate. You said he's really repetitious, right? So are you!" Theo actually seemed excited by his idea. "Maybe try to draw the music he's playing. Make it visual."

"Oh, so I should give up everything I'm doing for him." She pulled away from him. "He wins?"

"I didn't realize it was a competition. It was just a suggestion."

"Then go 'suggest' to him that he practice his music somewhere else."

"Emma," he said, cupping her face in his hands and squishing her cheeks together the way he still likes to do when she's acting nuts. "I don't know how to help you."

"Did I say I needed help?" she chirped back through fish-puckered lips.

He didn't answer, kissed her instead. Every marriage, Emma remembers thinking, goes from kissing being an act of passion, to an act of shutting up the other person before you clobber them.

Emma had needed help, even if she couldn't admit it. Headphones weren't working, venting to Theo wasn't working, even escaping the apartment wasn't working. She took long walks all over Providence with a sketchbook in her bag, hoping she'd find a place to draw, though she never did. She just walked and walked, getting angrier and angrier and obsessing about whether the jazz man would still be playing when she returned. On these walks, peculiar things started to happen. First, she started stepping over pavement cracks. It was a silly thing really. She just noticed she was doing it one day. Except that when she tried to stop, she realized she couldn't. She started to feel superstitious about what would happen if she did step on them. What was that old saying from her childhood? "Step on a crack, break your mother's back." She didn't think *that* was going to happen, but she started to wonder what would. Would the piano man start practicing earlier in the mornings? Would a drummer move in downstairs? One day, just to prove to herself that she could, she jumped up and down on a big pavement crack eight times. She had to do it an even number of times, because an odd number felt unfinished. After that, she avoided cracks by searching out routes that had fewer cracks in the sidewalks. On one new route, she passed a house that had a big football-size rock leaning up against the mailbox. On any given day, she would decide whether she was having a good or a bad day based on whether she wanted to throw the rock through one of the house's bay windows. Most days she wanted to. Most days she wanted to shatter everyone's windows with that rock. She wanted these people to notice her, to ask her what was wrong, to assure her that her fears of cracks and her hatred of the piano player were understandable and not at all irrational. But nobody ever came out of their homes, which made her resent them, those lucky bastards with their own houses, their own four walls that they didn't have to share with anyone. They were all assholes, every single one of them. How could they live with themselves, knowing the paint was peeling around their attic windows, that their roof tiles were falling off? The bastards didn't deserve their own houses. If she had a house of her own, it would be a temple. She would never forget, not even for a second, how lucky she was to have it. So she changed her route again, this one comprised of houses she liked, that she could picture herself living in, that made her feel safe. The other houses, the ones with the peeling paint and loose roof tiles, didn't just make her angry, they frightened her. The bubbling paint reminded her of boils, the peeling paint of open wounds, the loose roof tiles of welts. *If* all those ugly houses *and* the cracked sidewalks *and* the fucking jazz pianist were to disappear, she told herself, she'd be okay.

Within a few months, she was walking a very specific route to a tiny park with just a couple of benches—the kind of space that people pass through but don't stay. There Emma would sit, always on the same bench, headphones on, staring at her feet. On the fourth day, after sitting there for an hour, she pulled a ballpoint pen out of her purse. She missed having a pen in her hands. She had her sketchbook, too, but she left it in her purse, and instead started tracing the lines of the veins on her arms. By the following week, she was tracing the veins on her legs, too. People would walk past and they'd look at her strangely, but in Providence, a town full of artists, very few things caused genuine alarm, least of all a white girl drawing on herself with a ballpoint pen. Back home, she'd take a shower and scrub off all the ink with a loofah. After a few weeks her skin was dry and rough from all the scrubbing. Even so, the ink marks were becoming permanent. She started to panic about the possibility of ink poisoning, which she looked up online. Google provided plenty of photographs of what the extremely rare condition would look like. In most, the skin was red, bumpy, blistered, but the worst photo was of an arm with raised black veins and capillaries, like the rotting roots of a tree. She couldn't get the image out of her mind. She saw it each time she closed her eyes and she begged herself not to trace her veins the next day on that park bench, though she always did.

Theo, who saw so little of her, didn't notice the changes. She bought pajamas with full-length sleeves and pants, so he couldn't see her skin. They basically stopped having sex; their competing schedules made intimacy difficult, and Emma's anxiety made it worse. Sensing she was recently getting more anxious, Theo thought a night at their old grad student bar, the site of their first date, would loosen her up. He even called the place beforehand and asked the barman to hold their favorite booth for them.

"Come on," he said, pulling her into their old vinyl bench, its big, gaping, polyester-foamy wound staring up at her.

"Can we sit somewhere else?"

"What? This is our booth." He smiled, but she could see he was hurt.

"There's barely anything left of it." Pulling herself out of the booth, she searched for another place to sit, pointing to a small table with two rickety wooden chairs. "How about there?"

He regarded her strangely. "That's way worse. I want to curl up."

She buried her head in his chest to signify she wanted to be near him, just not the torn vinyl.

When two frothy beers arrived at their small wooden table, Theo took her hand. "I'm worried about you, babe."

"I'm fine," she said, unconvincingly. "Things just aren't how I imagined."

"They'll get better," he assured her. "You only just graduated. In a couple years, you'll have more exhibition offers than you know what to do with." He squeezed her hand and craned his neck so he could meet her downcast eyes. "You'll be much busier, way more successful than the piano man. You won't even notice him."

Later, back home, they'd talked about the future and everything they wanted in life: a house with a big backyard, galleries to represent them, and universities where they'd one day teach. When they fell into bed together all Emma could think about was how lucky she was to have this wonderful man who loved her so much. She would stop all this craziness for him, she told herself. Tomorrow was a new day. He took off her shirt and tossed it on the floor. Holding her close, he rolled her over onto her back, straddling her, locking her arms under his thighs so he could tickle her neck, an activity that never failed to unleash an incredible barrage of laughter. But when he finally looked down at her arms, which were bruised and chapped, he stopped cold. Blue and black lines appeared and then faded away. Her skin was rough and peeling. There were cuts, scrapes, and dry, scaly patches. He climbed off her and turned on the light. When he threw back the covers to examine her legs, she burst into tears.

"Emma, what have you done?"

"I can't stop," she said, sobbing. "It hurts."

The next week they put down the first and last month's rent on a tiny house in suburban Pawtucket.

||||||||||||||||||||||||||

When she enters the master bedroom again, she sees the box of colored pencils and a large white eraser sitting on top of the dresser. She stuffs the eraser in the front pocket of her jeans, but lingers in the room, her back to The Crack. On the floor, barely visible, is the thin indigo line she drew yesterday. She hasn't heard from Theo yet today. Maybe *if* she knew Charlie didn't overdose last night . . . *If* Charlie could start to help himself, then *maybe* Emma could get to work on the drawing she's supposed to be doing, instead of what she's about to do. Rather than close the lid on her pencil box, she picks it up and sets it on the floor. Sitting down next to it, she removes the indigo blue.

||||||||||||||||||||||||||

By the time Theo finally calls, she's already traced twenty floorboards with thirty colors. "We're nearly in Manchester," he says.

"Manchester is a big city. Do you know where he is?" she asks, tracing in walnut brown.

"I think so. I found his mate on Facebook. Doubt we'll be back tonight. I'll call once we're booked into a hotel."

"Yeah, okay," she says. "Have fun."

She chooses light purple-pink as the thirty-second color. She probably wouldn't have picked it if Theo hadn't distracted her. She should have picked grass green.

"'Have fun'?"

"Good luck, I mean," she says, propping herself up on her knees. The purple-pink line hugs the walnut brown. She goes around each plank in four steady lines, twirling herself around on her knees every time she needs to change direction.

"Am I bothering you?"

"I'm working on my drawing." Not a total lie. "I don't just sit around waiting for you to call."

"Emma . . . I gotta go, Mum is waiting."

Hanging up without saying goodbye, she drops the phone on the floor and shoves it, like an air hockey puck, under the bed. With nothing obstructing its path, the phone glides, twirling, all the way to the opposite wall, where it bounces off the skirting board and continues to spin about six inches before finally stopping. She continues tracing the herringbone pattern with the light purple-pink, holding the grass-green pencil in the other hand so she doesn't forget which color she wants next. After that she picks deep cadmium yellow because it reminds her of Bennett's canvas, followed by Venetian red, then juniper green, ultramarine blue, orange glaze, pink carmine, and raw umber. She mumbles the numbers of *Einstein on the Beach* to herself as she traces the floorboards: "1, 2, 3, 4, 5, 6, 7, 8, 2, 3, 4, 2, 3, 4."

When she hears her phone vibrate, she gets to her feet for the first time in hours and hobbles to the other side of the room to retrieve it.

It's a text from Theo: *I've told Mum that I'm spending tomorrow night with you. Nonnegotiable XXX.*

She stares at The Crack and then down at the rainbow floorboards. "Fuck."

She can't let him see what she's done. She kneels down before the traced floorboards, running her fingers over one of the planks, caressing the rainbow of colors, forty lines deep. Pulling the large white eraser from her jeans pocket, she twirls it between her fingers. What are the chances that Theo really is coming back tomorrow night? He's made promises like this before and broken them. It's probably best she erase it now, before things get really out of hand. She rubs the eraser along a cross section of the forty colors, which causes them to bleed into each other. She examines the bottom of the eraser, streaked with color. This time she presses harder, but the rubber acts more like a squeegee, moving the color around instead of lifting it. Fuck. She hasn't even considered what to do about The Crack.

She lies down on the floor and picks up her phone. *It's okay*, she types. *Stay with your mum tomorrow. She needs you.* She tries to think practically. On her phone, she searches for nearby hardware stores. The nearest one is more than a mile away.

Sitting up straight, she shimmies over to the window, where she rests her arms and chin on the sill. From here she can watch Bennett while he paints. He holds his brush to the canvas, makes a stroke, steps back to look, his head cocked to one side, and then steps in again. It's nothing like the way Emma works, hunched over a table, making small marks, forgetting to breathe or stretch until it feels like her back might split in half. Bennett paints like he's going for a leisurely walk in the park. Emma's drawings are more like marathons where she tries to cover the greatest distance in the shortest amount of time, never stopping to sniff a single rose along the way.

Back when Emma was a nervous kid, her older sister tried to convince her it was impossible for anyone to count to a million in his or her lifetime. This theory terrified little Emma: How many seconds had already passed and how many more were left? As she got older she continued to puzzle over it. Deep down, she understood her sister's claim was bullshit, but it came with a profound message: her time on earth was quantifiable. It would be possible to count her life away. What if she started counting and couldn't stop?

She wonders what it's like to not think about these kinds of things, to have the kind of brain that's like a walk in the park. Doesn't it bother Bennett that his life can be broken down into a number of seconds? That some things can't be quantified at all? She thinks again of *Einstein on the Beach*:

> *How much do I love you?*
> *Count the stars in the sky.*
> *Measure the waters of the oceans with a teaspoon.*
> *Number the grains of sand on the sea shore.*
> *Impossible, you say?*

Looking over at the traced floorboards, she wishes Bennett could understand all this. She can't help it, but his process, his competency, it fills her with rage. She wants it to be as hard for him as it is for her. Across the way, he puts on his coat and checks his hair in the studio window. While she was daydreaming, he must have changed out of his studio clothes. Dressed now in his going-out clothes, he reaches back into the studio to hit the lights, turning the space dark before locking the door behind him. She's surprised by the disappointment she feels at knowing that he's gone for the rest of the day and possibly the night. She wants him to keep working. *If* he kept working, then *maybe* she could get back to her drafting table and do the real work she needs to do. They both *need* to work. He needs to finish that painting, sell it, and fix this crumbling house, the bastard. She'd like to chase after him with the tainted avocado. She'd like to tell him that if he doesn't go back to work on his painting, she's going to smear it all over his precious fucking hair. And fix the damn crack in his wall. And tell her that he's sorry for touching her avocado. She knows then and there that she's through fighting it. She's going to trace every damn floorboard in his bedroom. The dickhead deserves it.

||||||||||||||||||||||

It takes her all day and night. She moves the dresser first, tracing the boards underneath with the same forty colors she used earlier, then moves it back into place. Next she pushes the chaise lounge out of the way and traces that area. Her wrists and elbows ache, but she finds a rhythm, shaking out her arms after every board. The left side of the room is nearly finished by seven. When she allows herself to get up for a drink of water, she sees that Bennett's studio is still dark. She tells herself that when she's a famous artist, she won't let it slip away like he has. When she can afford a house like this, there won't be any cracks.

She lies flat on her stomach and shimmies under the bed with a flashlight she found in the laundry room. Starting at the head, she works her way down. Theo calls while she's under there, so she tells him she's curled up *in* the bed. He says that Charlie is with them at a Travelodge. He sounds so relieved, it breaks Emma's heart. Relieved to find his brother alive, Theo has forgotten that nothing's changed. There's still no rehab, and Charlie still doesn't believe he has a bad enough problem to warrant it. He's just *not dead*. The bar of success keeps getting lower.

A couple hours later and she's out from under the bed, tracing faster now, feeling the need to finish by sunrise. She's memorized the order of the colors by now, racing around each herringbone plank. She's not even shaking out her arms after every board, anymore. She's gotten used to the pain.

By two a.m. she's made it to the other side of the room. Bennett definitely never came home. She imagines him fucking Claire in some dank apartment in the center of town. She's not sure why, but Claire just seems like someone who might have a tiny, crowded flat full of knickknacks.

It's 4:37 a.m. when Emma traces the last floorboard. She stands up, her legs numb and wobbly. At the entrance of the room, she takes in what she's accomplished. It's not as striking as she imagined. It's more like a light hum emanating from the floor, subtle and rhythmic. She looks over at The Crack, bulging and pulsing like a rupturing varicose vein, even more garish and grotesque than before. She recalls the image of the ink-poisoned skin that so haunted her in Providence, capillaries running thick with brown rot. The Crack is like that, its veins raised and full of blood. The room beats around her like a stethoscope against a guilty heart.

||||||||||||||||||||||

She wakes up under the covers of the master bed. She remembers lying down just for a second, but that was eight hours ago. Looking left to right at the sketchy lines drawn on the floorboards, she's perplexed. What she thought was delicate and cadenced last night, just looks manic and messy this morning. She looks up at The Crack, which is not gaping and oozing like it was last night, just thumping, stupidly, like the headache after a night of too much drinking. She puts her head in her hands, thinking a hangover would be preferable to the feeling she has right now. A hangover, she could wait out, whereas none of this will go away until she fixes it. She starts to weep, knowing that even if she can fill The Crack and paint the walls and floor, that won't erase them from her mind. The Crack will still pulse. The floorboards will still hum.

She stumbles over to her phone, which is resting on the windowsill. She's missed five calls from Theo; he left two voicemails. The first is an update; they are on their way back to London. Charlie is reconsidering Crossroads if "it'll make Mum happy." The second, two hours later, is a little more panicked. "Emma—you haven't called me back. I'm getting worried. Call me." She takes a deep breath before hitting the callback button. As it rings, she rests her chin on the windowsill. Bennett has returned and is back in his paint clothes. She wipes the tears from her eyes, happy to see him.

"Hi, babe," she says when Theo answers, trying to sound chipper.

"I've been worried, are you okay?"

"I'm fine. Sorry. I left my phone downstairs and didn't realize."

"You must be working really hard," he says, his voice relieved and proud.

"Yeah." Her heart sinks.

"I started panicking, thinking maybe Bennett had poisoned your avocado after all."

"No," she says, chuckling. "You were right, I think he's harmless. Are you back?"

"No. Right after I called you we stopped at a service station and Charlie did a runner."

"Shit."

"Took us a while, but we eventually found him in the little M&S buying discount Valentine's Day sweets . . ." Emma can hear his voice choking. "He wanted to do something nice for Mum."

"That's heartbreaking."

"She doesn't want any bloody sweets, Emma, she just wants him to get better. He can't see it. He can't fucking see it."

"I know, babe." She feels herself choke up, too.

His voice crackles and waivers. "I'm so tired, Emma."

She'd take him in her arms, if she could. "You need to take care of yourself," she tells him. "You're no use to anybody like this."

"I know. I'm trying."

She can hear her husband chewing something on the other end of the phone. "Are you eating the discount candy?"

"I haven't had Love Hearts in ages," he says, laughing through tears. "They're so chalky."

She laughs, too. "Yeah. They're disgusting."

"What did we do for Valentine's Day?" he asks.

"Nothing. I was working at the restaurant and you said we'd celebrate once we got to London."

"Shit. I'm sorry."

"It's okay," she says, rubbing her socked foot along the colorful floorboards, hoping to remove some of the pencil, but it doesn't even smudge.

"I don't think I'll make it back tonight."

"I know."

"I'm going to make this up to you."

After hanging up, she goes down to the kitchen, pours herself a bowl of granola, and sits down at the kitchen island. She watches Bennett work, fleshing out Claire's breasts on canvas. She smiles, wondering if they're that perky in real life or if that's just wishful thinking on Bennett's part. The yellow from a few days ago is nearly gone, covered up, hardly a trace of it left on the canvas. It's just a memory now, the painting's origins—an unintentional secret she'll share with Bennett. As though he can feel Emma's eyes on him, he turns around. This time, she waves first, catching him by surprise. Turning back to contemplate the painted tits, he runs a hand through his hair before turning back to Emma and offering a goofy grin. She gives him a thumbs-up. There's something different about him today, something oddly comforting about his consistency. He's there painting every day. Maybe it's not easy for him, maybe it's just practice? He's resilient. She's going to fix the mess she's made in his master bedroom.

Still exhausted from staying up all night, she resolves to take a quick nap before heading to the hardware store to get the paint and brushes she'll need to paint the walls and floor. It'll probably take two trips to get everything, but she tells herself that's fine. She can do this; she can fix this. Now that Theo isn't coming back tonight, she's got time. She'll paint through the night, when Bennett's asleep. By morning, everything will be back to normal. Maybe not for her, but for everyone else. "Not everything is about you, Emma," she tells herself, thinking that Dr. Gibson would be pleased with that conclusion. She writes it down on a slip of paper and adds it to the fact jar.

But the nap isn't quick. She falls asleep in the small guest bedroom, where she moved her drafting table the day before. She curls up under the covers and falls asleep before she can even set an alarm. She dreams of Theo. He's wearing a nice shirt and tie and he smells good, like he did when she met him, clean, like cucumbers and mint.

"Emma?" He's there, sitting on the edge of the bed and tucking her crazy brown curls behind her ear.

"Hi!" She wakes, startled to realize he's not a dream. "What are you doing here?" She blinks a couple times; he's actually wearing the nice shirt and tie. His green eyes are beaming down on her.

"I wanted to surprise you," he says, distracted and maybe a little angry. He pulls back the duvet and looks at her legs, but she still has her jeans on.

She sits up, confused and groggy.

"I went upstairs to look for you."

The Crack pulses again in her mind. "You did?"

"Give me your arm," he says.

"I know what you're doing, Theo. It's fine."

"GIVE IT TO ME!"

She holds out her arm to him and he rolls up the sleeve of her shirt above her elbow, checking for bruises and ink lines.

"Other one."

"Theo, I haven't been doing that, I promise."

He looks her in the eyes, but rolls up the other sleeve, anyway.

"I'm going to fix it," she says. "I was going to go to the hardware store this afternoon. I must have slept too late."

"I never should have dragged you to London."

"You didn't drag me!" She throws off the duvet.

"I can't worry about you and Charlie both. Maybe you should go back home. I'll talk to Bennett about getting a refund on this place."

"No!"

Sitting on the edge of the bed, her mind races, thinking about all the things Theo might tell Bennett: "My wife is ill," "Wife suffers from anxiety," "Wife is OCD," as though there's nothing more to her than these facts. She cringes at the thought of Bennett knowing any of it. Making fists, she says, "You don't get to make decisions for me, especially when you're not even around!"

"That's our bedroom, Emma," he says, pointing to the stairs.

"OUR bedroom? You're. Not. Here. Your bedroom is at your

mother's house." She points in the general direction of Theo's mother's house, but she has no idea if she's pointing the right way.

"Okay, I get it."

"No, you don't. You're spending all your time there and you're just enabling your brother. He's no closer to admitting he needs help. No closer to rehab. Did you even search his bag for Vicodin? He wouldn't have left Manchester unless he had a good supply."

"No . . . Mum was worried he would see it as a violation of trust."

She throws her arms up in the air. "So you want to send me home for drawing on a wall, but Charlie gets to do whatever the fuck he wants?"

"It's not comparable, Emma."

"Why can't you be as hard on him as you are on me?" she asks, thrusting herself back under the duvet.

"It's not the same." He takes a deep breath. "Tomorrow I'll go to the hardware store to get some paint. I can fix what you've done, but I need you to promise me you won't do it again."

"Did you say that to Charlie?" she yells, muffled, from under the covers. "'I'll bring you home from Manchester, but you have to promise me that you won't take any more drugs.'"

"Something like that."

She pops out from the duvet. "Let me know how that works out for you," she says, before pulling the duvet on top of her again. "I'll do the painting myself."

Theo storms off. She can hear him swearing at the bedroom walls and floor.

She wants to apologize, but her blood boils when he scolds her like that, like she's a puppy that's just chewed up his favorite shoe. She knows she made a mistake drawing all over their bedroom. She even knows she'll have to be honest about all of it with Dr. Gibson when she gets home, but if she's learned anything from Charlie, it's that the best way to get Theo's attention is to behave badly. She tells herself she will apologize tomorrow.

They spend the night in different rooms, Emma in the small guest room, Theo in the master. As far as Emma is concerned, he might as well have stayed at his mother's house. He doesn't feel any closer to her by being in the house. In fact, he feels farther away.

||||||||||||||||||||||

The next morning, she hears Theo moving purposefully around the house. Even his footsteps sound patronizing.

"Hi," he says, when he sees her coming down the stairs.

She stands on the staircase, still wearing the clothes she's been wearing for two days now. Her hair must be crazy, because he's looking several inches above her eyes. Or maybe he can't bear to look her in the eyes anymore. Hopefully, it's the hair.

"This should do it," he says, holding up supplies. He's been to the hardware store.

"Thanks," she says, sheepishly. She wants to be angry, but in truth, she's thrilled that he went to buy the paint, even more thrilled that he did it without asking.

"Granola?" he asks, pointing to the kitchen island.

"Yeah, alright," she says, although she's not hungry. She hasn't eaten anything since the granola she had yesterday, but she's not going to tell him that for fear he'll go ballistic again. Okay, not ballistic. A better word to describe Theo would be *concerned*. That's the word she would use if she were writing it down for the fact jar.

He pulls down two bowls from the cabinet and pours granola into each. He slides one bowl down the island to Emma, followed by a spoon, before filling his own with milk. He eats his granola standing up, facing Emma from the other side of the island. "I'm not the only one that needs to take better care of myself," he says, not in a patronizing way this time, but like someone who knows what's at stake when you don't.

From where Emma sits, she can see Bennett looking out his studio window, but he turns around quickly to make it seem like he hasn't been watching. Normally, she'd tell Theo, try to prove to him that Bennett's been spying, but this morning she lets it go.

"I'm sorry," she says. "About upstairs. Do you want some help?"

He smiles. "No. That's okay. I'm kind of looking forward to it. Something I can actually fix." He lifts the lid off the fact jar and stares in at the full contents. "That's a lot of truth. Does every one of these pieces of paper say, 'Theo is a jerk'?"

"No," she answers. Just one, she thinks. "Besides, that's a feeling, not a fact."

He nods, impressed, and puts the lid back on the jar. He looks around, clearly hoping to reacquaint himself with both the kitchen and the wife he left behind. When he picks up one of the avocados from the fruit bowl, it bursts in his hand.

"Eww . . ." he says, looking down at the brownish-green slime on his palm and fingers. "Why did you keep this?" He chucks it into the bin, but his hand is still coated in green slime.

Emma watches, bewildered at how quickly he dispenses with the piece of fruit that's been taunting her all week. He's forgotten all about the circumstances of that avocado—that it needs to face the laundry room, that Bennett touched it, that it represented a "good challenge" she could never quite bring herself to face.

He looks down at his hand, his fingers splayed out and sticky, and she can sense him plotting something. Wiggling his fingers, he smiles mischievously and reaches across the island to rub the sticky, rotten avocado flesh all over Emma's face. Leaping off her stool, she shrieks with laughter. Game on, he chases her around the island as she continues to scream and swear at him. When he catches her, she freezes in his grasp. No laughing, no screaming. Just eye contact.

How much do I love you? Count the stars in the sky . . .

To Theo, an avocado doesn't have a set of circumstances, it's just fruit.

. . . Measure the waters of the oceans with a teaspoon. Number the grains of sand on the sea shore. Impossible, you say?

He leans in, tongue out, and licks the green gunk off her face. She starts to shriek, again, but he holds her tight.

For Emma, an avocado will never be just an avocado. Fact.

MIND TO MOTION

Claire's got him running. "A spring cleaning for the body and soul," was how she put it, except it doesn't feel like spring. The blooms on the trees are still covered in a light frost. Early April mornings might as well be January, Bennett thinks, following his breath as he chugs along toward the river in dark grey sweatpants and a long-sleeved blue T-shirt—the two least offensive fitness items he could find on the sale rack at M&S. Both are made from really soft cotton and wearing the outfit doesn't make him want to run at all. It makes him want to curl up on the futon and eat Doritos.

When he passes Ravenscourt Gardens, where he grew up, he doesn't even look down the road. Since his mother died five years ago, he hasn't walked, run, or driven down it. There's no reason to. It's someone else's house now, someone else's street. Though, sometimes, he does wonder if the whiskey bottle that his father hid in the garden fish pond is still there. Back when he was in school, his mother, Helen, wouldn't allow her alcoholic husband to drink in the house, so once she had gone to bed, the bastard would drink in the garden under the stars. Gary Driscoll would happily sink into a patio chair, whiskey bottle in hand, his feet up on the wooden picnic table, with Helen's beloved fish pond bubbling and trickling nearby. From his bedroom window, Bennett had a perfect view of his father's ritual, the old man groaning as he got down on both knees next to the fish pond where he wedged the whiskey bottle under the water between two rocks, so it couldn't float up to the surface. A couple times he got so pissed that he returned the bottle to the pond without screwing the cap on tight. The next morning the fish would be dead, floating on the water's surface with the cap. On these occasions, Bennett would rush out to the garden, retrieve the cap, and throw it over the fence before his mother saw it. One time he even grabbed the dead fish, stuffed them in the pockets of his school blazer, and flushed them down the toilet after English class. When he got home, he told his mother he'd seen a heron near the pond. It wasn't that he wanted to protect his old man, he just hated to see his parents fight. He hated the way his father would never pull back in an argument, always determined to win, no matter the consequences, no matter the tears he caused. To Gary Driscoll, nothing was below the belt and there was no such thing as an unfair fight.

||||||||||||||||||||||

Bennett likes to run before it gets busy out. He's prone to groaning, especially when he just starts out and his knees are popping and cracking. The other people out at seven a.m. are similar over-the-hill wankers running because of bad cholesterol, high blood pressure, diabetes. Bennett's running for sex, and for that reason alone, he feels smug. Claire has taken to grabbing his love handles and acting impressed. She swears they're shrinking. He's pretty sure she's patronizing him, but he doesn't care. Originally, she had wanted them to go running together, but there was no way he was doing that. "It's not a social activity," he told her.

"You just don't want me to hear you puffing and panting," she said, pinching one of those love handles.

"Yes, exactly."

Why does she always find the painful truth to be so adorable?

"I bet you look sexy in sweatpants. Send me a picture, at least."

Nope and nope.

He's reluctant to use the word *girlfriend* to describe Claire, but she's not. Like, a couple weeks ago, when she enquired about when she'd get to meet Mia. "What?" she said. "You don't want to introduce your daughter to your new girlfriend?"

Nope.

Truth be told, he hasn't said anything to Mia about Claire. It hasn't really got anything to do with Claire, herself, it's just that he and Mia have been a good pair ever since Eliza left and he doesn't want to ruin that. Besides, Mia doesn't tell him about the guys she's dating, so it makes sense that he affords her the same distance from his love life. He knows that when Mia meets someone really special, she'll introduce him. He worries sometimes that his and Eliza's divorce may have irreparably damaged her ideas about love and relationships, but she's still young. He doesn't want to know any of the twats she's dating now, anyway. He's never met a twenty-year-old he liked, including the one he was.

|||||||||||||||||||||||||

The morning after their first night together, Bennett came clean with Claire. Yes, the house was his, but he doesn't live in it anymore, he lets it on AirBed. As it turns out, it wasn't much of a secret. Claire had seen the fire exit map on the fridge, noticed that the door of the locked study was marked "private," and she even nicked one of the tiny bottles of Molton Brown shower gel from the bathroom. Bennett has since learned that sneaking around is kind of a turn-on for Claire. Since then, more than once, she's forced him up against the back wall of the walk-in fridge at the Claret, despite the fact that it's impossible for a fifty-five-year-old man to get hard in a cold metal box. After that first night, when they woke up in the guest bedroom of the main house, he confessed that he actually lived in the studio in the back garden. And, well, he didn't have a collector in Edinburgh waiting for a painting, either. She giggled, twirling the hairs on his chest with her index finger. The whole thing amused her to the point of arousal, so they had another quick fuck and then she helped him put the place back together before Emma came home. Apparently, the last guy Claire dated was an estate agent in Mayfair and the two of them used to screw around in all of his luxury listings. But she doesn't miss that guy. He was a twat, she claims. "He wore these really wide ties. He put this gel in his hair that always made it look wet all the time," she continued, cataloging all of her ex's undesirable characteristics. "But those flats!" she added, gasping. "You wouldn't believe the luxury. Well, maybe *you* would." Bennett just smiled. *Would she ever shut up?* "I like the way you look more," she assured him. "Dapper, but soft." Bennett had no idea what she meant by that, but then she put her hand down his pants, so he didn't care.

After they finished tidying up the house, he showed her the studio. She must have picked up every tube of paint on his workbench, stroked every sample of fabric stacked on the back wall. "I want you to paint me naked and sell it to some rich guy in Chelsea," she demanded, which sounded good to him, too. Since then, she's even let him take a few naked photos of her on his phone. Not just in the studio, but around her flat as well. So long as he says something flattering like, "I love the way the sunlight falls on your hips," she'll stay in the position and reply, "Go on, then." He's beginning to understand the point of camera phones.

Now, six weeks later, he's still working on the painting. He's running in the morning, painting late morning and on through to the afternoon. Most evenings he spends at Claire's place in Stoke Newington. On the nights she works, he'll show up late at the Claret and have a glass of wine while she finishes her shift. (This is when she tries to ravish him in the walk-in.) On Saturdays she works the day shift, so he meets her outside her flat in the early evening. They order takeaway and curl up on the sofa to watch *Britain's Got Talent* (her favorite), a program that to Bennett's mind only exists to prove that the exact opposite is true. The show seems to have a one-to-one ratio of human to dog contestants. "Is that dog British?" Bennett asked, pointing at the TV last Saturday night. Claire was curled up in his arm, eating chicken tikka masala out of a white carton. She studied the little dog, which was performing some sort of dressage routine. "It's a Norwich terrier," she replied with an implied *Duh*.

It's strange for Bennett to be spending so much time in Northeast London, not far from where his daughter and her friends live in Dalston. He feels like he's sneaking around. When he leaves Claire's place in the mornings, he risks bumping into Mia at the station, where he waits to take the Overground back to West London. He's banking on the knowledge that she doesn't really "do" mornings, and she takes the bus most places, anyway.

Though he may be reluctant to call her a girlfriend, Claire is definitely a lifestyle change. Recently, she's been talking about joining one of those food services that deliver the recipes and ingredients to your door. "It's perfect!" she claims. "They deliver everything for three meals a week. That's how many nights I have off! We wouldn't even need to go to the store."

We.

Roots Manuva pumps in his ears as he plods along to the river.

Off beat . . . lost the key and can't find it
Representation of the spit in the grit
The devil on my shoulder keep tellin' me shit
Constantly got me feeling like I'm losin' my grip.

He keeps the iPod in one pocket and his phone in the other. The two devices bump along, bulbously, on his upper thighs as he runs. Claire suggested he get one of those iPod holders that straps to your upper arm, but Bennett told her that he'd look like an agent for MI5 with one of those things. Not his vibe. Claire looked at him funny when he used the word *vibe*. When the phone vibrates, he takes a quick look, not breaking stride—an AirBed booking request. He picks up his pace a little, rejuvenated by the inquiry. Bookings have been slow recently. He's convinced it's because of the recent review Emma left: **Bennett's house was suitable for our needs,** it read. *Suitable. The rainfall shower was suitable, was it? How about the six-hundred-thread-count sheets? The free posh soap? The marble countertops and six-burner gas range? All that was suitable for you, Emma?* It continued: **FYI. While you do get the whole house to yourself, Bennett lives very close by in a studio behind the house.** *For* your *information, Emma, some people like that.* It was still a five-star review. He has to remind himself of that. He's still a Super Host. It just wasn't a glowing review, which he prefers.

Maybe, in hindsight, he shouldn't have responded to the review. It could, he supposes, look petty to potential guests. **Emma—**he wrote and then stopped, letting the cursor pulse. **I'm glad my house suited your needs. I hope you had a comfortable stay. As stated, in the available property description, yes, I do live in a studio on the premises. Other than a shared yard, the entrance to the house is completely separate and entirely private.** He felt bad typing that last part, remembering how Claire had tried on Emma's ballet flats the morning after they slept together in the house. "Oh, I like these," Claire had said, swanning around the kitchen while Bennett washed out the amaretto glasses. But he couldn't help it, he responded because Emma's review disappointed him. By the end of her and her husband's stay, Bennett thought they were starting to become friendly. Her husband wasn't around much, so Bennett was sure to wave to her whenever he was leaving the studio. She waved back, even started to smile, eventually. One afternoon they bumped into each other in the garden and she told Bennett about her drawing project, something to do with a Philip Glass song. It sounded really boring to him, but she was clearly really into it and he thought he'd love to be that passionate about an idea again. The painting of Claire was going well, but still, it's an old idea, not a new one. "It's very classical," Emma said about his painting of Claire, "her pose." *Classical.* That's the thing about Emma, he could never tell what she meant. *Classical? Suitable? Close by?* Were these good or bad things? Partly to prove his versatility, he went back into the studio and stretched and primed a few small canvases. Perhaps he could make some smaller paintings of Claire that would be more intimate. After all, she's his lover, not a Roman statue. *Classical.*

‖‖‖‖‖‖‖‖‖‖‖‖‖‖‖

The tide is out along the Thames, but the water is rising, slowly. Geese and swans collect along the bank, picking through the sand and sludge. For Bennett, the houses along the river are the stuff of fairy tales, so grand that many of them have names, beautifully lettered on their stone gates, like "Windroffe House." This one has been his favorite ever since he was a child, with its lavish garden that abuts the river. When he made the mistake of telling Eliza about this, she decided to interpret it as more of a goal than a fantasy, and when the house came on the market a couple years ago for five and a half million, she came excitedly into Bennett's studio to show him the listing. "Look! Your dream house is for sale!" She held her iPad right up to his face, scrolling through the images. "Look at their back garden office," she enthused, "so much nicer than this shed!" And she was right, it was beautiful, far too beautiful to paint in, though he knew she'd never understand that.

"Yeah, it's beautiful," Bennett agreed, secretly preferring the interiors of his imagination to the actual images on the screen.

She shrugged her shoulders at him expectantly. "Well?"

"Well, what?"

"Should we go look?" she asked, taking the paintbrush out of his hand and setting it on his workbench. She had a habit of doing that when she wanted his attention and it pissed him off.

"We don't have five point five million," he pointed out, picking up the paintbrush again, defiantly, and turned back to his painting—a large canvas, featuring radishes and a loaf of bread on a ticking-stripe fabric.

"That's what mortgages are for."

They'd been lucky enough to buy their current house with cash during Bennett's heyday.

"I'm fifty. A mortgage will outlive me."

"This is your dream," she said, angry now.

"No. It's a fantasy. I also have a fantasy where you wear a French maid's outfit. You don't seem as eager to make that a reality."

She stormed out.

That was, now that he thinks about it, her storming-out phase, the part of their marriage where she was so desperate for change, any change, to alter the monotony of their days. His fantasy house had become her dream. She had co-opted it and nurtured it. She'd actually put a property alert on that house, so she'd be prepared, at a moment's notice, to tell Bennett that his dream (her dream) was coming true. And in an instant he crushed it. To Eliza, it didn't matter that they couldn't afford that house. That was just an obstacle to overcome. The larger issue, she believed, was that Bennett never wanted to share his fantasy house with her in the first place. "You think I stole your dream," she told him later, after divorce papers had been filed. "But only because you refused to share it."

|||||||||||||||||||||||||

He slows down, approaching the back gate of his house. Leaning on the fence, he stretches out his calves, or pretends to, while catching his breath, then paces around the garden while his heart rate slows, the sweat turning from liquid to sticky sap on his skin. Plopping down in the middle of the grass, he empties his pockets of the phone and iPod, dropping them onto the lawn. Lying down on his back, he stares up at the airplane exhaust–streaked London sky, music still playing:

Mind to motion. Know the notion.
Notion! Know shun, No. No -shun . . .

There's no one renting the main house at the moment, which means Bennett can once again pace around shirtless in his own yard if he wants to. Emma's no longer holding court at the kitchen island, watching him. Of course, he was watching her, too. That, it turns out, she knew. After they'd checked out, Bennett found a cookie jar full of little slips of paper, all with strange and angry observations written on them. Obviously, he had to read them all. Mostly, she was really mad at some guy named Charlie . . . but two slips of paper had Bennett's name on them: "Bennett touched my avocado." *What are you on about? No, I bloody didn't.* And "Bennett is spying on me." God knows what the purpose was for this random selection of accusations or what the fuck they were doing in the cookie jar, but Bennett kept the last one that pertained to him. He liked the matter-of-factness with which Emma wrote it. *Bennett is spying on me.* Full stop. Not, *Is Bennett spying on me?* She knew. There is something strangely comforting about knowing that she noticed him. She could have included that in her AirBed review, but she didn't. Maybe they were friendly after all. Also, did she paint his bedroom? It smells like fresh paint in there. Who does that?

Of course, he could also move back in until the next guest arrives, but the house doesn't feel like home anymore. Looking at it from the lawn, he can feel it bearing down on him, unfriendly, full of past mistakes and the promise of a future that at one time felt so certain he'd somehow let it slip right through his fingers. He's thinking about selling it, though he doesn't want to tell Mia yet. She's been trying to get him to sell it ever since Eliza left. He doesn't want to get her hopes up that he might finally be ready to move on. After all, it's more necessity than personal growth that's led him to consider a sale. London has recently changed its policy on AirBed lettings. Hosts must now live in their properties three-quarters of the year and rent it out no more than ninety days. He doesn't want to live in his old house for two hundred and seventy-five days a year, and the ninety night maximum won't generate enough income to pay taxes and his living expenses. He can either let it long-term or sell it. But a long-term letting is tantamount to kicking a can down the road. That's something he's good at doing. As with so many things, what he's hoping for is his next chapter to be presented to him on a silver platter. All he has to do is accept it. A new house, new wife, new gallery—like bundling your TV, phone, and Wi-Fi. He hasn't brought up this idea with Claire, either. He's worried she'll take it as an opportunity to discuss their future. It's only been six weeks.

Six weeks.

He likes Claire; she's a good reason to take a shower and wash off all this crusted-on sweat. They don't have a lot in common, though, except a deep need for companionship. He hates *Britain's Got Talent*, but he likes watching it with her because he can complain to her about how stupid it is and she listens. It's nice to have someone who'll listen when he's telling her that her taste is stupid. She just smiles and sometimes, if she really wants him to shut up, she'll stick food in his mouth. Or kiss him. Both are good results for insulting another person's taste. But he never says anything too mean and by the end of the show she always agrees that the singers can't sing, the comedians aren't funny, and no dog can be inherently British. He likes her best when she's tired, especially on the nights after a long shift when she says, "I just want to curl up with my book." On those nights, she'll lay her head in his lap and read a Ruth Rendell, holding the paperback open above her head, until she falls asleep and the book slips from her fingers right onto her face. He's started reading *The Shining* while he's at her flat. She has all the Stephen King books, the ones his father never let him have. He's going to read *Misery* next, if the relationship lasts that long—*The Shining* is a big book. It'll probably last, they have a nice rhythm going, so long as she doesn't want to talk about the future. He'd like for things to last at least until autumn, because Eliza asked Mia to spend the summer with her in America and she agreed. Bennett hates the idea of his daughter being away for two whole months, but he knows it's the right thing. Mia has been cold with Eliza ever since the affair. Her loyalty to him is very touching, but he knows she needs to have a relationship with her mother. So long as she doesn't come back saying things like, "Jeff isn't so bad."

Jeff is the worst.

Still, he can't very well tell Claire that he wants to continue dating her until the end of the summer, so she can distract him from his daughter being gone. Chief distractor can't be the future she has in mind.

He runs his hand through the grass, searching for his phone. The AirBed request is still on the screen when he locates the phone by his ankles. A woman named Kirstie: **Hello, Bennett, I'm a recent divorcée looking for my first place in London,** the message says. **I've lived the last thirty years in Devon and I'm looking to escape my small town and my ex-husband!**

He clicks out of the message for a moment and clicks on her photograph. She looks about his age, and she's standing on a beach in a floral wrap dress with a plunging neckline, the effect enhanced by a push-up bra. She has one hand on her hip and a cocktail in the other, her eyes concealed by giant sunglasses. She's smiling, but it doesn't strike him as a happy smile. It's more of a possessive smile, a queen in her kingdom smile. Sort of like Eliza.

It looks like your place is available from next week, but that seems too good to be true?! she continues. **I'd like to book for a few months, with the possibility of extending until I find the right place to buy. I have three grown children who might be in and out (when they're broke or hungry!). Would this be a suitable arrangement for you? You live in a studio behind the property? How delightfully bohemian!**

How delightfully patronizing.

Does he really want to live behind this woman for several months? The money *would* be good and it *would* give him a chance to think longer about whether he wants to sell the house.

But her? Eliza 2.0?

He could live at Claire's for a couple months, but then he'd have to concede that she's his girlfriend. He'd have to introduce her to Mia, too. Suddenly, the future feels very present.

||||||||||||||||||||||

Back in the studio, using photos now, he spends the morning painting Claire's legs, trying to perfect the moment where her thighs cross, pressing against each other, creating a crevice of deep purple. Against the original yellow background of the painting, the blues and purples had been easy to achieve, but as the painting has progressed and the yellow is vanishing, it's starting to look muted and dull. He thought the yellow, left over from his last fabric painting—the one he named "Alicia yellow"—was an inspired choice for the background of Claire's painting, but Claire wrinkled her nose when she saw it.

"I'm not going to look jaundiced, am I?" she had asked.

"No, of course not," he'd answered, though truthfully, he wasn't sure. It had been a long time since he'd painted flesh. Looking at it now, Claire doesn't look jaundiced or ill, rather, she looks porcelain. No, that's too fragile. Maybe stone? Actually, stone is no better. Hardly flattering, especially for a woman he knows for a fact is soft, warm, and supple. He adds a little ultramarine blue to his pinky flesh tint and a bluish-purple forms. Then a little brown ochre to tamp it down— *let's not go crazy*—holding the color up to the painting and then tweaking it with a little more flesh tint. When he finally gets the color right and applies it to the fleshy blob on the canvas, just like that, her legs really appear, ample and round, grope-able. Suddenly, he's hungry. Taking a break for lunch, he pulls out a block of cheese from the fridge—the block of English white cheddar that Claire demanded he have stocked at all times. A lover of seriously mature and crumbly cheddar, she's offended by the mini Babybel he prefers at lunchtime. For Bennett, the small red-waxed circular cheeses are more a matter of convenience than taste. It's a cheese you can eat without thinking. Mature English cheddar is a thinking cheese. It requires a cutting board, a knife, and at least a fraction of your attention. Today, he decides to forgo the cutting board and the attention, slicing the cheese straight on the countertop while looking back at his painting of Claire on the easel. Most of what he cuts is cheddar, but he soon realizes he has also sliced the cord for his phone charger. With only ten percent battery left, he has to halt his afternoon painting session and make a trip to the phone shop.

In his paint clothes and flip-flops, earbuds in and head down, he rushes down the high road, eager to finish his errand and get back to the studio. The deadline for the Royal Academy Summer Show is coming up and he intends to enter the painting of Claire. In the late nineties and early two-thousands, Bennett was a fixture at the Academy's yearly salon hang of the best U.K. art, but he hasn't had a painting in the show since 2011. Lacking confidence, he hasn't entered a painting in five years. When he strides past Bedford House, an exclusive West London club where he and Eliza used to be members in his heyday, he recalls drinking overpriced mojitos with other self-aggrandizing artists and media-types.

"Benji! Oi, Benji!"

Bennett pulls the earbuds out of his ears and sees Carl Willis, an old classmate from the Royal College, sitting at a table outside Bedford House, drinking a glass of white wine, a pit bull asleep at his ankles. Carl has long believed that Bennett's name is actually Benjamin and there's nothing he can do to convince the guy otherwise.

"Alright, Benji?" Carl asks, waving his old friend over to the table. "You looked deep in thought just then." He takes a swig from his large glass of wine. He's got on Ray-Ban aviators, despite the overcast day. His pink Dolce & Gabbana T-shirt clings tightly to his chest and spray-tanned biceps.

"Fine, thanks." Bennett hovers over Carl's table, shifting his weight between legs, anxious to get to the phone shop. Never Bennett's favorite person at art school, Carl was loud, opinionated, and "touchy," always asking the other blokes to flex their muscles, grabbing their behinds, and giving them unwanted embraces, because, apparently, he was in touch with his feminine side.

"Sit, mate. Take a load off."

Bennett looks down at the strange beast at Carl's feet, a pit bull with a lazy eye and faux leather booties. The dog raises its head and growls.

"Keep cool, Rosie. It's just Benji." He pushes out an empty chair with his foot, signaling Bennett to sit down. "You look like you've been *working it,"* he says, pointing to Bennett's paint clothes, but seeming to insinuate prostitution in the tone of his voice.

Wanker.

"Yeah, studio day," Bennett explains, sitting down across from Carl. "Just need to replace my phone charger."

"What? There?" Carl points in the direction of the phone shop down the road. "Don't go there, mate. I got a geezer sells them discount." Carl's always got a geezer.

"My phone's almost dead. I just need to get one now." He starts to get up, but Carl gestures for him to sit back down.

"You got an exhibition coming up, then, mate?"

Fuck. Not this.

He doesn't want to talk about the stagnation in his work, certainly not with Carl, who has never suffered from a lack of confidence, having just recently finished an exhibition at the White Cube, where he showed a selection of large-scale paintings of biblical scenes set in working-class London locations: *The Crucifixion* in East Street Market, *The Annunciation* in a Council Flat, *The Virgin and Child* in Primark, *The Last Supper* at KFC. Bennett didn't see the show, but it was a hit, at least according to the *Daily Mail*, the rag that also happens to be currently on Carl's table. At art school, Carl claimed to read the right-wing paper ironically. Bennett suspects he just reads it, now, full stop.

"No, nothing specific," he responds.

"I haven't seen any of your work in a while. I was worried maybe you wasn't painting anymore, nuhtamean?"

Here it comes. Every time Bennett has the displeasure of this guy's company, his fake, working-class accent gets thicker and thicker. He's pretty sure Carl grew up in Tunbridge Wells and moved to Chiswick five years ago after a stint in the East End. Bennett suspects he's putting on the inflection to challenge the stiff upper lips of West London. He always had a strong command of grammar in art school. Either that or the guy's had a stroke.

"Nope. Still painting." When Bennett shifts in his chair, the dog growls again.

"Come on, Rosie. He ain't so bad." Carl speaks to the dog in a baby voice.

"Rosie?" Bennett can see Carl has "Rosie" tattooed in large cursive on his forearm.

"Yeah, named her after my lil' sis."

Jesus. Does she have a lazy eye, too?

Bennett raises an eyebrow. "How does your sister feel about that?"

"She's passed on, mate."

"Oh, I'm sorry."

"Thirty years, now, but she's in the old ticker, nuhtamean?" He points to his heart.

Bennett nods, solemnly. He can't just get up and leave now. He's trapped.

"You a member?" Carl asks, sipping from his glass of wine, nodding at the entrance of Bedford House.

Bennett runs his hand through his hair. "Not anymore. I wasn't here enough to justify the cost." That's better than saying he flat out can't afford it.

"Let's get you a glass of vino, my friend." Carl looks around for a server.

Bennett puts his hand up. "No, that's okay. I just need to get the charger, then it's back to work."

Carl ignores this and waves down a waitress in a tight black cock-tail dress. "Hello, love. He'll have a large glass of chardonnay, as well," he says, his posh Kent accent returning. "On my account, darling."

She nods, saying nothing. Carl's eyes follow her bum as she heads back inside. When the waitress is out of earshot, Carl continues, "Fuck, mate, they always dress like that 'ere. It's fuckin' Saturday night at all hours of the bloody day. You eaten?"

"Yeah," Bennett says, his belly full of mature white cheddar, thank God.

"They got this wicked pheasant 'ere. Bloody delish, mate. You gotta pick the bullet out your teeth, nuhtamean?" He mimics picking a bullet out from between his two front teeth, the whiteness of which suggests he's as liberal with bleach strips as he is with the spray tan. "Proper fuckin' grub."

Bennett just nods. What else can anyone do when Carl is talking?

The waitress returns with Bennett's chardonnay. He gives her a half-smile when she sets it down, hoping to convey more sympathy than gratitude. He takes a sip and tries not to smile, thinking how much Claire would hate this disgusting, woody wine.

"Now, that's vino!" Carl says, pointing at Bennett's glass.

"It's nice," he says, though it tastes like the inside of a moldy barrel.

"I'm into my wines now. The missus wanted me off the hard gear—snow, 'shrooms, K—nuhtamean?"

I have no fucking clue what you mean.

"She's worth it, though, my Keeley. True ride or die, that bird."

What?

"And I'm a dad, mate. Did you know that?" Carl sits up straight, excited.

Bennett looks down at Rosie. Can it be that this mutt is what Carl means by fatherhood? "No, I don't think I did know that."

"Eighteen months, now. Best eighteen months of my life. I'm well into it. Participant father and all that," he says with his voice rising, full of pride. "You've got a lil' girl, don't cha?"

"Not little. She's nineteen." Bennett shifts uncomfortably at the thought of Carl picturing Mia.

"Bloody hell! You'll be a grampy soon."

Bennett grips the arm of his chair so he doesn't lunge at Carl like a pit bull. One with two good eyes.

"I hope not. She's at St. Martins now."

"Good on her. Following in Daddy's footsteps."

By the time Mia was six, Bennett had instructed her to stop calling him "Daddy." It never sounded right. Now he knows why.

The foul chardonnay has gone straight to his head and he's thinking about heading to the Claret as soon as he can escape Carl. Claire's on the day shift, and he might as well drink something nice. He's thinking he'd like to kiss her with the taste of this disgusting wine still in his mouth, just to see what kind of face she makes.

"How's your good woman?" Carl asks.

Carl's forgotten Eliza's name. He has no idea about the divorce, which would have happened around the same time this wanker was changing his first diaper.

"You'd have to ask Jeff."

"Mate." Carl lets his head hang low, as though he feels Bennett's pain. "You living alone in that big gaff?"

"Renting it on AirBed these days."

Carl's ears perk up at this. Bennett immediately regrets letting down his guard.

"I've been curious how that works, actually."

Bennett braces himself, sensing the cogs turning in Carl's mind.

"Like, have you got to let to everybody? What about the Muslims and all that?"

And all what?

Carl leans in. "I was reading 'bout this geezer in Lancaster that was letting out his gaff on AirBed to these two Syrians . . . Well, they was British technically, but Syrian, really, nuhtamean? They was letting the place for two months or somefink like that. Anyway, six weeks in and the coppers are raiding the place. Figured the carpet-kissers was building a bomb in there."

Bennett glances down at the *Daily Mail*, no doubt the source of this twisted tale.

"Aren't you worried 'bout that happening at your gaff?"

Nope.

"Were they actually building a bomb?" Bennett asks.

"Fuck, mate, how would I know?"

"I thought maybe it was in the article you read."

"Don't think it said. Basically, it was warning about letting to foreigners on AirBed and that."

Bennett shrugs. "I had a couple from Jordan a few months back. They were visiting London to meet their new grandchild. She made the best falafel I've ever tasted."

"Oh, I do love a good falafel," Carl concedes. "With a bit a halloumi?" He kisses the tips of his fingers, signaling perfection.

Bennett drains his glass. "Good to see you, mate," he says, pulling himself out of the chair and noticing Carl looks hurt. "I've got to get that phone charger, then back to work," he adds, putting one earbud in.

"What you so keen about on those buds?"

Drowning you out.

"Oh, you know . . ."

"No idea, mate. That's why I'm asking." Carl shifts in his chair, looking up at Bennett earnestly.

Rosie looks up, too, waiting for an answer.

Shit.

"Roots Manuva. You know him?"

"I didn't peg you for a gangsta, Benji."

Bennett smiles. It *is* ridiculous.

Carl, excited, pulls out his phone. "I got a geezer that books one of them clubs in Brixton. I'll find out if Roots's got anything coming up. I'll text you."

"Right," Bennett says, popping in the other earbud. "I'll catch you later," he says, confident Carl doesn't have his number.

IIIIIIIIIIIIIIIIIIIIIIII

From the phone shop, he heads to Soho. He surprises Claire at the bar with a sloppy chardonnay kiss. She loves hating it, pulling him across the bar by his shirt collar and shoving her tongue inside his mouth with all her customers watching, an act they no longer find all that surprising. She then tells him he looks sexy in his paint clothes and he should wear them out more often. When her shift ends, she changes out of her low-cut, navy blue cotton frock, the one that clings to her body—her *tip dress*, she calls it—and puts on a pair of jeans and her favorite "FEMINIST AS FUCK" T-shirt. He would prefer her to stay in her tip dress, but he can't complain, not when he was wearing paint-spattered clothes. He suggests they go back to Townhouse for her favorite lavender martini; they endure dirty looks for their attire. After that, they head across the street to some tapas place for charcuterie and cheese and those little fried peppers everyone is always banging on about. On the cab ride home, Claire has one hand on the door handle and the other on his crotch, looking over at him every few seconds to enjoy his dilemma. How exactly is he supposed to look aroused for her, but not aroused for the cabbie? She loves doing this kind of thing, making him play two roles at once. He is starting to feel like he has two lives, the one with Claire and the one before Claire, all of which seems to be going, effortlessly, out the window. The whole day would've been different, if he hadn't switched from Babybel to English cheddar, but Claire's right—the cheddar tastes better and life is better with her than without her. They have sex twice when they get back to her place and both times she is on top. She doesn't like missionary, because she can't orgasm that way. According to her, no woman can. "If a woman cums in missionary, she's faking it," Claire assures him, a sentence that explains so much about his marriage. They fall asleep buck naked, as they often do, and now he can't decide which he prefers—the feeling of her soft skin against his or the feeling of her Egyptian cotton sheets.

||||||||||||||||||||||

In the morning, he wakes up in Claire's tiny double bed to the sound of his phone vibrating on the bedside table, his dick pitching a tent under the sheets. The only people that ever text him are Claire and Mia. Claire is fast asleep next to him and Mia would never be awake at six-thirty unless something was wrong.

Oh, shit.

Startled, he grabs the phone, his penis shriveling at the thought of Mia in danger.

The text is from an unknown number. *Strangest thing, mate.*

Roots is playing Brixton Phoenix tonight. Secret show. Got us on the guest list.

Carl? How the fuck did he get my number?

"Everything alright?" Claire groans, barely audible from her side of the bed.

Setting the phone down on the table, he rolls onto his side and puts an arm around Claire's waist. "That guy I was telling you about last night? He wants me to go to a gig with him tonight."

"That sounds nice," she says, still half asleep.

Bennett grunts, too groggy to explain to her why it's not nice.

It's never occurred to Bennett to go see Roots Manuva. He's never looked up the artist's tour dates or even wondered when his next release might be coming out. As far as Bennett is concerned, Roots Manuva performs every day in his ears and that's all he needs to know. He's never thought about what other Manuva fans might look or act like. He doesn't really want to know. The music is personal to him. Why would he want to share Roots Manuva with a whole bunch of strangers, people who are probably more obsessed with the man than he is? Why would he want to know who loves the thing he loves more than he does? That'd be like finding out about Jeff all over again.

As it caresses the cheeks of Claire's behind, his dick returns to life. He's not even in the mood, but recently his penis has developed a mind of its own, ready to go even when his mind is preoccupied by other things and indifferent to the crucial moments of arousal. Nevertheless, when she feels it growing, Claire rolls around to face him, buries her head under his neck, nuzzling and kissing his collarbone.

"I got an AirBed request yesterday morning," he blurts out.

"Yeah?" she asks, confused by why this should come up now. She continues kissing his chest and down to his abdomen.

"This woman wants to let for a few months."

She props her chin on the palm of her hand. "You have an erection. You do know that, right?"

"You can just ignore it."

She grimaces and he can tell she's wondering if his ambivalence has something to do with her.

"I'm just not sure what to do. I need to respond in the next four hours if I want to keep my Super Host status," he says, staring up at the ceiling, where there's a weird damp stain that looks like Mr. Potato Head. "If I decided to let to her, I'd probably need to do a contract outside of AirBed."

"If that's the case, then your Super Host status doesn't matter, yeah?"

"Maybe, but I don't want to give it up."

"It's not the Nobel Prize, Bennett," she tells him, turning his chin to her so that he's looking her in the eye.

No shit.

It's not that he thinks his Super Host status is akin to world peace, obviously, but he has earned it and, like most people, he wants to keep the thing he's earned. She doesn't understand that what he's considering here is bigger than an online status. It's a possible big life change— selling the house he's lived in for twenty years, or at least letting it long-term. He's thinking about finally moving to East London, like he's always wanted to do, and he's wondering whether all this planning should take Claire into account. And here she is bloody teasing him about being a Super Host; a status that means he can charge top prices. And what does he do with that money? He takes her out to a bar where she can sip her disgusting lavender martinis, made from the very same flower that his grandmother used to keep in a vase on her toilet. If there were such a thing as a Super Bartender status, wouldn't she take *that* seriously?

"Yes, I know," he says, kissing her forehead.

"Do you think you could live in your studio for all that time?" she asks.

Tread carefully.

"I don't know. I might need to find something else."

Claire looks around her bedroom, which is crammed with the bed and built-in wardrobes. Only one wall is furniture-free and it has a big window looking out onto Stoke Newington High Street. Around the window, paperbacks are stacked up to shoulder height. "There's probably not enough room here, right?"

He smiles. He doesn't want to say no, especially not when she already knows the answer.

"You could continue to work in your studio during the day, but live here. That's pretty much what you've been doing anyway."

She's not wrong, but for Bennett, the magic of this arrangement is that it's unspoken. He's not sure he's ready for happy circumstance to become blueprint. She raises an eyebrow, keeping her eyes locked on his. He can tell that she's not going to let him wriggle out of this.

"Don't you enjoy getting nights off from me?" he says.

She hits his chest with the back of her hand. "What you mean is, *you* enjoy getting *your* nights off. Don't turn this around on me."

Damn, she's smart.

"It's a big decision," he concedes.

"I guess you'd better make it in the next four hours," she says, throwing back the duvet and standing up stark naked in the morning sun, "or you'll lose your precious status."

|||||||||||||||||||||||

It wasn't a full-fledged argument that ensued after that, but certainly some passive-aggressive sparring, the kind of thing Bennett was used to having been married. Claire's suggestion that he stay with her while he's letting out the house is sensible; after all, he can still use his studio, which would alleviate the necessity of finding a larger residence, at least for now. Still, it seems obvious to him that what Claire's suggesting is more of a life trajectory than a practical solution to a problem. What happens when his house becomes vacant again? Does he move back? What happens if he decides to sell it? When he's looking for a new place, is he shopping for one or two people? Once you move in with someone you don't then move out, not unless you're breaking up, right? By moving in with her for a few months, what she's really suggesting is the first in a line of dominoes, set to tip over—and God knows what's at the end of that line. When he told her he needed some more time to think it over, she suggested that, yes, he should do that; in his own home, not hers. He wanted to point out, that *if* they were to move in together, she wouldn't be able to kick him out every time she's angry with him. But she didn't look like she was in the mood to let him have the last word, so he let it go.

|||||||||||||||||||||||

By nine, he's on the platform waiting for a train back to West London. Not sure what to say, he still hasn't responded to Carl about the gig. He's inclined to make an excuse, because he's worried Carl will ruin his love for Roots Manuva. Carl ruins everything. He looks up at the timetable. Still fifteen minutes until the next train.

"Mr. D!"

Fuck. Fuck. Fuck.

He doesn't need to look up. Richard's presence comes with an olfactory warning, a potent, sweet and sour combination of BO and Lynx body spray. If only the young man could understand that covering up bad smells isn't the same as getting rid of them.

Bennett smiles as Richard and another young man approach, probably the guy he pulled at some club last night, although he doesn't look like Richard's type, meaning he doesn't look like Bennett. This kid is kind of preppy, wearing an oxford shirt, khakis, and boat shoes with no socks. It's a look Bennett would normally criticize if he wasn't himself currently in his paint clothes, flip-flops, and yesterday's underwear.

"What brings you to Dalston this fine morning, Mr. D?" Richard slaps him playfully on the arm, looking him up and down, "In your studio duds, no less."

The preppy kid stares down at his Sperry Topsiders, his wavy blond fringe falling in front of his eyes.

"Heading home," Bennett says. "You?" Because if he can get Richard talking about himself, maybe there's a chance he won't have to explain his own circumstances any further.

"Off to work. The people need their coffee! Oh my God, we have to call Mia!"

"No need," Bennett says, trying not to sound panicked. "I'll call her later."

Richard strokes Bennett's shoulder with one hand, as he pulls his phone from his bag with the other. "Don't be ridiculous, we're all just standing here!"

The other guy's eyes wander around the platform. Bennett gives the kid an awkward smile, because he looks like he might throw up, probably from the combination of last night's vodka and Richard's stench. And it can't be easy to watch the guy you went home with last night, stroking the arm of an older man. Bennett backs up a few steps, out of Richard's reach, while the kid fiddles with his phone.

"MIA! You'll never guess who I am standing next to on the train platform!" He uses his paparazzi voice, like he's a reporter for *TMZ* and Bennett is Ed Sheeran.

Bennett considers ripping the phone from his hand and throwing it onto the tracks. He can hear Mia's muffled and indifferent voice, "Okay. Then tell me."

Richard's date starts jumping in place, like he's nervous or really needs a piss.

"It's your dad!" Richard sings through the phone, smiling a reality-TV smile.

"Seriously?" Her voice elevates, so that Bennett can clearly hear her. Oddly, she's the one that sounds panicked. "Is Calum still with you?"

The other guy looks at Richard and shrugs his shoulders. All the color has drained from his face.

Who the fuck is Calum? This guy?

Richard looks over at Bennett, dumbfounded, and then at Calum, terrified, and his TV smile disappears. "Yeah."

"Put my dad on the phone," Mia demands.

Bennett takes the phone from Richard and walks down the platform, away from Richard and Calum.

"Hello, darling," he says, sounding fatherly, jammy, and warm.

"Why are you in Dalston?" There's no warmth in his daughter's voice. He can picture her on the other end with the phone, standing with one hand on her hip, the way she did when she was a little kid, demanding an explanation.

"Who's Calum?" He smiles at her, even though he knows she can't see it.

"Fuck sake, Dad."

"You can tell me over breakfast."

||||||||||||||||||||||

They agree to meet at a greasy spoon a couple doors down from Mia's flat. After giving Richard his phone back, Bennett introduced himself to Calum. A not entirely unpleasant introduction, considering the little shit is probably fucking his daughter. Polite and shy—bordering on sheepish—he, like Bennett, played with his hair when he was nervous, which he had parted heavily to the right. He could be a spokesman for Tory youth, this kid—a young Boris Johnson with a slightly more appealing face, Bennett thinks, though he intends to reserve judgment. After all, looking like Boris Johnson isn't so much a judgment as an unfortunate coincidence.

As he approaches the cafe, he can see Mia through the large window, reading a book by someone called Zadie Smith. He's seen that name on Claire's bookshelf and he thinks Claire and Mia would probably get along.

"Why are you in your paint clothes?" Mia asks as soon as he enters. He blends right in with the rest of the clientele, builders covered in paint and dirt.

"Well, hello to you, too," he says, leaning over and kissing her on the head, before taking a seat across from her. "What's good?"

She just looks at him, cocking her head a little to the side with confusion.

"Full English for me, I think. I'm peckish." He taps his fingers on the Formica table and looks up at the menu board. "Do they have something vegetarian for you?"

What are the chances she'll answer the vegetarian question and let the rest go?

"Dad." She squints at him. "What are you doing here?"

Zero.

"Are you dating someone?" she asks with a half-smile.

"Possibly," he says with a smirk.

"And she lives nearby?"

"Stoke Newington." It feels like a role reversal, answering her questions like an awkward teenager.

"Does she have a name?"

"Claire."

"Come on, Dad. More dirt."

"Alright, but one for one." He leans forward, pressing against the table, as if to say, *Game on.*

"What does that mean?"

"For every question you ask me, you have to answer one yourself."

She looks up at the menu board. "Yeah, there's something vegetarian."

"Great, let's eat."

They order and spend the next few minutes talking about the Picasso exhibition at Tate Modern.

"I just don't understand why they're still giving shows to misogynist wankers," she states with fiery indignation.

"Being a wanker doesn't make him a bad painter," Bennett argues, but he beams with pride: not everyone's got a kid with principles.

When the food arrives, Bennett's done with the Picasso conversation. There are more pressing issues on his mind. "So, is Calum on your course?"

"No." Mia takes a bite and finishes chewing before asking in return, "Where did you meet Claire?"

"At the Claret. She's a bartender." He stabs his fork into a sauteed portobello mushroom. "Is Calum a Tory?"

"What?! No!" She drops her fork, so outraged she forgets it's her turn to ask a question.

"Sorry. He looks a little, you know, conservative," he says.

"We can't all be as hip-hop as you, Dad."

Shit. The gig. He's forgotten all about it. "Speaking of. I got invited to a Roots Manuva gig tonight. Think I should go?"

"Why wouldn't you?" she asks, biting into her toast. "You're obsessed with the guy."

"I don't know. Think I'd enjoy him live?"

She gives him a shrug with the toast still in her hand, like *How am I supposed to know?*

"It's with this guy I met back at the Royal College. Not sure I like him well enough to spend a whole evening with him."

"So? Just listen to the music and ignore him," she says, dropping the crust of her toast on the plate. "Honestly, you're always looking for problems. You and Mum, both."

Ouch.

"Does Claire find you this infuriating?"

|||||||||||||||||||||||||

On the train home he thinks about what it would be like to introduce Claire and Mia. He imagines taking Mia to the Claret so she could see

Claire in her element, then taking them both out to dinner, maybe at the expensive vegetarian restaurant that Mia likes. Claire would like it, too, he's pretty sure. They'd like each other, actually. They'd probably start off by talking about books and art, but by the end of the night the two of them would be united in a common goal: taking the piss out of him. Eliza and Mia always teamed up against him. Does he really want to be outnumbered again? He likes his one-on-one time with Mia, same with Claire. He can't help thinking, if the two of them get together, he'll be the loser.

He gets a lot of thinking done on the long train rides from East to West London. Honestly, though, he's not sure he likes thinking. He often feels heavy and burdened by the time he reaches his back gate in Chiswick. Another reason to move east, maybe—fewer trains, fewer thoughts. Plugging in his earbuds, he turns up the volume high, bobbing his head as he stares out the window at London racing by.

Hither to! Bear Witness . . .
The brute!
The birth of the brute . . .

Bennett mouths along to the lyrics, really feeling them this morning. Maybe Claire thinks he's a brute. Maybe Eliza did, as well. Maybe he is. Maybe he doesn't care.

And furthermore
The Brute . . . shall stay . . . Brutish!
Yes . . . Yes . . . and Furthermore . . . Yes

His phone vibrates in his pocket, shocking him out of his personal *brute assessment.* A message from AirBed: **Hello, Bennett! Have you forgotten about Kirstie? For the best possible guest-host relationship we suggest responding within twenty-four hours of the original request. Make Kirstie's day! Let her know that your Four Bed Detached House in Leafy West London is available!**

Make my *day, you cocksuckers.*

He has thirty minutes to respond to Kirstie, but he's no closer to deciding what to do. He can probably live in the studio for a few months. This Kirstie chick will probably let him use the laundry room. That's his biggest concern, though, really, it shouldn't be. Maybe he could offer a discount if she lets him do his laundry in the main house. He doesn't have to make a decision about his relationship with Claire right away. If she really likes him, she'll be patient with him, surely? He looks again at Kirstie's picture—her on the beach, in a low-cut wrap dress tied tantalizingly at the side.

Hi, Kirstie, he types. **Sorry for the late reply. The AirBed rules are changing in London such that I am only allowed to let through the site ninety days a year. We can talk about a potential letting by other means over the phone.** He adds his phone number, putting a space between the digits, so the website can't detect it and block it. **I look forward to hearing from you. Best wishes, Bennett.**

"Best wishes." Hardly the language of a brute.

Just as the train docks at the next station, she sends him a text: *I'm in London today and tomorrow. Would it be possible to come by and look at the house?*

He checks his watch. It's late morning. He needs to do *some* painting today.

Certainly, he types back. Another word he's pretty sure he never used previous to AirBed inquiries. *How about this afternoon, around five?*

Perfect! X, she replies almost instantaneously.

A kiss? Interesting.

Great! he writes back, trying to match her energy. *I'll look forward to meeting you then.* No kiss. You can't be too careful these days. It's possible her kiss was an accident. He sends her the address and gets comfortable in his seat for the remaining seven stops on his journey and tries not to think about anything.

IIIIIIIIIIIIIIIIIIIIII

The painting of Claire stares at him, suspiciously, as he opens the door to the studio. He knows it's impossible for the painting to have changed expression overnight, but this morning, Claire's smile looks more skeptical. *You're an idiot, Bennett*, it seems to be saying. The bleach-stained duvet that she ruined the first night she stayed over in the studio is curled up in a ball on his futon. The mattress looks hard, like a sack of potatoes. Claire has one of those soft egg-crate mattress pads on her bed. He's been getting used to that. Will she want him to come over tonight or will she want him to stay away until he's made a decision about moving in?

All the lights are off in the empty main house. It looms over him, like a giant question mark. He'd sooner enter a haunted house than his own at the moment. *Too much thinking.* He plugs his iPod back into the dock and hits Play.

He still hasn't replied to Carl about the gig. He should just go, he tells himself. Claire is probably still angry with him and won't want him to come over tonight, anyway. He pulls the giant block of mature white cheddar out of the fridge and sets it on the counter, eyeing the severed phone cord that sent him out on yesterday's adventure from which he's only just returned. He decides to forgo slicing the cheese and instead takes the entire block, the size of an old videocassette, and sits down in his rolling chair across from the painting of Claire. He takes a big bite out of the cheese, swiveling from side to side, staring at her painted breasts. The tits are done, he thinks. Her milky-white skin and perky pink nipples are perfectly rendered. As usual, it's her face that needs work; her expression isn't quite right. What was she thinking, he wonders, that day she posed for this painting? Was she skeptical or content? Was she comfortable? Warm? Why didn't he ask her any of these things? She was sitting there for five hours, most of it silent; she had to have been thinking lots of thoughts. He sets the brick of cheese next to his palette of flesh tints; the gnawed corner of the cheese dips into the titanium white paint. He pulls his phone out of his pocket and starts typing a text message.

What were you thinking about when you posed for this painting? he asks.

The bubble pops up quickly, indicating Claire's responding. *That's a strange question.*

I'm trying to read your expression.

I thought you knew exactly what I was thinking the whole time.

Fuck. Walked right into that.

That's one of the things I liked about you, she adds.

Liked? he writes, hopeful for a correction, but she doesn't respond.

He grabs the cheese and wipes the paint-coated corner onto his jeans, before digging in for another bite.

He stares at the painting. She stares back—cold, arrogant, and unfamiliar. Not Claire. *Fuck. Maybe it* is *classical.* He thinks again of his renter Emma's comment, then he remembers something a tutor told him at the Royal College, "All portraiture is self-portraiture." *Is that true?* Is this actually a painting of Bennett Driscoll on his pedestal? Was it his personality Emma saw in the painting? Was she trying to tell him he's pompous? Even ancient?

He eyes the three small canvases, the ones he stretched almost in rebellion a few weeks back, perched behind the easel. He picks one up and flips it around in his hands, while continuing to contemplate the big painting. Getting up, he rests the small canvas on his chair, then takes hold of the large one and marches it outside into the garden, propping it up against the front of the studio. "Just for now," he assures the Claire in the painting, though he's not sure he can bear to bring that judgmental stare back indoors. Back at the easel, he places the small canvas on the bar and grabs his phone. Scrolling through his photos, he finds one he took of Claire a few weeks back where she's naked, sprawled out on her duvet. The light streams in through her second-story window onto her torso and hips. She looks away with a slight smirk, all too aware of her photo being taken. He remembers she didn't shrink up like so many women would have, wasn't ashamed of her own exposure. If anything, he'd swear she stretched herself out longer to let the sun drench even more of her skin, willing Bennett to just go ahead and take the photo, while simultaneously reminding him that he was on her turf now. He sets the phone on the easel next to the canvas, which he then coats in a light wash of brown umber. With his eyes on the photo, he begins to sketch her form in a peach-hued flesh tint.

His phone vibrates on the easel. He squints to read the message, hopeful for Claire's reply, but it's from Carl. *Lads nite, 2nite?*

Bloody hell. He doesn't want to be antiquated, he wants to be relevant. *Yeah,* he responds. *Let's do it.*

Didn't expect that, did you, Emma?

I knew you'd cave, mate. Meet me at Krafty Hops. Solid boozer.

||||||||||||||||||||||||

Kirstie pulls up to the house at five in a dark blue Mercedes. Typical, Bennett thinks. Eliza had the exact same car before she moved to America. He watches her through the front window of the house as she steps out of the driver's seat in yet another low-cut wrap dress like the one in her AirBed photo. This one is white with bold pink flowers. As she makes her way to the front door, he follows the line of the dress from her right shoulder, across her chest, and down to her left hip, where the two sides of the wrap meet. Two strings, tied in a bow, keep the whole operation together. Pull those strings, he thinks, and she's naked.

As he opens the door, she pushes her sunglasses up to the top of her head, lifting back her blond fringe and revealing her shiny Botoxed forehead.

"Bennett!" she says, smiling, like he's an old friend she hasn't seen in years.

He holds out his hand, which she accepts, pulling him in and kissing him on both cheeks. He attempts to keep up, each of his kisses a second behind hers.

"Please, come in," he says, stepping aside and running his hand through his hair. He took a long shower in the master bedroom en suite before she arrived. He'd forgotten how wonderful the water pressure is up there. He even used one of those little Molton Brown soaps he leaves for the guests, and he now smells like a grapefruit. After thirty minutes of hemming and hawing about what outfit would work best for meeting a wealthy divorcée *and* going to a hip-hop gig, he settled on his favorite dark wash jeans and a black cashmere V-neck jumper.

"This is lovely," she says, crossing the threshold into the open-plan living space. "Do you have good taste or an ex-wife?"

"I can't have both?" He smirks, closing the door, then stuffing his hands in his pockets.

"Good for you," she cheers him on.

"Downstairs is all open-plan, as you can see"—he directs her eyes—"chef-quality kitchen."

"I'll be sure to bring my chef's hat," she quips.

Maybe it's because of her blond hair or the low-cut dress, but he hadn't expected her to be so sarcastic. *Sexist thought.*

He wanders into the living room area and opens two cabinet doors, behind which is a large flat-screen television. "Telly is here. It's got Sky, Netflix, all of that stuff."

She looks off in the distance, regarding his studio out the window, where the naked painting of Claire is still propped up against the outer wall of the studio, her breasts glowing in the afternoon light. He probably should have brought it inside, but he forgot about it until just now.

"Well, well. You keep busy over there, don't you," she says with a raised eyebrow. She wanders over to the window for a closer look. "Will you be in the studio much of the time?"

"I'll be in and out," he says. "My girlfriend lives in North London, so I'll be there a lot, too."

My girlfriend?

"What does your girlfriend think about you painting naked ladies in your garden?"

"That's her," he clarifies, stupid grin on his face.

"Well done, you," she says, like she's awarding him an "A" on a test.

"Would it be a problem for you?" he asks. "If I am in the studio a lot? I do sleep there sometimes."

Possibly all the time, if Claire dumps me.

"Of course not!" She sounds almost offended by the question. She saunters back to the living room area, the back of her dress clinging to her thighs. "Heck, you're more than welcome to stay here. We can be housemates!" She laughs. "Might be fun!"

What kind of fun? Only one type comes to mind.

He's standing with one hand on the bannister, meaning for her to ascend the stairs behind him, but instead she sits down on the sofa, taking care to make sure her upper legs are covered by the flaps of her dress—the flaps which so naturally want to part. "Does it get easier?" she asks, hopeful. "Divorce?"

No.

"Yes, a little. I'm still working through it."

"But you've got a lovely looking girlfriend. That helps, I'm sure."

He smiles. "She's very patient with me."

I hope.

"Would you like to see the rest of the house?" he asks.

"Yes, let's. I'm sure you've lots of things to do."

Pulling herself up from the couch, she smooths the fabric of her dress, as though she needs to collect herself. Bennett catches her eye and sees the tears welling up.

‖‖‖‖‖‖‖‖‖‖‖‖‖‖‖‖‖‖‖‖‖

An hour later they decide that Kirstie will let the house on a monthly basis, until either she or Bennett make a decision about buying or selling property. She confides she's relieved to hear that he has also become more indecisive after his divorce. It's not just her. If Eliza were here she'd say Bennett's chronic indecisiveness was one of the grounds *for* the divorce, but Kirstie doesn't need to know that. It's almost as though she sees Bennett as a potential role model, as well as landlord, helping her navigate the complicated emotional stages of divorce. Maybe he'll write a self-help book. Maybe call it, *Yes, You Do Need to Change Your Underwear.*

He calls Claire on his way to the Tube. She'll be on her shift, but he wants to leave her a message, tell her he's decided to let the house. He wants to tell her he'd like to keep things as they are for now, that he's looking forward to exploring all possibilities in the coming months, that he hopes she'll explore them with him.

"Hi," she answers.

"Oh," he says, surprised. "I wasn't expecting you to pick up. I thought you'd be working."

"I am. Just on a fag break."

"You don't smoke," he says, stunned.

"I do, sometimes. When I'm in a bad mood."

"You're still mad."

"You're a genius."

He can hear her taking a drag from her cigarette and blowing out the smoke. He's completely forgotten the message he intended to leave.

"Want me to hang up," she asks, "so you can call back and leave the breakup message you intended?"

"I wasn't going to do that." He knows that much, at least.

"Are you still a Super Host?"

"For now," he replies, embarrassed. It sounds so stupid when she says it like that. "I decided to let the house to this woman on a monthly basis." He pauses, but Claire gives no reaction. "She's looking for a house to buy. Once she has that, then maybe I'll put my house up for sale."

"Right."

"She said she didn't mind me being in the studio and she's happy to share the laundry room with me—"

"Sounds like you have it all worked out," she interrupts.

Nothing could be further from the truth.

"Well, it means you and I don't have to make any big decisions. Maybe just keep things as they are for now."

"Right."

"I thought that would be a good thing, no pressure."

"Well, if that's what you think . . ."

Christ. He stops abruptly in the middle of the sidewalk; he can't walk and compute this passive-aggressive assault at the same time.

"I should get back to work," she adds.

"Okay. Listen, I decided to go to the gig with Carl tonight. Want to meet up after?"

Silence.

"I saw Mia earlier. I told her about you. She wants to meet you."

"Then send her in for a glass of wine. You know my schedule."

He runs his hand over his hair, but stops halfway to make a fist. "Claire. I'm trying here."

She laughs. "Enjoy your concert."

|||||||||||||||||||||

"Alright, Benji?" Carl asks Bennett as he approaches, setting a half pint of flat brown ale on the table in front of him. Bennett's found him scrunched into a corner table at the packed pub. At the other end of the table that's not meant to be communal, a young couple sits, huddled together. "I've been fighting off geezers right and left to save you this chair," he adds, kicking it out to Bennett.

"Thanks, mate. Can I get you another drink?" Bennett asks, pointing to the bar.

"No, thank you," Carl lifts his half. "Drinking mindfully these days." He takes a sip, pinky extended, like a little girl drinking tea. His T-shirt says, "Life Is Gucci."

Fuck sake.

The bar has thirty taps. All the beers are listed on a chalkboard above the bar, but Bennett doesn't recognize any of them. "Something light?" he asks the young woman serving him, who studies Bennett curiously, while he reads the chalkboard like he's looking for train times at Waterloo Station.

"What do you like?" she asks. "Bitter? IPA? Pilsner?"

"Just regular beer," he says, rubbing his forehead. "What's that? Lager, right?"

"You'd probably like the pilsner," she says, pointing to a tap. "This is a good one. It's light, but with a full flavor."

"Sure." He doesn't even bother looking at the tap.

"Pint or half?"

"Pint, please," he says, thinking he'd like to make as few trips to the bar as possible. He pulls a five-pound note out of his pocket.

"That's six-quid-eighty."

Christ. Seriously?

He fishes in his pocket for a two-pound coin.

"Seven quid for a pint!" he gripes, setting the beer down when he returns to the table. Carl is twirling his glass in his hand, looking at the reflections.

"That's quality shit you've got there, mate. Some Belgian monk probably spunked in that."

Bennett looks at the yellow liquid skeptically, afraid to taste it now. He takes his first sip, as Carl awaits his reaction. "It's just beer."

"You gotta loosen up, Benji. Open your senses to the subtleties of life and all that, nuhtamean?"

No fucking clue.

"What are you working on, anyway?" Carl asks, shifting effortlessly from moron to art critic.

"Oh. Um, I'm kind of getting back into nudes, actually."

Carl slaps the table hard. "Yes, mate!"

The couple with whom they'd been sharing a table rise, leaving a good third in each of their pint glasses. The young man puts his arm around his partner and escorts her from the table, after shooting them a dirty look. Carl doesn't notice.

"Yeah, it feels good," Bennett says quietly, though he wonders what Carl would make of the first Claire painting. Would he, too, find it *classical*, aka dated?

"When you started painting fruit, I was like, 'What the fuck's he on about?'"

Oh, right. I'm the confusing one.

"I don't know. I needed a break, I guess."

"Fifteen years?"

"Yeah, well, I had a little girl," he says defensively, taking another swig from his beer. "I didn't want her to think her dad was some perv that looked at naked women all day."

Carl's expression says, *So what?* "Nah. Daddy would be rich if he'd kept painting the ladies. Your girl would be nipping around London in a little pink Roadster and summering in the South of France. She wouldn't give a fuck how you made the money."

Every last word of that makes Bennett's skin crawl. Though it's true that Mia probably *wouldn't* have cared if he'd continued to paint nudes. It's not like she doesn't know about his past with the genre. It's never bothered her, that he can tell. And she's no stranger to painting the female anatomy herself. Case in point: that recent five-foot vagina painting.

"I didn't want to do it anymore," Bennett explains. "The fabrics and the still lifes were more interesting to me."

"And only you, geez."

"Yeah. Alright. I get it." He chugs the rest of his six-quid-eighty pint. The only thing he's "mindful" of is how much he wants to punch Carl in the face. *Nuhtamean?*

Carl drains his own half pint and turns the glass over on the table. The remaining beer drips down the inside of the glass, creating a ring on the surface.

"C'mon, Benji. You think I want to paint massive biblical altarpieces?"

Yes?

"I'd rather fuck off to Margate and paint seascapes, but nobody is going to buy those, not from Carl Willis. I got a reputation to uphold." He leans across, propping both elbows up on the table. "You're Bennett Fucking Driscoll, mate. Act like it."

Bennett swallows hard and nods. Carl is right; he didn't have to give up the nudes. He could have continued to paint them while developing other work. Maybe it was stubborn and stupid of him to just abandon them altogether. If he'd continued with them, he probably wouldn't have to worry about letting his house on AirBed. He'd probably still have his gallery, or *a gallery*, at least. Maybe he would have been able to afford that house on the edge of the Thames, the one he loved since he was a kid, the one Eliza kept tabs on for years. And maybe Eliza wouldn't have left him at all. Maybe he's the only man in the world who could have saved his marriage by looking at *more* naked women.

Wait.

"If you know my name is Bennett, why do you call me Benji?"

"I prefer it," Carl says, pointing at Bennett's empty pint glass. "Looks like you could use another."

||||||||||||||||||||||||

Before they even get to the venue, Bennett's consumed twenty-eight quid's worth of pilsner. It takes him a little while to add it up, his math skills severely impaired by the four pints. Even after two hours of drinking, they're still early to the small, dark venue. A crowd of die-hard fans is starting to form around the stage. To Bennett's surprise, most of them are white men in their forties dressed, ridiculously, in hip-hop themed T-shirts from Tupac to Dizzee Rascal.

"I need a leak," Carl says.

"Yeah, me, too."

"You just want to get a look at my cock?" Carl asks, somewhere between joking and serious.

No. No. No. No. No.

"I just thought maybe your missus left you because you're . . . nuhtamean?"

"I do know what you mean, Carl, and I'm not gay."

"Alright. If you say so. Men's loo is a good place to meet other blokes." They're making their way to the back of the club over floors so sticky their shoes actually cling. "No judgment, mate, if you meet a fella. We don't have to end the night together."

That, at least, is reassuring.

In the toilets, all the urinals, but one, are mercifully in use. Bennett makes a beeline for the empty stall and shuts the door behind him. Releasing his urine he closes his eyes, enjoying every second away from Carl—his voice, his gaze, his stupid fucking T-shirt. When he opens his eyes, he sees there's a message on the back wall: DAVE. SAD. BIG COCK. CALL ME. 07700987868

"Oi, Benji! You taking a shit or taking down phone numbers?" Carl snorts at his own joke.

Fuck you, Carl.

He hovers, dick over the toilet for an extra second, uncomfortable knowing Carl is waiting on the other side of the door. This whole thing was a mistake. He should be at home, painting. He should be spending the night at Claire's, not in this club with a racist, homophobic twat. It's bad enough that Carl is more successful than he is. It's even worse listening to the dickhead explain why that is, over extortionately priced pilsner. Bennett is zipping his fly when his phone vibrates. Text from Eliza. *Fuck, really?*

Mia says you're dating. Good for you.

He flings open the door of the stall, startling Carl and everyone at the urinals.

"Alright, Benji! I was just making a joke."

"What?" Bennett heads for the exit.

"About the phone numbers, mate. Just a lil' banter and all that."

"Whatever. I'll be right back. I need to make a call."

Outside he paces, wondering why Mia betrayed him by telling her mother about Claire. Surely, his daughter had to know that Eliza was the last person he wants to know about his personal life.

Good for you? The phrase has him reeling. If she really wanted *good* things for him she wouldn't have left him in the first place, right? You don't pledge to spend your whole life with someone and then fuck off just because you got bored. You don't get to pretend you know what's *good* for a person after you bail on them. You don't get to pretend you know them at all.

He presses Call, pacing like a leopard on the dark, crowded sidewalk, waiting for her to answer.

"Hi," she says, in a tentative, slightly defensive voice.

"'Good for you'? Are you fucking kidding me?"

"Alright, Bennett . . . I was trying to be nice." The resignation in her voice suggests she suspected his reaction.

"I don't know why Mia told you that, but you don't get to know anything about my personal life."

"I asked her, Bennett. She didn't want to tell me at first. She's very loyal to you, you know?"

His heart swells for a moment, causing him to momentarily forget his anger. He thinks about Mia and how much he knows she worries about him.

"When was it over between us? Before or after you met Jeff?"

"Bennett . . ."

"I deserve an answer to that. Did you know it was over before you met him?

"Yes," she says, taking a deep breath. "I think so."

"Good. I hate thinking you left me because of that smug little twat."

"You've been drinking."

"I'm at a gig."

"A gig?" she asks, chuckling.

He stops pacing. "Yes. Is that so unbelievable?"

"Kinda," she says, laughing harder now.

"You don't know me anymore."

"Rubbish, Bennett. You may have *gone* to a gig, but you're outside on the phone talking to me."

He wants to hang up on her, but he can't. It's too good hearing her voice.

"Mia says her name is Claire?"

"Yeah."

He lets silence fall over the conversation, like a petulant teenager.

"How did you meet her?"

"I'm painting her," he says. Not the full truth, but close enough. After all, when you paint someone, it's like meeting for the first time. He remembers how he and Claire stared at each other for five hours, both vulnerable, her naked and him with his heart on his sleeve and a perpetual lump in his throat.

"Right," she says, after a moment.

"Any more questions?"

"No."

"You're holding back. What?"

"You never painted me," she says.

"I didn't think you wanted me to."

"You're a fool, Bennett."

His heart ceases to beat, just for a second, the way it does when the simple solution to a problem presents itself far too late.

"Good night," she says, then hangs up.

⦚⦚⦚⦚⦚⦚⦚⦚⦚⦚⦚⦚⦚⦚⦚⦚

When he walks back into the venue, Roots Manuva has started. The crowd around the stage has swelled and Carl is in the center of it, jumping up and down like a six-year-old in a bouncy castle.

Mind to motion. Know the notion.

Bennett pushes through the crowd, giving Carl a shove when he finally reaches the center of the mosh pit. Carl has a giant grin on his face. "Fuck, mate. I thought you bailed!" Carl shakes him, excited. "This bruv is mint, geez!"

Bennett smiles as Carl continues to gyrate manically, off beat.

Roots Manuva jaunts from one side of the stage to the other in a coat with tails and a top hat.

Hither to . . . Bear Witness.
To the Birth . . .
Of the Brute . . . !

Bennett stuffs his hands in his pockets, swaying as he surveys the crowd that packs in around him—sweaty middle-aged men jumping up and down with their hands in the air and their beer guts wobbling like bowls of jelly. This is what it looks like to live in the moment, Bennett thinks. These guys aren't giving any fucks about how ridiculous they look. They're not thinking about their ex-wives or current girlfriends or the staggering price of a pint. They're just listening and misguidedly shaking out their suffering in the belief that the music was written especially for them. Mindfulness, Bennett thinks, is a truly disturbing sight.

Roots Manuva squats down at the front of the stage and points into the crowd. Right at Bennett, he could swear it. Bennett swallows, paying attention.

"Hither to!" the rapper shouts, and the hairs on Bennett's neck stand to attention.

Bennett removes his hands from his pockets and cups them around his mouth and shouts, "Bear Witness!" in time with the rapper. "And furthermore. The Brute . . . shall stay . . . Brutish!"

SINKING STONE

When he opens the door, Bennett is smiling, broadly. Kirstie is used
to the goofy man grin, usually accompanied by a gaze that's directed
right at her cleavage. It doesn't bother her that men stare at her larger
than average breasts. After all, it's a compliment. Most women don't
know the difference between a compliment and an insult anymore.

"Good to see you again, Bennett," she says, placing a hand on his
arm and kissing both cheeks. "I'm so happy this worked out."

"Me, too," he says. "Can I help with your bags?"

"Yes, please! I'm afraid I've brought way too much stuff!" She looks
back at her Mercedes, crammed to the gills with suitcases and tote bags.

"You do know the place comes furnished?" he kids, looking
through the window of the packed car. He opens the trunk and pulls
out a large, zebra-print suitcase. It drops with a resounding *thud* onto
the driveway. He groans a little, pulling it along. "What is this, your
rock collection?"

She just smiles, too embarrassed to tell him the truth—yes.

"I can't really judge," he offers, lifting the suitcase into the house. "I haven't gotten rid of a single thing since my divorce."

"Except the wife," Kirstie says, laughing. She removes several tote bags from the back seat. She looks over at him, expecting a shared laugh, but he's already disappeared into the house. Her kids are always telling her that her sense of humor is completely devoid of tact. She's been wondering recently if maybe the little shits are right. With two tote bags full of shoes in each hand, she struggles to the front door, teetering on a pair of high-wedge espadrilles. A stiletto heel pokes through the tote bag and digs into her thigh.

"Give 'em here," Bennett says, appearing in the doorway.

"Sorry about the wife gag," she says, embarrassed. "My kids say my jokes aren't funny."

"She got rid of me, actually."

She looks at him sympathetically, even though she doesn't quite believe him. "I won't pry. My kids say I pry too much, as well."

He smiles, not the goofy grin from before, but a kind of half-smile that suggests he'd like to change the subject. She can take a hint. Don't bring up Bennett's ex-wife. Got it. They unload the rest of the car in silence, with only the occasional sideways glance and polite curls of the lip.

"Can I take any of these bags upstairs to the master bedroom?" he asks once everything is out of the car.

She looks around at all her stuff. The answer is that it can all go upstairs, but she feels wrong asking him to do that, even though she'd like him to stick around. She's not looking forward to that first moment of being alone in this house.

"Let's have a cup of tea first, yes? Are you in a hurry?" she asks, hopeful.

"No. No hurry."

"Well, have a seat on the sofa. Let me make you a cuppa. I bet you're not used to that, are you?"

"I'm not." He smiles and does as he's told.

He's very obedient, she thinks. It's nice.

She kicks off her espadrilles by the front door, thereby dropping two inches in height on her way to the kitchen. People have said that she has an imposing presence. It's mostly her personality, but disproportionately large breasts and high-heeled shoes help. Without shoes she's lucky if she's five-foot-two.

"I don't think I picked the right attire for the day," she says, smoothing down her electric-blue top with a plunging V-neck, complete with a ruffled collar that frames her deep cleavage. Her kids are always telling her to dress *normally*, but she has no idea what they mean. "I think I might pour myself into my pajamas once you've left." She pulls on the belt loops of her tight black trousers and takes a deep breath. "Sorry."

She doesn't even need to look at Bennett to know that was an overshare. He's probably picturing her in a black satin nightgown. If he's picturing her in flannel bottoms and the oversize T-shirt she intends to put on, then there's something wrong with his imagination. "Do you take sugar, Bennett?" she asks, putting a tea bag each in two white mugs she pulled from the wooden mug tree.

"No, thank you. Just milk," he says, regarding her from the sofa.

"Aren't you good! I've tried to give it up several times, but I just love a lump of sugar. My ex-husband used to say I reminded him of a horse, I love sugar cubes so much."

She can see Bennett grimace, though he tries to hide it.

"Thank you," she says. "I thought it was a horrible thing to say, as well."

As she pours a little milk over the dry tea bags, the kettle begins to whistle.

"I used to take a lot of sugar," Bennett says, leaning over the back of the sofa. "My mum always made a really sweet cuppa while I was growing up. Sometimes I swear she left out the tea bag. It was just hot water, milk, and sugar."

"That's nice. That your mum made you tea," she says, coming over to the couch with both mugs.

He accepts his mug but regards her strangely.

"My mum doesn't believe in caffeine," Kirstie explains, sitting down next to him.

"Tragic," he says, swallowing a big gulp, then going in for another.

He likes it, she thinks. Good. Albert, her ex, never thought her tea was strong enough.

"Do you know your way around the area?" Bennett asks. "Can I help direct you to anything?"

"I'm getting my bearings, I think," she says. "It's such a shift—small coastal town to the big city."

Until now, Torquay was the biggest city she's ever lived in; she's not even sure if the coastal tourist destination is technically a city. She used to love living by the ocean. Its vastness and fluidity had a calming effect on her, but not anymore. She doesn't think she'll miss it. Not after what happened with Albert. The idea of hard concrete, as far as the eye can see, appeals to her now.

"Well, I've been here my whole life, so just let me know."

"I will, thank you." She smiles. He's so helpful. She wonders if he'd be this nice to her if she wasn't paying him eight thousand pounds a month. "It doesn't feel like the city out here."

"No, it doesn't, but everything you'll need day to day can be found on Chiswick High Road," he says vaguely, maybe even a little bored. "Lots of nice restaurants, too. Great parks."

"You sound like you've been doing this a long time." She laughs. "Does the tourism board know about you?"

He smiles, blushing.

"What would I do in a park, Bennett?"

He shrugs. "Sit on a bench? Look at the rose beds?"

"Sounds hideous."

"I don't go, either," he concedes.

"I can tell." She slaps him playfully on the arm. "You don't need to worry about me. I know my way to Harrods. That's all that matters."

He takes his final swig of tea and sets the mug down on the coffee table. Her own mug is still half full.

"I should let you get settled," he says, rising.

Not keen to let him go, she remains seated for a moment, then reluctantly stands as well. She glances at the window that looks out on the garden and his studio, which is where he's no doubt headed. "The lovely painting of your girlfriend is gone."

"I figured you wouldn't want that painting staring at you from the garden."

"I don't mind. I liked her. She looked confident," Kirstie asserts. "I guess you'd have to be to pose nude." Not something she could ever imagine doing herself. Not anymore.

"That painting was a headache," he says, brushing past her obvious lack of confidence. "I've moved on." He gestures to his easel, where a smaller canvas sits. She has to squint to make out a possible figure as its subject matter.

"Very exciting," she fibs. "I look forward to spying on your progress."

"Pop round for a cup of tea sometime. Have a look."

"Thank you, I will." She hopes his invitation is sincere. He's the only person in this whole city she knows.

"Off to meet the pretty girlfriend?" she asks, catching herself too late. "None of your business, Kirstie!" she scolds herself aloud.

"It's okay," he says. "Dinner with my daughter and her new boyfriend, actually. If I strangle him, I may need you to bail me out of prison."

She thinks back to Albert, his hands around her throat, telling her she's not worth the oxygen she breathes.

||||||||||||||||||||||||

She's lucky to be alive. He could so easily have pushed her over the glass balcony and right into Salcombe Harbor. "Ungrateful bitch," he called her. His house, his balcony, and his wife. To Albert's mind, he could do what he wanted with all of it.

Of course, he hadn't been like that when she first met him. That's the thing people can't seem to grasp. If he'd been like that when they were going out, she wouldn't have married him. She's not an idiot. His cruelty snuck up on her, starting out as a whisper, a tiny insult here, an undermining gesture there. But after Michael, their first son, was born, the "or elses" started to creep in. "Shut up, or else." "Smile, or else." "Fuck me, or else." She didn't know what the "or else" meant, but her imagination ran wild with it—everything from cutting off her credit card to running her over with his Land Rover. So, she shut up, she smiled, she fucked him. In return, she got a beautiful, contemporary house on a Salcombe cliffside that looked out over the harbor. She got a large stipend, plus a maid and a nanny. Her time was mostly her own, since Albert, an actor, was always on set. By the time Martha and Matthew were born, Albert was in Dorset most of the time filming *Criminal Coast*, the long-running drama series in which he played the lead, Detective Inspector Cliff Caswell, a troubled, but brilliant and handsome, homicide investigator. The character of Caswell was inspired by Albert's own father, a man who came back from war damaged, but more determined than ever to put the world right, a giant bleeding heart on legs. The character may have been a saint, a man devoted to justice and the service of his community, but Albert Cartwright was a prick and a control freak. A health-nut, he treated his body like a temple and, committed as he was to the art of manipulation, he rarely drank. He was also charismatic and charming. He enjoyed telling sentimental stories about his old man, while stroking his luscious white-blond hair that never went thin. The cast and crew of *Criminal Coast* were all his disciples. A die-hard Labour supporter, he defended the show's crew, men who frequently went on strike for better pay, though his passion for a fair, living wage never seemed to apply to the women on the show. Every season had a new female lead, each paid a small fraction of what Albert was. He slept with every single one of them, Kirstie suspects, though he never tried to strangle any of them. They would have sold their stories to the papers by now, if he had. No, she's the only woman he ever strangled, so in that respect, she told herself, sarcastically, she was special.

It was when *Criminal Coast* got canceled five years ago, after a twenty-year run, that things started to feel dangerous. Suddenly, he was at home all the time, a presence in the house and the town that, until then, had been her domain. He resented her constant closeness and seemed frustrated that she was no longer the pretty young thing he married. He was insulted that she wasn't more intelligent and didn't care to listen to his daily monologues on current affairs. "God, Kirstie! Think!" he'd say, looking over the top of his *Guardian*, trying to explain the day's news to her. "What do you *do* all day?" he'd ask her. Then he'd quickly add, "Don't answer that. I don't want to know." What *did* she do all day? Well, what she'd always done. She shopped. She watched a lot of property programs. She took classes, mostly in yoga and Pilates. She liked to walk along the beach and collect shells, but why tell him any of that? He would have considered all of that pointless and shallow. What did he expect? Hadn't he for the last twenty-five years methodically stripped her of her interests, her life of purpose? She kept her mouth shut, she smiled, she fucked him. That's what he asked for. Since when do trophies get to think? "I've met rocks with more common sense than you," he liked to tell her. The kids, too, picked up on his contempt. "Mum's dumb as a rock," she heard Martha whisper to Matthew when they were just eight and six, and they giggled. It was probably around that time when she began her slow transformation to the stone everyone believed her to be. She could actually feel herself harden.

||||||||||||||||||||||||

A retired couple happened to be sailing past their harbor-view house on the night Albert tried to strangle her on the balcony. She wasn't sure what frightened her more—being breathless because of his tight grip or the fear of gasping for air under water if he succeeded in pushing her over the ledge. As it turns out, it's the latter that's stayed with her—that fear of sinking to the bottom of the ocean. She's certain that Albert would have succeeded in sending her tumbling into the sea, had the man on his boat not shouted, "Let go of her!" In that moment,

Albert removed his hands from her throat and peered down into the harbor at the older man, who'd begun snapping photos of him. "Mind your own sodding business," Albert shouted, throwing one deck chair, and then another, out into the water, hoping they might land on the man or his boat. "That's Inspector Cliff Caswell!" the man's wife shouted, pointing up at Albert. "From telly! He's throwing furniture at you!" Kirstie heard all of this from the adjoining master bedroom, where she'd escaped to. While he was chucking chairs into the sea, she was frantically searching for shoes with no heels that she could run in.

Eventually, she found a pair of penny loafers and ran downstairs, while Albert was still shouting at the couple on the boat. Grabbing her coat and purse, she made a dash for her Mercedes parked out front in the center of their crescent driveway. She'd imagined that one day it would be her getaway car, and for that very reason she'd bought it under her own name with the money her father had put in an account for her twenty-five years ago—money he wanted to invest in a hotel she'd planned to open. He'd died before she and Albert started seeing each other seriously, but how he would have hated Albert! She wishes now that they'd met, wishes her father could've warned her against Albert, because she would have listened. She knows most feminists would disagree, but sometimes you just need a good man's opinion.

She drove around for a while that night but eventually ended up at the police station. Had the man on the boat not taken the photos, she's not sure she would have reported Albert. But she was pretty certain the guy would sell the pictures to the tabloids, and sure enough, he did. It made sense to get ahead of the story.

"I'd like to report a crime," she told the constable sitting behind the desk at the Salcombe police station.

"What's your name?" he asked, bored.

"Kirstie Cartwright," she replied, thinking this could have been in an episode of *Criminal Coast*. She'd watched this scene a million times. "My husband, Albert Cartwright, just tried to strangle me and throw me over our balcony."

The constable, an older man, looked at her in disbelief. "Albert Cartwright? As in Detective Inspector Cliff Caswell?"

"Albert. Yes. He's not really a detective," she added, feeling the need to clarify that, lest the constable think of her husband as a brother-in-arms.

"That would be a huge news story, Mrs. Cartwright. Are you sure you want to report that?"

She pulled back her hair and showed him the finger burns on her neck. "I'm sure. And there'll be photographic evidence, too," she added. "Some guy and his wife in a boat saw the whole thing."

The constable, looking unconvinced, pushed back his chair. "Alright, I'll have you talk to the sergeant."

The sergeant took her statement with as much doubt as the constable had earlier, even after she told him that the coast guard would no doubt find their deck chairs floating in the harbor, even after she provided him with the make and model.

"Floating deck chairs isn't really proof of domestic abuse, I'm afraid," the sergeant, a younger man with razor burn all around his Adam's apple, told her. "It only proves that someone in your house didn't like those chairs."

Actually, she loved those chairs. She sat in one every morning, from April until November, sipping her coffee and reading *House Beautiful* magazine.

"You don't seem very upset?" the sergeant pointed out.

"My husband is a bastard. It may be news to you, but it's not news to me."

"We'll go round and talk to him, but I suggest you find someplace else to stay tonight."

"No kidding," she said.

The sergeant looked at her, as if to say, *I'd toss you over a balcony, too, if I could.* She was used to men looking at her that way. They either want to fuck her or kill her. Not one that she can think of has ever expressed indifference.

"Will you arrest him?"

"That depends, Mrs. Cartwright."

"On what?"

"On what we find, Mrs. Cartwright."

"You're going to find a good liar and a deck with no chairs."

"We'll let you know, Mrs. Cartwright."

"For the love of God, please call me Kirstie."

"That's not how we do things, Mrs. Cartwright. I'll get you a case number so you can call for updates."

"You won't call me, I have to call you?"

"We're very busy, Mrs. Cartwright."

"With what?!"

"Well, someone just accused Albert Cartwright of domestic violence," he tells her. "The press will be all over this."

||||||||||||||||||||||||

After Bennett leaves, she makes herself a second cup of tea. The great British stalling technique, she thinks—making tea. When she's busy, when she's happy, she could go days without drinking tea. She's only brewing tea right now to trick herself into believing she's busy. She hasn't lived alone, ever. Not until today. For the last several months she lived with her mother in Totnes, a hippie enclave about an hour from Salcombe. Vivienne, despite being in her mid-eighties, owns and operates the town's most popular shop for medicinal crystals, believing wholeheartedly in their healing powers. Viv never liked Albert, said she always "had a feeling" about him. Viv's *feelings* come from what the crystals tell her. This makes them evidence-based, as far as she is concerned. "I can feel a lot of negative energy coming from him," she mentioned on her daughter's wedding night. Pulling a bag of rocks from her purse, she handed them to her daughter, saying, "Try resting these on his stomach while he's sleeping. They should help neutralize him."

On the night of the balcony incident, when Kirstie arrived, late, at her mother's house, Viv wasn't at all surprised to see her. "You never tried the crystals, did you?" she asked.

"No, Mum, I didn't."

The old woman, wearing a colorful, psychedelic-looking robe, her short, dark grey hair going in all directions, just tossed her hands in the air. "How 'bout a whiskey?"

||||||||||||||||||||||||

Kirstie takes her tea upstairs to the master bedroom, where Bennett has laid the four large suitcases on the bed, including the zebra one, which she unzips first. Inside is the collection of crystals her mother gave her before she left Totnes, all carefully bundled in Bubble Wrap. Kirstie thought about stopping alongside the A303, maybe around Stonehenge, and dumping the lot—let some hippie freak happen upon them and build a shrine to their magical powers. However, though she hates to admit it, part of her wants the crystals to work their magical powers on her. Wouldn't it be nice if the secret to serenity and fulfillment only required the presence of a few rocks? She pulls out the large hunk of amethyst and unwraps it. "This will bring calm to your life," Viv had said. "Whenever you're feeling stressed, just bring the amethyst into your orbit."

"My 'orbit'?" she asked. "I'm not a fucking planet, Mum."

She puts it on the windowsill, thinking it might be pretty to look at while she's doing yoga. Next, she pulls out the rose quartz. "This is for your emotional well-being," her mother had explained. "It will promote self-love." Unwrapping it from the bubble, she holds it up to the bedroom skylight, so the light can shine through the pale pink rock. It's true, she hasn't got a lot of "self-love." She doesn't even own a vibrator. What the hell is the crystal going to do? Give her a pep talk? "You're resilient," she tells herself in a goofy cartoon voice, wobbling the quartz as though it's speaking. "You're quick-witted, and your arse is the real deal." Kirstie decides to place it on the bedside table, thinking that she's hardest on herself first thing in the morning.

Lastly, she pulls out the citrine, her favorite of the three big stones her mother gave her. "This will help you realize and fulfill your dreams," Viv stated, with great confidence. It's this rock that Kirstie holds out the most hope for. She sets it on the opposite end of the windowsill from the amethyst, facing Bennett's studio in the backyard. Since leaving Salcombe, she purposely hasn't thought much about her future. She hoped that freedom would inspire her. Instead, it's only filled her with fear. What happened to the big dreams she had when she was younger? Actually, they were better than dreams. They were plans—to design and open her own hotel. It seems strange to her now, how close and certain those plans had felt. So certain, in fact, that it never occurred to her that marriage and children could derail them. She doesn't know what to hope for now. It's hard to imagine wanting anything beyond a life without fear and judgment. If she could have that, the rest is just details.

She unpacks her clothes slowly and methodically, careful to make sure the activity eats up a decent chunk of the afternoon. She finds she likes the feeling of the fabric in her hands; the whole process feels deliciously necessary. She never got to do such necessary things in Salcombe. They had a maid for all of that. Maybe she could get a job at one of the high street fashion stores, folding shirts and designing displays? She raises an eyebrow at the citrine crystal in the window. It stares back as if to say, *That's your dream? Folding clothes at fucking Topshop? Try again*. It's not like she needs the money. Albert kept the Salcombe house in the divorce, but she got most of the cash in their bank account, plus half of the continuing residuals from *Criminal Coast*. No small thing, since the damn show plays on a loop on ITV3 all day and night. Anything she does now, she can do purely for the love of it. It's just, what *does* she love?

She loved hotels and hospitality when she was younger. That was her first job straight out of school, cleaning rooms at a local seaside hotel. It was only supposed to be a temporary gig, but then she worked her way up to the front desk and even manager. She was good at it and it's always been hard for her not to fall in love with things she's good at. Back in those days, she used to study old issues of glossy magazines—ones she knicked from the lobby of the hotel where she was working—and cut out pictures that would inspire the design of her own hotel. She'd paste the cutouts in a red scrapbook called *My Hotel*, along with copious notes about how she'd use the designs and what she'd change. She'd considered calling it *My Dream Hotel* but decided this place wasn't going to be a dream—it would be a reality.

When she met Albert, she'd been managing the front desk at a waterfront Torquay hotel for two years. She knew everything there was to know about both the hotel and the town. In her opinion, there was no better feeling in the world than knowing how to do something really well. (She misses that feeling every day.) That year she applied to the University of Plymouth for the hospitality program. Her plan was to open her own boutique hotel in some small Devon village. A destination hotel with ten beautifully appointed rooms and a restaurant rated the best in Devon. These days, there are lots of such places, but back in the mid-eighties, her idea was an entirely fresh concept. She tells herself not to be bitter about that. She made her choice. It was the wrong one. Move on.

Albert, a guest at the Torquay hotel, had been in town for a wedding. Kirstie checked him in on a Friday afternoon. She didn't recognize him, but she thought he looked like Boris Becker, her favorite tennis player. A porter would later explain who he was.

He wanted to know where the wedding would be taking place, so she pointed through a large bay window into the hotel's beautifully manicured garden, where a tent had been set up. "Why come all the way to the seaside to get married in a garden?" he mused.

He had a point, she thought. She wouldn't learn until much later that Albert always had a point.

"A wedding on the beach would be better. Sand in your toes . . ."

She smiled, enamored by the idea. "Lots of lovely secluded coves around here."

When she handed him the room key, he winked at her. "They should have let you plan it."

Kirstie tucked her blond hair behind her ear. She'd had it cut and blow-dried to look just like Chrissy Evert, her other favorite tennis player.

"I don't suppose you'd like to have a drink later?" he enquired, feigning insecurity. "When you're done here. I'd like to hear more about these coves."

"I'm off at five," she answered, like this kind of thing happened all the time.

He jingled the key in front of her. "Perfect. You know my room number."

She went up to his room at five, bringing with her a handful of foldout maps and a pen to mark where all the secluded coves were. She was pretty sure that he intended to make a pass at her—she wasn't an idiot—but it was important to keep up pretenses. After all, she wasn't a prostitute. When she knocked on the door, he called, "Door's open," and there he was on the balcony—their first balcony—looking at the seafront, a pitcher of gin and tonic on a clear plastic table.

She showed him the maps, folding them out onto her lap, so that he had to lean over her in order to see. He held one corner, she another, while she circled spots of interest. She told him all about her life, what it was like to grow up in the so-called "English Riviera," all about her job and her plans to attend hospitality school and open up her own hotel. He listened to all of it and asked questions. He smiled a lot, leaning on the arm of his chair, his head propped up in his hand. He refilled her glass from the pitcher of gin and tonic, but never his own.

"How old are you? Do you mind my asking?"

"Twenty-three," she said. "And I don't mind. Ask me again in ten years and I'll say the same thing."

He smiled at her wit, which she could tell he found sexy, at the time. "For such a young woman, you have big aspirations."

She shrugged. "It's just an idea . . ."

Except it wasn't. It was a well-researched proposal. Comments like that haunt her, now. At the time, she didn't notice how quickly she downplayed her life's ambition just because she was drinking gin and tonics with a handsome and successful man.

The next day he called the front desk and extended his stay another five days. Every evening after work, she went up to his room. On the second evening they kissed and on the third she went to bed with him. She hadn't wanted to miss out on what might well be her only chance to have sex with someone from telly, someone who also happened to look like Boris, the dreamiest man alive. Once he had her in bed and her hotel uniform—a tight black skirt and white blouse, complete with name tag—on the floor, he asked, "Are you a virgin?" She replied, "No!"—as if to say, *Are you nuts?*—and, for a moment, she thought he looked disappointed. On her day off, they hopped in his MG convertible and she showed him all around South Devon. They went to Salcombe for the first time and he remarked that it was more civilized than Torquay, the kind of place where he could see himself settling down. By the end of the five days, she'd pretty much forgotten about her plan to open the hotel. She hadn't opened her scrapbook once. There was still plenty of time, in her mind, and a new idea was forming: *my dream husband.*

She'd like to slap that girl now.

||||||||||||||||||||||

After she ended up at her mother's in Totnes that night, Kirstie called each of her children. "You're probably going to see some photos in the press," she told them. It was important they hear about what happened from her first, she explained calmly. Michael, an aspiring actor, though he mostly does voice-over work, said "You went to the police? Oh, Mum . . . couldn't you have at least talked to me first?"

"What would that have done, Michael?"

"I could have told you not to. This is going to be everywhere."

"I'm sorry, darling. I know this is hard." Her heart sank, realizing for the first time that her kids would be caught in the media circus.

"So, what now? You can't go back there, not after you reported him to the cops."

"No. I'm going to file for divorce."

"I'm sure he didn't mean it, Mum. He's just got a wretched temper."

"He meant it, darling. I'm sorry."

Matthew had been more difficult to get ahold of. He was in some nightclub in Plymouth, when on Kirstie's fifth attempt, he finally answered his mobile. A once semiprofessional cricketer, he'd torn his ACL leaping over a fence at Dartmouth Naval Academy on a drunken dare. Now he's a full-time bum.

"'Bout time," he said, when she told him she was divorcing his father. "You two have never been happy together."

Well, that wasn't quite true, but probably not since Matthew was born, and Matthew was the kind of kid who believed, vehemently, that nothing at all existed before he did, least of all, other people's feelings.

Then there was Martha. She'd saved the conversation with her daughter for last because she knew it would be the most difficult, not because her daughter would be hurt, but because she wouldn't. A dentist outside Leeds, she spends her days whitening the teeth of the Yorkshire elite. Martha has insinuated, more than once, that she believes her mother has "wasted" her life, which hurts Kirstie deeply, in part because she agrees. Still, she suspects that she and her daughter have a lot more in common than Martha admits, like the time her daughter hinted that she liked Theresa May, calling her "brave in the face of a hostile nation."

"Nonsense," Albert scolded (just like he scolded Kirstie), "that wretched witch cares more about her shoe collection than she does the British people." Albert believed the working-class man was the most important asset to any civilization. He'd used his fame to stump for Labour candidates all over the country—well, male candidates, anyway. "Women don't use reason," he always explained. "They always want something." As if male politicians never want anything.

"That's such a stereotype, Dad," Martha had shouted back.

Kirstie remembered smiling at this, opening the refrigerator and putting her head inside where no one could see it. When she was young, she'd liked Margaret Thatcher. She remembers seeing the Iron Lady on her parents' TV screen and imagining that she, too, could one day be prime minister. When she looked at Thatcher, dressed in her red woven skirt and matching jacket with gold buttons, she saw a woman who could render a roomful of men silent. They hung on her every word.

"What did you do, Mum?" Martha wanted to know, after Kirstie told her the balcony story.

"What do you mean?"

"You must have done *something* to make him angry. Why do you always egg him on?"

This was one of her daughter's frequent misconceptions, that Kirstie did things, on purpose, to make Albert's temper worse. Like some kind of weird sex game, Martha is convinced her mother gets off on it.

"I didn't *do* anything, Martha."

"You've always wanted to leave him, don't make him out to be a criminal in the process. He wouldn't kill you, Mum. He just wouldn't."

She let the line go silent. He *would* have killed her. The problem with Albert was that he thought he could kill her and then bring her back to life. As if he's been writing her into the script of his life all this time. As if he could hit Delete and then start her story again.

"Right." She let the phone go silent for a moment. "I like Theresa May, too, you know," she said, feeling the tears well up. "I voted for her." Then she hung up.

|||||||||||||||||||||

She sends all the kids a group text saying she's arrived in London and misses them. *Come down anytime*, she says, even though she knows she'll eventually have to beg.

|||||||||||||||||||||

Morning bursts into the bedroom through the skylight by six. Light bounces off the crystals, refracting and casting light purple and yellow tones all over Bennett's white designed room. Kirstie rolls over and looks at the citrine on the windowsill, the keeper of her hopes and dreams. According to Viv, she'll look over at the crystal one morning and her future will become clear. Not *this* morning, though, not yet. It's hard to be patient with a rock. She rolls herself out of bed, keen not to stew in her own thoughts or analyze that strange dream she had last night, where she was standing on stage in front of an audience of old men wearing Thatcher's red wool jacket with the gold buttons and nothing else.

Opening the middle drawer to her dresser, she looks down at the clothes she folded so neatly yesterday, before pulling out a pair of black yoga pants and a hot pink elastic top. Dressed, she rolls out her yoga mat onto the floor by the window. Facing the garden, she starts stretching. She reaches above her head and to the side, letting her hips pull her waist in the opposite direction. She holds herself in this position for thirty seconds before switching to the other side. She and her mother did yoga together, while she was staying in Totnes. At eighty-four, Vivienne can't do the really difficult poses, so it's been a while since Kirstie has tried anything as challenging as a Crane Pose or her favorite, a Firefly Pose. She worked on her core strength for months in order to achieve this pose for the first time. She spent hours a day at the yoga studio in Salcombe with Thorbjørn, her blond-haired instructor, twenty years her junior. Everyone in town thought she was fucking the Dane, but it wasn't like that at all, though she did confide in him. He was the only person in Salcombe she'd told about Albert's temper, that she was worried that one day her husband might try to hurt her and she wanted to be ready. She might need her balance and core strength to save herself, she told him, and that turned out to be true. That night on the balcony, she felt her abs lock into place, a wall of defiance. She might be "dumb as a rock," but try snapping a rock in half.

She gets down on the floor in a squatting position, thinking that maybe when she gets better at doing the difficult poses again, she'll start doing her yoga in the garden. Maybe she'll ask Bennett to take a photo of her in Firefly Pose so she can send it to Thorbjørn and let him know she's still working hard. She had to say goodbye to him abruptly after the photos were published. Viv got a call from a friend that morning, who told her, all excited, that "Your daughter is on the cover of all the papers!" It was difficult to go back to Salcombe after that.

The town was suspicious. Had the photos been doctored? they wondered. Surely, not Cliff Caswell, national treasure. Not Albert Cartwright, upstanding community member and card-carrying liberal? Not possible, they wrote in the opinion section of the local paper. Sure, maybe he slept around a little; after all, boys will be boys. But she probably slept around, too, have you *seen* her? they whispered. They were convinced that Albert Cartwright would never hit a woman. It's true. Albert had never hit her. He just berated her and tightened his grip around her neck until she couldn't breathe. But no hitting. Why, everyone wanted to know, would she have stayed with him if he was so horrible? Only a moron would stick around if she truly feared for her life. Try being told you're stupid and useless for twenty years and see if you don't end up believing it yourself. That's what she wanted to tell them.

She squats on the floor, like a frog getting ready to leap, then shifts her center of gravity so that her hands are carrying most of her weight. Her knees hug her shoulders and she tightens her abdominal muscles, rock-solid, preparing to stretch her legs up to the ceiling. She gulps, letting out a groan as her legs extend, and her hands bear all the weight. She's just about to straighten her arms, pushing her whole body about a foot above the mat, when she tips over backward, landing on her bum. "Aw, fuck," she yells, rolling onto her side and rubbing her elbow, which she's pretty sure bent back in the wrong direction. She stands up, so she can shake out her arms and roll out her neck. From the window, she studies Bennett's studio, wondering if he slept there last night, or went to his girlfriend's. As if she's willed him into being, he opens the door of the studio in a navy blue T-shirt and pair of grey sweatpants. His eyes are pulled up to the master bedroom by the brightness of her hot pink top in the window and she waves down to him, smiling. He waves back with the same goofy grin he greeted her with yesterday, then exits his gate and begins to run. Her smile remains, even after he's gone.

|||||||||||||||||||||||

An hour later, she's sitting on the patio sofa, dressed in khaki capri slacks and a black top that wraps around her waist, tying in a bow at her side. She likes to think "the wrap" is her signature style, classy yet seductive, just like Catherine, Duchess of Cambridge—her favorite royal.

With a cup of tea and her iPad, she's on a property website looking at flats when Bennett reaches the gate, panting. She looks up, smiling. He's grasping the fence for support while he tries to catch his breath; he isn't aware that she's there, watching. When he finally comes through the gate, he's drenched in sweat. He shakes his whole body, like a dog after a swim, hoping to fling off some of the sweat.

"Morning, Bennett!" she shouts, her smile even broader now.

"Morning!" he says, startled, trying to mask his surprise with enthusiasm. He pulls the earbuds from his ears and the faint sound of rap fills the garden. She wasn't expecting that. "How was your first night?" he asks, fishing around in his pockets for the right device. First he pulls out his phone, then finds the iPod and hits Pause. "Sorry."

She waits for him to look up before answering. "It was fine, thank you. Lovely bed in the master."

"Good. Yeah. It's one of those mattresses that claim to keep you cool. So it should be really nice when the weather gets warmer."

She chuckles. "At my age, women are hot all year round."

His eyes twitch while he digs around in his brain for an appropriate response. She loves doing this to men.

"You're a runner?" she asks, letting him off the hook.

"No, not really, just trying to be healthier, I guess, in my old age." He paces around the garden. "Mind if I sit for a minute?" he asks, pointing at the ground. He looks as though he might collapse if he doesn't.

"Of course! Did you have some horrible guest that wouldn't let you sit in your own garden?"

He flops down on his back and stares up at the sky, emptying his pockets into the grass, then turns his head to look at her. "No, but you are the friendliest. Most want privacy. They don't want to see your face at all."

She rolls her eyes. She's never known a day of privacy in her whole life. People who demand it bore her. "Honestly, Bennett, I'm happy to share it all. I like your face."

He smiles back. "Even when I look like this?"

She brushes it off. "I raised two athletic sons. God, they used to stink."

He chuckles at that, stretching his arms across the lawn.

"Oh, how was meeting the boyfriend last night?" she asks, feeling like maybe they've got a bit of a rapport building.

He stops chuckling and sits up. He's cautious. "I don't think I like him."

"What's wrong with him?" She sets down her iPad to signal she's listening.

"I don't know if I can put my finger on it. He's too polite, maybe? Strong handshake and he called me 'sir.' In fact, he wouldn't stop calling me 'sir,' even when I asked him not to." She can hear the agitation building in his voice. "It won't stick, right? Am I going to have to deal with some kid calling me 'sir' for the rest of my life?"

She starts laughing before he can even finish stating his concerns. "Poor Dad. I'd be worried if you didn't hate him. That would mean you weren't paying attention."

He shrugs.

"You two are close? You and your daughter?"

"Yeah," he says, almost misty-eyed.

"She won't stay with anyone you hate."

"So, if I just hate them all . . ." he says, apparently hatching a plan.

She nods, laughing. "Well, one day she's going to bring home a young man that will remind you an awful lot of yourself, and you'll have no choice but to like him."

He flops back down on the grass. "I think you underestimate the power of my self-loathing."

They're both laughing now, Bennett so hard that he starts coughing and has to roll over onto his side to relieve his chest.

"I could use your help," Kirstie says, when he's finally stopped hacking.

"Of course," he says, pulling himself up.

"I don't need you to stand," she says, motioning him to sit back down and he complies. She loves that about him. He's like a well-trained dog. She picks up her iPad. "Where should I live?"

He looks taken aback, but then quickly smiles. "Big question."

"I'm looking at properties and maybe I'm in the minority, but I don't think I want one of those Victorian terrace houses. I want something modern. I want someplace with a real city feel to it." She realizes, of course, that she's describing the opposite of his house. "No offense."

"None taken," he assures her. He stares up at the sky, thinking. "I don't know what your budget is . . ."

"It's pretty big," she says. "Go on."

He looks right at her and she can tell he wants to ask where all the money has come from, but he doesn't. If he's figured out who she is and why she's here, he's given no indication. "Well, then maybe you want to look at the Barbican."

"Ohhh," she says, typing that into Google, saying it as she goes, "Bar-bi-can."

"It's right in the center of town. Very modern. Like a little city in the city."

She scrolls through images of the brutalist designed estate with its three towers looking out over the city. It's all concrete, as far as the eye can see, like it's grown straight up from the pavement. How on earth did Bennett understand, so effortlessly, a place she'd actually been imagining? She looks over at him, excitedly. "I love it. Oooo . . . Look at this one! Tenth floor, Lauderdale Tower . . . three bedrooms. Gorgeous kitchen . . . not that I can cook. Wow! The views!"

She spins the iPad around so Bennett can see. He comes closer, squatting in front of the screen, but clearly trying not to get too close. His sweat smells sweet, like old socks dipped in honey. He shrugs, looking at the images as she scrolls through them. "Well, yeah, it's amazing."

"This is perfect for me. How did I not know about this?"

"Happy to help." He sits back down, clearly satisfied with a job well done. "Maybe I should become an estate agent."

"For wealthy divorcées," she says. "You'd make a killing."

He seems to be genuinely mulling over this possibility.

"Yep. I love this!" she declares, setting down the iPad and clapping her hands together in one big boom. "Come have a look at it with me!"

He looks back at his studio, nothing on his easel. "Yeah, okay. Let me get cleaned up," he says, standing.

"What happened to your little painting?"

"Done." He smiles proudly.

She hopes he'll offer to show it to her, but he doesn't.

When he's gone inside, she looks up at her citrine crystal on the bedroom windowsill. She'd swear it's glowing.

||||||||||||||||||||||||

When Kirstie and Bennett step out of Barbican Station into the afternoon sunshine, she immediately looks up at the concrete towers that reach forty-two stories each in front of her. The glass-walled skyscrapers of the city shimmer in the distance.

"What time is the viewing?" Bennett asks, glancing at his watch.

"Three," she tells him, strutting down Aldersgate Street, confident, like she knows where she's going.

"That's it, there." Bennett stops in the middle of the sidewalk, pointing at the tower directly in front of them. "Lauderdale Tower."

She grabs his arm and shakes it with excitement. She wouldn't be here right now if it wasn't for him, and for that reason alone she thinks she has the right to touch him.

Almost a foot taller, he smiles down at her. "Still like it, then?"

Yes, yes, a thousand times, yes. She likes everything about this moment, though she reminds herself that she tends to get overexcited by things she really should think through. But, she loves a good gut feeling and still continues to trust hers, despite the fact that it's clearly led her astray before.

"We've got a little time. Want to see the pond?"

"There's a pond?!" She does her best to sound thrilled, not wanting to tell him she's recently developed a fear of water. After all, for the last two decades she's gradually transformed herself from woman to stone, thinking that was what she needed to do to build her defenses, to become impenetrable and solid. Until that night on the balcony, it didn't occur to her that there's one problem with stones: they sink.

IIIIIIIIIIIIIIIIIIIII

She can't tell how deep it is. That's Kirstie's first thought as they approach the man-made pond at the center of the Barbican Estate. The water is a dark, greenish-brown, covered with a thick green moss. An abyss, Kirstie thinks, stagnant and dense. She imagines her body sinking to the bottom, never to be found. Shuddering, she turns her attention to the fountain that spits and gurgles in its center. Around it, a few small, long-beaked birds wade through the water, picking at the moss. Bennett's looking at her, strangely. "Sorry," she tells him. "Got a shiver."

"I thought you were always hot?"

She scowls at him, then turns her attention back to the birds. "Aren't they cute. What are they?"

"Birds," Bennett says.

She looks over at him again, pretending exasperation, though in truth she enjoys his facetiousness.

"No clue. I'm not a bird guy."

"Ornithologist," she says. Her father was an avid bird lover. "You're not an ornithologist."

He shakes his head, no, he's not. Unlike Albert, Bennett doesn't seem to mind being corrected. They amble along the brick-lined terrace that surrounds the pond, where residents and city types have gathered to eat sandwiches out of triangular cardboard packages.

Bennett points to the restaurant that runs along the side of the pond. "That's the cafe, there. They serve chicken—also a bird, so I'm told."

She squints at him, trying to figure out if he's flirting or if he's just like this. Most men, when they flirt with her, just stare at her cleavage, but Bennett seems to prefer teasing, like a boy on the playground who doesn't yet know about sex, only proximity.

"You're going to go for a swim, Bennett. If you're not careful."

||||||||||||||||||||||

The estate agent is waiting in the lobby of Lauderdale Tower when they arrive. She's a younger Indian woman, probably in her thirties, even shorter than Kirstie, dressed in a grey pantsuit. "Hello, there," she says, reaching out her hand. "I'm Priya, and you must be Kirstie?"

"Yes! Hello!" she says, taking Priya's hand. She indicates to Bennett, who's several feet behind her. "This is my friend and second pair of eyes, Bennett." He takes his hand from his pocket and waves.

"Let's go! Let's go!" Kirstie persuades, adopting a sprinter's stance.

Priya looks surprised, possibly a little frightened, by Kirstie's enthusiasm. Kirstie is used to that look—equal parts intimidation and pity—from other women. Priya turns to Bennett for guidance.

"She's a little excited," Bennett says with the classic British restraint Kirstie's never been able to master. This is exactly why Kirstie brought him. He's more likable. He's handsome and he's got this little scar under his eye that gets really deep when he smiles, making him just rugged enough. Priya's noticed it already.

||||||||||||||||||||||

After a short elevator ride, during which Kirstie was effervescent, like freshly poured prosecco trying not to fizz over the side of the glass, they arrive at the flat. She's excited by the idea of changing her life so completely that, maybe, in a few years her old one will be unrecognizable. Maybe it's not the right thing to want that. Maybe she should want to hang on to some elements of her old life, but why? A butterfly, she suspects, doesn't long for the days it was a caterpillar. She hopes that when she steps into the flat, she'll be able to see clearly, for the first time in thirty years, what life without Albert—a life on her own—could look like. For a long time, solitude had been scarier even than death. That's what a guy like Albert does to you. He convinces you that your worst enemy is yourself. It hadn't even occurred to her to be frightened of him, fearing herself instead. She still hates being alone in a room, so she keeps the TV on in the background. Afraid of her own thoughts, she takes sleeping pills at night to avoid being left alone with them for too long.

She opens the door to a long corridor, Bennett and Priya trailing behind. She does this slowly and quietly, almost as if she expects to encounter a predator around any corner—old habits die hard. When she comes to the edge of the kitchen, where the flat really opens up, she feels her face stretch into a wide, mouthy grin, and she turns back to Bennett, grabbing his arm and dragging him up beside her. "This is it!"

He looks at her like she's nuts. "It's the first place you've seen. You haven't even seen the whole thing."

"Haven't you heard of love at first sight?"

His eyes seem to go dark, not exactly the reaction she'd hoped to elicit. Grabbing his shoulders, she shakes him, then goes over to the bank of wide windows that offer views of the other two towers. "Look at the view!" Light bounces off the glass of the skyscrapers in the distance. "Can you imagine waking up to energy like this every morning?!" Opening the door, she goes out onto the concrete terrace and peers over the edge. Below, the pavement bustles. "Ah! Men in suits everywhere! I wonder what they all do. Where are they all going?" It occurs to her that she's talking to herself. Neither Bennett nor Priya have followed her out. She watches them chat through the glass, and when they share a laugh her heart sinks, wondering if it's at her expense.

Bennett notices and joins her on the terrace.

"What was so funny?" she asks, when he leans his weight on the concrete ledge.

He looks at her strangely. "Oh. The rising cost of property in London. Suppose it's not that funny, really . . ."

She nods, relieved. "I know you think I'm crazy. But it's not just practicalities. I'm also looking for a gut feeling." Again, she looks down at the pavement below. Strange, but the concrete actually empowers her. If she fell over the side, she wouldn't sink, she wouldn't gasp for air, wouldn't disappear. She'd go *splat*. There's something comforting about a hard impact. No use trying to explain this to Bennett; though she wonders if he is thinking about death, too, as he leans over the edge. "'Look first with your heart and then with your head.' That's what they say on the property programs," she says, trying to convince herself as much as him.

He looks out to the city, deep in thought, before he finally shrugs. "Yeah, alright."

"Let's look at the bedrooms." she says, taking him by the hand and pulling him indoors.

"Do I get to pick which one I want?" He grins.

She realizes, their hands clasped, how elusive solitude still is to her.

||||||||||||||||||||

Back on Aldersgate Street, she says, "I need to make a list of questions. Will you help me think of all the practical things I need to ask?" Albert handled the purchase of their house in Salcombe. Before that, she'd lived at home with her parents or in a house share in Torquay. "I should at least try to make it seem like I know what I'm doing, but I don't," she adds. "I have no idea."

"I'm no expert," Bennett admits, running his hand through his hair. "It's been over twenty years since I've bought a house. You might want to consult someone else."

"I haven't got anybody else, so put your thinking cap on."

He smiles nervously.

"Have you got plans tonight?" she asks.

He glances at his watch. "I guess I thought I'd try to meet Claire at the end of her shift, but that's not until eleven."

"Perfect! Can I borrow you until closing time?"

He shrugs. "Yeah, okay."

"Let's find a pub and make a list. Then I'll buy you dinner."

She loops her arm through his to keep up with his pace. She wonders how long it will be before he starts asking questions about her past. She's amazed that he hasn't already. For such a sweet bloke, he seems rather self-absorbed. It's nice, though, she thinks, that he doesn't know her history. She's noticing that the more time she spends with him, the more she forgets it herself.

||||||||||||||||||||

They find a small pub tucked into a courtyard next to a church that Kirstie thinks must be five hundred years old, at least. Thousands of people walk past this church every day, she imagines, and they have done for hundreds of years. It reminds her of the vastness of history, and she likes that. The ocean used to make her feel that way—like she's only a speck on the vast earth, a tiny blip in this world. Comforting, somehow. "I feel like I'm in a Dickens book," she says.

Bennett pulls on the heavy wooden door to the pub, and they step into the empty, dimly lit room. "You like Dickens?"

Kirstie laughs. "I've seen *A Christmas Carol* on TV."

He smirks, like he's caught her in a lie.

"And you're an expert?"

"Yep. Dickens and birds." He grins as they hover by the dark wooden bar.

"Alright?" the barman asks. He's a pale, skinny guy in a black shirt and trousers, both covered in white, crusty stains. Kirsty wonders if they keep him in a cupboard when he's not on shift.

Bennett takes the lead. "Pint of lager, please." He motions to Kirstie.

"Nonsense, we'll share a bottle of pinot grigio," she tells the barman, whose pointy hook nose goes back and forth between the two of them.

"You still want that lager, mate?"

"No," Bennett says. "I guess not."

When the barman hands Kirstie two glasses, she goes off in search of seats, leaving Bennett to follow with the wine and cooler.

"I like this one," she says, choosing a table. "Nice view of the church."

Bennett sets the ice bucket and wine in the center of the table. "Oh. You're religious, now?"

She smiles. "Don't be daft. It's just pretty."

He stays standing, regarding the church.

"Come on, admit it!" she says. "It's pretty!"

"It's a pretty church," he concedes.

"Good. That's settled," she says, annoyed that he would take that long to admit something so obvious. What's this guy like when things get complicated? "So, how's your pretty girlfriend?" she asks, teasing, as he sits down.

He gives her a bitter side-eye as he untwists the cap on the wine bottle. "She wants me to move in," he says. "I blame you."

Kirstie is used to getting blamed for things, but in this instance, she's pretty sure Bennett is joking. Very few things are actually her fault. She doesn't have enough power for that. "*My* fault?"

"If I hadn't rented the house to you, our future probably wouldn't have come up. She thought a long-term letting was a chance to talk about our relationship." He regards her before tipping the wine bottle toward her glass.

She pushes it a little closer. "Just to the brim, darling."

He smiles and gives her a little more than he gives himself. "Don't you have questions to go over?"

"Yes!" She changes gears, pulling a notebook and pen out of her handbag, and settles in. Ready for dictation. "Questions. Go."

"Right, okay . . . I think you want to find out about fees," he suggests, businesslike. "Grounds keeping, rubbish collection, and stuff like that." He lifts his glass, but doesn't drink. "And council tax. All these things add up."

She writes all this down, furiously, as he brings his wineglass to his lips.

"Wait!" she shouts, holding out her other hand.

Bennett, startled, sets down his glass.

Dropping her pen, she raises her own glass and says, "Cheers."

"Cheers," he says, picking his up again, still a little tentative.

She's been looking forward to this moment, the opportunity to really look into Bennett's eyes for the first time. She believes you learn the most about people through their eyes. Albert mostly evaded her gaze. When he looked deep into her eyes on the balcony that night, she understood why he never had before. He hated her.

She and Bennett both take a sip, watching each other, Bennett with one eyebrow arched. If he doesn't ask any questions, he's never going to work her out. Why, she wonders, has this not occurred to him?

"How did you get the scar under your eye?" she asks him.

He hesitates. "I was a boxer."

"No, you weren't."

"I was. Chris Eubank did this in 1992."

"No! Really?"

"Of course not." He points to her notepad. "Do you want my help or not?"

She doesn't like it when men point out how gullible she is. She asked a serious question and was hoping for a serious answer. She wants to know him and for him to know her. Is that too much to ask? To have an actual friend? "Continue," she says, setting down her wine and once again picking up her pen.

"Getting a mortgage can be complicated after divorce, I hear."

"I can pay cash." She thinks he'll *have* to start asking questions now, taking a deep breath.

"Alright, then," he says, holding his wineglass in the air. "Oh. You probably want to research the market value of the flat, as well. It should be easy enough to find out what similar units have sold for."

She can't believe it. How could he *not* ask where she got the money? "Right," she says. "Makes sense." She taps her pen on the notepad, not bothering to write down this particular suggestion.

He watches, clearly confused, as the pen bobs up and down. "That's probably the most important stuff. I'm sure you'll think of more questions once you get the answers to those."

A large group of men in suits burst into the pub like a gust of wind, beer guts first, laughing and yelling, arms flailing. Bennett rolls his eyes.

They both watch the suits, all hovering around the bar, ordering their pints of bitter. There aren't any businessmen in Salcombe, so Kirstie finds them fascinating.

"You'll have to get used to them," he says. "They travel in packs." He turns around to watch them with an expression she recognizes as contempt. The way Albert looked at her.

"Do you paint every day?" she asks, attempting to regain his attention.

"Not today," he answers, with fake hostility. Then, "Pretty much. I try to."

"That's what *I* want to find! Something to engage me the way painting engages you. Do you exhibit?"

"I used to, quite a bit. It's a long story, but I'm trying to get back in the game. I've entered the painting I just finished into the Royal Academy Summer Show," he confesses. "That would mean a lot, if it got in."

"I'll cross my fingers for you."

He shrugs. "We'll see," he says, sitting back, looking up at the ceiling.

Fuck it, she thinks, if he's not going to ask about her. "There was a time when I wanted to own my own hotel. I married a man that I *thought* would support my dream."

Leaning forward, he pours more wine into their glasses. "Men are wankers."

Now there's a massive understatement. In a way she feels sorry for Bennett. He can't even bring himself to ask the right damn questions. Stroking the stem of her wineglass, she stares at him in disbelief.

"What?" he finally says.

"Do you own a television?" she asks him.

"The one in the house," he says. "That's it."

"So, you don't watch TV?"

"Not really. I've seen far too much *Britain's Got Talent* for my liking," he says. "Claire loves it."

"Did you ever?"

He shrugs, leaning away from her again, clearly confused, and maybe even annoyed by this line of questioning.

She presses on. "Mysteries? Cop shows? Anything like that?"

"Nope. Not really. Why? Am I missing something good?"

"No." She sits back, satisfied that even if she tells him her ex-husband's name, he'd still be clueless. "My ex was on telly," she explains, "that's all."

"Ah," he says, unimpressed. "He's not anymore?"

"No. His show got canceled five years ago."

Bennett nods at this, as though the same thing happened to him. "Too bad."

No, Bennett, it's not *too bad*, she thinks. The bastard deserves every bit of bad fortune that crosses his path. She takes a long swig from her wineglass and again resorts to tapping her fingers on the table. She's not giving Bennett any more information. Not until he starts asking the correct questions.

Nonplussed, Bennett picks up his own wineglass and tilts it to the side, staring at the light yellow contents. He straightens the glass again, studying the liquid's movement. "Huh," he says.

Kirstie watches him, fuming.

"No legs," he says, catching her eye through the glass. "That means low alcohol. Claire taught me that."

"Right." Like she could give a flying fuck. "She's got a lot of patience, hasn't she?"

"I'm sorry?"

"Your girlfriend. If you're like this with her, she must have the patience of a saint."

"Like what?" he asks, defensively.

"Nothing, never mind."

He rolls his eyes, like he's heard it all before. "So, what do you like to eat?" he asks, pivoting, knocking back the rest of his glass.

Amazing. She'd like to throttle him right now. On the other hand, at least he's finally asked her a question. She lets him hang in anticipation, pretending to think long and hard about it. "Steak," she says finally, though she knew all along. "A big juicy steak."

"Right," he says, pulling out his phone, presumably to find a good steak house nearby. "I wasn't expecting that."

"What were you expecting?" she asks, though she's not at all surprised that Bennett surrounds himself with the kind of women that prefer hummus to real food.

"The women in my life aren't big meat eaters . . ." he explains, typing on his phone.

"The women in your life are idiots," she tells him, letting her anger from the previous moment spill over into this one. She doesn't even know who these women are. His girlfriend? His daughter? She can't help but feel jealous, probably because she suspects Bennett gives them more attention than he's giving her right now. Finishing her wine, Kirstie waits for him to offer some sort of comeback, or at least put down his phone. When he does neither, she says, "Sorry. Tact again. I'm sure they make up for their boring diets in lots of other interesting ways."

"You're mean when you're hungry." He chuckles, scrolling down his screen with his thumb. "Alright. Found a place, but it's about a thirty-minute walk. Up for a stroll or would you rather get a cab?"

She looks at him like he's crazy. "Please, darling. There's no way I'm walking."

IIIIIIIIIIIIIIIIIIIIIII

They sit at a small wooden table for two at the back of the restaurant where it's dark and a bit romantic, though she wasn't so sure about the place when he led her into the black-painted Industrial Era warehouse. The hostess had given them a couple different options and this is the table that Bennett selected. Kirstie tells herself not to read anything into it, even as the couple nearest them is holding hands across the table.

She looks at the menu, licking her lips. Once again, he's gotten her taste exactly right, amazing for someone so seemingly oblivious, and to judge by the smug look on his face, he knows it.

"Go on and pick a bottle of red, darling," she tells him. "Get one with those legs you like." She pulls out a pair of bright red reading glasses and puts them on.

He looks over at her nervously. "If I am going to pick the wine, I should pay for it."

"Nonsense," she retorts quickly, putting down her menu. "Surely, we've established by now that you don't need to worry about my bank account."

"Still, the wine here is pricey."

"Excellent, pick a really expensive one."

He looks at her, mystified. She picks up her menu again, ignoring his pleading expression. "Crikey," she scolds him. "Just pick one."

"Rioja?" he asks.

"Sure. As long as it's not cheap. There's nothing worse than cheap rioja."

"It's not," he says, confidently.

She smiles at him. "Good. Was that so hard?"

He shakes his head, but she can tell he finds making decisions, any decisions, nearly impossible.

"What are you going to eat?" she asks him, taunting his indecisiveness.

"I don't know," he says. He holds out the menu at arm's length, trying to get it into focus. "I haven't looked yet. Steak, I'm guessing."

"Want to borrow my glasses?" she asks.

He looks across the table at her bright red glasses. "No, it's fine. I only need glasses when it's really dark."

"Like right now?" she asks, taking them off and holding them in front of his face.

He takes them reluctantly and tries to read the menu through the lenses without actually putting them on.

"You're ridiculous," she says, laughing. And vain, she thinks, but somehow manages not to say that out loud. "Just put them on. I won't laugh."

When he slides the glasses onto his face, of course she laughs. She can't help it.

"They have Salcombe crab," he says, looking right at her through the glasses, his grey eyes magnified.

"I didn't come to a steak house to eat crab. Disgusting little bottom-feeders. My kids used to fish them right off the docks in town. They're stupid little creatures, let me tell you."

"That's why we eat them. 'Cause they're stupid." He removes her glasses and sets them in the center of the table, suggesting that's his final thought on the matter.

She takes this as a personal insult, though she's not sure why. He's not calling *her* stupid, just suggesting that the unintelligent make good prey. Albert would agree.

The waitress approaches; her long brown braid rests over her left shoulder, falling down to her elbow. She twirls the end of it with her index finger. "Hello," she says, brightly. "Would you like to order some wine?" She smiles politely at Kirstie and then turns to Bennett for the answer.

"A bottle of rioja, please." He affably tilts the wine list in her direction, prompting her to take it.

"Nice. That one is super delicious," she says, balancing on her tiptoes with enthusiasm. "My name is Ellie, if you need anything."

"That's what happens when you tip them too much," Kirstie says, after Ellie has skipped away, her teardrop bum swaying weightlessly. "They get bubbly. Someone should tell her that's not an attractive quality."

Bennett sets his menu at the edge of the table and studies her with an irritating smirk. "You're a bit bubbly yourself."

"I AM NOT!" She'd like to reach across the table and smack him.

He sits back in his chair, enjoying her reaction. She could swear this guy likes torturing her. It's beside the point that she enjoys torturing him, too.

"Come on, back at the Barbican? That was bubbly," he says, arms crossed, cocky.

"That was controlled enthusiasm. I never said, 'Wow. This flat is super amazing!'" she offers, her voice raised, just as Ellie returns with the wine. If she registers the insult, she gives no sign, but holds the bottle out to Bennett like she's presenting him with a medal.

"Super," he says, straight-faced, causing Kirstie to chortle under her breath. She has to stare down at the table.

Ellie struggles to cut the foil around the mouth of the bottle. "Sorry!" she says, now twisting the corkscrew into the cork, fighting it with every turn. "This cork is super stubborn."

Bennett swallows a laugh and chokes on it, hacking until he can get a hand on his glass of water. The wrinkles deepen on his face as it turns red. It's refreshing, Kirstie thinks, to meet another person who is as easily amused as she is.

"There we go!" Ellie says, triumphantly, none the wiser about being the butt of a joke. She pours a little wine into Bennett's glass.

He gets serious again, sticking his nose in the wineglass and inhaling.

"It's wine, not perfume," Kirstie tells him. "Drink it."

"It's lovely, thank you," he tells Ellie, then rolls his eyes at Kirstie.

"What would you like to eat?" the young woman asks as she pours the wine.

"Yes," Kirstie states, confidently, grabbing her glasses from the center of the table and putting them on the edge of her nose. "I'll start with the beef tartare and then I'll have the rib eye steak with the bone marrow gravy and some triple-cooked chips. Please make sure there is enough of the bone marrow gravy for both the steak and the chips."

Bennett stares at her, wide-eyed. She squints, challenging him.

"Make it two, I guess."

||||||||||||||||||||||

When the rib eyes come, the bottle of rioja is nearly gone. Kirstie licks her teeth, convinced they must be dyed red—Bennett's are—but she doesn't want to stop talking, there's so much to say to him. So far there have been no awkward silences, the kind she's used to with her family, where they all stare at each other thinking, *Are we really related to this woman?* He still hasn't asked her about her divorce, but she tells herself it's because he's being polite. At least he's laughing at her jokes. And he teases her, which admittedly she likes. At the end of the day, she's still paying him; it's not really friendship, not yet. And there's no reason for him to expect there was anything extraordinary about her separation from Albert. She prides herself on how normal she feels after what happened. The red marks on her neck from Albert's grip have faded and his grip on her consciousness will fade, too, eventually. If Bennett can't see it, that's a good thing. No need to point it out. People who act like victims are such a bore.

"Does your daughter get along with your ex?" she asks him, curious in her own right, whether daughters can ever forgive their mothers for not being perfect women.

"It's been difficult for her," Bennett says, cutting into his steak. He pops the piece in his mouth. "I'm lucky, Mia likes to root for the underdog and that's me." It doesn't bother Kirstie that he talks with food in his mouth. The only man she's ever known to chew with his mouth closed is Albert.

"She blames your ex for the separation?"

He nods. "I wasn't the one having an affair."

"Right," she says, having figured that was probably the case. Some women are always looking for something better.

"They're trying to patch things up. Mia's going to spend the summer in America with Eliza. It's the right thing," he adds, though he shakes his head, seeming to negate his own sentiment.

"I can hear you gritting your teeth," she says with a chuckle.

He brings the white cloth napkin to his face, stained red with wine and gravy. "She should have her mother in her life. Don't know how I am going to survive two months without her, but I will."

"She'll be back before you know it. Two months is nothing when you're as old as we are."

He shrugs, apparently conceding her point, and then the dreaded silence sets in.

How many kids do you have? How old are they? What are they like? All questions he *could* ask.

"You don't ever ask questions," she blurts out.

He regards her, puzzled. "What do you want me to ask?"

"Anything that makes you sound interested."

His eyes grow wide and he stutters defensively before she cuts him off. "It's just some advice, darling. Women like to be asked questions."

"Okay." He nods after seeming to take this information in. "Your kids? They blame you?"

She looks down at her rib eye, her eyes filling quickly and unexpectedly with tears. *Wrong fucking question.*

After a deep breath, she responds, "I think so," blinking a few times and stuffing a chip in her mouth. It's possible, given how dark it is, that he hasn't noticed her eyes brimming over.

"That must be awful. I'm sorry."

"My kids . . . they're difficult. They've never really wanted to be close to me or their father. Sometimes I think they saw through both of us."

He nods. "Kids are good at that."

"I should stop calling them kids. They're not kids anymore. All in their twenties. Full-grown cunts now!" She laughs, in the hopes of fighting back the rest of the tears.

Bennett looks shocked, though he's quick to cover it up. "And I take it you and your ex don't get along, either?"

"Ha! No," she says.

"Stupid question, sorry. Has he"—here Bennett searches for the right words—"moved on?"

The questions are coming so thick and fast now that Kirstie wonders if maybe she'd like to go back to when he wasn't asking her any questions at all.

"No idea," she says. "I hope not."

He stops chewing and looks at her pityingly.

"I don't want him back! Is that what you think?"

"Maybe . . ." he admits. "I kept hoping my wife would ditch the twat she left me for and come crawling back."

"Do you still?" she asks, turning the tables, though she doesn't really think she needs to. It's pretty clear he'd take his ex back in a heartbeat.

He doesn't answer immediately. "I know she won't. That's the important thing. There was a fine line between hope and delusion there for a while." He draws the last of his wine. "Jesus. If we're going to continue this conversation, we're going to need another bottle," he says, trying to lighten the mood.

"We'll get a Châteauneuf-du-Pape this time." She smiles at him. She has the distinct feeling that he's never told anyone what he just told her about his ex. Furthermore, she suspects Bennett is still prone to delusion. She could share with him her firm conviction that *all* hope is delusional, but she doesn't want to break his spirit. He's the first person in a long time that she wants to rebuild instead of smashing into a million tiny pieces.

Waving down Ellie, she orders the bottle even though she knows she'll be incredibly drunk by the time they finish it. It should worry her that she has no idea where she is or how to get home. If Bennett leaves her to meet his girlfriend, she'll have to get back to West London all by herself, blind drunk. But maybe they'll go home together. Maybe Bennett's not the only one who is delusional.

"It's usually the other way around," Bennett explains, after tasting the new bottle of wine. "Most people order the expensive bottle first and the shit bottle last."

"No they don't, darling. Most people start out sensible, then they get pissed." She takes a sip for good measure. "Then they get depressed and the only cure is Châteauneuf-du-Pape."

He laughs. "You clearly know what you're talking about."

"Yes, I do."

He stops laughing, abruptly, and pulls his phone out of his pocket. "Sorry, it keeps vibrating. Just want to check it isn't Mia." He looks down at the screen, then holds the phone out at arm's length, across the table, to read a text message.

"You want my glasses?"

He gives her the stink eye. "No." He squints at the screen. "It's Claire, not Mia. She wants to know if I am coming to the bar tonight."

"We'll finish up here," she says, trying to hide the disappointment in her voice. "I've commandeered you long enough."

"If we finish this bottle of wine," he says, running a hand through his hair, "I'm going to be too drunk."

"Drink some water," she says. "You'll be fine."

He picks up his glass of water and takes a big gulp. Blimey, if she told him to walk in front of traffic, would he?

When the screen lights up, Bennett again looks at his phone. "Alright, I told her I'd be in Soho in an hour."

Kirstie nods, bravely. She's been lucky to have his company all day. It's time to let him go. He had a life before she stepped into his house and she needs to let him keep it. Tomorrow she'll start thinking about how to find fulfillment in her own life. She'll call Priya and ask the necessary questions about the Barbican flat. She'll look into adult education classes. She'll find a yoga group. She'll call the kids and she'll leave Bennett alone.

"Bollocks," he says, looking at her with the kind of expression a father gives his teenage daughter. "You don't know how to get back to West London."

"I'll head west," she says, taking her final bite of steak. She'd swear the look he's giving her now is pity. She doesn't want to be pitied. "I'll be fine."

"Alright . . ." He's unconvinced.

"Do you want me to send you a text when I'm home safe, Dad?"

He rolls his eyes.

She shouldn't be this way. He's only showing he cares. Sure, she's disappointed he's leaving her tonight, but she's also annoyed that he doesn't think she's capable of getting back on her own. "I'm not an idiot," she says, putting a cap on it.

"I didn't say you were," he responds, frustrated, putting his fork down and looking right across the table at her. "I brought you to a neighborhood you don't recognize and now I'm abandoning you and I feel badly about it. I just want to help. I'm not as oblivious as you think I am."

"I know. I'm sorry." She pushes her plate away.

"That was a lot of steak," he says, staring down at an empty white plate but for one lonely bone.

"Thank you for indulging me."

"Pleasure."

"Let's get the bill and get you to your pretty lady." She waves at Ellie to get her attention.

"Please, can we split it?" Bennett asks.

"Don't be daft. You've been a big help to me today. I owe you."

"I really didn't do anything, Kirstie."

She's not sure he's called her by her name until now. Her whole body tingles. "You did!" You made me laugh, she thinks. You re-minded me what it's like to hear another person laugh. But there is no point explaining this to him. It would only sound pathetic. "Let me do a nice thing for you."

"Okay," he says, putting his hands up in the air in surrender as Ellie puts the bill on the table.

||||||||||||||||||||||

On the cab ride home, she warns herself not to get too excited about her day with Bennett. Sure, he seems like a sweetheart, but she can't let another man derail her plans. Besides, men like Bennett, they never know what they want. To them, life is like the conveyor belt at a sushi restaurant: Just take what you want as all the choices pass by. Try lots of things and then forget about all of them once you've moved on to the next. His poor girlfriend. Maybe he's like this with all his guests. She did notice on the AirBed website that the majority of his reviews were written by women. All positive. His house might be nothing more than a conveyor belt of single women who come into his orbit and leave again. It's a perfect setup, really. Amazing more single men haven't thought of it.

|||||||||||||||||||||||||

The crystals look lifeless when she walks into the master bedroom. The citrine—the keeper of her hopes and dreams—is looking particularly dull in the dark room. Under the depressive curse of red wine, all the promise they held earlier now feels like a load of bollocks. They're all just rocks, good for nothing, except maybe propping open a door. Over the course of their marriage, Albert turned her to stone, now she's surrounding herself with rocks. It's like a fucking quarry in here, she thinks. She lied to herself about Albert for thirty years, telling herself that he didn't mean the things he did. Is she really going to lie to herself about the potential of these damn rocks for *another* thirty? No, she's going to learn to live with the truth, even if it's uncomfortable. She gathers up the amethyst, the rose quartz, and the citrine and takes them all down to the kitchen and dumps them in the bin.

She heads back upstairs with a glass of water. The hangover effects of three bottles of wine have already started to kick in before she's even fallen asleep. She takes off her clothes, but can't be bothered with a nightgown. Hot and sweaty, she doesn't want any fabric clinging to her. She stretches across the width of the bed in nothing but her compression underwear. Eventually she slips those off, too. Lying back down, on the bed, so that her feet hang over the side, she feels the tightly wound coils of her intestines begin to unravel in gentle ripples. She's falling asleep before she can even turn herself the right way around on the bed. Maybe she won't do any of the things she told herself she would tomorrow. Maybe she'll do nothing at all, she muses, as she starts drifting off. When she wakes up in the morning, maybe she'll just roll over and sleep through the day. She could sleep through all the days and nights until it feels like there's a reason not to. She has no idea what that reason would be, but that's been the problem all along, hasn't it? Maybe if she doesn't know what she wants to do or where she wants to do it, she should just do nothing in the place where she already is.

She wakes up when light comes cascading through the window facing the garden. Pulling herself up off the bed, she turns back the covers, preparing to climb in, when she sees Bennett is standing at the door of his studio. He's feeling for his keys. The clock on her bedside table says one a.m. He's looking up at her now, her breasts illuminated by the floodlight attached to the side of the house, and he doesn't move. She turns back to the bed, offering him nothing, not a wave or a smile.

He's not the answer, she tells herself. She has to decide what she wants, how to spend her days, and where to live them. And she has to do it alone.

DREAMY DAYS—COME WHAT MAY

It's mid-morning, but Bennett is still in his pants, the blackout curtain drawn. He really should give the damn thing back to Claire, but she hasn't asked for it. Right now, it's keeping the room cool during this improbable May heat wave that's making him feel both lazy and irritable. It's also creating some much needed space between him and Kirstie, who, now that the weather is hot, is spending all her time out in the garden with one of those little electric hand fans that sounds like a swarm of bees. He's been sitting on his futon for hours, hitting Refresh on his artist's account page on the Royal Academy website. Roots Manuva thumps quietly from the iPod dock:

> *Dreamy days, come what may, we feel no way*
> *there's gonna be fun and lots of laughter*

It's May 15. Today is the day applicants were told to expect results, when either "short-listed" or "not accepted" will turn up next to their name on the website.

Entering his small painting of Claire into the Royal Academy Summer Show feels like his last real chance at success, though there's no particular reason to think that way. There will be another chance next year, not to mention countless other painting competitions. Still, this feels like a punctuated moment. Maybe he feels this way because of all those poor sods he's been watching on *Britain's Got Talent*, all that bollocks about "This is my last chance to make it as an operatic juggler!" This *isn't* Bennett's last chance to make a comeback as a painter, he reminds himself, hitting Refresh yet again. It just feels like it, because he wants it badly and he's not used to wanting things badly. Until recently, he was used to *having* the things he wanted. He tells himself that he should feel privileged to have had one really successful career. It's probably selfish to want more, but he does anyway and hits Refresh one more time.

Of course, he nearly didn't apply when he realized his old art school classmate Carl Willis would be one of this year's selectors. He hates the idea of being judged by someone with whom he was once equal, if not more successful, but he swallowed what was left of his pride. It was also a risk to enter the smaller painting of Claire. The safer bet would have been to finish and enter the larger painting— Claire seated, statuesque. The wall of fabrics behind her. A Bennett Driscoll. The small painting is bordering on voyeuristic; Claire averts her gaze, looking out the window to the street, her legs tangled up in the billowing peach duvet. He knows that she was aware of him taking the photo of this moment, but still, previous models had always been painted head-on, seemingly competing for his attention with the intricate fabrics on which they were posed. None of that exists in this painting; neither model nor fabric is jealous of the other. Instead they seem more infatuated with each other than they are with the man holding the paintbrush. Everything about this painting is different; he's never painted entirely from a photograph before, let alone one on his phone. He zoomed in and out on the screen, but most of the painting was done from memory. Not just the memory of seeing her lying there naked on the bed, but also the memory of what she felt like, how she tasted and smelled. All the sensory cues he never had with any other models. And might not have again with *this* model. Not after that fight at the Claret.

Bennett Driscoll—Awaiting Status Update, the webpage says, as it has all morning and every day for the last few weeks. He can't help but chortle to himself; this phrase applies to just about every facet of his life.

He and Claire haven't been talking much since the enormous row they got into a couple weeks ago, when he showed up drunk at the Claret after having dinner with Kirstie. Today's news could be a good reason to call Claire. He told her she'd be the first person to know if he's short-listed, though he made that promise before she wanted him dead (her words, not his). Anyway, he intends to keep it, even though he hasn't yet admitted he decided to enter a different painting of her. Plus, he misses her. That night, he assured Claire that he and Kirstie were just friends, though he wonders if that's entirely accurate. It's just that he and Kirstie have a lot in common and sometimes it's nice to feel close to someone that gets you. He shouldn't have told Claire about the Barbican or the fancy steak house and he *definitely* shouldn't have told her about the expensive wine. It was the Châteauneuf-du-Pape that tipped her over the edge. Sharing such a special bottle of wine with another woman, in Claire's mind, was akin to fucking her.

"Châteauneuf-du-Pape!" she shrieked. It was after closing and she and Bennett were the only two people in the whole place. "How dare you?!"

"It's just wine," he mumbled.

"Fuck you! It's Châteauneuf-du-Pape!" she shouted, throwing a dirty rag in his face. She had her red hair down that night, which she doesn't do very often when she's behind the bar. It looked sleek, like she'd just been to the hairdresser. Her dress looked new, too, black and short, like she'd been expecting him to take it off.

"She ordered it, not me," he told her in a weak attempt to defend himself.

"But you *drank* it," she replied.

"Let's you and I get a bottle, then. A better one." He stretched his arms across the bar in exhaustion and defeat. "What's it called? Château Margaret or something?"

"MARGAUX!"

"Okay, fine. Let's get that." He tried smiling.

"You can't get that at eleven-thirty at night, Bennett. They don't sell it at the offie!"

"Alright, tomorrow night," he suggested, desperate to make this problem go away.

"Piss off, Bennett."

The room was starting to spin, so he rested his head on the bar.

"Go home to your new girlfriend."

He banged his forehead lightly on the wooden bar, thinking maybe that might stop the spinning. It didn't.

"We should take a break," she said, with finality.

"Because I drank Châteauneuf-du-Pape?" he asked, giving the name a hint of sarcasm, which he immediately regretted when he realized she was about to cry.

"Because you don't know what you want."

That's not true, he thought. He did know what he wanted. He wanted the argument to stop. He wanted to run his fingers through her silky hair. He wanted to sleep in her bed with the comfortable pillow-top mattress pad. And he wanted to wake up with an erection and somewhere nice to put it. He wasn't going to get any of these things, all because he drank some stupid bottle of French wine that, if he's honest, didn't taste any different from the plonk they sell at Khoury's.

Bennett and Claire: Awaiting Status Update.

The next afternoon, after the throbbing headache and the feeling of impending vomit had finally subsided, he went to the wine shop on Turnham Green Terrace and asked how much a bottle of Château Margaux would cost. "Depends on the vintage," said the toff behind the counter, who looked like an anorexic wax statue of Prince William.

"A good vintage would be around five hundred pounds," the man said, tapping the pocket square in his starched blue blazer, insinuating it was worth about as much.

Fuck that.

Kirstie was sitting in the garden reading a magazine when he returned sans Margaux. "How's your head?" she asked, a self-conscious smile on her face.

"Been better," he admitted. He ran his hand through his hair, remembering the sight of Kirstie, naked, at the bedroom window. He should have gone inside immediately, but he didn't. He just watched her until she crawled into bed. He had no idea whether he should mention any of that.

"Want me to fry you an egg?" she asked. "Helps me when I'm hungover."

His stomach churned, either at the thought of an egg or the

thought of the awkward conversation. Or both. "No, thank you," he said, adding, "I'm still full from that steak." Better than admitting there was no way he'd be able to keep an egg down.

When he headed back to the studio, she closed her magazine. "Is everything okay?"

"Yeah, fine," he said and immediately wondered why he hadn't told her the truth. "Have a nice day."

Bennett and Kirstie: Awaiting Status Update.

||||||||||||||||||||||

He hits Refresh, again. Nothing. Being short-listed doesn't even guarantee a place in the show. All it means is he'll get the privilege of taking the painting all the way to Mayfair, leaving it at the Royal Academy, and crossing his fingers that they'll hang it.

He looks out the window, through the curtain, at Kirstie, who is again sitting on the terrace sofa. She's in her yoga clothes, which she's taken to wearing more and more over the last couple weeks. Perhaps for both their sakes, she's stopped wearing the sexy outfits. Is she even doing any yoga? Mostly she just sits on that sofa, drinking tea, reading magazines, or playing on her iPad. All the energy and ambition she had earlier on seems to have vanished, and he wonders if it has something to do with the ex-husband. She's mentioned the guy being a wanker a couple of times, but Bennett hasn't enquired further. He's sick of hearing what wankers men are, though it's true, they are. But women can be total cunts, too, sometimes. The difference is that he's not allowed to say that. He hits the Refresh button on his computer really hard this time. Nothing.

Do something, anything, else.

There's a pair of jeans on the floor, so he picks them up and slides them on.

There. Something.

He hasn't started on a new painting since he finished the small one of Claire a few weeks back. His intention had been to go full steam ahead on a series of nudes, especially after Carl's assessment that he needed to return to his old subject matter, but he's found himself stuck, too apprehensive to move forward. He's never gone this long without painting. He's not sure which direction to go in. The old style or the new. Hearing back from the Academy would help. Plus, he'd thought he'd do a few more of Claire from life, instead of photos, but she's made it clear she'd rather not be in the same room with him. He's even thought about asking Kirstie. Hell, he's already seen her naked and he'd been struck by how perfectly still she could stand, reminding him of an Edward Hopper painting. And it's not like she's doing anything besides lounging around in the garden. Still, he hasn't asked her because he knows that would be crossing a line. After all, she's *paying him*. That leaves him with hiring a model, which he hasn't done in years. How does one even do that nowadays? Advertise on the Internet? God only knows who'd come through the door. He supposes he could ask for recommendations, but that seems awkward, too. *Seen any naked ladies you've liked, lately?*

He looks out the window, again, just as Kirstie looks up from her iPad. Seeing him, she waves, beckoning him outside.

Shit.

"You alright?" she shouts, when he opens the door.

"Yeah, fine," he replies, hands in his pockets, leaning in the doorway.

"I haven't seen much of you recently. Thought maybe you were avoiding me."

Yes.

"No. Of course not."

"I just got an e-mail from Priya, the estate agent," she says, lifting up her tablet. "Someone else has made an offer on the flat in the Barbican."

"What are you going to do?" he asks, stepping out into the garden.

"Let them have it, I guess," she says, deflated. "You were right, I was rushing."

He looks at his feet. She *had* been rushing, but now it feels like *he's* crushed her dream. Why would she take advice from a guy who makes life decisions at a glacial pace? "I'm rarely right, Kirstie."

She frowns at him, sensing his self-deprecation.

"I live in a shed in my back garden. You should never take advice from me."

"Sit," she commands, tapping the sofa cushion next to her.

She really needs a pet.

But he does as he's told. The waterproof fabric makes a crinkling sound when he plops down.

"I'm worried I've done something to upset you."

It's possible she was sleepwalking that night she appeared, naked, at the window. Maybe she has no memory of it. "No, nothing," he says.

She looks at him, curiously. "You're hesitating . . ."

"Claire wasn't so happy about our dinner."

"Ah," she says, setting down her iPad. "I'm sorry I got you into trouble."

He doesn't think she's really sorry at all. She sounds more irritated than sorry.

"I think she's looking for things to be angry about, honestly. I'm not sure I'm the man she had in mind."

"Who do you think she had in mind?"

"I don't know . . ."

"Yes, you do!" She slaps him playfully on the arm, as she's done several times before. Eliza used to do that, too, whenever he feigned ignorance, which was a lot.

"I think, maybe, she thought dating a painter would be more romantic."

Kirstie rolls her eyes. "Don't date someone that makes you feel bad about yourself." She has a way of making things sound so simple. Far simpler than they are, actually. After all, if life was as simple as Kirstie makes it out to be, she wouldn't be divorced and renting his house or asking him what she did to upset him.

"I find out about the RA Summer Show today. I just want to have good news for her."

"You want to have good news for *you*," she scolds. "You painted it, not her."

Yes, obviously. He stands up. "You been okay? Is everything alright with the house?"

"The *house*, darling, is fine."

He nods, slowly, absorbing the clear implication that the house is fine but the woman is not. He never knows how to respond to such insinuations. Do you acknowledge them or not? If she wants him to know something, she should just tell him.

"If you need anything, let me know," he says in his usual Super Host voice to his less-than-usual guest. By the time he reaches the door to his studio, she's picked up her iPad again. Returning to the futon, he immediately wishes he hadn't come back inside.

||||||||||||||||||||||||

It's four p.m. when he hits Refresh and he sees his status has finally changed. He's been staring at **Awaiting Status Update** for so long he can scarcely believe what he sees: **Bennett Driscoll—Short-listed.** He hits Refresh another time to make sure it's not an error. Maybe he should wait a little while before telling anyone, just in case the Academy wants to change its mind.

He looks outside at Kirstie who is still out on the sofa, this time with a magazine, a glass of white wine, and her stupid little fan. She sees him watching her and gestures both a thumbs-up and a thumbs-down, then throws her hand up in the air to ask "Which?"

He smiles, giving her a thumbs-up. *Technically, that's not* telling *her first, right?*

She gives him a little fist pump and settles back into her magazine.

His mind leaps, immediately, to what this could all mean. Maybe the *Guardian* will do a profile on him. "Bennett Driscoll Is Back and Better Than Ever" will be the headline. Under it will be a picture of him in his studio, an army of nudes behind him. He'll have his hands in his pockets, and he'll be staring straight at the camera, looking serious, dressed in his paint clothes. Everyone who looks at it will think: *This man lives and breathes painting. He IS painting.*

It's just short-listed. It's not in the show, yet. And just like that he's back down to earth. Maybe he should wait until it's definitely in before he tells Claire?

Jesus, just call her.

Even though it's been a while since they've talked, she's still near the top of his Recents list, just below Mia. He takes a deep breath.

"Hi," Claire answers, solemn, after a couple rings.

"Hi. Is this a bad time?"

"No. Just waiting for the bus. On my way to work."

"You don't normally work Thursdays."

"I changed my schedule." He can hear her feet scraping along the pavement.

"Oh."

"Did you expect me to consult you, first?"

"No." He doesn't want to tell her his news anymore, so the line goes silent.

"Why did you call, Bennett?"

"I wanted to tell you something."

"Alright, tell me." Her tone suggests that nothing he could possibly say would be what she wants to hear.

"The painting of you got short-listed for the RA Summer Show."

"Okay," she says after a moment's silence.

"It's actually not the one you posed for."

"Huh?"

"It's from a photo of you on my phone," he says, trying to sound nonchalant.

"Seriously? You painted a naked portrait of me without my permission?"

"You let me take the photo. It's beautiful."

"That's not the point!"

"Do you want me to withdraw it?" *Please say no, please . . .*

"Send me a photo of it." She hangs up.

Finding a photo of the painting on his phone, he texts it to her.

Keep it in, she writes back.

He smiles, responding, *Maybe I'll come in tonight for a glass of wine at the end of your shift?*

It's just a painting, Bennett.

What do you mean?

We're still at an impasse. It doesn't change anything.

"Congratulations, Bennett," would be nice.

He doesn't know how to respond. He's got no idea what she wants, and it's not like he can ask her. She'll only accuse him of not paying attention. He could spend five hundred pounds on the bottle of Château Margaux, but she might decide to smash it on the ground in front of him. If she did drink it, she probably wouldn't share it with him.

Fuck it.

He should be celebrating. He launches himself off the futon and grabs his tea mug that's sitting by the sink. He gives it a quick rinse before opening the door to the garden.

"Gimme some wine!" he says, and Kirstie smiles back.

||||||||||||||||||||||||

"Shall we order a pizza?" Kirstie asks, two hours and two bottles of white wine later. "I'm starving."

"Sure." He's getting hungry, too, and he knows he hasn't got anything in his fridge except for a block of cheddar that's getting dried out and crusty at the corners.

"A big, dirty pizza," she explains. "Like a Pizza Hut. None of that healthy, thin crust bollocks."

"You really hate healthy food, don't you?" he asks, thinking back to their big steak dinner.

"My ex was a health nut. Nothing processed. Everything organic. I'm rebelling." She fiddles with her phone, but then stops, abruptly. "Don't you ever do that?" She looks at him, keenly. "Do something just because your ex-wife would hate it?"

He thinks about Roots Manuva and smiles. "I started listening to rap."

Kirstie grins, pleased with that response. "Well, hopefully the fatty food is just a phase or I'll end up looking like a blimp."

Now he can't help wondering if she's been wearing the stretchy yoga pants because she can't fit into tight jeans anymore. He really wishes he wasn't facing her head-on at the moment. "Nah," he says, "it's very difficult for people our age to gain weight." He tries to keep a straight face but breaks out into a wide grin.

Making her face tight as a fist, she grabs one of the sofa cushions and throws it at him. It's dense enough that when it hits his face, he can feel the cartilage in his nose click.

"What are your preferred toppings, you bastard?" she asks, returning to her phone.

He tries to wiggle his nose back into place. "I don't mind. You choose."

"I'll choose ham and pineapple," she warns him.

"Ham and pineapple, it is." He smiles, because that actually sounds good and also because unlike Claire, Kirstie is so easy to please. He tucks himself further into the sofa, getting comfortable.

"Done."

"How?!" He leans forward. "You haven't called yet."

She holds out her phone to him. "It's called an app, old man." She tosses the phone on the sofa and slouches down. "Beautiful evening," she says. "Finally, a breeze."

They both relax into the sofa and listen as the air rustles the leaves on the trees.

"You must miss the sea?" he asks, thinking that with her famous actor husband, she must have had an ocean view in Salcombe.

She smiles at him. "I was ready for a change."

"I should have guessed," he says. "The Barbican is about as opposite to the Devon coast as you can get."

"I should start looking again. Either that or you and I have to live like this forever." She studies him, no doubt trying to gauge his reaction.

"This isn't so bad," he says, taking a sip of his wine. Kirstie hadn't let him drink out of his mug, instead making him go inside the house for a proper glass. When he pulled the glass from the hanging rack in the kitchen, it squeaked so familiarly along the cast iron that, for a moment, it was like the last two years of his life hadn't happened at all, like Eliza would be there, standing at the kitchen island, when he turned around. She'd be wearing her bright red apron with her rusty brown ringlets falling in front of her face as she chopped an onion. She'd look up at him, tears streaming down her face, and he'd wrap his arms around her and say, "Don't cry, baby. It could be so much worse." Then he'd kiss her until the onion juice made his own eyes burn.

A lot worse.

"Why don't you move back into the house?" Kirstie suggests.

He's thought about it a few times—sharing the house with Kirstie. The company would be nice and so would a comfortable bed. But he can't shake how melancholy it would make him feel to be inside its walls again.

"I don't think I can," he explains. "Too many memories in there. It's not you."

"You don't have to explain," she says, and genuinely seems to mean it.

He feels his phone vibrating and he's instantly terrified it's Claire. Has she changed her mind about tonight? Will he have to admit he's gotten drunk again with the very same woman? But no, it's Mia's name flashing up on the screen.

"Sorry." He shows Kirstie the phone. "It's my daughter."

"Go on, please."

He walks over to the center of the garden. "Hi, darling. You alright?"

"Dad . . ." He can hear her voice trembling on the other end.

She's pregnant.

"What's wrong?" Pacing the lawn, he makes a face at Kirstie, like this might take a while.

"Calum and I broke up."

Thank fuck.

"Oh, Mia, what happened?" He can hear her sniffling and gurgling, trying to hold back sobs.

"He punched Richard!"

"What? Why would he do that?!"

Aside from the fact that Richard's obnoxious.

She takes a deep breath. "He thought Richard and I were too close."

Bennett does his best to stifle his laughter. "He does know Richard is gay, right?"

"Yeah." She manages a little giggle herself.

"So why did he think that?" Bennett asks, pacing the whole width of the garden, now, trying to drag out the necessary information.

"Because Richard told Calum he is too controlling."

This is getting complicated. "Is he?" *What does that mean?*

"Maybe. A little."

"Mia, has Calum ever hit you?" He looks over at Kirstie, who visibly stiffens at this question.

"No. It's okay, Dad."

"Right . . ." He has no choice but to believe her. "Is Richard okay? Where did he get hit?"

"His left eye."

For a split second Bennett imagines taking his thumbs and pushing Calum's eyeballs into the back of his skull. "Do you want me to come over?"

"No," she says, sniffling loudly. Bennett can hear all the snot being vacuumed back up into her nose. When she was a baby, he used to extract all her bogeys by putting a little pipette up her nostril. It's probably not useful to remind her of that now. "I'm gonna watch romantic comedies and eat Ben and Jerry's with Richard and Gemma," she adds. "I'll call you tomorrow."

"Okay. Tell Richard to put some ice on that eye."

"We don't have any ice. He's got a frozen pork pie on it."

"I'll buy you some ice trays."

"Dad . . ."

"Let me do something," he says, shaking his head to show Kirstie his exasperation. "Please?"

Kirstie smiles back, putting a hand on her heart to show she understands.

"Okay, Dad. Buy ice trays."

"I love you."

"Love you, too, Dad."

"What happened?" Kirstie shouts from the sofa, when he hangs up the phone.

"I guess I don't have to worry about the boyfriend anymore," he answers, still staring down at his phone, confused. "When Mia says he was 'too controlling,' what does that mean exactly?" He turns to Kirstie, worried.

Kirstie's face has gone pale. "It's not good news. Have they broken up for good?"

"I think so."

"Good." She nods, aggressively.

"He punched her best friend, Richard, who was apparently trying to warn her that the guy was a creep."

"That's a good best friend she's got."

Bennett is surprised to find himself in full agreement. "She claims Calum never hit her."

"He probably did everything but . . ." Kirstie says, quietly. She taps the sofa, again, encouraging Bennett to sit back down.

He remembers his own father, the way he used to torment his mother emotionally, and how bloody proud of himself he was for never actually hitting her. Bennett flops back on the sofa like he's just finished a marathon. Kirstie puts a hand on his shoulder and strokes it. He'd love to curl into her right now. He'd like her to stroke his hair the way Eliza used to when he was worried about something.

"She's a smart girl for getting rid of the bastard. Guys like that don't get better. They get worse."

Bennett recognizes the expression on Kirstie's face as she says this. He's seen it before, not long ago, back in January when his guest Alicia was staying. He recalls her striding across the garden to his studio door, distraught. When he joined her in the garden that morning, she told him she had to go home early. At the time, he thought he was looking at someone who was profoundly lost. But she wasn't just lost, he realizes, she was broken. He knows that now, looking at Kirstie.

He swallows hard, remembering the tears in Kirstie's eyes the first day they met and how she clearly wanted to linger and talk. She was broken, too. And he'd been pushing her away. How had he not understood she was hurting? Or worse, had he understood and not cared? Turning to her now, he asks, "Your husband. He hit you?"

She rolls her eyes, then looks away, unwilling or unable to meet his eye. "No. He was too smart for that. Didn't want to damage my face, one of the few good things about me. Mostly he berated me. A few times, when he was particularly angry, he tried to strangle me."

"Jesus." Without thinking, he reaches out to take her hand.

And what of Mia, he wonders. How much damage did Calum do? Will she ever have to move across the country or travel halfway across the world just to repair the damage that bastard did?

Kirstie smiles, resolutely, fighting back tears. "Anyway, it's all over now."

"I'm sorry," he says. "I should have realized."

"Don't be daft. How on earth could you know if I didn't tell you?" She squeezes his hand. "No need to apologize, just keep making me smile."

He makes a mental note to do exactly this. Until she mentioned it just now, it hadn't occurred to him just how much he enjoys making her smile. No easy task, though, making someone smile, day in, day out. In fact, it might be the hardest thing in the world.

"Your girlfriend wouldn't be happy about this, either, would she?" she asks, looking down at their clasped hands.

"No. I guess not." He removes his hand. He hadn't even been thinking about Claire and now he feels bad about that, too. "We're not really talking. I have to decide between moving in with her or ending it."

"Okay." Kirstie sits up, looking him in the eyes, now. "Which is it?"

He stares at her, blankly. Doesn't have the answer.

"Oh, poor Bennett." She shoves him. "You have no idea what you want."

He rolls his eyes. "That's what Claire says."

"That's alright, you know? Not knowing." She sits back again and stares out into the garden. "I don't know what I want, either."

They sit quietly for a moment and Bennett thinks that what he wants more than anything is not to feel stuck anymore, to feel like he's moving toward something. He'd like to have more nights like this one, enjoying the breeze. He also wants to eat pizza.

||||||||||||||||||||||||

The next morning, after his run, he resolves to do something he thought he'd never do: go see Richard at the coffee shop. He owes the kid, because Kirstie was right—having a best friend like that is rare. Bennett knows that well enough, because he doesn't. Last night, in the back garden with Kirstie, he wondered if maybe she could be that friend for him. It feels like she's looking out for him, and he thinks he'd like to look out for her, too. There's just one problem. He's worried he might be falling for her. In bed last night, he fell asleep thinking about how soft her left hand was and wondering if the right one is the same.

There are *so* many reasons to banish his feelings for Kirstie, all of which he lists to himself on the Tube journey to Soho. One: Their relationship is still, technically, a business one, and you shouldn't fancy someone who's paying you. Two: He has no idea how *she* sees him. If he tells her about his feelings and she doesn't reciprocate, that could be bad for both their business relationship and their budding friendship.

Three: Even if she does have feelings for him, her divorce is very recent and he doesn't want to be her rebound. Four: He's worried that he only finds her attractive because she's more damaged than he is. Five: She reminds him a lot of Eliza, and Eliza left him. Six: She's a pain in the arse. Seven: Claire. Claire. Claire. Remember her?

Sitting across from him on the train, a little boy smiles every time Bennett lifts a finger, counting. The child shifts himself to the end of his seat in eager anticipation of the conclusion—the eighth, then the ninth, then the tenth (Jackpot! Ten fingers!). When Bennett drops both hands in his lap at seven and slouches back in his seat, the kid frowns and buries his head in his mother's breast.

Bennett reaches into his coat pocket and turns up the volume on his iPod:

> *I got the sudden urge to miss behave*
> *I want to take you away from all the stresses*
> *Buy you nice flowers and expensive dresses*
> *You don't believe me, you think I'm cheesy*

Last night, after they finished their pizza, Kirstie asked if he wanted to come in and watch a movie, but he declined. He'd probably have felt like teenage boy on his first date at the cinema, so he lied, saying he wanted to call Mia to check in on her again.

He hasn't seen Kirstie yet today, probably because it's been drizzling all morning. The heat of the past few days has finally been broken by a cloudburst. He glanced in her windows a couple times this morning, hoping to catch a glimpse of her moving around in the kitchen with her hair tied up in a high, messy ponytail and her tummy compressed by her tight spandex top. There we go, eight: The spandex. (The little boy has given up on Bennett and is playing with his own fingers, now.) If Kirstie actually fancied him, she'd go back to those sexy wrap dresses.

|||||||||||||||||||||||||||

It's midday when he enters the coffee shop on Berwick Street, the spitting rain coats his blazer. His leather boots, light tan when he left the studio, are now a medium umber. He'd passed by the Claret on the way, though on the other side of the street, and he'd only half-glanced inside the pub from under his large umbrella. There was a silhouette in the window that looked like Claire's.

The coffee shop is small, only a half dozen tables, all white Formica, each decorated with a small terrarium of succulents. More plants hang in baskets from the ceiling, their leaves and vines dangling. Bennett has to duck under one to get to the counter, where Richard is sulking behind the large espresso machine, not at all his usual chipper self. He doesn't even look up as Bennett approaches.

"Hello, mate, what can I get ya?" says the girl behind the register with a bull ring in her nose and a thick Australian accent.

"Can I have a flat white, please?" He leans over the counter to get a better look at Richard's black eye, which confuses the Aussie.

"'Course, mate. We can do that for you. Anything else?"

"Make that two, actually. One for Richard here, as well."

When Richard looks up from scraping espresso grinds out of the filter, he's wearing the expression of one of those sad, abused children from the NSPCC ads—the ones that aren't really sad or abused, just paid to act like they are on TV. His left eye is puffy and purple, the lid swollen. "Mr. D!" he shouts, brightening considerably. He comes out from behind the counter at a trot to give Bennett an enormous hug. "You came!"

"How's the eye?" Bennett asks, trying his best to loosen Richard's death grip and get a better look at the bruise.

Richard steps back, striking a silhouette pose. "Do I look tough?" he asks. The purple eye is shiny like the butt end of an aubergine. Richard puts up his fists and growls.

"Terrifying." *Honestly.* "Does it hurt?"

"Fuck, yes! I got it, Misty," Richard hollers when his coworker leaves the register for the espresso machine. "I want to make Mr. D's coffee. And I'll take my lunch break now," he adds, putting his hand on Bennett's shoulder. "So we can catch up."

Oh, Christ.

While Richard makes the coffee, Bennett takes a seat at one of the white Formica tables by the window, where he can watch the rain. Outside, the market men of Berwick Street huddle under their plastic tarps, checking their phones, likely for evidence that the rain will let up.

Richard arrives, smiling ear to ear, with two coffees.

Bennett gets right to the point. "I wanted to say thank you," he explains, when Richard sits down.

"What for?" Richard says, brushing off the gratitude.

"You're a really good friend to Mia. I appreciate you looking out for her. I'm sure it's not easy for her to come to me with these types of problems."

"Omigod! Are you kidding? You're the best dad ever, Mr. D!"

Well, maybe.

"That's very kind . . . But the boyfriend stuff is hard to talk about, so I'm glad you're around. Thank you."

"We make a good team, you and I," Richard says, looking at Bennett, seductively, through his one good eye.

Gotta hand it to him, Bennett thinks, sipping his coffee. Richard's commitment to flirtation, despite his face looking like an exploding vegetable, is admirable.

Bennett taps his finger on the white Formica that's chipping away to brown at the corners. "So do I have to worry about this guy coming around again?" Because last night Kirstie had wondered if Richard and Mia might need a restraining order.

Richard waves that off. "I don't think so."

Bennett groans, unconvinced. "How's she doing? I haven't heard from her yet today."

"Omigod, she is *moping* like you would not believe. But yeah, she's totally fine."

Wonder where she gets that from?

"Should I call her or let her mope?"

"Are you asking me for parenting advice, Mr. D?!"

"I'm asking you your opinion, Richard, as her best friend."

Richard puts his hand on his heart, like it hadn't occurred to him before that this is what he might be. "I'd leave her for a bit. I bet she calls you later tonight."

"Alright," Bennett says, taking a deep breath. "I'll try to back off. One more question?"

"Anything," Richard says, reaching across the table to graze Bennett's hand. "Anything."

Bennett pulls back his hand, clears his throat. "Has she told her mother?"

"I don't think so. I mean, you're the one she tells things to, Mr. D. She hates the idea of her mum discussing her personal life with that tosser, Jeff."

Bennett grins. "Thank you, Richard. I needed that." He surprises himself by reaching across the table to grab Richard's hand this time, just for a moment.

"Rumor is, there's trouble in paradise," the boy says, then covers his mouth in pseudo shock, like he hadn't expected the words to come out.

At this, Bennett swallows hard, fearing his flat white might come up. "What do you mean?"

"Mia says Eliza is on this American visa that's about to expire. She was expecting to be married with a green card by now, but Jeff has yet to put a ring on it." Richard flashes his ring finger for emphasis.

"Right," Bennett says, sweat gathering at his temples. Under the table, his legs begin to twitch violently. It's been a long time since he'd considered that Eliza's relationship with Jeff wouldn't last.

"You alright, Mr. D?"

Bennett runs his hand through his hair. "I didn't know any of that."

"Yeah. According to Mia, Eliza might be headed back to London."

|||||||||||||||||||||||

Five minutes later, Bennett is back outside in the rain. He sits down on a bench in Soho Square, ignoring the rain that's pooling on the wooden slats. Burying his head in his hands, he tries to calm his churning insides. His jeans are quickly becoming soaked, but he doesn't care. For months after Eliza left, he dreamed of this exact scenario—his wife coming home with her tail between her legs. Now that it could actually happen, he feels sick, like a sudden onset of the flu. He's not an idiot; he knows that if she comes back, it won't be for him and he hates the idea of having to share London with her again, having to share Mia with her. The best thing about their divorce was that she went far away. If he can't have Eliza then he wants an ocean between them. He rubs his face in his hands, trying to collect himself, then glances over at a Tudor-style hut in the center of the square. When Mia was little, he convinced her that it was made entirely out of gingerbread and frosting and that every year the best behaved children in London were allowed to eat it from the inside out. In the months that followed, Mia behaved like a saint, hoping to earn a piece of that hut. Finally, of course, he'd had to tell her he was kidding, which made him feel so terrible he'd gone to Fortnum and Mason and bought her a gingerbread house to make up for it.

Don't call her.

Mia has her own struggles right now, he reminds himself. When Richard gets home later, he'll tell her about the visit to the coffee shop and she'll surely call him after that. He just has to wait until then. His phone vibrates in his pocket. Maybe that's her now, so he pulls it out.

It's a text from Claire: *Was that you walking by earlier?*

He doesn't even reply, pulls himself up from the bench, and heads back in the direction of the Claret, wiping the wet off the back of his jeans as he walks.

|||||||||||||||||||||||||

"Are you stalking me?" she wants to know, when he walks through the entrance. She's behind the bar, her expression halfway between a smile and a panic attack.

Would stalking her be a good or a bad thing?

She's wearing the same red shirt with the ruffle sleeves she wore the day they met, though it seems to hang on her differently now.

In the back of the bar a group of tourists have pulled together most of the tables and are spreading out a giant folding map of London. Otherwise, the place is empty.

"No." He smiles at her, sweetly, he hopes, because she really does look frightened. As if over the last couple of weeks she's managed to convince herself that he's a monster. "Mia's best friend works at a coffee shop nearby. I needed to thank him for something."

"What?" she asks, clearly not believing this story.

"He took a punch for Mia. She's been dating a creep."

"Oh, wow," she responds, looking guilty now for doubting him, maybe even a little disappointed that he hasn't been stalking her after all. "Is he okay?"

Bennett stuffs his hands in his pockets. "Yeah, fine."

"And Mia?"

"She's alright." He moves closer to the bar. "A little heartbroken."

"Yeah," she says, letting her voice drop, like heartbreak is something she knows all about. "You want a glass of wine?"

"No." Though he takes a seat at the bar, his wet jeans squishy.

"They're not drinking, either," she says, rolling her eyes to the tourists in the back. "They ordered Cokes."

Her annoyance with the tourists reminds him of just how easily irritated she can get and how charming he finds it, until, of course, it's directed at him. "I've missed you," he says.

"Not now," she says, looking down at the bar.

Just that quickly, he's confused. "What, not now?"

"We can't talk about us right now. Not while I'm working."

"That's all I wanted to say," he tells her. Feeling unwelcome, he rises from the stool. "I'll let you get back to work."

At the door, he stops, turning around to look at her. Her face is heavy and tired in a way he's never seen before, even after she's worked a busy shift. He senses that whatever is causing this exhaustion, it isn't something you can just sleep off.

"What?" she asks, as he stares at her, trying to work it out.

Though he knows he probably shouldn't, he says, "You look different."

She nods. "But you don't know why?"

You look knackered and heavy. Can't say that . . .

"No." He wishes he could understand her. Wishes he wasn't always letting her down by requiring an explanation. He thinks about Kirstie last night in the garden, how effortlessly they seemed to intuit each other's needs. "Don't make me guess, Claire, please."

She turns, showing him her profile. He remembers their first meeting in this very bar, when he sketched her standing behind that same counter. He thinks about his hand drawing the contours of her body, the thinness of her neck, the slight lift of her breasts, the curve of her hips. His eyes stall at the slight curve of her belly.

Wait.

He swallows hard before meeting her eyes. He can't possibly tell her what he thinks he sees. That it might be the same thing he saw for the first time twenty years ago, a sight that changed every little thing in his known universe. Life growing because of him, in spite of him.

"It's yours," she says. "Just in case you're stupid enough to ask *that* question."

"I wasn't going to." That's all he can get out. He thinks there must be a million questions he *could* ask, but all he can think about is Eliza moving back to London and Kirstie sitting on the sofa in the garden with a home decor magazine and a glass of wine. Neither of which should matter in the present moment. "How long?" he manages, sitting back down on a barstool.

"I'm ten weeks," she tells him.

We've only been seeing each other for that long.

"Okay." He reaches his hand across the bar, hoping to take hers, but she pulls away. "How long have you known?"

"A while. I thought I was starting menopause," she says, chuckling to herself, even though she clearly doesn't find it funny.

"Why didn't you tell me?" He holds his face in his hands.

"I was trying to make up my mind."

Have you? He watches her, hoping that question doesn't have to leave his mouth.

A couple of older men, regulars, walk into the bar and pull up stools annoyingly close to Bennett, considering the rest of the bar is empty. They nod at him familiarly.

"Hiya, gents," Claire says, throwing beer mats in front of them. "Bottle of Syrah?"

"Summer's coming, doll," one of them says. "How about a rosé?"

"Branching out," she says, smiling at the man wearing an oversize, khaki, button-down shirt with two enormous breast pockets, like he's just come from a safari. "I like it when you keep me on my toes," she adds, filling up a bucket with ice.

Bennett watches her effortlessly flirt with the old men. He remembers how she'd flirted with him the day he sketched her, thinking he could have left it at that, same as these blokes do. Come in for a flirt and then go home a little tipsy. Why hadn't that been enough? Why did he have to go and get her pregnant?

"I'm going to keep it," she whispers, leaning over the bar, their faces just centimeters from each other. "Who else is going to pay for my funeral, right?" This time, even Claire can't laugh at her own morbid joke.

He nods, managing a smile, although to her it must look like the sham that it is. He doesn't want to be a father all over again. He's worried he'll never be able to love anyone else even half as much as he loves Mia. Until this moment, he never thought he'd have to.

"I know it's probably not what you want," she tells him.

"Well, it certainly wasn't the plan, if that's what you mean?"

"There was a plan?" She steps back now, as if she means to include the other men in the conversation. "I'm not going to be one of those women that tells you you don't have to be involved if you don't want to." She points to her stomach. "You did this and I expect you to take responsibility."

He looks over at the other two. They seem to have heard her but are decent enough not to engage. It angers him that she'd even suggest he would abandon her, even though he hasn't yet decided that he definitely won't.

"*We* did that," he clarifies, adding, "And of course I will." He's surprised to hear himself say this with such authority. "What time do you get off work?"

"I'm working a double," Claire tells him, turning toward her regulars. "Not until eleven."

"I'll be back then," he says, getting up from the stool.

"No," she says. "I'll be knackered." The look in her eyes conveys the truth of this.

"I'll call you in the morning?" he says, desperate to make a plan.

"Call me," she says, "when you know what you want."

||||||||||||||||||||

Coming in through the back gate, Bennett regards what he's come to think of as *Kirstie's sofa*. On the journey home, he's imagined her curled up with a cup of tea and flipping through a magazine by lick-ing the tip of her finger to turn the page—a habit that he finds repul-sive when done by any other human being. He knows she won't actually be sitting there, it's pouring out, but his heart still sinks when she's not. He thinks about knocking on her door but wonders if that will break what he feels is an unspoken rule between them—to com-mune only in the garden, their shared space. After all, she hasn't knocked on his door yet, so maybe he shouldn't knock on hers. Even so, he wants to tell her everything: about Eliza, about Claire, about Kirstie herself. He needs her, literally, to hold his hand through all of this.

He takes a few steps toward the main house, changes his mind, and heads instead to the studio. He tosses a plastic bag of ice trays, the ones he bought for Mia—the most useful thing he could think to do after his conversation with Claire—onto the counter. From his shoul-der bag, which hangs by the door, he removes his sketchbook and an HB pencil. He's going to make a list. When he opens the sketchbook, a folded napkin falls out, the one with the stick figure drawing that Claire made for him. He'd forgotten he tucked it in there next to that first drawing he made of her. The two sketches are paired in his mind, and he allows himself to linger on both. He hadn't known her then as he knows her now. He's surprised by how hopeful both sketches are, the beginning of a new chapter he didn't even know he was writing. Taking a seat on the futon, he turns to a blank page and writes *Ques-tions* at the top, underlining it several times. He'd thought Claire was on the pill. Did she forget to take it? he wonders. The answer doesn't matter, so he doesn't write it down, but still, how did this happen? Can he ask her that: *How did this happen?* No. He had sex with her, a lot. *That's* how it happened. Isn't it really hard for women over forty to get pregnant? He read something in the *Guardian* about how women in their forties who want children usually have to rely on expensive therapies like IVF. How has he managed to find the only fertile forty-something on his first try? *Don't write that down.*

Getting up, he puts his iPod on the speaker, thinking some music might loosen up his thinking.

Dreamy days, come what may, we feel no way
there's gonna be fun and lots of laughter

Or maybe not.

Claire's made it clear that she wants him to play a role, but what kind? She can barely stand his presence at the moment. Does she just want money? Does she still want him to move in with her? Does she want to *be* with him? Be a family?

Fuck. A family?

Why does that make him cringe? He's been in a family before and he loved it. It nearly killed him when it all fell apart. Now, he has another chance, why should the word *family* feel like a synonym for *prison*? And what kind of mother will Claire be, anyway? He's never even heard her mention children before, in either a good or a bad way. He can't picture her rocking a baby, or singing one to sleep, or biting off its tiny fingernails. He's guessing she doesn't know about the fingernails or about the pipette and the bogeys. It probably hasn't occurred to her yet just how fucking helpless this little person is going to be. It hadn't occurred to him until he held Mia in his arms for the first time and she made a tiny little fist around his thumb, unable even to close it. And Mia! How will she react to having a sibling?

Jesus.

The thought of Mia having to share his love breaks his heart. She's his whole world and he got *so* lucky with her. As kids go, they don't get any better. And last night, when she called in tears . . . *That never gets any easier.* Can he handle twice as much of that?

And what if he doesn't feel the same way about this kid? What if it cries and he doesn't give a shit? What if he feels no emotions at all and to him it's just an alien in a basket? What would it feel like to wake up every morning and admit to himself that he doesn't love the second child as much as he loves the first? That he doesn't love Claire the way he loved Eliza.

Fuck.

What if the second family isn't nearly as good as the first?

Fuck. Fuck. Fuck.

Christ, last night when he was falling asleep he thought about the Barbican flat, imagining himself and Kirstie living there together.

What a bastard.

Still, maybe none of this matters. Not with Eliza coming back into town. Is it possible to feel anything for any other woman with Eliza back in the picture? It's a crazy thought, but what if she knocks on his door tomorrow and says, "I love you. Paint my portrait." He can't, right? Because of Claire. Because of the baby.

Goddamnit, motherfucking, cocksucking, fuck, fuck, fuck.

He tosses the sketchbook onto the floor, immediately regrets doing so and picks it up again, checking to see that none of the drawings are creased. There must be questions he can ask. He can't just leave that page blank, but his questions are all existential, not practical. He recalls when his guest Emma was staying at the house and the cookie jar she filled with notes to herself—more like strongly held convictions about her circumstances and the world around her. Not facts, exactly, but personal truths. What had she used them for? He can only assume she had a problem she was trying to solve and the slips of paper were the circumstantial evidence. He turns the page and writes down *FACTS*, underlining it several times as well. Below that, he writes, *Claire is pregnant*. This isn't going to change. He has to accept it. She's a bartender and she's going to need money. Her flat isn't big enough for a baby. Whether or not they end up living together, she'll need a bigger place. He tries to picture Claire and the baby moving into the big house with him. Could he be happy with a different family in the same house? *I need to sell the house*, he writes.

Setting the sketchbook aside, he searches for his phone in the folds of the futon, only to realize he's sitting on it. *I am going to sell my house*, he writes to Claire, pressing Send. It makes him feel a little bit proud, like at least he's done *something*.

He imagines that whatever problem Emma was trying to solve was far bigger than the small conclusions she collected in the cookie jar—so big that maybe the problem she was trying to solve was *What's the problem?* Maybe the same could be said for him. His small conclusions: Claire is pregnant; he needs to sell the house; he's stopped painting; he fancies Kirstie; Eliza is coming home. *What's the problem?*

Through the kitchen window, he sees Kirstie approach her kitchen sink with an empty plate and glass. She looks out to the studio and smiles, not directly at him, but at the thought of him, or so he imagines.

Claire's text pops up: *Is that what you want?*

Goddamnit.

Looking down at the sketchbook he sighs, heavily, and writes down the big problem: *You don't know what the fuck you want.*

||||||||||||||||||||||

Mia calls that evening, just as Richard had told Bennett she would.

"You alright?" he asks. "Doing any better today?"

That afternoon he'd started another painting. Unable to face the big problem he'd written down, he turned back in the sketchbook to the drawing of Claire and was surprised by how vividly he remembered the palette and mood of that day. He grabbed another small canvas and placed it on the easel, with the sketchbook next to it, before covering the canvas with a light wash of raw sienna. First, he drew the shape of the bar onto the canvas in dark brown, just like he remembered doing the day he'd made the sketch. Next, he mixed a deep crimson and started to draw Claire's flared shirt sleeve that dropped just below the bar. The same shirt she wore today.

"I don't know," Mia replies, slow and quiet. "I guess? Calum called a couple of times."

Leaving the painting, he goes over the kitchen counter to fill up the kettle with water. "You didn't answer, did you?"

"I did the first time."

"Oh, Mia."

"I know. I learned my lesson."

"What did he say?"

"I don't want to tell you. You'll just get angry."

"Well, I'm worried, Mia," he says, putting the kettle on to boil. "I wonder if we need to think about a restraining order." It's nice, he thinks, to have a different problem to solve.

"Dad, no. Don't be ridiculous."

"Am I?" He leans on the counter, back to the kettle. "What did he say?"

"He called me a bitch, that's all."

"That's all?! That's horrible."

"I won't answer again. I'll block him."

"How about a new phone number?"

"I like my phone number, Dad," she tells him, sounding exasperated, which makes *him* exasperated.

"That's silly. No one *likes* a phone number. Let's get you a new one." When she doesn't respond to this, he begins to ramble. "I bought you some ice trays today. If I'd been smart I'd have bought them before I went to see Richard. Hey, when is your lease up? I bet you guys could break it if you explained the situation. I don't like the idea of this guy coming around at night and banging on your door—"

"DAD! Stop."

He'd like to, but he can't. "You didn't give him a key, did you?"

"Of course not. Fuck sake, Dad."

"Okay." He reaches out and taps the side of the counter a few times, attempting to slow down his brain. "Sorry."

When the kettle starts to boil, he tosses a tea bag into his mug and pours the steaming hot water on top.

"Richard shouldn't have told you about Mum. That's why you're acting crazy, right?"

Not entirely. But he's not ready to tell her the rest of it yet.

"It was a pretty big surprise." *Not the biggest of the day, but still.* He picks up the tea bag by the corner with the tips of his fingers and bobs it up and down until the hot water turns brown. "Why didn't you tell me?"

"I didn't want to worry you, not until I knew for sure whether she was coming back. I wasn't expecting you to go see Richard."

"So, what about your trip this summer? Are you still going?"

"It's on hold for now."

He smiles to himself. Maybe Mia is staying put. Good.

"I think she's planning to give Jeff an ultimatum," she adds.

Sounds about right. Eliza loves her ultimatums. During their twenty-year marriage, Bennett was subjected to several. Most involved withholding sex, which actually didn't bother him as much as she liked to think it did.

"Do you think she'll come back?" he asks.

"I don't know. Possibly."

"Where would she live?" He pulls the milk from the fridge and adds a dollop to his mug. Looking around for a spoon and not finding one, he gives up and stirs it with his paint-coated index finger. The tea is scalding and he pulls it right out.

"She was talking about renting something on AirBed," Mia tells him, acknowledging the irony with a little snicker.

"Is that so?" He, too, lets out a little laugh, wiping his finger on his jeans. "Well, tell her I know a bloke."

"Ha. No way."

"Seriously, though, you will tell me if she's coming back?"

"Of course."

"Maybe I'll send her a little housewarming gift." *A dead rat.*

"Dad . . ."

"What?" he asks, smiling into his cup of tea. "I'm just trying to be nice."

"No, you're not. I can tell by the tone of your voice."

"Who knows, maybe Jeff will come through at the eleventh hour?"

"Is that what you want?" Mia asks. "For Mum not to come back?"

"She's not coming back for me, darling."

"I know, but what if she decides to come back *for me?*"

He sets his mug on the counter, stung by the painful realization that he, on his own, might not be enough for his daughter.

Of course she needs her mother, of course she does.

"I can't think of a better reason for her to come home. I hope she does."

He can sense she is blushing on the other end of the line. Compliments always make her go quiet.

"How's Claire?" she asks, keen to change the subject.

Bugger.

"Yeah, she's alright."

"Don't tell me you're having relationship trouble, too? Jesus, what a family . . ."

"No," he assures her, unconvincingly. "Everything's fine."

"Does she work tomorrow tonight? Maybe you and I can go for a drink at her bar?"

Fuck.

"Let me find out if she's working. Her schedule has changed recently and I can't remember if she's on." *Not a total lie.*

"Well, if she's not working, maybe she can join us for a drink somewhere else?"

Fuuuuuuck.

"I'll find out. You and I should go for a drink and dinner, either way," he says. "I miss you. How long until your end-of-year show?"

"A couple weeks."

"You going to be ready?"

"Barely. I decided to do four smaller paintings rather than one large one."

"Any subject matter you want to warn me about this time?"

"I'll tell you all about them tomorrow night. No surprises."

He wishes he could promise her the same.

||||||||||||||||||||||

Wide awake, he continues painting until two in the morning. He brings the sketchbook to bed with him, laying it on the floor next to the futon, open to the FACTS page. That way, when he wakes up in the morning, he won't wonder whether it's all been a dream. Claire *is* pregnant.

Tomorrow he has to drop off his small Claire painting at the Royal Academy. That, at least, will keep him busy. He looks over at the new painting of Claire. It pleases him that he and Mia have both started making small paintings at the same time. It feels like they're inextricably linked, working from the same genetic paint box. This new one is coming along nicely. A mixture of memory and imagination, Claire fits perfectly into the background of the Claret. He's spent a lot of the evening thinking about what makes the sketch so different from his earlier figure work. Even though she was unaware of him making it, the drawing was still on her terms. Like the other small painting, he didn't pose her. He didn't stage the backdrop. He remembers what she told him at Townhouse—how the woman in the painting there looked uncomfortable. In the sketch, Claire doesn't look uncomfortable at all. She looks in control. It was all Claire, all Claret. This concept, he suspects, is what's been missing all along, the blending of figure and ground. People cannot really be understood without understanding the space they occupy. How had he not realized that? Maybe this is why his old work feels "classical," as Emma called it. The word still haunts him even after abandoning his first Claire painting. It's the reason that painting is currently facing against the wall, unfinished. Furthermore, maybe this is why he's *always* had such a hard time reading his models' expressions. He was treating them as props instead of people. Maybe his preoccupation with capturing Claire's expression has been all wrong. What if her expression doesn't matter? She can make any face she wants. It doesn't change where she's standing, what she's doing, who she *is*. Claire is the Claret and the Claret is her, both richer for the presence of the other. A figure in her ground.

Still wide awake, he sits up and rests his chin on the windowsill, looking at his house, all dark. Kirstie's bedroom window is opaque, but he imagines her naked body, lit up, staring down at him. He can see the image as a painting. They still haven't talked about that night. They probably never will. Maybe they don't need to. Some moments are like paintings—no words necessary.

What the fuck do you want, Bennett?

The question pulses in his mind, perhaps because he's no closer to the answer. He again regards his new painting of Claire on the easel. After a few weeks of no productivity, it felt really good to hold a paintbrush again, to remember what made him fall in love with painting all those years ago. It would be nice, he thinks, to be inspired once more, to wake up in the morning and wonder how he'll pack everything into the day, instead of wondering how he'll fill it.

||||||||||||||||||||||

He's up early in the morning, having barely slept. Eliza, Kirstie, and Claire were all present in his dreams, though not, blessedly, together. They hadn't joined forces to murder him, though it may be only a matter of time before that idea occurs to them. He opens his front door to the garden at seven a.m. and starts unraveling a roll of Bubble

Wrap on the lawn. When he gets down on his knees, he feels a twinge in his lower back and groans. *Honestly, a baby?* He looks up at the sky. *Whose fucked-up plan is this?* He cuts the Bubble Wrap into equal strips, which he tapes together again with packaging tape, the kind that shrieks when you pull on it. A few minutes later, Kirstie comes outside in one of her wrap dresses (*Finally!*) with her hands over her ears. "What on earth are you doing?" she asks.

He smiles up at her. He'd like to leap to his feet and wrap his arms around her, but he can't. Foremost among the many reasons, because his days of leaping are long over. "Taking my painting to the Royal Academy today. Just wrapping it up."

"Can I get a closer look?" she asks. "Before you wrap it?"

"Why not?" he says, and immediately thinks of several reasons. She hasn't been in his studio yet.

She watches as he gets to his feet in stages. "Need help, old man?" *Cheeky little . . .*

She smiles wide. "I could show you some yoga poses that'll make you feel young again."

"I don't know what you're talking about," he says, arching backward, hands on his hips, for a stretch. He gestures for her to enter the studio and follows when she does. She smells amazing, like wildflowers and fresh linen.

"So, this is where the magic happens?" she says. But then she notices the futon, and her curiosity turns to horror. "Are you sleeping on *that*?!"

"I thought you wanted to look at the paintings."

"I do, darling." When she puts her hand on his shoulder, he notices she's painted her fingernails a deep purple. "But no wonder you have a stiff back. Are you sure you don't want to sleep in the house?"

Haven't you heard? I have no idea what the fuck I want.

"It's not so bad."

"I'm offended that you don't want to share the house with me when you're sleeping on that!"

"Don't be. It's not you." He'd give anything for a pile of sand to bury his head in.

She shakes his arm. "Prove it! Stay in the house tonight."

Breathe. He has to remind himself every couple seconds. *Breathe.* Where would he sleep? Mia's old room? In the guest room where he probably impregnated Claire? Or in the master with Kirstie, where he spent twenty years sleeping next to Eliza?

"I'm going out with Mia tonight. I won't be back until late."

"Who cares?" She looks at him, genuinely flabbergasted. "You're a grown man, for Christ's sake. Come back whenever you want."

"Okay."

"Good. Was that so hard?"

Yes.

"Now," she says, rubbing her hands together. "Let's look at this painting."

He picks it up from the floor, where it was leaning against the backs of larger canvases, and hands it to her.

She grips it gingerly and grins at it. "Yes," she says, "I can see why you wanted to start anew. This is so much more visceral. None of the useless details, but so much more *depth*."

He feels a lump the size of a walnut in his throat. "Thank you."

"It's beautiful," she says. "Really," then turns to look at him. "I'm so jealous. God, how I'd love to be this good at something."

He wants to tell her that he finds her perfect just as she is, but he knows it doesn't matter what he thinks.

She puts her arm around his waist. "I find you quite inspiring," she says.

Really?

"The way you just keep working. You could have given up, but you haven't."

He wants to draw her in close, because so far nobody has understood, not even him, that painting this painting was hard. It meant admitting mistakes, it meant stepping back in order to move forward. He feels a tightness in his gut, the kind that comes with realizing your responsibility. A responsibility he feels for Kirstie, to inspire her, to make her smile. The kind of responsibility he hasn't had in a long time and, until now, he hasn't realized he's been missing desperately.

||||||||||||||||||||||||

"Why don't I drive you?" Kirstie asked, after Bennett made the mistake of complaining about how difficult it would be to protect the painting on a congested Tube train.

"The traffic will be terrible. There will be nowhere to park."

"I don't need to park. I'll just drop you off and head home."

"Kirstie, that's too much," he said, and meant it. Sometimes someone else's kindness is far too much to bear, he thinks, especially once you've realized that all you want is to absorb that person's kindness and give it back tenfold, except you can't. There's no way.

But after the initial protest, she wears him down. As she barrels down the Great West Road at forty miles an hour in second gear, he realizes her city driving needs more than a little work. The engine shrieks bloody murder until she finally shifts into third. "Oh. That's better," she says, turning to Bennett, who has a death grip on the car door's handle, the veins in his hand fit to burst.

He surrenders a nervous smile. They've been in close proximity before, but this feels more cramped—the two of them, plus a painting of a naked Claire—all jostling for space in her Mercedes, the physical embodiment of a love triangle he'd hoped would remain in his mind, where it belongs. That's why he had to put the painting in the back seat, out of view. It's now lounging back there, effortlessly, just like Claire always does. Kirstie senses something is up with him, he can tell. She's too astute not to. She keeps looking over at him, trying to read his face.

"My wife had this car," he says, cutting through the silence.

"Then I'm surprised you haven't keyed it." She laughs, slamming on the brakes to avoid running into the back of a red Vauxhall Corsa.

"I never even considered it," he assures her, reaching his other hand out onto the dash.

When the car in front of her moves, she downshifts into second again, causing the car to lurch forward. A moment later she has to break again. "Such a Cub Scout, you are. Where's your sense of menace, Bennett?"

I'm thinking about grabbing the wheel from you. Maybe diving out of this moving car.

"Your mother raised you well," she adds, resolutely.

"She'd have liked to hear that."

"When did she die?"

He likes that she uses the word *die*. He hates it when people say *passed on*. Lives end. Relationships end. They don't pass on to anywhere, they die. "Five years ago." He shifts in his seat, remembering Helen hooked up to all those monitors, gasping for air. She had said her heart felt "like an anvil pressing on her lungs." How was it that she should be the one to get congestive heart failure, while his father got to drift away peacefully during a dream?

"Were you as close to her as Mia is to you?"

"No," he admits, though he immediately feels the need to clarify. "She was a good mum, but I couldn't tell her most things."

"Why not?"

He feels his eyes getting misty. *This is torture.* "She wasn't very interested in the truth. She preferred things with a thick coat of sugar." He stares straight ahead, feeling that if he looked at Kirstie right now, he'd surely cry. "Hey, there's your favorite store," he tells her, pointing at Harrods.

She gives him a wry smile. "You can just say, darling, if you want to change the subject."

Darling. She's been calling him that since day one. She probably calls everyone that, but the way she says it now, with a combination of sweetness and frustration, makes him feel like he's her only darling.

||||||||||||||||||||||

The Royal Fucking Academy. Hello, again.

Waving goodbye to Kirstie, he stands just outside the entrance to the Academy's magnificent courtyard, where a giant orb sculpture glows orange in front of him, looking as hot as the surface of the sun. The artists' entrance is technically through the rear of the building, but he felt bad asking Kirstie to drive around the back; plus, it's nice to look at the grand entrance, to feel grand beside it. After a moment of taking it all in, he enters the opulent Burlington Arcade, moving past all the fancy jewelry shops, to the Academy's back entrance. In one of these shops he bought Eliza's antique 1920s engagement ring, a central sapphire surrounded by six small diamonds. This city, he thinks, is nothing but a map of the past, even as he tries desperately to move forward. Kirstie's words—*you could have given up, but you haven't*—sing in his ears.

||||||||||||||||||||||||

"Oi! Benji!"

Confused and turned around, Bennett searches the Academy foyer. *Where is the fucker?* Finally, he locates Carl Willis at the top of the staircase, arms wide open, a giant two-liter bottle of Volvic Touch of Fruit water in one hand.

"Let's see this beaut'ee," Carl says, descending the staircase and crinkling the plastic bottle like it's a stress ball. There's an artistic rendering of a snarling dog on his tight black T-shirt.

"That Rosie?" Bennett asks, indicating to the dog on the shirt.

"No, Givenchy," he explains without a hint of irony. He extends his free hand to Bennett. "Alright, mate?"

Bennett reciprocates for what starts out as a warm professional handshake, but quickly devolves into an embrace. As Carl pulls him in, Bennett nearly drops the painting. "Yeah, good," Bennett grunts.

"Come on, then. Let me get a look." Carl takes hold of the painting, regarding it. "You're shagging her, I hope?"

Bennett looks down at his toes, runs his free hand through his hair. "No comment."

"Nice one, geez. She gonna be with you at the opening?" Carl looks Claire up and down, not letting the Bubble Wrap spoil his view.

"Yeah, maybe. I don't even know if you guys are going to hang it."

"Of course we're going to bloody hang it, mate. You're Bennett Driscoll."

Bennett suppresses a smile. He doesn't want to give Carl the satisfaction of knowing how happy he's just made him.

"Get your bird a shiny new frock. We'll toast Bennett Driscoll's return to fame." He uses his water bottle as a prop, pretending to pop its top like a champagne cork.

Though he should be thrilled by Carl's enthusiasm, he's overcome by a sense of dread and guilt. *No champagne for Claire.* If she comes at all. He changes the subject. "Where should I take this?"

"I got it, mate." The pervert seems all too happy to hang on to it. "I'll text ya a pickie as soon as it's up on the wall."

"Thanks. That'd be great," Bennett says.

When he moves toward the exit, Carl draws him in for another embrace, then slaps him hard on the back several times. "Proud of you, Benji!"

"Thanks," Bennett says, finding himself welling up again. "I should—"

"Yep, yep," Carl says. "I gotta get back to judging all the other shit-munchers." He laughs. "I kid ya."

No, you don't.

||||||||||||||||||||||

You working tonight? He texts Claire from a bench in Trafalgar Square. He's not sure why he's there. He just started wandering when he left the Royal Academy. Teenagers bounce around in the stone fountains with their pant legs rolled up, splashing each other and screaming, announcing to the world that summer will soon be here.

Yes. Claire writes back. She's a woman of few words these days, especially considering it used to be impossible to shut her up.

Mia asked me to meet her for a drink at the Claret tonight. I'm not sure what I should tell her, he types.

That's strange, you're usually so decisive, Claire texts back.

Walked into that one.

What do you want me to do, Claire?

The three dots come up indicating she was responding, then they disappear. This happens a couple more times, before a short message finally pops up, *Have you told her?*

This is ridiculous. He decides to call her just as a young mother and her little girl, sharing an ice cream, sit down on the bench next to him. Both have tight blond ringlets, and he wonders, for the first time, what the baby will look like. Will it have ginger hair like Claire's? His grey-blue eyes? Mia's infectious smile?

"Hi," he says, when Claire answers. "I haven't told her. I think we should talk more first. But you two really should meet," he says, with as much authority as he can muster. He's surprised to find himself coming to this conclusion, but he wants Mia to meet Claire like he did, in her element. He wants her to meet the Claire from the sketch.

"Alright," she responds. No argument.

"That's what I want. I want you to meet Mia."

"Okay."

"Have you been to a doctor?"

"Yes. A week ago."

"So when we had that big fight, did you know?"

"Just found out, that's why I wanted you to come in." Her voice is getting thinner and thinner. "So I could tell you."

"Why didn't you tell me it was important?"

"Jesus, Bennett," her voice cracks, her anger returning. "I shouldn't have to tell you it's important."

"Sorry," he says, his tone suggesting more aggravation than remorse.

"You were on a date with another woman. I'm clearly not important to you at all."

"It wasn't a date."

The young mother glares at him. Claire's voice is now loud enough for her to hear.

"Bollocks, it wasn't."

"Of course you're important to me, Claire."

"You *have* to say that now."

Yes, I do.

"It's true." He glances over at the little girl, her blissful face planted on the top of the ice cream cone, her mother giggling at the mess. "You've had a scan?" he asks.

"Yes."

"The baby is healthy?"

The young mother stops giggling and stares at him again.

"Yes. Strong heartbeat, the doctor says."

Fuck me. That hits him like a ton of bricks. "Yeah?"

The mum takes a napkin from her purse and wipes chocolate off the little girl's face. Only when her previous look of disdain morphs into concern does he realize there are tears streaming down his face. *Here we go again.* He quickly wipes them away.

"Did they give you a photo?"

"Yes. You want to see it? I can text it to you."

"Really?" *Things have changed a lot in the last twenty years.*

He puts his head in his free hand, holding the phone away from him so Claire won't hear him sniffing. The mother picks up her little girl and leaves him to weep alone.

His phone vibrates and there on the screen is a photo of the sonogram. His child, a barely visible ball of mucus.

Putting the phone back to his ear, he says, "Wow." That's all he can manage.

"I can't get it out of my head that it looks like a turtle without a shell," she says, worried.

He laughs. "That's 'cause my uncle was a turtle. I didn't tell you that?"

"You really think your lame jokes are a good idea right now?"

"No," he says, feeling scolded. "Wait 'til you meet Mia," he says, trying a new tack. "She's beautiful, smart, and not at all annoying, even with my genetics in the mix."

He can hear her breathing, measured and mindful, like breathing exercises.

"Alright. Come in later." She takes another deep breath. "And, Bennett?" she says, wearily. "Come back to mine tonight. Please."

"Oh," he says, remembering the deal he made with Kirstie to stay in the house. "Sure. Of course."

He sets down his phone, the sonogram of the baby still up on the screen. When the image goes dark, he refreshes it, telling himself that if he and Claire can come up with a plan tonight, he'll get excited about whatever that is. Maybe they'll decide he should sell the house and use the money to buy something more modest in Stoke Newington. There's a nice family vibe there. He thinks back to that Saturday when he and Claire were walking down Church Street and she got clobbered in the ankle by a stroller, not once but three times, on the way to Clissold Park. She'd been desperate to have a picnic. "It'll be like an impressionist painting," she'd said, to sell him the idea. They'd gone to Whole Foods, bought a whole lot of fancy cheese and crackers, laid out a picnic blanket just by the pond, and he kissed the bruises forming on her ankle.

Just add your own stroller and a screaming baby to that image.

Was that so hard? He hears the question in Kirstie's voice.

Yes.

That's the thing. Every time he comes up with a suitable scenario for a future with Claire, his thoughts immediately return to Kirstie. Where will she be when he's in Clissold Park playing happy family? Will she be alone? Lonely? Earlier, she asked him to keep making her smile. How can he do that now?

|||||||||||||||||||||||||

When he arrives at the Claret, Mia is already sitting at the bar, leaning forward, showing Claire photos on her phone. Claire is in her tip dress, her cleavage plunging at Mia's eyeline. He watches them through the window as they laugh. Claire reaches across the counter to grab Mia's phone and gasps.

My daughter and my pregnant girlfriend are bonding over a painting of a giant vagina.

He has to linger outside a little longer than intended, because he's getting emotional again. It's an odd thing to get emotional about. *Of course Claire would love that painting. How have I never thought to tell her about it?*

Claire spots him through the window and smiles like she hasn't smiled in so long, like she doesn't hate his guts. Mia turns around and waves her arm like, *Get in here.*

"Don't be a stalker, Dad," she says as he comes through the door.

"I wasn't stalking," he says, putting his arm around his daughter and kissing her on the head. "Just enjoying the view."

Mia gives him her *Don't be weird* look. He loves that look. It only makes him want to be weirder. He glances at Claire. He hadn't really thought about this moment. Will she want him to kiss her or stay away? Before it all got complicated, she would have wanted a kiss, she would have instigated it, but now he's not so sure. He smiles at her. "Hi."

She smiles back. "Hi."

When he puts out his hand, open, across the bar, she places hers in it and he pulls her forward, giving her a gentle kiss on the lips, not the sloppy kind she usually goes for to rile up the regulars. "How are you?" he asks.

She rolls her eyes. "Tourists, all damn day."

He can see out of the corner of his eye that Mia's watching them with a proud little smile, like she's the parent. He gives Claire's hand a squeeze before letting go.

Taking a seat next to Mia, he says, grinning, "You were showing her a picture of that painting, weren't you?"

Mia grins back. "You mean the *vagina* painting?" She winks at Claire, who's pouring Bennett a glass of wine without even asking what he wants. "Dad can't say the word 'vagina.'"

Both women look at him now.

Right. This is why I didn't want these two to meet.

"Seriously?" He looks back and forth between them.

"Go on," Claire says, also grinning now.

"Vagina?" He says the word, slowly, quietly, like it's a secret password, sending both Mia and Claire into fits of laughter. He throws his hands up in the air and then, exasperated, lifts his glass of wine and says, "Cheers."

Mia, still cackling, rests her head on Bennett's shoulder for stability. He sets down his glass and puts his arm around her, then runs his other hand over her hair like he did when she was little. He looks over at Claire on the other side of the bar, who is watching them, misty-eyed either from laughter or the sight of father and daughter, he's not sure.

|||||||||||||||||||||||

Mia and Claire are getting along like a house on fire, as he suspected they would, so well, in fact, that these two women would be just fine without him. They talk about art, about books, about their bordering neighborhoods. And, of course, they talk about Bennett, as if he isn't sitting right there. From time to time, he lets his mind wander. Mostly, he thinks about Kirstie in that big house all by herself, remembering how lonely it was for him after Eliza left. It makes exactly no sense, but he wishes she could be at the Claret with them, even though he suspects that neither Mia nor Claire would like her that much. Well, Claire definitely wouldn't, but he's pretty sure Mia wouldn't, either. Kirstie is brash, assertive, and opinionated. She treats Bennett like a pet, which he finds endearing, but these two surely wouldn't.

He hasn't told Kirstie he isn't coming back tonight and he can't get it out of his head that she might be sitting in the garden with another bottle of wine, waiting to hold his hand and fight through the loneliness together. He knows that what's in front of him, right now, is the opportunity not to be lonely anymore: a girlfriend, a daughter who likes her, and a baby on the way. If Kirstie herself had such an opportunity, wouldn't she take it? Does she see Bennett as that opportunity? If he chooses all this, Claire and the baby, what does Kirstie have left?

What the fuck is wrong with you?

"Dad?!"

"What? Sorry."

"You were a million miles away," Mia says. Both she and Claire are staring at him, Claire's face distinctly more sour than Mia's.

"Nope. I'm right here." He smiles at Claire, but she doesn't soften and he fears she might be able to read his mind.

"I'm just going to pop to the loo," he says, then glances at Mia. "Then you and I should consider getting some food."

Upstairs, he opts for a stall rather than the urinals. He shuts the door, thankful for a moment of solitude. He needs to collect his thoughts and to think what to say to Kirstie. After relieving himself, he sits on the toilet, pants still down at his knees, to compose a text. *I won't be coming home after all*, he writes. *Claire wants me to come over tonight.*

Back in the game, she responds only seconds later. *Well done, you.* I guess so. And though he knows he shouldn't: *Everything okay? Don't be daft, darling. Everything is fine. XXX*

He can picture her brave smile, the one she used when she told him about her wanker ex-husband trying to strangle her. He tells himself maybe it's not a brave smile at all. Maybe it's just a smile. Maybe she's actually, genuinely, happy for him.

||||||||||||||||||||||

Back downstairs, Mia has her purse over her shoulder, ready to go.

"Alright, kiddo, what are you hungry for? Barbecue?"

She huffs, irked. "How about Thai?"

"You got it."

He looks over at Claire. "You want something for later? Take-away?"

"No, thanks," she says, her expression suggesting that she'd rather stay angry than accept any favors from him.

"No spring rolls? You love spring rolls."

"Yeah, alright," she concedes. "Some spring rolls."

He smiles. "Good. How about the wine? What do I owe you?"

"On me," she says, through pursed lips, her arms crossed.

"Don't be ridiculous."

"Buying my boyfriend and his daughter a couple glasses of wine is ridiculous?"

Jesus Christ.

Mia heads toward the door, probably sensing they need some space.

"Thank you." He leans over the counter. "I'll see you back here in a bit."

She nods like a little kid, forced to obey an infuriating set of instructions.

He stands on his tiptoes and leans across to kiss her. She's unwilling to meet him halfway across the bar, so he really has to stretch, his feet finally lifting off the ground.

"Bye," she says with a weak smile.

Mia's already pushing on the door, desperate to escape. "Nice to meet you, Claire! See you soon!" she shouts.

Following Mia out, he glances back at Claire before letting the door close. Her arms are stretched across the bar, propping her up. This stance used to express confidence. The queen in her kingdom. Now it looks necessary for stability.

"She's cross with you," Mia says, once they're out on the street.

"I know," he says, putting his arm around her shoulders.
"Why?"

He swallows hard. He hates lying to his daughter. "Not sure."

|||||||||||||||||||||||||

They have dinner at the Thai place on Wardour Street, the one with the name he can't pronounce. The place with all the communal tables and the heavy smell of incense. Mia shows him images of the paintings she's working on for her end-of-year show. Her interest in feet and hands is paying off, and he's thankful for the anatomical shift. The new paintings, close-ups of couples holding hands and caressing each other's feet, are warm and delicate. They show a tenderness he's relieved she still possesses after his and Eliza's divorce, not to mention her own recent breakup. He wonders if they aren't done from photos of her and Calum, but he doesn't ask. He just beams because she's so excited about them. Nothing, it seems, is weighing this girl down. He knows she hasn't forgotten Calum; she probably still questions her decision to break up with him and probably fears, like everybody does, she'll never find her partner in life. She'll have her pick of partners, of course, but for now, Bennett thinks *he* still makes a pretty good one.

"I have news for you, too," he says, rubbing his fingers, greasy from crab rangoon, on a napkin.

"What's that?" she says, her chopsticks piled high with fried rice.

"I'm going to be in the Royal Academy Summer Show."

"No way!" She shoves him. "What painting?"

"You haven't seen it. It's of Claire, actually."

"Is she naked?" Mia asks, acting scandalized like Richard.

He raises an eyebrow. "Possibly."

"Dad! All my friends go to that show!"

"So what?"

"So everyone's going to know what your girlfriend looks like naked!"

"I'm going to assume most of your friends have seen a naked woman before." He shovels a spoonful of green curry with beef into his mouth. "Hell, if they want to know what a vagina looks like, they can just ask you."

She shoves him again, hard this time. He very nearly brushes up against his communal bench neighbor, a German man in a salmon-pink polo shirt. "You're disgusting!" Mia shouts.

"So," he asks through laughter, "you don't want to be my date for the opening?"

"No way! That would be way too weird. Besides, you should take Claire. You need to score some brownie points there if you want to get out of the doghouse."

"Yeah, alright. I don't need relationship advice, kiddo."

She scoffs into her bowl of fried rice. "The hell you don't."

He bends down to meet her gaze. "Excuse me?"

"Come on, Dad . . ."

Come on, what?

He'd love to sit back and get comfortable for whatever advice this nineteen-year-old is about to dispense, but it's a fucking backless bench he's sitting on and the German has pulled it up close to the table, so his chin is directly above his bowl. Every time the guy plunges his chopsticks into the rice and lifts them, they come up empty.

"What, Mia?" He uses a tone with her that he hasn't used in years, the don't-lie-to-me tone.

"You never fight," she says, assertively.

"I'm sorry?" *That's supposed to be a good thing, right? Not fighting.*

"You didn't fight for your career. You didn't fight for Mum. You're not going to fight for Claire, either, are you? You're just going to let her go."

So this is what a knife through the heart feels like.

"You wanted me to fight harder for your mother? After she had an affair?"

"Yes."

"Mia, she wanted to go," he asserts.

"Maybe in the end, but what about before that? When she just wanted you to pay attention to her and you wouldn't. You spent all your time in the studio. She thought you were hiding in there. Hiding from her."

"What? Of course I wasn't. She told you that?"

She puts down her chopsticks. "Yeah."

You don't ever ask questions, he can remember Kirstie alleging. *Your girlfriend . . . must have the patience of a saint.* Is he really as inattentive as everyone keeps saying he is?

She scoots down her bench to get closer to him. "Dad, when your paintings stopped selling, you kind of disappeared back there."

He looks down, running a hand through his hair, aware he's doing exactly what she's telling him not to: hiding.

"We kept waiting, waiting for you to get your fight back. We watched while you painted still lifes all day, every day, and then just stacked the finished work against the wall, never to be seen again."

"You were watching me?"

"Well, yeah . . . We loved you."

"I loved you, too." he says, taking her hands. "Both of you. You know that, right?"

"I do. Mum didn't."

He lets go and rubs his forehead with both hands. The guy in the salmon-colored shirt glances over at him, but only briefly. He's got his own problems with his rice.

"It's fine, Dad. She's fine."

Well, I'm not . . .

He wipes his eyes with his thumbs. "Doesn't sound like she is, not after what you told me."

"I spoke to her earlier today," she says, cautiously. "Looks like Jeff came through after all. They're getting married at city hall when I arrive in July. She wants me to be her witness."

"Right." He tries to smile, tries to be okay with what he knows is the best possible outcome, even though he despises it.

Jeff. Fucking Jeff fought for her.

"Are you disappointed?" he asks, remembering their conversation from last night. "You were hoping she'd come home."

"I'll be okay," she says, "I have you, right?"

Right???

"Of course, you do."

IIIIIIIIIIIIIIIIIIIIIII

They share a longer than usual hug outside the restaurant, Soho buzzing around them, before Mia makes her way to the Tube and he heads back toward the Claret. She tells him she loves him, even though he's an idiot. "I know," he says. "Thank you for that," and he really means it. It's both discouraging and comforting to have someone know you that well, and to love you in spite of being the fucked-up mess you are. Still, to know that his daughter has seen and identified his cowardice isn't something he'll be able to carry around with him lightly. After all, disappointment is far worse than anger. He knows that from parenting. He always assumed Mia blamed Eliza for their split, as he did, but he wonders now if, in her heart, she blames him.

He doesn't get far before pulling out his phone. He stops, determined, in front of a lingerie shop, Agent Provocateur.

"I hear congratulations are in order," he says, when Eliza answers.

"Bennett . . ." She groans on the other end.

"In a few weeks?"

"July first," she says. "Once Mia arrives." He can tell she's trying to sound proud.

"Good," he says, nodding to himself.

"Good?"

"Yeah. Good." He glances at the lingerie shop window. Eliza once bought a tight lace nightgown from this shop, because she thought Bennett would like it. He thought it was too scratchy. He wonders if she still has it? If Jeff likes it?

Don't ask her that.

"Is that the reason you called, Bennett? To say 'congratulations'?"

"Were you going to tell me?"

"I don't know. I guess I figured Mia would."

"We shouldn't expect her to pass on our news for us. That's not fair to her."

"I don't know, Bennett. Do we even need to pass on news? What's the point?"

What's the point?! Twenty years of our fucking lives?!

"Well, my girlfriend is pregnant. I'm having another kid." The words just tumble out of his mouth, unexpected.

Eliza says nothing, but he can hear her breathing over the sound of talk radio that plays faintly in the background. "Wow," she finally says. "You trying to one up me?"

"No. Not intentionally." *Maybe a little.*

"Wow. When?"

"She's ten weeks." It occurs to him that he doesn't even know the due date of his own child.

"Congratulations to you, too."

"Thank you," he says, though he feels hollow, aware that he doesn't deserve her good wishes even a little bit. "Mia doesn't know yet."

"Right . . ."

"I'll tell her before she comes to visit you, but don't say anything, please."

"I won't. But tell her, Bennett."

"I will."

"Is that it?"

"Pretty much."

"Pretty much?"

"I'm sorry," he manages, half choking on the words. Then, "I'm sorry I made you feel invisible."

The line goes quiet, again, as he tries desperately to fight back sobs.

"You're an excellent father, Bennett. This baby is going to be lucky to have you."

But a terrible husband, she seems to imply. He's getting better at understanding insinuations. Still, he thinks, the compliment is more than he deserves. "Thank you. That's it, I guess." It certainly feels like that's it. He waits a beat, just in case it isn't, before hanging up.

|||||||||||||||||||||||

By the time he gets back to the Claret, the blood vessels in his eyes are broken, throbbing. Claire doesn't seem to notice. She's in her own world, polishing wineglasses and stacking them on the shelves behind her. He sets her spring rolls in their plastic container on the bar.

"Hungry?"

"Not really," she says.

"You should eat."

She squints, stuck between anger and relief. At least he's thinking about her that much. Even he can read that thought.

"I'll polish the glasses, you eat." He pushes the spring rolls toward her and holds out his other hand for the polishing cloth, which she hands over, reluctantly.

"How was dinner?" she asks.

"Illuminating."

"What does that mean?"

"It means you're not the only person in the world that wants to punch me. You'll have to get in line."

She looks like she'd like to smile, but there's no way she's giving in that quickly.

It occurs to him that Kirstie is probably the one person that doesn't want to punch him. Strange. Mia accused him of giving up too easily, but earlier Kirstie praised him for *not* giving up. He'd like to accept Kirstie's opinion and reject those of the other women in his life, but he knows that's not right. He wants to believe Kirstie understands him best because she likes him best, but liking and understanding aren't the same thing, no matter how much he wishes they were.

Claire dips a spring roll in the accompanying sweet chili sauce. "I don't want to punch you," she says in a less than convincing tone. "I don't think that'll have any effect on you whatsoever."

Bit harsh.

"Might make you feel better?" he says, wiping the rim of a wine-glass with the cloth.

"Only one thing is going to make me feel better."

For the love of God, what is it?

"I want you to think about me the way you think about her."

He's not sure whether she's talking about Eliza or Kirstie.

Don't ask.

She looks him in the eye, like she's challenging him to another staring contest, but he lets her win right away, averting his eyes back to the glass in his hand, before she can see he's been crying.

"You pushed me away," he says. *That's true, isn't it? Didn't she?*

She drops her spring roll back in the plastic container. "Actually, I asked you to move in with me, which is quite the opposite."

Oh yeah. Right.

"Well, I think we should revisit that conversation."

"Do you?"

"I'm going to sell my house."

"Are you?" She leans forward, predatory.

Jesus, the questions.

"Because you mentioned that yesterday," she says, accusatory. "Have you called an estate agent? Told your 'guest'"—she uses air quotes—"that she needs to find another place to live?"

"Not yet."

"Exactly."

"It's been one day. You wouldn't even talk to me yesterday," he says, raising his voice, which sounds hoarse, unfamiliar.

"So you need me to hold your hand? Stroke your head and say 'good boy' every step of the way?"

"Come on!"

"In order to do the right thing, you need me to stop being angry with you? Is that right?"

Yes.

"Bennett, you'd put a crib in that stupid studio of yours, I know you would. I don't want my baby breathing in your paint fumes."

You loved that "stupid studio."

"I'm *telling* you, I'll sell the house," he says, emphatically.

"Tomorrow? You'll call an estate agent tomorrow? And you'll tell *her* tomorrow that she needs to move?"

"Yes," far less emphatic this time.

She shakes her head in disbelief.

"Claire, I'm trying."

"You always say that. You shouldn't have to try so hard."

This can't be what she wants, he thinks, for the two of them to have a baby. Why can't she just admit that this isn't ideal for either of them? Not right now. It's like she wants him to say this baby is everything he's ever hoped for.

Well, it's not.

"I'm still getting my head around this. Can you be patient with me?"

"I think you have feelings for that woman in your house."

"Claire—"

"Tell me you don't," she interrupts.

"Claire . . ." She doesn't interrupt this time, so he just lets his voice fall because he doesn't know what to say.

"I think if I wasn't pregnant, you'd have left me for her by now. Am I right?"

Why does she insist on knowing the truth, even when it'll crush her?

"We've become close friends."

That response seems to hurt her just as much as the truth would have, and she puts her face in her hands. After a couple seconds of silence, he can hear her start to weep, her stomach pulsing with the tiny gasps.

He abandons the cloth and the wineglass and walks around to the other side of the bar, uninvited, to wrap his arms around her. She wails in a way that he remembers Eliza wailing when she was pregnant and hormonal over any little thing. This though, he knows, is not little. She eventually gives in to his embrace and wraps her arms around his waist.

"We're not friends, are we?" She sobs into his collarbone.

"Of course, we are."

"I slept with you too soon."

He can't help but laugh a little at that, as though none of this would have happened if they'd just gone to dinner and a movie first.

"Don't laugh."

"Sorry," he says. He kisses her forehead and sways her gently, back and forth. "I started another painting of you."

"Are you asking for permission or forgiveness this time?"

He steps back so he can look at her and smiles. "It's from the sketch I made of you here. It's going to be even better than the other two."

"Have you done any paintings of *her*?"

"No. None."

She smiles, but only for a second. "You never painted your ex-wife, either." She buries her head under his chin.

"If I do a painting of Kirstie, will that make you feel better?"

"No," she says, muffled, but it still sounds assertive.

Unsure of his next move, he just holds her, feeling the front of his shirt getting damp. Their child is probably about the size of an avocado pit, he thinks, as her stomach presses up against his. He wonders if she knows she's carrying around a human the size of an avocado pit. *Probably.* He decides to take a different approach.

"Mia really likes you," he says, when her crying begins to subside.

"I know," she says, wiping her eyes on Bennett's sleeve. "She said she thought I was good for you."

He tries to picture the moment they had this exchange, maybe when he was in the bathroom, when Mia could sense that Claire was angry? What had possessed his daughter to make such a bold claim? If Mia knows him better than anyone, as she certainly established tonight, maybe she's right? Maybe Claire *is* good for him. He just wishes he knew why. He lifts her chin and kisses her, a strategy that's worked for them up to this point, whenever they've run out of words. She's reluctant at first, but it's not long before she gives in, gripping the back of his neck and pulling him down to her. She runs her fingers through his hair, always her most sincere form of affection. It makes the hairs on his arms stand up. "Let's finish up and get you home." He pulls away, intending to return to his polishing, but she pulls him back to her, clasping both his hands in hers. He smiles at her because she looks, suddenly, very serious—not upset, just serious. "What?"

"I love you."

When it comes to love, Bennett's only ever had three solid reference points. The first is his mother, the only member of his family that he loved voluntarily. He supposes he loved his father out of obligation, because when he was growing up he was told that he did, even though he wasn't so sure. His mother was different. He would've loved her regardless. Kind and sweet, she might have been naive, but she possessed an optimism that was like an alien force in the Driscoll family, always making lemonade out of the rotten piles of lemons that life kept tossing her. For whatever reason, Helen saw herself as the keeper of an alternative, syrupy reality, and she believed in Bennett probably more than anyone with a lick of common sense would have. It was her belief that had allowed him to dream, to imagine, to paint.

Loving Eliza had been a whole different story. Unlike Helen, reality was her default mode. She was the first person to trust him, which is what makes Mia's recent revelations about his ex-wife's feelings of abandonment all the more difficult to bear. She was the first woman he slept with who didn't immediately cover herself with a sheet after the act. As cruel as she was kind, she'd been driven by her dedication to the truth. Her standards were impossibly high. She was a pain in the arse. She absolutely could not relax, ever, and she wanted Bennett at her side for every jaw-clenching minute. In the early going, her love for him could only have been described as fierce. She rallied behind him when he was down, encouraged him when he was unsure, and more than once called her father-in-law a "spineless twat" to his face, because, to her mind, he deserved to know. Bennett had never known love like it before. It didn't come easily. He had to earn it. He wanted to earn it.

His love for Mia came the easiest. Well, it rolled in like a freight train, but it's certainly the purest, the most all-encompassing form of love he's ever experienced. The one that he knows is truly unconditional.

He's not sure where any of this leaves him, now, standing here with Claire. The truest expression of his feelings in this moment would be "I *want* to love you," but he knows he can't say that. He can't even be sure that what he feels for her *isn't* love. If all love is different, how can anyone ever be sure? It's not like he can expect himself to feel for Claire what he felt for Eliza. There are lots of things he loves *about* Claire: her smile, her feistiness, her tits (of course), her confidence behind the bar, even her impatience. Maybe, if he hadn't met Kirstie, he'd be in love with Claire. And who's to say you can't love two people at once, if they give you different things?

Claire, that's who. He has no doubt she'd tell him exactly why he can't love two people at once. It would probably be a really smart, really simple answer that he could never come up with on his own. He loves that about her, too, her clarity.

Would she even believe him if he said he loves her, too? After all, she accused him of having feelings for another woman not thirty minutes ago. Behind all her worrying, her eye rolls, and her complaints, he knows that, ultimately, Claire is a hopeful person. She's a born optimist who's burned, daily, by the shortcomings of everyone around her. In this moment, she's still hopeful that he'll say he loves her, too. What's worse? To say "I love you" when he's not sure, or to tell her he needs more time, which could crush her? Maybe she didn't mean it as seriously as all that? Maybe it's just like, "Love you, man."

Probably not.

She's been watching him this whole time, although he's not sure how long that's been. Nor can he judge what expression he's wearing on his face. Brave smile? Sheer terror? Eventually, he runs out of time and she has her answer.

"Just promise me"—she tells him, looking at her feet—"you'll love the baby like you do Mia."

You're a twat, Bennett.

"Of course, I will."

She pulls away. "You should head home. I'll finish up here."

"I thought I was coming home with you?"

She looks up at him, her eyes bloodshot, finally out of tears. "What's the point?"

What's the point?

He runs his hand through his hair and looks at her one more time, hoping to convey with his eyes what he's too cowardly to put into words.

I want to love you, I will love you, just give me a little time.

"Go on, go," she says.

"I'm calling an estate agent tomorrow," he tells her, coming out from behind the bar, still determined to show her he's doing his best, though he knows he should be capable of more than this.

"Okay," she says, picking up the cloth and the glass Bennett abandoned.

"I'll call you when it's done." He lingers between the bar and the door. "When is the baby due?"

Her back to him, she answers, "November second. Mark your calendar."

"Are you sure you're alright?" *Of course she's not alright.*

"Bennett . . ."

"Right." He pushes on the door. "Good night."

"Thank you for the spring rolls."

Spring rolls? Is that all I have to give?

|||||||||||||||||||||||||

When he gets back to the house, all the lights are still on. He knocks on the back door and Kirstie turns around on the sofa. She's been watching some crime show; two cops are chasing a man to the edge of a cliff where stones cascade to the water below. Bennett waves sheepishly through the glass. Kirstie returns his wave with a frown before turning down the volume and getting up. She's changed out of her wrap dress into a loose fitting pink T-shirt and a pair of gingham pajama bottoms. Her hair is tied up in a bun that reveals her grey roots.

"Why are you knocking on your own door, you daft banana?" she asks, letting him in. "What happened? What are you doing back?" She takes his hand and leads him to the sofa.

"I'm not sure where to start."

"The beginning, darling." She sits down on the sofa and pulls him down with her.

He takes a deep breath. "I need to sell the house, Kirstie," he just says it, like ripping off a plaster. "I need to list it tomorrow."

"I know." She nods, sensing his urgency.

"I'm sorry, really I am. Wait. How?"

She puts her hand on his leg. "She's pregnant? Your pretty girl-friend?"

"How did you know all this?"

"If I said women's intuition would you believe me?"

Probably.

"In your studio this morning, there was a notebook open to a page that said, 'Facts: Claire is pregnant' and 'I need to sell the house.'"

"So, the exact opposite of intuition, then."

She smiles. "Just nosy. What happens now?"

"Fuck, if I know," he says, staring at the TV screen, where a clean-shaven silver fox is putting handcuffs on a scruffy-looking man, who Bennett can't help but think looks a little like him. "I need to sell this house. That's as far as I've gotten."

"You'll figure it out," she says, stroking his knee. "You've done this before."

"Not like this, I haven't. This isn't ideal."

"Oh please, when was the last time anything in your life could be described as 'ideal'?"

He thinks back, but nothing in the last ten years, maybe even further, comes to mind. "Fair enough," he concedes. "If you found out you were having another kid, how do you think you'd handle it?"

She chuckles. "Darling, that ship has sailed."

He looks at her. *Oh yeah.*

"You'll be fine," she reassures him. "You two will figure it out, together."

"Claire thinks I have feelings for you."

She takes her hand off his leg. "Well, tell her you don't."

He faces her. "What if I do?"

She scoots down to the other end of the sofa. "Tell her you don't."

When he starts to say that he does a second time, she cuts him off. "Being a single mother is lonely. Lonelier than anything you can imagine." (Yes, even lonelier than a divorced man in his fifties—he twigs this implication as well.) Her eye contact is suddenly very urgent and very serious. He doesn't like it, but he doesn't dare look away.

"I'm not going to let her do it alone."

"That's not enough, Bennett."

Uh-oh. No more "darling."

"She needs a real partner, someone who intends to sacrifice as much as she *has to* for this child."

He nods, aware he's been caught out. He's somehow forgotten that above all, courage involves sacrifice. Fighting for something isn't a real fight unless you know what you're prepared to give up and what you're willing to break bones to keep.

The silver fox on the TV now has his arm around a young blonde.

They stand on the cliffside looking out to sea. "How can I ever repay you?" she asks.

"I think you should put a competing offer in on that Barbican flat," Bennett says, determined to repay Kirstie with a small nugget of wisdom or whimsy, even if he doesn't actually know which it is.

"I already did," she says with a cheeky grin.

He shakes his head in confusion, both relieved and surprised.

"After I dropped you off at the Royal Academy."

"When do you find out if it's yours?"

"Tomorrow, but I know I'll get it. I made sure of that."

He smiles. "Good," he says, standing up in what feels like an involuntary motion, as if a changing wind has pushed him. "Sorry. I'll let you get back to your show."

"Oh, I've already seen it," she says. She points to the silver fox. "That's my ex-husband." He takes the blonde in his arms and they kiss, passionately, as the credits roll.

"Why would you torture yourself like this?"

"That's rich, coming from you," she says, her eyebrow raised.

Fair point.

She pulls herself up from the sofa, as though she intends to escort him out. "No one knows Albert the way I do. Everyone thinks they do, but they just know Cliff, his character. I guess, every once in a while, I like to forget what I know and just see what they see."

"I probably would, too." He'd like to take her hand again, but he doesn't.

"I know you would, darling. That's why we get along."

"Come here," he says. She steps forward, timidly, into his embrace. With both arms wrapped around her for the first time, she feels unyielding and blunt, like a tiny stone, someone who's not remotely willing to love again. Not even close.

||||||||||||||||||||||||

Cramped on his hard futon, he realizes he had offers of two different, comfortable beds tonight and lost them both. "We get what we deserve," his father told him when he was eight, after Bennett asked why there were so many homeless men outside Hammersmith Station. He knows that's not strictly true. Gary Driscoll, the bastard, was himself a flesh-and-bone rebuttal of his own assertion. Still, tonight, Bennett suspects he deserves this stupid futon. Though he wishes it wasn't true, so much of what he has in life came too easily. He worked hard, sure, but his degrees, his success, the galleries? It all came quickly, before self-doubt could creep in. When he was a young man, it never occurred to him that he wouldn't have those things, just as it hadn't occurred to him that when he proposed to Eliza she might say no. Things went as they were meant to go.

We get what we deserve. Surely, he isn't the only person stupid enough to have believed that? When it came time for him to fight for what he had—his career, for Eliza—he hadn't realized he could really lose it all. He just expected it all to return to him, eventually. After all, it was his. So, he just hunkered down and did everything the way he'd always done it, even harder and less yielding than before. He wonders if during that time, he felt like a stone in Eliza's arms, the way Kirstie felt tonight. No, it was more likely the opposite. He wasn't a stone, he was a sponge, soaking up all of Eliza and Mia's love and giving nothing back. Even worse, he's still behaving like that. It took Kirstie to point out to him what a self-absorbed bastard he could be.

He pulls up the sonogram photo on his phone. He hasn't looked at it since Trafalgar Square. He's been afraid to, worried he won't be able calibrate the correct levels of love and fear. Recalling what Kirstie said to him about sacrifice, he wonders if he's prepared to give up, now, all the things he previously didn't truly believe he could lose.

I'm sleeping on this rock-hard futon for you, kid. I'm selling my house for you. I'm giving up my Super Host status for you. What are you going to do for me?

Another photo pops up on his screen as he contemplates how the amorphous blob in the sonogram will somehow morph into a human.

Oi, mate! Looks brill x, the attached message reads. The picture: his painting, hanging proudly on the wall of the Royal Academy, the first in more than five years. He zooms in and out with his thumbs, trying to get a better look at the work around it, inspecting his painting in far more detail than he did the sonogram. His mind wanders to opening night: the throngs of guests, the canapés, the collectors with little cocktail napkins, whispering, "Is that a Bennett Driscoll? Is he back?"

Is he back?

He flips back to the sonogram.

Please don't make me give up painting.

Quite the opposite, of course—he's going to have to start selling paintings again. Without the income from letting the house, he'll need to find it elsewhere, somehow. Turning over onto his side, he looks at the new painting of Claire, half-finished on the easel. There's just the faintest trace of her laughing, as she had been that day. Maybe even at him. It hadn't occurred to him until now that maybe what she found so amusing was the twat in the back of the pub with the sketchbook. The guy who thought he could sketch her without being noticed. The guy who thought he deserved to interpret her every angle and appropriate her every curve with his pencil without knowing one single thing about her. And yet he must have gotten something right, he thinks. She wouldn't have slept with him if there wasn't something in that sketch that rang as true to her as it did to him. Maybe he can paint his way into understanding Claire. Maybe he could he have done the same with Eliza, he thinks, but it hurts too much to contemplate that now.

The other night, when he was sitting in the garden with Kirstie, listening to the cool spring breeze in the trees, he thought that what he wanted more than anything was to find some real momentum and a reason to keep moving. It seems obvious to him now, staring at the painting, that Claire is that momentum. It was Claire that got him moving.

Bloody hell, she even got you running.

He picks up his phone again.

The painting of you got into the show, he types, looking at the half-finished painting one more time before pressing Send.

I thought it would, she writes back. *You're a good painter.*

It probably pained her to send that compliment.

Thank you. I couldn't have done it without you, he writes, hoping she'll understand his deeper meaning. *I hope you'll come with me to the opening.*

I hope it sells. It's worth a lot of nappies.

We'll be fine, Claire. You don't need to worry about any of that.

He can picture her lying on her bed in her dingy flat, probably naked, rolling her eyes. He's going to paint her in every room of the flat, he thinks, before they move somewhere else—a woman in her ground. There won't be as much time for painting once the baby is born. Even less time when Claire eventually opens her bookshop. This is the sacrifice he'll need to make.

I love you, too, he writes, though compared to any love before it, it's unrecognizable. He doesn't press Send just yet. It's because she worries so much, he thinks; that's why she's good for him. People who worry think about both favorable and unfavorable outcomes. Some just fear the worst, but others, like Claire, almost suffer more because they've dared imagine the best. The Bennett she's imagined is no doubt better than the real one and what worries him more than anything is that he'll disappoint her. But there's no worry without hope, and Claire, bless her, remains hopeful about him. He wonders for the first time in a long while, if his burdens and his desires might not be just his own, but shared. He hits Send.

The little bubble pops up and hovers. He waits, anticipating a complicated reply.

You're joking. A fucking text message?

No, he writes.

You're such a bastard.

I know. He smiles, aware that outrage is better than defeat. *It's better this way,* he types. *Now you have it in writing.*

Am I going to need it in writing? Are you planning to deny it later?

He rolls onto his back. *No. But you worry. So I thought you might like to have it.*

It's another minute before *Thank You* pops up on his screen. *You will say it, though? Like a proper human being?*

Kirstie's TV still flickers from the main house into the garden. It's nice, Bennett thinks, that he won't have to remember Kirstie this way, living in his house. He can think of her in her Barbican flat, leaning over her balcony, watching all the suits go by. He *is* going to think about her, he knows that. Maybe, in five years' time, he'll go sit by the Barbican pond, just to see if she's there. By then, he'll have a four-year-old. And a twenty-four-year-old, too. Maybe a new gallery. And Claire. He'll have Claire. Of course he will.

Tomorrow, he writes. *We've got lots to do tomorrow.*

ACKNOWLEDGMENTS

I suppose it makes sense to start at the beginning. A huge thank you to my family: Mom, Dad, and Emily. The phrase "I couldn't have done it without you" is probably said too much, but in this case it feels especially true. Your support and advice mean so much. Your love means everything. My dad read a couple drafts of this book, and it was his belief and encouragement in the early drafts that made it possible to keep going.

To Steve, Molly, and Henry, who listened to me talk about this book every Sunday night for two years; you deserve some sort of award.

To my friends and family in London; it's for you that I keep returning. Thank you for welcoming me and giving me a second home—Jon, Maha, James, Clare, Jenny, Luke, Maya, Ruth, Peter, Simon, Karina, Adam, Anna, and Ollie. Thank you to my tutors at the Slade School of Fine Art who told me I didn't have to choose between painting and writing. It took me a long time to believe you. And thank you to Ziella Bryars for including my early plays in Love Bites and prompting me to think of myself as a storyteller.

Thank you to Nicole Aragi, my wonderful agent, for knowing all the things I don't, for encouraging me to always trust my gut and for giving me so many reasons to dance in the street. Thank you to everyone at Aragi—Maya Solovej and Gracie Dietshe.

ACKNOWLEDGMENTS

Thank you to my fantastic editor, Sally Kim. I knew from our initial phone conversation that you truly cared about these characters. Working with you has been such a joy and a privilege. Both Bennett and I are the better for it.

Thank you to everyone at Putnam for their belief and hard work on this book—Gaby Mongelli, Alexis Welby, Ashley McClay, and Ivan Held. Thank you to the art department, who've designed a beautiful cover and layout.

Thank you to Imogen Taylor and Tinder Press for bringing this book home to the UK.

Thank you to Gabrielle Brooks for the early read and sage advice.

Thank you to Philip Glass for use of *Einstein on the Beach, Knee Play no. 5.* Every once in a while you hear a song that stops you in your tracks. This piece of music is such a gift.

A huge thank you to Roots Manuva for the music that inspires me every day to laugh, cry, dance, and fight. Thank you for soundtracking Bennett's life and mine.

Tom. To whom this book is dedicated. Anything I write here would fall short of communicating just how thankful I am. All you need is someone to go along with, right? In short, thank you for going along with me.